PUBLIC
INFORMATION

PUBLIC INFORMATION

COMING OF AGE DURING
THE KOREAN WAR

◆ ◆ ◆

Rolf C. Margenau

Public Information is a work of fiction.

Names, characters, incidents, places, and organizations are the product of the author's imagination or are used fictitiously. Any resemblance to actual persons, living or dead, events, organizations, or locales are entirely coincidental.

Second Edition Copyright© 2016 by Rolf C. Margenau
All rights reserved.
Published in the United States by Frogworks Publishing
ISBN: 0997615826
ISBN: 9780997615821
EBook ISBN: 9780997615838
Library of Congress Control Number: 2016959371
Frogworks.com LLC, Lebanon, NEW JERSEY

www.frogworks.com

By Rolf Margenau
PISTILS AND POETRY
MASTER GARDENER
HIGH ANDES
THE COMMODE COMPANION
NATIONAL PARKS

AUTHOR'S NOTE

◆ ◆ ◆

MOST READERS KNOW ABOUT THE people of the "greatest generation" who served during World War II. Yet the Korean War, which began five years after World War II ended, remains obscure for many Americans, most of whom were born after that conflict ended. Thirty- five thousand of our troops died in that war and two million people, all told, did not survive it. I hope that this story of a young soldier's odyssey during and after that conflict will enlighten those who are unfamiliar with the details of that "police action." I have tried to capture the jargon of the times and report on the military's sometimes peculiar approach to its mission. Specifically, I have attempted to show the "Army way" in all its splendor, confusion, and humor.

The sources for this novel are numerous and varied. The three hundred or so letters I wrote to my future wife from Korea, Japan and other "Far East" locations served as a primary source. Like Wylie and Judy, ours was a postal romance. Nancy numbered and preserved the letters, which I reread carefully in preparation for writing this book. If Wylie seems callow and immature, so, I confess, was I in the early fifties.

Thanks to the resources of the internet, I could read newspaper accounts of many of the historical events that occur in the novel. I also relied on recollections of soldiers that I recorded while a correspondent, and public memoirs of soldiers, marines, and airmen. In this second edition, I have added recollections of veterans who commented on the original.

A splendid aide-mémoire is John Toland's *In Mortal Combat – Korea, 1950-1953*. The lucidity and depth of his book are remarkable. I also relied on William Manchester's American Caesar to recall Douglas MacArthur's role during the Korean War.

I apologize for some of the dry historical information included in the book. Since one of my reasons to write the novel is to provide an accurate understanding of the war's genesis and how it was for the people involved, some accurate historical background is necessary. Also, fanciful as some of the scenes and chapters may seem, most are grounded in fact. The chapter on Marilyn Monroe's visit, for example, includes a scene of her waving to troops from a helicopter. It really happened. So, amazingly, did the diversion of the frozen lobsters and the capture of a train load of vodka.

The scenes of combat in this book are based on recollections of those who experienced it, many of whom were still there when I arrived in Korea a few months after the armistice. Luckily, I never experienced firsthand knowledge of combat, although I did manage to dodge a few bullets while I was there.

I dedicate this book to the dwindling number of those who served in the "forgotten war." They are some of the finest people I have ever known in a time when simple heroism and devotion to duty were routine. Their example has sustained me through some tough times. They deserve continuing recognition for their service to our country, as do all the young troopers who came before and after them.

The characters in this book are fictional, though I have cherry picked quirks and fancies of friends and compatriots with whom I served to make more real the people found on its pages.

I owe particular gratitude to two Army buddies who, so many years later, shared their stories and reminiscences with me and offered encouragement as Wylie floundered through the pages of the novel. To Professor Lee P. Herrington, Professor Emeritus of Resources

Information Management, State U. of New York, Department of Natural Resources, and Dr. Harry Roselle, renowned New Jersey Cardiologist, sincere thanks and appreciation. I also thank my editor, Carol Bere, for smoothing over rough spots and helping Wylie come to life. I am also grateful to my friend and copy editor, Tom Schroth, who provided the final edit for the book.

This book's publication in 2011 generated many responses from men and women who served—in Korea and other theaters. Their comments were both helpful, informative, and encouraging so, in 2016, I decided to edit the book to reflect information in some of those comments, and add historical facts recently come to light.

Partly because of this novel, I returned to Korea in 2013 with other veterans under that government's "Revisit Korea" program. The changes in the country since the war are spectacular. We felt proud that our intervention had been so successful, and humbled by the warmth and courtesy offered by the Korean people during that visit. Even today, they remember and honor those who served there.

I hope this book serves a similar purpose.

Rolf Margenau, Tewksbury, NJ November, 2016

CHAPTER 1
BEDCHECK CHARLIE

◆ ◆ ◆

As BEDCHECK CHARLIE RUMBLED OVERHEAD, PFC Wylie Cypher cowered in the latrine, fearing that his life would be over during his first week in war-torn Korea.

Wylie crouched in the center of the small frame building as though glued to the rough oval wood of the seat, listening to the drone and sputter of the enemy aircraft. He massaged the brown stubble of his military haircut and clamped shut his eyes, trying to ignore the icy feeling in his bowels, trying to shut out nameless fears. Danger was on every side.

Sweat dotted his brow as he focused on his greatest concern — how to survive a sixteen-month tour of duty in battle torn Korea and stay alive.

Thoughts of Judy kept interrupting. Brimming with self-pity, he thought, Jesus, my plans sure haven't worked out very well so far. Here I am in combat with the strong possibility of getting my ass shot off. What's my life expectancy as an infantry leader? What's …

The sound of Bedcheck Charlie's sputtering engine intensified. The latrine walls shuddered. That would just be it, he decided. That fucker drops his bomb on this latrine and my worries are over. His throat tightened and his buttocks went numb. He felt vulnerable, impotent, constipated, and frightened. It sounded as though the airplane was landing on the roof.

His nemesis, named for the hour of its arrival, was a Polikarpov PO-2, a small Russian biplane. That evening, like many evenings before, its pilot intended to drop bombs by hand on enemy troop concentrations. He focused on the replacement depot in Uijongbu, close to the latrine where Wylie cowered.

More seasoned troops at the depot had departed vulnerable areas for trenches and foxholes and fired on Bedcheck Charlie with M-1 rifles and carbines. A few aimed 45-caliber pistols at the plane's engine, an elusive target that might, however, succumb to a few well-placed ounces of lead and steel. The troops did not consider it sporting to use heavier arms. It would be like shooting deer with a howitzer, as happened the week before when an overzealous forward observer confused some grazing animals for a group of Chinese volunteers on the attack.

Kim Ky Yung, pilot of the Polikarpov, was not enthusiastic about this mission. With undiagnosed myopia, he had failed all aspects of Russian flight training in North Korea with the exception of the biplane he now controlled. Although instrument reading was easy, his haphazard approach to target sighting and abysmal navigation were serious drawbacks, but not enough to ground him. His coolness under fire counter-balanced those failings. His instructors were thoroughly impressed with his bravery, not realizing he could not see the puffs of smoke from weapons discharged below.

Pilots being in demand at this stage of the conflict, he sputtered forth almost every evening searching for targets beyond the lines of conflict but not too far from home.

Kim hazily noticed the latrine and buildings below and tried to ignore the buzzing of steel hornets rending the fabric of his wings. He concentrated on finding a suitable target below. There it was— large, dark, shimmering, and very hard to miss. With practiced movements, Kim tossed his dirigible shaped bomb over the side behind his lower wing, and headed north toward home.

Wylie had already heard references to the ungainly biplanes that harassed troops along the front lines with early evening bombing raids. UN troops almost considered them a joke because their erratic flight patterns made them seem awkward as gooney birds. In the first year of the war, the small, wooden Polikarpov biplanes provided by Russia to its North Korean clients flew slowly in darkness at such a low altitude they eluded allied radar and attacked their enemies with impunity. Though outdated Russian trainers from World War II, they were highly effective night bombers.

The United States Air Force tried to stop this deadly nuisance with Saber jets, but they were day fighters and flew too fast to neutralize them. For half a year, they tried other planes to destroy Charlie but the equipment was too sophisticated to do the job. Finally, in the first months of 1951, Marine pilots flying Corsair night fighters succeeded in killing Charlie.

With the number of their Polikarpovs diminishing, the North Koreans selected allied targets close to the front lines and deployed Charlie at odd intervals. Kim understood that the early, golden days of biplane combat were over and that now, in the spring of 1953, he could well become an easy kill for a Marine Corsair. That accounted for the hasty selection of a large target and the abrupt turn north.

The dark, shimmering mass that attracted Kim's attention was the lagoon next to Wylie's latrine. Frogs, leeches, and small fish populated it, and herons stared bleakly into the wind-ruffled water. The sudden appearance of a cylindrical object falling from the sky alerted the herons, but the frogs, leeches, and fish continued business as usual. Wylie, hearing the plane leave, felt it might be safe to venture from the latrine. As he raised himself from the seat, an explosion rocked the little building, followed by a geyser of dark water containing recently demised fornicating frogs, small fish, and other forms of detritus. Eerie plopping noises accompanied the sound of water striking the corrugated roof above him.

His senses already on edge, the impact of the bomb blast heightened Wylie's feeling of vulnerability and utter inability to control his life. He feared he might be wounded and, in the dim light, took inventory, patting himself from head to foot, searching for holes and wetness. None. Relieved, he wiped drops of sweat from his brow and relaxed, finally using the latrine for its intended purpose.

Kim, meanwhile, was dealing with control cables severed by small arms fire and severe buffeting as wind whistled through new holes in the plane's fabric. He passed over the 38th Parallel and sighed with relief at the sight of flickering lights illuminating the airfield below. Now, if only his wheels remained intact.

CHAPTER 2

WYLIE AND JUDY

◆ ◆ ◆

IT WAS QUIET BUT FOR the susurrus of small, dead creatures slipping down the corrugated roof of the latrine and plodding to the wet clay below. Wylie felt blood rushing back to his head and listened intently for Charlie's return. There was no sound of his coughing engine. At least he would survive another day. Would it always be like this, he wondered, this fear that chilled his spine and sent nasty tingles of apprehension to the base of his scrotum? Oh God, he wondered, how will I manage in combat?

He slowly pulled on his fatigues and found his gun belt, rifle, and helmet. He cracked open the door and saw other soldiers moving in the compound. No further visits from Charlie were expected that evening.

As Wylie made his way back to the squad tent, the sounds of distant artillery fire reinforced his troubling thoughts. Almost as scary as death by combat was the prospect of never returning to Judy. He smiled ruefully to himself, considering the irony of how his deep and abiding love for Judith Elizabeth Castelnuevo had placed him in harm's way.

The peril of his situation was reinforced upon his arrival at Pusan three days earlier when the Sergeant who reviewed his personnel folder said, "Oh yeah, another infantry leader MOS (Military Occupational Specialty). Young trooper, welcome to the land of the morning calm where you will have a most excellent chance of getting your ass shot off when you join your unit around Uijongbu. Good luck!"

Constantly on the move to reach his next destination, Wylie had not fully considered this unsettling comment until his visit to the latrine. There he examined the chain of events that delivered him to this Army replacement depot near the 38th Parallel in Korea, awaiting assignment as an infantryman to a platoon in an unknown company of an unknown regiment where he fully expected to have his ass shot off.

Wylie's childhood was pleasantly unexceptional. His father, an attorney specializing in animal law, and his mother, the canasta champion of Hope's Crossing, New Jersey, were indulgent but vaguely distant in raising their three children. Wylie and his two younger sisters benefitted from benign neglect, followed their muses, and developed skills in arcane areas of interest, which had relevance only to themselves. Wylie, for example, became a second-grade champion at marbles, snatching aggies and cat's eyes from the fists of defeated playmates. His accuracy with a knuckle was notorious in the schoolyard and foreshadowed the development of a previously unknown skill during Army basic training.

He was good at his studies and passionate about baseball. He was lanky and spry and, even in the eighth grade, excelled at first base, making seemingly impossible catches to the chagrin of runners to his base. The Great Depression had little effect on Wylie and his family, and World War II ended when he was thirteen. He soon forgot his ability to identify all types of allied and enemy aircraft and to distinguish among classes of Army tanks. There were other things on his mind, since the end of the war coincided with the beginning of that hormone cocktail known as puberty.

There were growth spurts, nocturnal emissions, confusing and rapid emotional changes and, finally, at the age of fifteen and one-half, an unyielding submission to an eternal yearning. He became fascinated with soft female protuberances, watching eagerly with shielded eyes the swaying hips of girls in his high school class self-consciously clutching notebooks to burgeoning bosoms.

Wylie was relieved to learn from class and teammates that most boys in his high school class shared this fascination. There were many conversations about the forbidden and forbidding subject—sex.

Pre-game, in the dugout.

"Stan says he got to third base with his girlfriend," said Wylie. "You think he's bullshitting?"

Charlie answered, "Stan doesn't know what third base is. Thinks first base is a warm handshake."

Confused, Mike asked, "Warm handshake? I though first base was French kissing."

Charlie, suspected of having gone all the way and therefore an expert, said, "It's debatable. Regular kissing is first base for sure. But French kissing and bare tit are usually considered second base."

Charlie practiced a major-league saliva expulsion, accidentally hitting the toe of his cleats. He wiped his mouth and added, "Everybody knows that below the waist is third base. It's a given."

Tubby Wilson, quietly listening, asked, "So, where does a hand job fit in? Is that like a home run?'

Wylie, not exactly certain what a hand job was, paid attention.

Charlie, the expert, obliged. "Naw. A hand job is still third base, like maybe getting ready to steal home."

No one needed an explanation of what getting a home run was. But, all had yet to experience it. Wylie still needed to work out what a hand job was.

Tubby, resentful of Charlie, asked, "So how do you know all this stuff? I don't see you going out with any girls."

"My sister told me, butthead!"

Aha. An unimpeachable source.

An umpire whisked dirt from home place, and they turned their attention to the game.

At the beginning of his senior year in high school, Judy Castelnuevo, of raven hair and sparking brown eyes, slipped while passing Wylie in the lunchroom and accidentally dropped a bowl of raspberry jello with fruit cocktail in his lap. His great romance grew from such a mundane beginning.

Judy was in the junior class, robust, well liked, and athletic. She had an impeccable religious upbringing, having transferred the previous year from a Catholic high school in New York State. Among her many goals was to remain a "good girl" as long as reasonably possible. A disinterested observer might have foreseen conflict in the blossoming relationship between Wylie and Judy based on thwarted expectations.

Nevertheless, mutual respect and shared goals, aided by Wylie's good humor and Judy's optimistic outlook resulted in growing affection for each other. He was her "bean pole," she was his "main squeeze," and they were going steady during the spring of Wylie's senior year. As for their close encounters, passionate and lengthy kisses, gentle groping, and the occasional hicky were their sum. Second base remained over the horizon

When Judy began her senior year, Wylie became a freshman at Princeton University. He found the curriculum challenging and the freedom of being away from home exhilarating. He joined the glee club and tried out for The Daily Princetonian, played baseball fall and spring and visited Judy whenever possible. Newly opened vistas tugged against ill-formed suburban beliefs, as did the beer and bull sessions with classmates who seemed more sophisticated.

His mind expanded as his grades fell. He believed that he had potential for greatness, but had no idea what or how to achieve it. At the end of his first year, his grades hovered between C and D, his love for Judy was cruelly poised between platonic and lustful, and his future direction was unclear. A still, disturbing voice somewhere in the back of his mind worried that he had wasted his past year. He was nineteen and confused.

During the summer of 1952, the Truman administration continued to refer to the Korean conflict as a United Nations "police action," even though the fighting was cruel, unrelenting, and extremely bloody. By then more than twenty-five thousand young Americans had lost their lives in obdurate efforts to take and retake godless pieces of real estate with names like Old Baldy, Pork Chop Hill, and Heartbreak Ridge. The draft was in effect, and the nation called up inexperienced young men to serve in the Army, Marines, Navy, and Air Force.

Young men were aware of the choices facing them as they considered military service. Volunteers for officer training in college committed to at least four years of service after graduation. Draftees were obliged to serve for only two years, but could not choose which branch of service they joined or their assignment. Enlistees in the Navy, Air Force, and Marines signed up for four years. Those who enlisted in the Army served for three years and could choose special training that interested them. Like all veterans, they qualified for a generous G.I. Bill that defrayed future costs of college. Length of service determined these benefits, so enlistees could look forward to more financial support than those who served only two years.

Wylie returned to Hope's Crossing after his first year at Princeton and took a summer job at the local ice cream factory as a stirrer. He spent his free hours, days, and weekends with Judy. It was a summer of delight. At its end, they were best friends, exchanging their deepest thoughts and concerns, sharing explicit trust. Their physical relationship moved only slightly past first base, curtailed by Judy's religious beliefs and Wylie's fear of embarrassing himself. However, at summer's end they tentatively considered a future together.

"That's a long way off, though," said Judy. "We've both got to get through college, and you have to worry about the draft. I love being best friends with you, but I'm not planning to make a commitment to anyone until I get a degree and start on my path in life. You get that, don't you?"

Wylie got that. He wished he were as organized and focused on the future as Judy was. His plans for the future were hazy, a situation clearly noticed by his father, who decided to discuss it with his son.

"Wylie," he offered, "I know you had an enjoyable freshman year at Princeton, but you really booted it academically. Has anything happened since May to make you think you will do better this fall?"

Wylie drew a blank. No magic wiffle dust had descended during the past three months to improve his academic motivation. Working as a stirrer convinced him that he would rather work with his head than his hands, but he was unsure whether that would help him excel in Physics and Spanish. He confessed that uncertainly to his father.

"Perhaps a break from college would be in order," said Cypher Senior. Wylie saw merit in the suggestion. They plotted an alternative path for Wylie for the next three years. It hinged on enlistment in the Army.

Soon after their conversation, Wylie visited the Army recruiting office in nearby Morristown. Guided by his father, he enlisted with the written understanding that he would receive eight weeks of basic training at Fort Dix in the New Jersey Pine Barrens, followed by almost a year of study in the Russian language at the Army's language school in Monterrey, California. Father and son believed such training would stand Wylie in good stead, insulate him from combat, and provide him with valuable future benefits.

CHAPTER 3
THE ARMY

◆ ◆ ◆

CORPORAL JESUS MARTINEZ STARED WITH feigned disbelief at the dusty group of recruits disembarking from the olive drab school bus. The recruits awkwardly held duffel bags stuffed with newly acquired uniforms and gear in their arms, pairs of brown boots dangling from hands or elbows. Their heads glistened from quarter inch long GI haircuts, and they stood apprehensive and hot before the Corporal, who occupied a shady spot in front of the Company C Day Room. Some of the recruits were woozy from the series of injections received earlier that day, and the dense, humid air of the Fort Dix parade ground in late August did not make them feel better. The attitude of the short, muscled Corporal with lush dark brows and sharp eyes under a lowered campaign hat was discomforting.

He bellowed in a voice accented with a hint of Spanish, "My name is Corporal Jesus Martinez and I will be your drill instructor for the next eight weeks, you disgusting maggots. You will obey my every command, fulfill my every whim and desire, and be attentive to the needs of my Army every waking minute. In case you didn't hear it, my name is Corporal Martinez. You do not call me 'sir' or salute me and you never call me by my first name that is pronounced 'Hay-Soo.' What did I just say?"

The confused recruits mumbled inaudibly, prompting the Corporal to thrust his face within an inch of Wylie's nose and scream

"You miserable maricas! I just said what did I say? I said Hay-Soo. And you pussies didn't answer me. Let me hear it!"

"Hay –Soo" came from the scattered ranks.

"I can't hear you."

"Hay-Soo!" echoed loudly against the day room wall.

"Thass right. Never call me that."

Corporal Martinez excelled as a drill instructor and wore his campaign hat with pride. He understood instinctively the Army's philosophy and practice of breaking down and rebuilding recruits during their period of basic training so they would function as effective warriors with pride and obedience. Humiliating the young men and creating confusion worked reasonably well in the initial stages of the training.

The Corporal employed these tools vigorously during the next two weeks while the recruits became familiar with niceties of military dress, various Army manuals, inspection of barracks, footlockers and weapons at 0200, close order drill, KP (kitchen police), the calisthenics daily dozen, marching in formation, and developing an extremely close relationship with their M-1 rifles.

Wylie learned to recite with the others the full military nomenclature of all parts of his rifle and could break down and reassemble his weapon with record speed. If a single member of their platoon mistakenly referred to his rifle as a "gun," Corporal Martinez dispensed corrective training. Late in the evening, all platoon members paraded around the barracks in their skivvies, holding their M-1s above their heads with right hands, their private parts in their left. Back and forth they went, shouting, "This is my rifle (pump right hand), and this is my gun (grab crotch). With my rifle I shoot; with my gun I have fun."

A half hour of that seemed sufficient to drive that lesson home.

With physical activity more vigorous than required of a dairy stirrer, Wylie's lanky frame began to fill out and his physical endurance strengthened. So occupied with military necessities was his every moment that he had little time to write Judy. He longed to see her and eagerly awaited his first leave - not scheduled until the end of basic training. That changed, however, with Wylie's first day on the rifle range.

Corporal Martinez banged on the barracks' butt cans with his bullet tipped swagger stick at 0400 hours, yelling, "All right ladies, drop your cocks and grab your socks. Today's the big day, I say the BIG day. You will have the great pleasure of marching seven miles to my rifle range and fire your rifles with real bullets. Remember what you learned and remember that anyone who fucks up will earn my undying displeasure. And make sure your rifles are scrupulously clean. Saddle up!"

In the cool dawn of that September day, the one hundred and twenty-two recruits in Company C marched over the sandy soil of the Pine Barrens to the Fort Dix rifle range. They were encouraged on their way by their four drill instructors, the Company adjutant, Lt. Randolph Butz, and the company "top" Sergeant Titus ("tightass" to the troops) Branch. The Sergeant had seen action in the Battle of the Bulge and helped supervise a camp for German prisoners of war. Stationed in Japan as the North Koreans invaded the South, he participated in the Inchon landing and led green troops of the 25th Division for 14 months beginning in August 1950. He helped push the invaders back to the Yalu River and engaged in bitter combat that began when Chinese soldiers joined the North Koreans. More than any other noncom in Company C, he understood the importance of the training his recruits would receive.

Sergeant Branch called cadence in his mellow southern voice as the sun crested the scrub pines beside the sandy path.

"Reettep, Reettep, Gimme a Reettep" ran the cadence as the soldiers changed their shuffle to a quick step.

"I donno, but I been told, Eskimo pussy's mighty cold. Am I right or wrong?" The troops agreed he was right and the other noncoms chimed in.

"I don't know but I been told, Sergeant Branch has a heart a gold," sang Corporal Martinez. "Keeps me marchin, keeps me fit, tells me when to take a sh-ower. Am I right or wrong?"

The company swung along and the bawdy cadence continued until the rifle range came into sight.

Wylie lowered himself to his stomach, spread his legs apart as instructed, and aimed his rifle toward the large bull's eye fifty yards to his front. His instructor lay at a right angle, his hand next to the bolt of the M-1. Wylie opened the chamber and the instructor inserted a single bullet. The bolt slid forward and Wylie waited for the firing line to clear. At the ready command, he followed his instructor's advice, sighted on the target, and squeezed the trigger.

The spotter showed perfect alignment with the bull's eye but a foot to the left. The instructor offered to adjust the sight, but Wylie, who had never fired a rifle before, asked if he could try another round. Using his first shot as reference, he sighted to the right and fired again, intersecting the bulls eye at a precise dead center. Instinctively, he used what Army sharp shooters called Kentucky windage. Wylie repeated his shot twice again and the instructor beckoned Sergeant Branch, saying, "Looks like we got some talent here."

"Give that sumbitch a full clip and another target and let's see what he can do," commanded Branch. "Even a blind hog finds a acorn ever once in a while. You a blind hog, boy?"

No, thought Wylie. But he remained uncertain of his newfound gift until seven of the eight rounds in the clip dissected the center of the black target in a shot group smaller than, as Branch said, a ferret's eyeball. The first shot had been quite high, to the left.

Early the next morning Corporal Martinez rattled his bunk. "Hey college boy, you some kinda exceptional marksman? You been holdin out on your DI? Top says you got the best score in Division this month. He said, and I quote him directly, that sumbitch got himself a three day pass this weekend."

"Outstanding, Corporal!" said Wylie as his feet hit the deck and his thoughts turned to his inamorata, his Judy, his main squeeze.

Judy greeted him warmly the following Saturday upon his return to Hope's Crossing, an expert rifleman's medal pinned to the left side of his olive brown Ike jacket. She kissed his lips and nuzzled his neck, then held him at arm's length for closer observation.

"You look pretty good, bean pole," she said. "Seems like the Army agrees with you."

At that moment, happier than he had been in weeks, he agreed.

Later that day, as dusk darkened the Crossing Cougars football field, they walked slowly toward Judy's home. She caressed his arm and said, "I've been thinking that, what with you being away and all and we're not sure how often we'll be seeing each other, maybe I could make myself more available to you."

A thunderbolt of anticipation struck Wylie. Could this mean that his private fantasies about Judy, conjured up in his dreamlike state while marching before dawn to ranges and fields at the Army base, would be made real? Could this mean there were attainable bases ahead?

He forced out, "Like what?"

"Well, Mom and Dad are at Uncle Leon's helping him with his abscess so they won't be home till late. Come home with me and I'll show you what I mean."

Wylie's pace quickened and he stumbled over the threshold to Judy's front door, preparing to hold it for her. There was a quick kiss in the foyer and Judy invited him upstairs, to her room.

Judy decorated her bedroom in high feminine style with ruffles, light pastel wall colors, and stuffed animals and dolls piled carefully on her bed. Based on past conversations, Wylie knew each animal represented an important occasion in her life. Pooh, the bear, for example, was a gift from her parents for completing Winnie's first book at the age of seven.

Gingerly, Wylie moved some of the stuffed creatures to the side of the bed and sat on its edge, looking a Judy a few feet away. Smiling, with a graceful motion Wylie had seen his sisters use, she pulled her blouse over her head, and, in a movement Wylie has not seen before, removed her bra and held it in her hand while turning back to Wylie.

It was the first time Wylie had seen a live, naked young woman's torso. He stared at her breasts, perfectly shaped like large lush peaches with raspberry nipples, each pointed at Wylie's astonished eyes. He gulped, and instantly decided her breasts were the most beautiful objects he has ever seen. A desire to reach up and caress them, to suck the nipples, to bury his face in the abundant cleft between these glorious globes almost overwhelmed him. With self-restraint worthy of a saint, Wylie forced his hands together on his lap. He looked in Judy's eyes, his heart overflowing with gratitude and longing, his undisciplined appendage beginning to rise. He could not move.

Judy raised a breast in each hand, saying, "Meet Rosie and Freckles."

Wylie was disappointed that the breasts already had names. In his fantasy, he always was the one to name them.

Judy paused, slowly raising and lowering Wylie's objects of desire. "My girlfriends and I don't know why boys are so fascinated with them and want to hold and kiss them but I'm pretty sure you'd like that too. Isn't that right?"

Wylie, concentrating in trying to reduce his erection, was temporarily distracted and forgot how to breathe. Recalling that involuntary process, he inhaled and croaked, "Yes."

In Wylie's absence, Judy had given the question of moving to a higher level in their relationship considerable thought, balancing the dictates of her Catholic school education against her tender feelings and desire for Wylie. Seeing him in uniform, she decided that some forward movement in their relationship was both inevitable and desirable, but it must be tempered with compromise.

"All right. From now on when we're alone together you can play with either Rosie or Freckles, but not both. I don't want either of us to get too excited because you know where that might lead. I'm not going to go all the way, and you better know that. Will you agree to that?"

Wylie agreed, returning his gaze to the lovely objects of his desire. He was overwhelmed by resolving a single difficult question: which one was it to be tonight?

When he returned to barracks the following day, he remained excited about progress in his relations with Judy. He was unable to resist sharing these momentous developments with his new best friend, Scott McIlvane, who slept in the bunk next to him. Scott had little or no reticence when it came to wooing and bedding women. He listened with well-disguised disbelief as Wylie outlined his new arrangement with Judy and poured forth paragraphs of undying love. There was a pause as Wylie, smiling broadly, finished his paean to Judy.

"How old you, anyway?" asked Scott.

"Almost twenty."

"Man, you're pretty young to be pussy whipped."

Wylie was not sure what that meant.

CHAPTER 4

INTO THE INFANTRY

◆ ◆ ◆

SERGEANT BRANCH CAREFULLY MONITORED WYLIE'S performance with all
the weapons available to the Army infantryman during the next few
weeks of basic training. Wylie demonstrated his aptitude for bisect-
ing distant targets with the carbine, BAR (Browning automatic rifle),
.45-caliber pistol, bazooka, and even 60 and 81-millimeter mortars.
After firing a single registration round, the others would find their
way to the center of a target, whether near or far. Pleased as he was
with this new talent, Wylie had no idea where his keen eye, steady bearing, and intuitive sense of distance arose. He was, however, thankful
for the grudging admiration of fellow recruits and the three-day passes received for his marksmanship. Judy seemed impressed with the
growing ladder of designated weapons attached to the expert marksmanship badge on his chest.

"Lootennet," said Sergeant Branch to Randy Butz as they raised
their second pints of beer at the Dew Drop Inn in Bordentown, "we
got ourselves a phenomenon here in Company C. That Cypher kid
can hit any fuckin' target with any fuckin' weapon the Army has. That
sumbitch can sever a gnat's pecker at a hunnert yards with a BAR. That
sumbitch is a natural born infantryman! And he thinks he wants to go
lollygagging out to California and mess around with Russki when he
could be a real asset to us and the glorious infantry"

Lt. Butz stared thoughtfully at the golden liquor in his glass.

"I'll see what I can do," he said.

As the end of his eight-week basic training course approached, Wylie was called to the base G-1 office and informed by the Sergeant responsible for his Regiment that the language training program for which he had applied operated on a semester basis and that he would be enrolled in mid-January.

"So, son," he said, "you got a choice. You can stay at this fort as a member of my casual company and pull KP, guard, and fireman duties until mustering out to California, or you can transfer to California after basic training and do the same chickenshit stuff there. You need to let me know by next Monday so I can cut the orders."

The next morning, after Wylie completed his daily dozen calisthenics, Lt. Butz motioned him over to the side of the bleachers.

"Private, I got a call from G-1 about the delay in your going out to the language school. I know you did well on your tests and it seems like a real shame that you've got to pull scut duty while you're waiting."

There was a pause that Wylie would have considered pregnant, had he given it any thought.

Butz continued, "You know you've been a real asset to your platoon; you've got the makings of a good soldier, and you're a hell of a marksman. So, the Captain and I were thinking maybe you'd like to go on for another eight weeks of advanced infantry training right here in the company instead of pulling KP and that other shit."

What, wondered Wylie, would advanced infantry training entail.

"Well, we do more things with infantry weapons, have live fire exercises, like with grenades and BARs, and give you more training in survival and tactics. We blow shit up. We do a couple of weeks of bivouac and combat exercises. It's also leadership training and the way you've been going you'll have your first stripe when you graduate."

The Lieutenant waited a moment before releasing the snapper. "Of course, as an advanced trainee you'll have a pass almost every week end."

As chill November air invaded the Pine Barrens, new members joined recruits continuing their infantry training at C Company. Most were draftees, not there by choice. Failing admission to other branches such as field artillery, armor (tanks), signal corps or engineering after their basic training, they were destined to wear the robin's egg blue neck scarves of the infantry.

The Army desperately needed fresh combat troops to replace infantry soldiers engaged in the worst of the battles in Korea. Clerks in Division G-1 directed any qualified young body to infantry training, followed by assignment to Korea.

An overzealous but harried Army PFC in a stuffy Headquarters G-1 office overlooked the notice of admission to the Army language school that was on a back page of Wylie's personnel file. He saw Wylie was beginning his second eight weeks of infantry training and marked his file with an ominous red "K" on the upper right hand corner of its cover.

During his new training regimen, Wylie was a happy young man. He continued to excel in all military endeavors involving the discharge of weapons and blowing things up. As Lt. Butz had promised, he saw Judy almost every weekend. He reveled in their tender moments together and his infatuation with all things Judy grew. He was troubled, however, by the recurring painful sensation in his scrotum after a few hours of nibbling and kissing. He confided his concern about this condition to Scott McIlwain, who confirmed that it was a normal condition for young men afflicted by unrequited love.

"Wylie, buddy, what you got there is just a mild case of blue balls," he said. "A hand job will take care of it."

Preparing to cure himself, Wylie now understood what a hand job was. Was that something girls could do too?

Wylie stood with other recruits in a bunker awaiting his first nighttime live fire exercise. He was now in his sixth week of advanced infantry training, and Corporal Martinez and others had carefully explained the importance and seriousness of the night's exercise. It was as close a simulation to actual battle conditions as possible, designed to introduce the recruits to the sounds and dangers of actual combat. Instructors advised about the importance of staying cool under fire and keeping their heads down. Real thirty caliber bullets would be whizzing over their heads.

His cheeks glowed with anticipation of the macho exercise ahead, yet a queasy feeling in his stomach and a chilly spot between his shoulder blades betrayed sensible dread of the moments to come. Wylie glanced at his grim-faced squad members on the line. He recalled the talk at chow that evening about recruits from previous training units who froze and couldn't bring themselves to move under the hail of fire or, in hushed tones, those who "lost it" and were wounded or worse from the friendly fire.

Wylie looked at the muddy field in front of the line. He tried to imagine himself slithering toward the far end and realized he had no idea whether he could make it. Braggadocio was gone; he was scared. He gripped the stock of his rifle tightly, but it did not help.

At the "go" signal, he managed to throw himself to the ground in front of the bunker and moved forward. They all crawled on their stomachs across the muddy field in full battle gear with packs, holding rifles in the crooks of their arms, avoiding barbed wire entanglements placed strategically in their paths. Machine gunners opened fire, sending a steady stream of bullets and tracers, red neon comets, a few feet above their heads. To add to the realism, demolition squads exploded C-4 in pits at the edge of the field at random intervals, sending clouds of smoke, sand, and grit into the simulated combat area.

Wylie had traversed about half the field in a state of panic, concentrating on keeping head and rear down while fighting a sense of total disorientation and repeatedly swallowing stomach acid that rose to the back of his mouth. Shooting accurately at antiseptic targets was fun. Experiencing a highly realistic battlefield situation was not. Whatever killer instinct the Army had imbued in him evaporated. This is crazy, he thought. I'm gonna get killed. As he struggled, he heard his friend, Scott, who was crawling slightly ahead to his right, crying for his mother.

In the eerie white light of a phosphorus grenade, he saw that Scott was pressing his body into the muddy earth as though seeking to inhabit it. His shoulders were shaking and his rifle had fallen to the side. The whites of his eyes became large and reflected the chalky brightness of the flare. He moaned. "I got to get the fuck outa here. Outa here. OUTA HERE!"

He began to press his palms against the earth, as though to raise himself to a runner's starting position. Wylie realized Scott was at risk of having portions of his head blown away. Wylie's fear dissolved as he concentrated on helping Scott.

"Hey, man, take it easy. You just got a few more yards to go," yelled Wylie as he inched forward to place his mouth close to Scott's ear.

"Oh Jesus, Wylie, I pissed myself."

"So, that's a problem for the guy behind you."

"Shit, I'm scared shitless. I mean it, Wylie. Shitless."

"Well, that's a relief, "said Wylie.

He placed his arm across Scott's shoulder and Scott slowly relaxed. Wyle's calmness and humor surprised even him. Scott released his hold on the earth and began to crawl forward. Both young soldiers were covered in mud, indistinguishable and anonymous.

A range officer who was preparing to order a cease-fire and extricate Scott from the field witnessed the incident. He watched as Wylie calmed his friend and saw the two crawl forward through the muck. He had no idea who the tall Private was, but noted his coolness under fire. Good man, thought the officer.

Scott and Wylie slid under the safety marker at the end of the field, raised themselves from the kneeling position, and tried to shake off some of the grime and muck. In the bright lights shining from exercise towers, they could hardly recognize each other.

"Pissed yourself, huh?"

"Man, you had to be there."

"Well, I was."

"Yeah."

Then the laughter began. Uncontrollable, air-gulping gobs of laughter that made their sides hurt and tears fill their eyes and course down mud-spattered cheeks. They held each other and wobbled toward waiting trucks.

I made it through that one, thought Wylie. But what if I hadn't been distracted by Scott? What if I'd been too scared to make it to the end? He did not dwell on those distressing questions. He thought instead of attending Russian language school in balmy Monterrey, California.

Colonel Alfonse C. "Chuck" Warfinger pointed to a vacant spot on his map of the Fort Dix war games area and announced, "We'll call that Hill 123 and that'll be the engagement point for Companies C and D." Originality was not his forte, but he was an experienced infantry officer and expected a well-orchestrated combat simulation.

"Sir, that's not a hill. There are no hills in that area."

"I damn well know that, Major," said Warfinger. "But a lot of these guys are going to be trying to take real hills pretty damn quick and they better get used to hill nomenclature. We got simulated combat with simulated ammunition, so we got a simulated hill. I can simulate any goddam thing I want. You decide who will be the defender and aggressor and tell the aggressor company to take the hill with speed and alacrity."

Company C became responsible for holding simulated Hill 123 during three snowy days in February 1953.

Lieutenant Butz and members of his platoon stamped feet encased in black rubber "Mickey Mouse" boots in front of their CP on Hill 123 as a half-moon withdrew behind scudding clouds. Scouts reported their perimeter was secure, but, knowing that Lt. Rusty Miller of D Company was a crafty poker player, Butz suspected a flanking movement from the aggressor Company. Admittedly, flanking movements on an open field masquerading as a hill would be problematic, but darkness would be an advantage and there were a few scrub pines for cover. The Umpire seemed uneasy too.

Butz called to his Corporal, "Martinez, take four men and out-flank our flank on the left. Stanley, you take four men and outflank our flank on the right. Slow and easy."

Outflanking a flank actually meant something to the noncoms, but seemed like gibberish to Wylie and the other three who joined Corporal Martinez. They clutched their weapons and followed the Corporal. Martinez expanded his chest with deep breaths and rotated his shoulders. He grimaced, imitating what he thought his Indian ancestor must have looked like as he prepared for battle. He was now in his Geronimo mode.

The eight members of Rusty Miller's Company D assigned to out-flank Lt. Butz' left flank and defeat the defenders were in difficulty.

The practice in chow lines during field maneuvers was to place two large steel water containers heated with gasoline burners in front of the line. The first container held boiling soapy water, the second boiling clear water. Troopers were expected to dip their mess kits first in soapy, then in clear water to clean and sterilize their cups and utensils before joining the chow line. Mess Sergeants selected soldiers at random to organize and set up the field mess under their supervision.

On the night that Corporal Martinez segued into Geronimo mode, the Private in charge of Company D's chow line unfortunately reversed the placement of the water containers. In the approaching darkness, no one noticed the change, although there were pointed remarks about the peculiar taste of the food ladled into their mess cups.

The ensuing laxative effect struck Company D's attackers a few moments before Corporal Martinez and his team crept from a small copse of scrub pines toward the sound of movement ahead. The sounds they heard were the unfortunate noises of a group of men suddenly afflicted by the drizzly shits. As the presumed attackers squatted for relief, bereft of weapons and fatigues about their ankles, they surrendered to

Corporal Martinez who attacked with his bayonet drawn. He detailed Wylie and the others to march the captives back to the CP once they were capable of doing so.

At the CP, the Umpire informed Company C the exercise was over. An unfortunate combination of unforeseen circumstances had felled their enemy. This event thwarted Colonel Warfinger's efforts to orchestrate an excellent exercise.

Wylie joined his platoon in gathering up gear and prepared to march to the trucks awaiting their return. As he picked up his pack, his rubber boots struck a patch of ice and he slipped into a sand bag lined slit trench where he broke his leg.

CHAPTER 5

FAREWELL FORT DIX

◆ ◆ ◆

THE VANQUISHED OF AGINCOURT, CULLODEN or Gallipoli would have empathized with a distressed Wylie, lying on his hospital bed observing his plaster encased leg. It was now six days since he would have graduated from advanced infantry training and spent a weekend of leave-taking with Judy before heading to California. Instead, he needed to nurse his boot top fracture in bed for a few more days before beginning to hobble around the ward on crutches. Yesterday a Sergeant from G-1 visited to inform him that his injury would cause him to miss the beginning of language training at Monterrey.

The Sergeant said, "Sorry, but the way this works, you miss it, you lose it. As far as personnel is concerned, it's open season on you. Once you get your leg healed, you will be reassigned at the discretion of the Army."

Noticing Wylie's anguished expression, he added, "Good news is that we credited you with completion of advanced infantry training. You are now a Private First Class with an infantry leader MOS. Congratulations!"

So now, thought Wylie, all my plans about serving as a Russian interpreter somewhere in Europe are out the window and I'm lying here with a future in the infantry, just about the last fucking thing I wanted to do. He stared blankly out the ward window, unhappily thinking, I'm up shits creek without a paddle and I think that's a waterfall ahead.

He poked a chopstick one of the nurses had given him under the cast and scratched a particularly itchy spot. It did not help his mood.

Three weeks later, he returned to Hope's Crossing, moving gracefully on his military issue crutches and wearing a new stripe on each arm. His parents were of three minds about recent developments in his military career - proud with his success in training, concerned about his injured leg, and aghast at the prospects of combat service in lieu of language training. While assignment to Europe or another base in the United States remained possible, the news about Korea with photographs of weary troops and stagnant combat lines was frightening. That seemed to be where recruits were being deployed —especially ones with sixteen weeks of infantry training. On the other hand, the Cold War with the Russians demanded a strong and ready American military presence in Europe, especially Germany. It was a dangerous world and time and neither Asia nor Europe boded well for Wylie.

Judy understood those challenges, but put them out of mind with loving concern about Wylie's injury. He told her it itched more than hurt and showed her how he cut his trousers to accommodate the cast. "Poor leg," she said, hugging Wylie to ease any discomfort. Recognizing that Wylie's limited mobility would hamper any unwanted sudden moves, Judy decided to go to the next step in their relationship. After all, Wylie was expecting new orders within a month and might not return to Hope's Crossing before he left. It would be, she felt, a kind of a going away present.

After helping Wylie hobble up the stairs to her bedroom, she told him that it would be a double-breasted weekend, and offered him complete access to the treasures above her waist. He was overwhelmed, delighted, breathless. It never occurred to him to demand more.

Wylie spent the next few weeks on light duty helping the C Company clerk process the innumerable papers associated with military record keeping. He relearned typing skills used while he edited his High School newspaper and watched new recruits crumble under

Corporal Martinez' tender ministrations. He continued these duties after doctors removed his cast, and was settling in as an assistant clerk when his personnel file arrived from Division.

One glance at the large red "K" on the upper right cover was enough. He was certain of his next destination.

However, there was time for farewells at Hope's Crossing. High school friends were home for spring break, now old enough to drink legally, and they plied Wylie with beer and manly hugs. He regaled them with stories of basic training. They paid attention. With the draft operative, many of them were destined to suffer through that training as well.

During awkward goodbyes, mother and sisters were tearful and his father reminded him to keep his head down. Judy's trembling upper lip soon gave way to a Niagara of tears and they exchanged wet kisses. They would write; they would write every day.

Wylie arrived at Fort Lewis, Washington four long days later. Lengthy waits to board the DC-3 aircraft at McGuire Air Base and more lengthy waits at each stop over as they flew across country prepared Wylie for the interminable lines for processing at the Fort. There, he was surprised to discover his good friend, Scott, standing in line with him.

"You got orders, man?" asked Wylie.

"Yeah - big K. Gonna get me some. You goin to Japan or Korea?"

"Korea."

"Fuckin' A, man. We're gonna be asshole buddies, get in that fox hole butt to butt, cover each other and get us some serious gooks."

"Yeah," mumbled Wylie surprised to discover what a warrior Scott had become.

They made a silent pact. They would look out for each other on leave in Seattle and on the troop ship that would carry them to Sasebo, Japan before the hop to Korea. Scott, strong and darkly handsome, soon violated the pact with an especially friendly young woman who frequented the bar they visited in Seattle. Wylie employed the interlude scratching a few lines to Judy, beginning a postal romance that would end only when and if he returned to Hope's Crossing.

The General Parker troop ship left its mooring for Puget Sound midafternoon, arriving at the open sea that evening as a light squall arrived from the southwest. The ship's movement through choppy waters churned the stomachs of hundreds of young soldiers who, throughout that night, revisited the last meal served at Fort Lewis.

The troops were packed into bunks four levels high in the hold of the ship. The worst location was the bottom bunk. Its occupant was at the mercy of potential projections from the three above him. Fortunately, Wylie and Scott occupied top bunks, cramped but clean. As the ship rocked in choppy waters, many soldiers raced up stairwells to the upper decks. A large minority did not quite make it to the railings in time. By the morning's gray light, the lower ranks busied themselves with buckets of seawater and mops cleansing steel decks and railings. This employment continued throughout the voyage.

Ironically, Scott, who was unable to eat anything for three days, reported for mess duty, cleaning tables and carrying metal trays. Three days out, however, he gained his sea legs. Wylie suffered seasickness for only a few hours and, as a PFC and infantry leader, led a squad in physical exercise—rounds of daily dozen calisthenics and volleyball games on the fantail. He organized weapon cleaning drills and target practice using slingshots and dried Army meat balls

Orchestrated high jinks as the ship passed the International Date Line helped relieve the monotony of cruising a now glassy Pacific Ocean. Grizzled King Neptune made his way to an upper deck, took a seat on a capstan, and placed over his potbelly a trident that suspiciously resembled a mop handle with wooden tines. He glared at the assembled soldiers, shook his stringy hair (probably the mop from the trident handle), and demanded to be worshipped by Captain, crew and cargo. Ship's crew, masquerading as mermen, selected unfortunates who were prodded to their knees before King Neptune. He meted out appropriate punishment for invading his kingdom, all of which involved dousing with buckets of salt water. When a score of young warriors stood dripping near his throne, he was satisfied and ordered the delivery of buckets of grog for the gathered assembly.

Scott and Wylie discovered the grog was none other than near beer, a malt brew with a 3.2 percent alcohol content that they had first encountered at Fort Dix. The ship's cargo, consequently, were obliged to drink approximately twenty percent more to achieve the same level of stupefaction as with proper beer. They consumed historic quantities. During the course of the next few hours, the troops returned the borrowed grog to King Neptune's domain.

As the festivities ended, a freshening wind and pelting rain drove in from the west. The storm battered the ship for three days, causing fresh misery for the ship's cargo. The skies finally cleared as the ship sailed through the Sea of Japan toward the Yellow Sea. Jeju Island was visible in the far distance. In another two days, they would dock in Inchon. As Scott and Wylie navigated a still slippery deck unsteadily heading for the railing, they looked forward to being on dry land, even if it was in Korea. It couldn't be worse than being cooped up in this fucking boat, could it?

Two days later, they disembarked at Inchon, going ashore in bumpy landing craft toward green hills. They clambered aboard semitrailers to be packed like oysters in a can. Wylie sat near the outer edge of the trailer and saw peaceful mist shrouded mountains contrasting with nearby devastation. Ruined, burned out vehicles hugged the shoulders of the slippery road they traveled. Gutted, crushed building foundations rose like ancient ruins from the charred landscape. Shabby Korean shacks cobbled together from sticks, cardboard, and mud seemed so fragile that the shuddering earth under the trucks' wheels would cause them to collapse.

Korean men carrying farm tools moved beside the road, and Wylie saw an ox cart loaded with manure plod along a path leading toward the mountains. Dark skies emphasized the charcoal gray and olive drab on all sides. Wylie hugged his duffel bag, uneasy in these grim surroundings.

The truckloads of soldiers prompted little interest from the villagers beside the road except for dirty small boys in tattered remnants of army fatigues. They ran alongside the slowly moving trucks, holding up cartridge belts, lighters, and other trinkets for sale. At a temporary stop, Scott amused himself by bargaining with one of the boys.

"Two dollars is too much for the hat," he said. "I'll give you 50 cents."

The five-year-old pointed his right middle finger toward Scott and declared, "Bullshit. Two bucks!"

I wonder, thought Wylie, whether future cultural interactions will proceed along the same lines.

At the processing center north of Inchon, the new arrivals exchanged their clothes for new fatigues. Medics inspected short arms; they filled up on hot chow; and a Second Lieutenant who appeared to be about fourteen years old delivered warnings about Korean diseases, food, controlled substances, and women. Among the various risks itemized, Wylie noted that he did not mention the dangers of facing North Korean and Chinese troops.

Before dawn the next day, a staff Sergeant who sounded like air brakes on a trailer truck when he whispered banged on a gong and announced to the barracks in his normal tones:

"All you young troopers pissing stateside water prepare to fall out and get processed. You WILL be moving to your new units post haste."

As dawn rusted corrugated metal above the doorways, Scott and Wylie returned their blankets, grabbed some coffee, and reported to the building designated by the dulcet-toned staff Sergeant. Inside were rows of counters that created narrow pathways for the troops to navigate before exiting at the rear of the building. Scott preceded Wylie and moved down the nearest pathway.

A scrawny, bespectacled soldier leaned toward him and demanded "Orders!" It took a moment or two for him to realize he was being asked to produce the mimeographed orders issued at Fort Lewis. He plucked the tattered paper from his breast pocket and handed it over. His interrogator moved his glasses to the top of his head and squinted at the paper.

"Private Scott McIlvane, Uijongbu Repple Depot!" he shouted. A disembodied voice a few paces away repeated the phrase, followed by an ominous "Seven!" Scott moved forward and passed another soldier who quickly inscribed the number seven on the back of his jacket with a stick of chalk. Startled, Scott turned and the chalker wrote the number again on his chest, defacing the clean fatigues issued the day before.

"That's your transport number. It's the train up North. You're going to 53rd Infantry. You get your gear and march to the train depot from here."

The transportation cadre enjoyed their chalk game and tried to distract incoming troops by blocking their view of the man ahead. The soldier requesting orders thrust himself in front of Wylie so he, too, was surprised with the chalk attack. The number seven blazed whitely from his new green fatigues as he pushed his way to the rear exit of the building.

After the customary long hours of waiting, he and Scott clambered aboard a rickety Korean train in full battle dress, wedging themselves onto wooden seats and avoiding the hole in the floor that was the latrine. As they crossed the Han River, Wylie saw the devastated city of Seoul through the framework of a wrecked and sunken bridge. In the shadow-less light of a cloudy day the crumbled and jagged buildings, still marked with fissures caused by the arsenal of ordinance employed against them by two armies, appeared two dimensional, as though the entire city had been flattened against the distant hills. In awe at the destruction still in evidence almost two years afterwards, Wylie considered what the impact of such forces would have on an infantryman in combat.

Less reflective, Scott said, "Holy shit; they really blew this place apart. Think they have any poon tang and liquor left there? I'm sure as hell gonna take my first leave here and find out!"

Wylie wished he could so nonchalantly ignore the Army's warnings about these things.

Later that day, the little train arrived in Uijongbu and the soldiers were processed again — more gear, further indoctrination, a meal more dependent on C ration staples, and a cot in a tent suspiciously patched to cover 50 caliber bullet holes. Wylie and Scott stowed their gear and awaited their new assignments, scheduled to be delivered in a day or so, hoping they would serve together.

For the first time in days, Wylie was able to pause and reflect on what he had seen and heard since arriving in the port of Inchon. He thought of the dangers surrounding them hidden in now lush hills, deceptively blooming with wild azaleas. The Sergeant's observation on the future prospects for his ass, combined with the stark evidence of the war's impact on Seoul and Inchon were frightening. Interlaced with such thoughts were all too fleeting mental images of Judy.

As dusk fell, his thoughts darkened and he became overwhelmed with bitterness, self-pity, and an unnamed sense of impending doom. He sped to the latrine, closing the door just as Bedcheck Charlie rumbled over the horizon.

CHAPTER 6

53RD INFANTRY DIVISION P.I.O.

◆ ◆ ◆

THE NEXT AFTERNOON, STAFF SERGEANT Waldo Oppenheimer motioned Wylie to his portable desk under the fly of a tent alongside the repple depple parade ground. As Wylie stood at ease by the desk, the Sergeant carefully reviewed a file that he pulled from the stack of folders on the desk. Wylie, who had been waiting in line for almost two hours, was surprised at Oppenheimer's first question.

"How did you like your freshman year at Princeton?"

"Well, I guess I really enjoyed it. There were lots of interesting people and I liked being in the Glee Club and the Dramat. Most of the courses I took were good even though I..."

Oppenheimer held up a hand and interrupted.

"It was really a rhetorical question. I figured that enlisting in the Army after your first year indicated a certain paucity of performance. Is that right?"

Who is this guy using alliteration and a fancy vocabulary, wondered Wylie? Am I in deep shit right now and don't know it?

Warily, "I guess that's right."

"Truth be told," said Oppenheimer, "I graduated two years ago with a degree in PolySci, got drafted and was assigned to G-1. I'm at about the end of my tour but I like to look out for us Ivy League guys. I can see you're a good marksman and have the Infantry leader MOS.

If you go up to the line, there's a pretty good chance you'll get your ass shot off within the first couple of weeks."

There it is again, thought Wylie. Everybody seems to be convinced my ass is not long for this world. There's absolutely nothing I want less than getting my ass shot off. But, wait a minute, didn't he just say "if" I go on the line? What is...

"Fortunately, combat duty is not foreordained. We have personnel requests from outfits up here that could use other talents. Right here," perusing a mimeographed list on the table, "there's a need for someone who can type at Special Services, orderly work at the M.A.S.H., writing for the Division paper at the P.I.O., and someone with mechanical experience at the motor pool. Does any of that interest you?"

"I worked on my high school newspaper, mainly doing stuff about sports. I was a staff writer for The Princetonian. What's P.I.O stand for; I never heard of it."

"That's the Division Public Information Office. Their mission is to report stories about the troops over here and to record interviews for local radio stations in the States. They also send articles to Sergeant Jules Pike in Tokyo who edits the weekly Division paper. The nice thing about this job is that you don't have to pull KP or guard duty, although you have to be combat ready. And you work in a tent with lights and sleep on a cot that's not in a bunker."

"I think that would be really good," said Wylie with perceptible relief.

After a moment's reflection, he added, "You know, one of my buddies is a really good mechanic. He's got an Infantry MOS too, but that motor pool job might be just right for him. He's right over there. His name's Scott McIlvane."

"Is he from a good school?"

"I don't think so, but he's a really good mechanic," lied Wylie "and we are trying to stick together."

Sergeant Oppenheimer said, "Okay. Send him over now."

Oppenheimer agreed that Scott would be suitable for the motor pool. Since he and Wylie were to be assigned to the Headquarters Company of the 53rd Infantry Division, the Sergeant briefly explained the Division's current situation and handed them a pamphlet entitled "53rd Infantry Division TOE" (Table of Organization and Equipment) and the official history of the Division prepared by its historian. He suggested to Wylie in particular that he look the material over before "the morrow" so he wouldn't appear like a complete asshole when the P.I.O. Sergeant looked him over. Scott might as well read it too.

According to the history, the 53rd Infantry Division was formed in Minnesota in 1916 and was known as the "Fighting Swedes." In Korea in 1953, however, it would be difficult to identify those of Nordic extraction under steel helmets, with grimy faces and shoulders hunched from packs and weapons. The Division's patch was crossed sabers on a field of barley, surrounded by a circle of emerald green. The Division fought valiantly at the Marne during World War One and returned to Fort Ord in California in recognition of its valor.

Apparently, something unspeakable involving members of the Division and a group of Girl Scouts occurred along California's lovely beaches in 1940. The division was dispatched quickly to a remote island in the Philippines, to be evacuated soon thereafter to Australia as Corregidor fell. Division troops fought during the Pacific Campaigns throughout World War II and, with the defeat of Japan in 1945, took posts in Korea. Because of what happened in California, however, top brass determined never to let the division return to CONUS (the Continental United States). The Fighting Swedes were also Flying Dutchmen, whether they liked it or not.

The bulk of the Division withdrew to Japan from Korea in 1949 and served under General McArthur in southern Japan. When North Korean armies invaded the South in massive numbers in June of 1950, a garrison from the Division stationed south of Seoul was supporting one of Syngman Rhee's Republic of Korea ("ROK") divisions. Overwhelmed by Russian tanks and waves of NK soldiers, the

ROK division crumbled and ran, and the Fighting Swedes retreated with them.

Few in the garrison survived, but a handful of its soldiers joined the United Nations forces defending the perimeters of Pusan in southern Korea. Those elements of the Division stationed in Japan returned to Korea during the Inchon landing in September of 1950 to fight with General Walker's Eighth Army and repel the North Korean invaders.

Wylie knew that the American and United Nations troops massed during the Inchon Landing joined with the troops defending Pusan to push the northern invaders back up the peninsula. That late summer and fall campaign succeeded with such speed that the troops' supply lines from Pusan and Inchon were stretched thin.

As a frigid October arrived, many of the soldiers were still fighting in their summer uniforms. At the end of that month, the 53rd Division was supporting the 1st Marines at the Chosin Reservoir, within striking distance of the Yalu River, the boundary between North Korea and China. Their mission was to drive the invaders to their northern border, and General McArthur urged Washington to let him take Manchuria, China's territory, to thwart communist aggression in the region.

Chairman Mao, communist China's leader, supported the invasion of South Korea as a way to extend communist rule over the entire peninsula and was prepared to help the North Koreans in any way possible to achieve that goal. When North Korea's forces began to retreat, Mao ordered tens of thousands of Chinese "volunteers" to gather north of the Yalu River as reserve forces. Toward the end of October 1950, as the United Nations troops fought their way north, Mao waited until they had extended their supply lines and no longer maintained cohesive unit contacts. He directed his generals to attack from all sides with overwhelming force and destroy the Yankee Imperialists.

The three Regiments of the 53rd Division were close to the Yalu River in Northeastern Korea when their patrols reported masses of troops clad in quilted brown uniforms wearing what looked like tennis shoes approaching their positions from all points of the compass. Mao had arranged to ferry some volunteers down the east coast of the peninsula to attack the enemy from the south as well. Trapped, the Division's only recourse was to attack to the rear in an effort to break out. What followed, during one of the coldest Novembers and Decembers in Korean history, was the destruction of five ROK Divisions and the bloody slaughter of UN troops as they fought their way southward through treacherous mountain terrain.

As would happen so often in this war, the retreating forces regrouped, reinforced, and reengaged the enemy. By the spring of 1951, Eighth Army and the other UN forces had established a see-saw perimeter north of Seoul. Fierce battles for blood-soaked real estate ensued; as men died, both sides considered the possibility of ending what seemed more and more like an unwinnable contest. A classical solution would be declaring a ceasefire. In June of 1951, negotiations between the two sides to establish an armistice began. They continued as battles raged and soldiers on both sides of the lines were killed, wounded and captured.

In April 1953, as Wylie conferred with Sergeant Oppenheimer, the talks and the battles continued. Wylie was only vaguely aware of this history, though he remembered vividly photographs of haggard men in combat retreating from the Chosin Reservoir. Such images strongly influenced his thwarted plans to avoid the place where he now was.

Major General Bart B. Black, whose adjutant was Brigadier General Henry "Hank" Walnut, commanded the Division. There were three Regiments led by Colonels with the customary support of artillery and armor. The Air Force and Marine Corsair squadrons conferred air superiority. Headquarters Company, where P.I.O. was located, was north of the replacement depot, and two Regiments were on the line, confronting NK and Chinese forces as they had for more than a year. One Regiment was in reserve to the East, below the 38th Parallel.

The pamphlet noted that a Captain commanded the P.I.O. with a cadre of ten enlisted men. The motor pool, on the other hand, seemed of higher importance, since it was commanded by a Major and had scores of enlisted men and a designated location.

The following morning, Wylie and Scott awaited transportation to Division headquarters. They were in full battle dress, shouldering M-1 rifles and holding duffel bags packed with their clothes and personal items. The dirt roads approaching the repple depple generated strawberry blonde clouds of dust. The two men saw a dirty Jeep plow through such a cloud and scud to a stop in front of them.

The grimy figure behind the wheel wore his fatigue hat backwards and sported an empty cigarette holder clenched between sparkling teeth.

"One a you guys McIlvane?" he asked.

Scott stepped forward and Sergeant Pangluss, who drove the Jeep, said, "Toss your gear in the back and grab a seat. Good to know you. You can call me Gus. We're heading for your rack behind my motor pool, and then we got work to do. The gooks are bustin up our stuff faster than we can fix it! Hang on."

Scott complied, waved goodbye to Wylie, saying, "Catch you later man," and clambered onto the passenger seat. With the anti-wire bar welded to the front of the Jeep leading on, Pangluss and Scott plunged down the rutted road to Headquarters.

Wylie waited expectantly, considering each newly arrived vehicle as his potential transport. After some time, two figures in a Jeep approached and stopped by the tent housing the G-1 section. A Sergeant walked to the tent, received direction from those inside, and strolled over to Wylie, who noticed the Combat Correspondent patch above his right breast pocket. Sergeant Richard Heron held out his hand and asked, "Wylie Cypher?"

Sergeant Heron was hardly older than Wylie was. He was fair-haired, tall and solidly built, but there were unexpected lines at the corners of his eyes and mouth. He carried a side arm, usually reserved for officers, and his boots were miraculously clean. A combat infantry badge was embroidered on the fabric of his blouse, an unusual decoration for a correspondent.

Two years earlier, Heron graduated from Gonzaga University in Indiana with a degree in journalism, was drafted immediately, trained, and sent to Korea. Army Personnel, in a decision that confounded customary practice, assigned him to a position that took advantage of his college training. Sergeant Heron joined the Division as its members were engaged in mortal combat, and he had stories to tell. The combat infantry badge and his rapid promotion to Sergeant attested to that. During the past nine months in Korea he developed the ability to assess quickly the quality of men he served with, an important factor in self-preservation. He examined his new recruit closely as he walked toward Wylie. As he held out his hand, he thought, looks okay.

Wylie took Heron's hand, saying, "Thanks for coming to get me, Sergeant. I'm really, really excited about working for you. I wasn't sure how things were going to work out for..."

"First of all," said Heron, "you call me Dick unless there's an officer around. Second, do me a favor and don't bullshit me. The reason I'm here is because Oppie thought you might have more on the ball that most of these peckerheads, and I need a quick replacement for one of my guys who's rotating in a couple of weeks. You don't work out, it's off to a bunker with your rifle. We clear?"

"Crystal, Sergeant."

"Okay. Grab your gear and toss it in the Jeep. We should be at Division in less than an hour."

As Wylie took his place at the rear of the Jeep, Heron gestured toward the driver, a grinning young man with the beginning of a non-GI stubby beard.

"Oh, uh, that's our driver," he said. "You call him 'Shit Dad'."

CHAPTER 7

COMRADES IN ARMS

◆ ◆ ◆

"Shit dad," said Private Rowe in his syrupy Cajun accent as he helped Wylie secure his gear, "it's fine you gonna be with us, man. This Sergeant here is one kinda good fella. He take care of his men and we take care of him. We a good group, work hard, have fun. Get shot at a little, but not too much." He laughed, cranked up the engine, and eased the Jeep on its way south.

For reasons he later disclosed to Wylie, Private Rowe volunteered for a second tour in Korea. He combined a unique mixture of irreverence and amiability in his approach to life, fostered by the easygoing life style of the Bayou and the fact that he had survived on his own since the age of twelve. Wylie soon learned that his skill in survival techniques helped preserve Shit Dad and his comrades during combat.

He prefaced most utterances with a cordial "Shit dad" as in, "Shit dad, Major, sir, I do believe we should take the fork to the left." He was so agreeable and friendly that his superiors ultimately tired of disciplining him and accepted him as pleasantly incorrigible. His skills as a driver and his sixth sense of impending danger also tempered thoughts of punishment, especially since these abilities had saved the lives of more than one of his passengers.

Myles Standrich, the Captain leading the Public Information Office, was one. Private Rowe had maneuvered the Captain to safety through a gauntlet of small arms and mortar fire in a Jeep with a flat tire and steaming radiator some months before. The Captain arranged with Sergeant Pangluss of the motor pool for Rowe's permanent attachment to the P.I.O.

After a few weeks as P.I.O. driver under the Captain's supervision, Standrich became concerned for the Private's immortal soul. He suspected him of fornication, ungodliness, corruption, and an unhealthy disregard of Army regulations. Standrich intended to guide him toward goodness. A first step was to change his odious nickname. He always referred to him by his rank. Nevertheless, Rowe continued to be known as Shit Dad, and he cheerfully addressed all by his unique salutation, without consideration of rank or fortune.

As their Jeep sped over the dusty road to Division headquarters, Dick Heron provided more details about the P.I.O. operation.

"Basically, we're the Division's public relations arm disguised as journalism," he said. "We create stories favorable to our interests and coordinate with civilian reporters whenever they visit division locations. We help the people from AP, UP, INS, the TV networks, and newspapers with transport, getting interviews and so on. Our job is also to hook them up with Signal Corps to make sure they have lines to get their stories out. Occasionally, we go with them to the combat zone and try to keep them from getting killed."

Shit Dad found that piece of information amusing. He wobbled the steering wheel to encourage great puffs of dust from the Jeep's wheels.

Heron continued, "Some of the reporters have a pretty high opinion of themselves and are interested in either interviewing generals or reporting from the front, but not too close to the lines. Others want to report things from the G.I. point of view and spend time in the bunkers and trenches. They all want to get the story first and scoop their rivals, but they really are a congenial bunch. You can learn a lot by hanging out with them."

The prospect of hanging out with such luminaries excited Wylie. He visualized rubbing shoulders with Marguerite Higgins, David

Douglas Duncan, Walter Cronkite, and reporters for the Times. It was heady stuff for a twenty-year-old.

"I saw copies of the Division newspaper and the Stars and Stripes in the repple depple day room. Does P.I.O. work with them?" asked Wylie.

"Yeah, the Saber is printed in Tokyo every week and copies are flown over here and distributed to all Division personnel. We get our stuff in the Stars and Stripes every once in a while, but it's more pictures than copy. If you manage to get a good story, you'll have a byline there every once in a while."

Wylie had yet to learn of the importance of a byline or what a good story was. Heron's information and casual manner made it all seem easy. It would be simple, he thought, to transform an ability to write about high school sports to becoming a combat correspondent.

"We also have a team that does what we call hometowners. They go all over the Division with a tape recorder and interview the troops. It's like 'What's your job?' and they say 'I'm a machine gunner' and then they explain they kill the enemy and say Hi to Mom back home. We edit those tapes and they get played on home town radio stations in CONUS.

"Do we see any ... action?" asked Wylie.

Shit Dad laughed at that, and Dick Heron said, "As much as you want. It's pretty much up to you, but it won't happen right away. You've got to get your feet wet before we send you out to the JAMs."

"The JAMs?"

"Yeah. That's what the black guys on the line call themselves. They are Jive Ass Mothers. The Army likes acronyms so we call them JAMs. You'll see"

Wylie watched the road and tried to absorb Heron's comments. Maybe there was more to this than he first thought.

A large crescent wood sign over the entrance to the camp showed crossed sabers and proclaimed, "Stay sharp! You are entering 53rd Division HQRS." A tent city interspersed with Quonset huts unfolded into a flat valley surrounded by steep hills. Stones painted white created paths and identified several of the huts: MASH, HQRS, MESS, and MP and, as the Jeep moved ahead, P.I.O.

The Jeep slowed, and Heron said, "We'll drop you off at the Company Clerk so you can hand in your two oh one file. He'll show you our tent where you can stow your gear. We've got eleven cots instead of ten today because the man you'll be replacing is still here. Our houseboy, Kim, should be there and he'll take care of you and take you to the office when you're ready. Then I'll show you around and you can eat with the enlisted. See you later."

Heron and Shit Dad drove off after depositing Wylie at the clerk's office.

Kim Yon Dung, the houseboy, was a slender Korean boy of, Wylie guessed, about fourteen. As Wylie entered the tent, he smiled broadly and took his duffel bag. He pointed to a cot and footlocker in the middle of the tent saying, "You bed; I fix it all. You name?"

"I'm Wylie."

"Ho, you funny sojer. Have Korean name - Why-Lee. Very funny, very funny. Don't look Korean."

Kim laughed at his excellent joke, and Wylie joined in.

As Kim busied himself unpacking the duffel bag and carefully placing its contents in the footlocker, Wylie examined his new home. The large olive drab tent stood on a wooden platform and was held up by two poles supported by guy wires. There were flaps at both ends and four cots on each side with three in the middle. Two wash basins stood beside the main entrance and two light bulbs dangled on wires from above. In the exact center of the tent stood an oil-fueled iron stove that Kim had decorated with wild flowers in a K-ration can.

Not bad, thought Wylie, whose standards had been drastically lowered during his voyage across the Pacific. Electric lights, heat, a wood floor, a clean cot, my own footlocker, a place to wash up, a houseboy, and nobody shooting at me.

I better not screw this up!

A sea of olive drab canvas and the sounds and smells of hundreds of soldiers busily attending to their duties surrounded Wylie as he walked with Kim toward the P.I.O. office tent. Curious about the makeup of his new comrades in arms, he wondered if they would resemble the stock characters he remembered from the war movies he watched so intently when he was younger.

Would there be a wisecracking Italian kid from the Bronx or a sincere, blond Midwestern boy who always seemed to carry a machine gun? Maybe there would be a gruff Sergeant with a heart of gold or a scrawny intellectual writing a journal, which would later become a war novel. Would there be a tough guy who breaks in combat and is rescued by the quiet Jewish kid everyone thought was a fuck up?

He reached the door of the P.I.O. office, which Kim opened, then ushered him in.

"Have good time, Why-Lee," he said.

Heron sat at a desk near the entrance, commanding a telephone, a typewriter, piles of papers, and green in and out baskets. He was marking up one of the papers with a blue crayon as Wylie entered. Beyond the Sergeant was another, larger desk containing framed family photographs, a telephone, a rock with a crudely painted yellow sun weighing down a small pile of papers, some newspapers, and a massive coffee cup. Captain Myles Standrich leaned back in a comfortable chair, preparing to sip from his cup of coffee. He had a stocky body with a large, pink face topped by close-cropped reddish blonde hair. My God, thought Wylie, he's a cherub! But he was also a Captain, and Wylie saluted him as he entered the tent.

Standrich waved back a salute, saying "No need for that inside Private, otherwise we'd be saluting all day and never get any work done." Chuckle.

The Captain stood and turned to Heron.

"Well, Sergeant, now that I've met our new man I'll be off to the Battalion skeet range. Private Rowe will drop me off and I'll find my own way back tonight. If there's anything that needs my attention, just give a note to my houseboy. Nice to meet you, Private Cypher."

As the Captain left with his coffee, Wylie noticed he carried a bullet tipped swagger stick under his arm. Incongruous, thought Wylie. This officer's swagger resembled a pig on ice. However, he remembered one of his mother's frequent admonitions: don't judge lest you be judged and found wanting. I won't be taken in by first impressions. Maybe the Captain is a ball of fire and great leader of men.

Heron introduced Wylie to the others in the tent. There were two tables holding reel tape recorders, earphones, and microphones, boxes of tape reels and cardboard containers. A tall, dark haired Corporal offered his hand. "I'm Phil Nordman and this Neanderthal back here is Boomer Flatley."

He gestured to the Corporal behind him who Wylie expected should be carrying the machine gun, a tall, blonde, taciturn looking young man with a wide grin behind full lips, as sunny an expression as fully grown wheat at noon. Boomer was loading recording gear into a wooden case.

"Phil and I do the hometowners," said Boomer. "I think Dick already explained what they are. I run the equipment and Phil, who used to broadcast from a 50-Watt station in Idaho, does the interviews. We try to knock off about fifteen interviews a day and then edit them all the next day. Nice to have you here. We'll see you later tonight."

At the other side of the tent were four metal desks with typewriters occupied by two Privates, a Corporal, and a Sergeant. Helmets, ammunition belts, and M-1 rifles were neatly stacked along the wall of the tent. These men had all been typing as Wylie entered the tent and stopped to greet him as Sergeant Heron made introductions.

"Sergeant Cranford is rotating back in about three weeks; you are his replacement as our general reporter for Division. Corporal Izzy Flint is our sports editor and these other guys are Lamar Trenchant and Barry Sonnenfeld. They are clerk typists and crank out the final versions of our stories. Lamar is the one who operates the telex. We also have a correspondent in each of the regiments and they send news and hometowners for us to pass on.

"The Captain's job is to review it all and make sure none of it will show the Division in a poor light or bite us in the ass. We have to be careful that we send out nothing that gives 'aid and comfort' to the enemy. That's especially true about pictures. An editor at the Stars and Stripes got canned last month for publishing pictures of American POWs looking as though they enjoyed playing volley ball up North."

Heron directed Wylie to a spare desk supporting an old typewriter in the rear of the tent and asked him to rewrite an article about a regimental baseball game. I can do this, thought Wylie, happy and relieved. He began working the keys of the typewriter. The clacking noise almost covered the sound of artillery in the distance.

CHAPTER 8

LETTER TO JUDY

◆ ◆ ◆

BY FREE AIR MAIL
2 April 1953

My Dearest One -

A typewritten letter again, but honest, darling, it's the only way I can get all my jumbled thoughts down on paper tonight. First of all, I love you; second of all, it is not a mere infantry PFC who is pounding out this epistle, but an Official U.S. Army combat correspondent (I pause to bask in the glory of it all). Seriously, though, my luck has held beyond my wildest dreams. I now live in a tent with real wooden floors, sleep on a cot with an air mattress, have the use of electric lights and a typewriter, and am assigned to the Headquarters Company of the 53rd Infantry Division, a stone's throw from the general's home.

Naturally, it's got to be pretty fine here, and aside from the fact that we can see the enemy lines and hear sounds of combat on a clear day, it's got everything of the best— as far as that goes in the land of frozen Chosin. I forgot to mention there's a latrine (no plumbing, but quite serviceable) and a shower point a spitting distance from the door of the tent and we have a houseboy, Kim, who does our washing, polishes our shoes and cleans the tent for five bucks a month from each of the ten of us. To say that I've got it knocked so far is the understatement of the year, nay the century!

Well, now that the logorrhea is over with, down to the stark facts. The kid is working with the Public Information Office. I have the use of a Jeep driven by an amazing character called, believe it or not, Shit Dad Rowe. We run around and collect stories that are sent to the Stars and Stripes and other publications, both Army and civilian. There will be times when I'll be off to interview the characters who are periodically dropping over to Korea to get the "big picture."

Our job here is to make the Army look good and our Division look best. At least that's what I understand from my boss, Dick Heron, who is the Sergeant in charge of this lashup. It's pretty hypocritical, but at least I'll be on the "inside" as it were and can take notes and such rot for my personal use when the Army is a thing of the past. This is one point I dwell on a hell of a lot, and most of it has got to do with you, darling. I know it's not exactly the best to be thinking of this all the time, but I think that every once in a while, I should tell you how much I miss you and love you and wish I were holding you in my arms again - especially on those cold spring nights here. But I digress.

The guys in our office all seem to be budding literary brains, so conversations ought to be stimulating. The Captain in charge is what one might call a "hot shit" and is always coming up with statements like "he didn't know whether to defecate or become sightless" - little quaint ways of making the vulgar sound sophisticated. He doesn't spend a lot of time in the office and I still can't figure out why he's still in the Army; he may be lazy or something.

Did I mention the bugs? We really have bugs here. We are constantly on the alert with the aerosol bomb, but it seems they only thrive on the stuff and grow fatter and more dangerous; but along with my carbine and other field gear I was issued (I just know I'll <u>never</u> get a chance to use them of course) I was issued mosquito netting and lots of repellent that does come in handy — instead of stinging or biting right away, the bugs whet their appetites on the stuff before getting down to the meat course, but I must remember never to complain.

The things our Infantry line companies do is almost beyond imagination— I'll write more about that when I've seen it firsthand.

We did have a bit of a scare today. Seems like every time they think they see an enemy plane in the air they have an alert and we have to get our weapons and ammo and take up positions on the hill, scanning the skies. I got sort of shook when all sorts of whistles went off and the artillery crews got set for action. Those guys are really fast! It turned out to be a false alarm and my relief was great. Maybe I'll get used to this stuff after a while, but, for now, Schmuckville!

Must draw to a close for the dusky venetian blinds (too modern to say "shades") of sleep are closing around and I'm fighting a losing battle in doing pushups with my eyelids. Must say good night, my sweetest one.

My thoughts are with you every moment -
Wylie

CHAPTER 9

IDLE CONVERSATION

◆ ◆ ◆

STANDING NEXT TO THE CORPULENT Australian, Dick Heron said, "This is a friend I've been working with for over a year, and though he looks fat and sloppy and doesn't speak the King's English very well, he is a damn good reporter and deserves to be listened to."

"Deeply honored; deeply honored, Dick," said Alistair Benchley, foreign correspondent for the Australian Times, as he settled more comfortably in his chair and sipped from his tumbler of Glen Morangie.

Sergeant Heron was his host at the Enlisted Men's Club, lowering his NCO status so Wylie and Izzy Flint could join him and Alistair, who had arrived that morning from a frustrating week at Panmunjom. Peace talks had been in progress there for almost two years and had resulted so far only in an agreement for the exchange of wounded prisoners from both sides. Operation Little Switch was to take place in about two weeks.

Izzy and Wylie were in awe of this battle-hardened reporter, especially since he hardly looked like the dashing foreign correspondent they imagined before meeting him. He was large and flabby, and his upholstered flesh moved only grudgingly when demanded. Bronze hairs that might have slipped there from his balding head covered his chin, and he clutched a cigar between yellowing teeth. He was able to drink his Scotch without removing the cigar, which he did, however, to speak in an accent devoid of "r"s.

They had been discussing his views on the possibility of an armistice when he excused himself, saying, "Solly, lads, got to bog. That ride down shook up my insides." Heron passed around the bottle of Scotch, noting that Alistair had been reporting from Korea since June of 1950, and acquired as detailed an understanding of the political and military situation on the peninsula as anyone. Further, he was no fan of General McArthur and believed that his discharge by President Truman had saved many lives.

Heron said, "Alistair will provide you with a really good understanding of what is going on in Korea, and he'll do it for half a bottle of Glen Morangie."

The Australian correspondent resumed his seat.

"Let's see - the armistice. First, you've got to understand that each side is trying to prove it has the bigger penis, but without actually dropping its pants. So, as the talks go on, the Chinks and the NKs attack the UN units, especially the ROK divisions, as though they had unlimited resources — which they probably do, as long as we're talking about people.

"Likewise, the UN units decide that some bloody hill or other should belong to them so they attack, lose more of their men, take prisoners. Since the UN has almost complete air superiority, that side can inflict greater damage and, among other things, can toast more of the enemy with phosphorus and napalm, to say nothing of completely destroying every major northern city in Korea.

"Meanwhile South Korean President Syngman Rhee (you know he has a Ph.D. from Princeton, Wylie?) refuses to accept the idea of partition and demands the unification of the country, under his rule, of course. And he's making matters worse by continuing to kill suspected communist sympathizers in the South."

Jeez, thought Wylie, I didn't get any of this from our orientation lectures. They told us we were the cavalry in the white hats, here to liberate the downtrodden. Since Dick Heron earlier assured Wylie and Izzy that Alistair was as unbiased a reporter as could be found in

Korea. Wylie listened carefully, prepared to learn, ready to consider challenges to adolescent beliefs.

"And, Dick," continued Alistair, "I have a bone to pick with the so-called UN information officer at Panmunjom, Brigadier General Quohog. He censors almost everything of importance or delays telling us what's going on. We get more accurate news from the French and Aussie correspondents working for commie papers that are wired in to the other side."

"You're telling me? It's my job to do that at Division level," laughed Dick.

"Anyway, lads, it all boils down to two issues right now—where to locate the demilitarized zone and whether POWs held by the UN can choose where they will be repatriated. The North says they must all return above the DMZ while the UN insists they be given the freedom to choose whether to go to Formosa, South Korea, or North. The DMZ issue isn't hard to resolve, staff people on both sides have got that decided already, but the repatriation thing is a standoff. Whatever happens, they have to get President Rhee on board, and he's a squirrely bostid."

Izzy and Wylie assimilated Alistair's colorful analysis. They realized that Dick Heron probably understood this background well but, coming from this Aussie with his reputation for solid reporting, it would be imprinted indelibly on the young reporters.

"Thanks, Alistair," they said almost in unison.

"Not to mention it lads; it's been great to meet you."

The Scotch bottle now empty, he rose somewhat unsteadily.

"I'm off to my billet and then I'll be stopping at the NAAFI tomorrow to replenish necessities of life — cigars and chocolate. Hope to see you young reporters soon. There's always an extra bunk at the press billets in Seoul," said Alistair as he moved to the door and ambled out into the evening.

Wylie and Izzy later swore to each other they never saw him refill his glass; perhaps he had little suction cups at the end of his fingers.

CHAPTER 10

WYLIE ON THE LINE

◆ ◆ ◆

A ROUTINE STORY FROM A Regimental stringer about two soldiers on their second Korean tour, reunited after fighting their way south from the Chosin Reservoir in November of 1950, piqued Dick Heron's interest. Both had been Sergeants at that time but now only one was. Heron thought there might be a story in that and assigned it to Wylie.

Shit Dad had left to drive Captain Standrich to important business that required his presence elsewhere, but Sergeant Pangluss was willing to do without Private McIlwain for a couple of days. Scott greeted Wylie with, "Hey, asshole buddy, we're goin' up on the line, you and me, just like I predicted. Bitchin', man. Bitchin'!"

Wylie climbed onto the passenger seat, and punched Scott in the right bicep by way of greeting. They both laughed, anticipating a day together, as Scott rammed the Jeep into gear and headed northeast through the village of Tongduchon-ni toward Dog Company of M Battalion.

Now seasoned by four weeks as a combat correspondent, Wylie was excited about visiting a company on the line. Combat veterans at headquarters told him what he believed were tall stories about their experiences, and he was eager to learn how the front line warriors really lived and fought. Dog Company was on a front flanking three ROK Divisions that anchored the eastern end of the UN line.

Sergeant Heron understood there was little activity in that area, other than routine patrols probing the front and looking for prisoners.

In fact, there seemed to be a hiatus in serious combat after the terrible, bloody, and inconclusive battles that March. It seemed reasonable to send his green correspondent into harm's way when there seemed little chance of serious action. At the same time, he was impressed with the quality of Wylie's writing and his quick grasp of story lines. A little exposure to the JAMs was in order.

As they drove, Scott described his experiences at the motor pool. Scott did have mechanical aptitude and had worked on cars with his dad while he was growing up. Sergeant Pangluss had him changing Jeep transmissions, which tended to burn out rapidly from the muck and dust of Korean roads. This week he was transferring to heavier equipment, something he really enjoyed. However, a couple of days driving with Wylie would be a treat. Losing their way was also not likely since there was only one well-traveled road to their destination. Scott expected the trip to take about three hours.

They arrived at the Dog Company hilltop CP midafternoon, since Scott had wildly underestimated driving time. He failed to consider detours up mountains, slowing for oncoming traffic, and maneuvering around crater like potholes.

Second Lieutenant Percy Swift, a platoon commander who seemed younger than Wylie and friendly as a Labrador puppy, greeted them. "I was wondering if you were going to make it," he said after returning their salutes. "The Captain said you were supposed to be here this morning."

Scott took responsibility for the delay. "It's okay," said the Lieutenant. "It's just that my guys could use a little diversion, and the chance of recognition for their contribution would be a good thing. I hope you have a chance to visit with them all. You probably will because there's no way you're going back to Headquarters today. It gets dark in about two hours. So, is one of you the photographer?"

Wylie pulled the 4 x 5 Speed Graphic from the back of the Jeep and explained that he was really the correspondent. The Signal Corps couldn't spare a photographer that morning, but he could use the camera if needed.

"Outstanding! Let's get you set up with Tully and Sergeant Yeoman. They were both here about sixteen months ago and ended up in my platoon by coincidence," said the Lieutenant.

He went into the bunker to confer with the company clerk, returned, and said, "There's some kind of a screw up. Yeoman's over at the Battalion CP, but Tully's here. You can talk to him first, I guess."

In Wylie's brief military experience even small screw ups did not bode well. Things that started on the wrong foot seemed to limp all the way to their conclusion.

"Yes, sir. Let's have a chat with Tully," said Wylie

Tully McGregor could have been a model for an Army recruiting poster. Late twenties, steel blue eyes, ramrod straight, powerful build, square jaw, and an aura of competence. As he rose from a seat in the corner of the bunker there was enough light for Wylie to notice he wore the Queen of Combat Infantry Badge, signifying his participation in two combat areas, and the outline of Master Sergeant Stripes on his faded fatigues - where no stripes now resided. Well, thought Wylie, Heron's instincts were excellent. This guy's distinguished himself in two wars and has been up and down the enlisted ranks. Must be a story here.

"You're SOL if you think you're going to see Yeoman any time soon. He's with the clap doctor over at Battalion. That cock hound is going to be out of action for a while," said Tully with a hint of Tennessee in his accent. Wylie warmed to him immediately.

After introductions, Wylie wrote down the details of Tully's meeting Sergeant Yeoman on their second tour in Korea and learned more about their retreat in the brutal cold from the Chosin Reservoir with hordes of Chinese charging after them. He took a few pictures of Tully, using side light that came through the bunker's openings.

Asked if anything in particular stood out in his mind about that action Tully said, "It was disorganized while we were running south. I got stuck alone in a trench with my BAR holdin' off those Chinks for two days. I had K rations, beans and franks and spaghetti with meatballs, and plenty of rounds with me. On the second day, I ate the franks and beans, but I never could stomach the spaghetti. I got some of the enemy, though, before our guys came along and let me pull out."

It was now dark, and Scott found Wylie and asked if he would join him for a meal with some of the men in the bunker. Tully decided to join them, and Wylie sensed that Tully had not yet finished their conversation.

Later, Wylie drew Tully to a corner of the bunker and, as they each drank a can of near beer, asked, "Feel like telling me what happened to your stripes?"

Tully considered the question carefully. "Yeah, why not? It's not like it's a secret," he said.

Tully explained that he had enlisted in the Army as soon as he was seventeen, fought in North Africa, Anzio and up the Italian boot. There were hairbreadth escapes and moments of valor, recognized by advancements in rank and, ultimately, a battlefield commission as a Second Lieutenant as he led a platoon across Germany. At war's end and demobilization, the Army revoked his commission and he became a top Sergeant again.

"I spent some time in Georgia and then I was stationed in Hawaii. Never did get the hang of women and I've stayed single with no kids that I know of. Like they say, the Army is my home.

"When the war of northern aggression began here I came right over from Hawaii and served with the 24th Regiment of the 7th Division, and we took the brunt of it when the Marines pulled back from the Yalu. I rotated back to Oahu, got bored as hell, and volunteered to return — back to the 7th. About three months ago was when I lost the stripes, not too far from here"

"Tell me about it," said Wylie who had long since put down his note pad.

"All right. I was honchoing the guys in my company that was being commanded by a Major from Battalion. Our Captain got shot and he was filling in, but he was from quartermaster or something and was shy of combat. Anyway, we had one of those mass attacks with trumpets and screaming and all that shit and our guys were hanging in there like it was business as usual. The Major discovers that the ROK Regiment on our right has melted away and is yelling on the phone for orders, of which there aren't any because the lines are down. Then he panics and starts screaming at my guys on the line to fall back, which was inappropriate because we were doing all right. It was then that I made my big mistake"

Sensing the drama of the moment, Tully drew in the remainder of his beer, and then continued.

"See, if I'd done the sensible thing and shot the Major, he would have just died in combat. Instead, I cold cocked him and sat on him till I was sure he wouldn't be a bother and then tended to my guys. Sure enough, the Chinks withdrew after a while and the Major woke up. We all tried to convince him he'd hit his head or something but he was sure I'd done him damage.

"It was a ticklish situation for the Major because unfortunate items might come out in a Court Martial, so he knocked it down to company punishment, and I agreed to keep my trap shut and lose the stripes. So as not to be a further embarrassment, he booted me out of the Company and had me sent here. That make a good story for you?"

"Tully, it's one hell of a story," said Wylie, "but you can bet your ass it'll never make any paper you and I know of. Thanks for telling me, though, and I hope things look up for you soon."

With that, they both joined the other men in the bunker as guards were changed and the lookout focused his binoculars on the valley below. Everything seemed quiet, and a conversation arose about determining a baby's sex. One of the JAMs pronounced that if you did it doggy style it would be a girl, missionary style it would be a boy. "Bullshit," said another, "It depends on how high you ride, the higher you get it'll be a girl."

The argument continued as theories moved from positions to the kind of food consumed during pregnancy. Wylie guessed that okra made male babies and collard greens insured female children.

Near a lantern in the corner, an exasperated black Corporal attempting to read a romance novel wrinkled his nose at the rumble of misinformation surrounding him. Finally, exasperated, he stated, "You dumb fuckers don't know anything. Anybody with at least half a brain knows it all depends on whether you hit the right or left ovalry."

There was silence as the company digested this piece of information, for the Corporal was recognized as a sage by those assembled. Wylie, Scott, and Tully held their tongues, waiting for the next verbal gem.

Instead, the lookout manning the field binoculars loudly said "Oh, Shit!" and the silence was broken by the sound of trumpets, whistles, and thudding mortars released from the valley below.

CHAPTER 11
HOLDING THE LINE

◆ ◆ ◆

"GRAB YOUR GEAR AND FOLLOW me to the trenches. The enemy has this bunker zeroed in on their mortars and will also attack with flame-throwers. We're better off in the open," yelled Tully above the sound of the incoming rounds.

Wylie and Scott ran from the bunker and followed Tully for about 50 yards where he scooped up a BAR located atop boxes of ammunition and pointed to locations along the trench. Fearful of flamethrowers, the others took positions in the trench on either side of Tully.

From the other end of the trench Lieutenant Swift ran toward them, brandishing his 45. He had experienced a communist attack before and his first thought was for his men. Relieved that Tully had marshaled them in the trench, he cautiously tried to observe what he could of the enemy moving across the valley, ready to clamber up the hill to his CP. A new moon gave little light, but he could make out some movement; it seemed close. As he turned to his men he raised his head slightly above the top of the bunker and a bullet pierced his forehead. He died without a sound. Wylie watched him fall backward. There was, no doubt that the Lieutenant was dead.

Wylie squatted in the trench, his eyes fixed on the dead officer who lay with his arms spread wide. His mouth was open as though he was about to rally his troops, but his brow was wrinkled in confusion. As a phosphorus flare rose above them, Wylie saw that his eyes were open and had a dull sheen. Though he was fully aware of the noise and smoke around him, the advancing Chinese troops, and the need for immediate action, he could not move. It was as though all his resources were engaged on processing the event of the Lieutenant's death. His fear that he would be unable to function in real combat resurfaced and he imagined himself in the Lieutenant's place, his eyes clouded and lifeless.

A mortar struck the ground twenty yards in front of his position and dust from the disturbed sand bags lining the trench flew into his eyes and mouth. As he spat it out, anger suddenly replaced his fear. These bastards are trying to kill me. I'm not going to let that happen. He was recharged; the steely grip of self-preservation asserted itself. This is it, what I trained for. This is infantry on the line and I can handle it!

He heard the thud of mortars coming up the hill toward the bunker. Tully was right about being zeroed in, but the bracketing was imperfect. An enemy forward observer must be somewhere below, helping aim the deadly mortars. To his left, Scott uncovered a box of grenades, preparing for close combat. "He's steady," thought Wylie, "and he's got a hell of an arm." Tully was readying the BAR and the strands of ammunition at his side. The others were calm, ready. To his great surprise, so was he. He ignored the wet chill of fear creeping up the small of his back.

Wylie was holding a carbine, a weapon suitable for close combat but certainly not for an enemy hundreds of yards away. Scott leaned his M-1 against the wall of the trench as he scooped up an armful of grenades and Wylie asked by a gesture whether he could exchange it for the carbine. Thumbs up. Wylie retrieved the rifle, chambered a round, and waited. The comforting sound of their own artillery shells now began and explosions shattered the valley below. Flares arose in the night sky and the garish blue-white light illuminated the trench and the slope before them. Wylie and the others defending the hill peered through slits in the trench wall and saw hundreds of Chinese soldiers, clad in khaki pajamas and canvas sneakers, scurrying across the valley and beginning to ascend the hill toward their CP. The shrill sound of their whistles pierced the night and the noise of muffled drums and cymbals rolled toward the CP. Inky shadows surrounded the attackers' feet, sharp as bayonet points. Most of them carried grease guns; a few had heavier weapons.

At first, Wylie was mesmerized by the activity below, unable to look away from the lines of approaching enemy infantry. A mortar shell burst twenty-five yards in front of his position. The impact encouraged him to search for the forward observer who would be exposed and using either a whistle or hand signals to adjust mortar fire. There, to the left, behind an outcrop eighty yards below!

With cool precision, he sighted and fired at the Chinese soldier. His first round raised a cloud of dirt in front of the observer's position; the second hit the soldier in the head, generating the pink cloud he had heard described by veterans at Fort Dix. The soldier lay lifeless, sprawled under the harsh glare of phosphorus flares, his whistle dangling from inert lips Wylie stared at him briefly, but now accepted the killing as a matter of fact. No more forward observer reduced the danger he and his companions faced.

Withering small arms fire surrounded their position, but the mortars ceased. UN artillery was decimating enemy soldiers as they rushed across the valley below, but still they kept coming up the hill. The men in the trench could make out enemy faces and Wylie thought fleetingly of Bunker Hill and seeing the whites of their eyes. Tully was directing fire at men with heavy weapons while Scott rolled grenades toward the attacking troops. The din was terrible, the light from the flares undiminished. He followed Tully's lead and searched for burdened Chinese soldiers struggling up the hill with machine guns along with their ammo bearers carrying boxes of shells.

Wylie had the correct aim now and almost all of his shots found an enemy soldier. The advancing troops seemed undeterred by the sight of their comrades falling from the hill. He could hear their screaming, saw their open mouths, watched them advancing Coolly, he assessing his target and carefully squeezing off one round after another. There were more pink clouds, more enemy soldiers suspended in slow motion as they fell to the ground. Clip after clip made its peculiar "ca-ping' sound as it flew from his rifle. He soon lost track of everything but assessing a target and sending a bullet into it. Yet they kept coming.

As Wylie wiped the sweat from his eyes, he saw Scott alternating between rolling and throwing hand grenades toward the enemy, saw in his peripheral vision steel shards cutting through earth, body armor, flesh, and bone. A head, still encased in a helmet, rolled into the valley below. The horns, trumpets, cymbals, and whistles died down, as Tully's rat-a-tat-tat staccato BAR fire echoed in his ears. An almost perfect crescent of khaki-clad corpses mottled in dark maroon and black stains lay sixty yards in front of the BAR position. Heat waves rose from the barrel, visible in the stark white flare light.

Wylie's fatigue shirt was soaked though and rivulets of sweat ran from beneath his helmet. Salt stung his eyes as he stared into the valley. The little men stopped coming up the hill. They clustered behind boulders, shrubs, corpses, carts, and mortar emplacements.

He turned to look at the others in the trench. A medic was placing a compress at the side of the man next to Scott, who monitored the area in front of the trench. Scott was breathing hard and his hands shook. He looked at Wylie and grinned wildly. Just past Scott, Wylie saw the black corporal dancing with an invisible partner, slowly turning and staring at the place here his left hand had been. Tully was leaning forward against the stock of the BAR. He had loosened his fatigue shirt and his chest glistened in the fading light of the flares.

The men in the trench heard bugle calls sounding retreat. They realized that the approaching soldiers now had hands raised in surrender or waved little white handkerchiefs. They threw their weapons aside and moved cautiously toward the trench, calling out "Okay, G.I. Sullendah!"

Wylie recognized that his first combat experience was over. He had survived. His relief became physical, as his hands began to tremble and his legs weakened. He saw a field of contorted bodies on the slope in front of their line, and he believed that each one of them had been intent on killing him. There was no pity in him. He became overwhelmed with elation, with victory, with power. He raised his rifle over his head and howled. Scott did the same.

They helped their wounded to the aid station, corralled the prisoners, and placed them in custody of Military Police, who marched them to a temporary POW location. The threesome reassembled in the bunker. "Jesus, do I have to take a wicked piss," Scott confided to Wylie, who was in the same condition. "That's right," said Tully. "It's the adrenalin. Makes you piss like a race horse."

The Regimental historian responsible for reporting the battle counted two hundred and seventeen dead enemy soldiers in front of their bunker, with fourteen of their own killed, including Lieutenant Swift. The battle had lasted almost three hours.

Two and a half weeks later, the Army promoted Wylie and Scott to Corporal and awarded them the Combat Infantry Badge. Sergeant Heron gave Wylie a brass pin engraved with "Badass Combat Correspondent" and his peers in the office pretended not to be in awe of his experience.

Wylie knew something in him had changed. Sleeping was difficult and his reflexes were on edge. He jumped when one of his tent mates dropped a wash basin. He felt as though something was missing, but could not identify it. He mentioned it to Dick Heron.

The Sergeant put an arm around his shoulder. "Don't worry about it. Combat screws you up a little. It will pass." He glanced at the Sergeant's crow's feet and the lines around his mouth and wasn't sure he could believe that.

The next day notice of Tully's promotion came across his desk. Tully became a First Sergeant with his own platoon.

CHAPTER 12

KIM KY YUNG

◆ ◆ ◆

AFTER HIS RUDDER FAILED TO respond, Kim shifted quickly in his seat to discover the tail of his biplane was gone. He knew that his foray over enemy bunkers would not be ending well this evening. Small arms fire had ripped apart the primary navigation system of his aircraft and he had only the ailerons at the wing tips to control the plane's tendency to pitch and roll. With great difficulty, he managed to turn to the north but was still far from the safety of his own lines above the 38th parallel. As the plane gradually lost altitude, he felt a sticky, hot wetness on his chest and neck and smelled oil. Blinding black smoke followed and, as his heart sank, the engine stopped.

Barely scraping the rugged hills and treetops, his altitude was too low to attempt a parachute descent. However, air speed was fast enough to permit rudimentary control so he quickly searched for a spot where he could direct his mortally wounded aircraft. Dusky gloom and poor distance vision made this an almost impossible task, but necessity forced Kim's choice. The Polikarpov descended in silent and ungainly flight to a tiny field below a terraced hillside surrounded by large evergreens, many of which were either uprooted or shattered.

The plane landed on its damaged tail and bounced on its wheels back into the air as various bits fell off. It landed again, struck a tree stump that removed the lower left wing, plowed onward into a still standing tree, which eliminated both right wings. What remained of the plane stopped when the engine contacted the tall tree stump previously felled by an 82 mm mortar. Like an abandoned teeter-tot-ter, the plane rested on its upper left wing and damaged landing gear.

Unconscious, Kim did not hear the ominous gurgling sounds and the creak of fatigued metal and wood. Fortunately, the plane's journey through trees and underbrush had extinguished the engine fire and fuel dripped harmlessly to the ground.

Private Milo Walker was among the G.I.s in the frontline X Battalion bunker watching the final descent of Bedcheck Charlie into the copse of trees in the valley below. They waited eagerly for an ex-plosion and the fiery disintegration of the enemy but none occurred. Disappointed, Milo's squad leader ordered him and two others to "check it out, but stay frosty; the chinks are out there."

Three of Kim's senses were excited as he woke. A powerful light was shining in his eyes; a harsh voice was screaming in his ear and excruciating pain radiated through his chest with each breath. He raised his hand to shield his eyes and tried to make sense of the for-eign sounds. He nearly fainted again from the pain caused by mov-ing his arm. "Foo-king guk ge fuk oot" resonated in his ear as rough hands pulled him from his seat and thrust him to the ground. He blacked out again.

Milo focused his flashlight on Kim's face and, speaking loudly to enhance communication in a foreign language not understood by the listener, screamed at Kim, "Fucking gook, get the fuck out!" Apparently, Milo felt Kim's response was too slow and he tossed his carbine to his squad member so he could grasp his lapels and wrest Kim from the cockpit.

Kim conveniently collapsed on the ground, allowing Milo to pro-ceed with the time-honored practice, followed by both sides in the conflict, of relieving prisoners of all valuables. Kim's watch, two rings, a pocketknife, and some paper money quickly disappeared into the pocket of Milo's field jacket. Then, suspecting Kim's lifeless state in-dicated an injury, he called a medic and the two carried Kim toward the bunker.

The medic confirmed that, except for some cuts, bruises and two or three broken ribs, Kim had miraculously survived the crash. He taped the ribs and administered morphine to help with the pain and Kim woke to the warm and comforting arrival of the drug's numbing waves. No more nighttime flights, no more starvation, no more fear as a constant companion, no more lip service to the crazy demands of a communist regime, thought Kim as he drifted into deep sleep.

Early the following morning, an Army truck carrying wounded prisoners arrived near the bunker and medics transferred Kim carefully to a seat in the back. He was beginning to tolerate the hurt in his chest but the choppy ride south was challenging. He noted that the G.I.s scorned the olive drab cans of K rations offered the prisoners but decided it was the best food he had eaten in months. Their guards were well fed and clothed, accustomed to riding Jeeps and trucks instead of marching to move from place to place. They carried a wide range of new weapons and had excellent boots. Their escorts all seemed to be able to read and had an easy familiarity with their officers. They in no way resembled the image the North Korean propagandists had presented. Not a single UN soldier seemed to breathe fire or eat babies.

Badly wounded prisoners were taken to hospitals south of Seoul while the walking wounded like Kim were dispatched by train to a holding area in Pusan. From there they traveled by LST [1] to Koje Island, the main UN prisoner of war camp. Upon Kim's arrival in late March of 1953, over one hundred thousand North Korean POWs were in residence in the overcrowded camp.

The previous May, one group of prisoners revolted and captured the camp commander, General Francis Dodd, and released him only after extracting a confession of inhumane treatment from his replacement. The North Korean propaganda machine broadcast the "confession" around the world, emphasizing what was arguably one of the United States' most embarrassing events of the war.

---

1 Landing Ship, Tank

The new camp commander restored order through artful reorganization of the compounds and the imposition of strict rules enforced by US soldiers supported by tanks. His firm discipline changed the camp from one dominated by a cadre of trouble-making communist leaders demanding self-rule to the orderly and regimented camp Kim discovered. Gradually, the U.N. moved POWs to compounds on the mainland to eliminate overcrowding and the potential for future riots. Kim, unaware of this history, was simply grateful for the issue of new clothing and blankets as he found his straw cot in the adobe walled barracks.

During the next few weeks the pain in his chest subsided. He listened carefully as his fellow prisoners described their experiences before and during the war, explained the details of their capture, and considered future prospects. Kim soon understood that there were no Chinese soldiers in their camp and that the administration divided captured NK soldiers into three groups.

Those who had been pressed into service against their will came from North and South Korea. They served because they feared being shot by their senior comrades, and many took the first opportunity to surrender, having concluded that the odds were at least even that being a prisoner of war would improve their present condition. They found this was so, and were happy being fed, clothed, and trained in mechanical skills on Koje Island.

Others, like Kim, eagerly joined the military, convinced they would play an important role in uniting their homeland under communist rule. Youthful gullibility and little formal education helped them accept the golden promise of a new and fair society with equality for all. The grinding miseries of combat altered their views. They were disillusioned but still shared guilt about their capture. That feeling, however, was not strong enough to encourage serious thoughts of escape.

The third group, many of whom had surrendered on orders of their superiors, was comprised of diehard communists charged with infiltrating prison camps and organizing the POWs to create disruption and difficulty for their captors. This group enforced its authority through lectures, beatings, even murder. These zealots were responsible for the notorious capture of General Dodd. Although many were relocated to other compounds, there were still some in Kim's adobe barracks. One of them took a special dislike to Kim; he refused to forgive him for surviving his plane crash.

CHAPTER 13

A LETTER HOME

◆ ◆ ◆

BY FREE AIRMAIL
April 23 1953

Dear Mom and Dad, Betty, and Ellie,

I really apologize for not writing in a while, but I finally have some time to catch up a little and let you know how I've been doing here. As always, I miss you all, but the weeks are going by fast. As you can see from the return address, I can now call myself a Corporal. I guess it's true that you make rank fast in a combat zone, though I haven't seen much of that! Your news about the new car is great and I can't wait to drive a Lincoln when I get back. And, yes, Mom I did receive the sweater and it looks great under my field jacket, even though royal blue is not really Government Issue. You girls sound as though you are doing just fine. I'll bet I won't recognize you when I get back home.

Dad, I certainly remember your advice about not taking unnecessary risks over here, though sometimes that's not always easy to follow. Part of my job is reporting from some places that aren't too stable, but it seems to be worth it because one or two of my articles have been published in Tokyo. The Army Times used one of my pieces last week. I promise to be more diligent about sending you some of the clippings.

As you can tell from the typing, I'm back in the Division office now after learning about a situation that's sort of smelly, and I thought I would mention it to Dad and get it off my chest. Any guidance would be appreciated.

But first, I should mention that there might be a piece in our local paper about me getting a commendation for a thing I was involved with a couple of weeks ago. It was no big deal because I was just interviewing some guys about their prior service here and the outpost we were in came under fire. It let up after a while and everybody got a commendation, which seems to be the "Army way," and of course P.I.O. sent the story to all the local papers. Anyway, I'm fine and trying to stay out of trouble.

But what I learned yesterday was pretty disturbing because it might affect our houseboy, Kim, who really is a swell kid and working hard to take good care of all ten of us in our tent. The other day he nearly ripped my boots off my feet so he could clean off the dust and polish them.

To answer Dad's question, as far as President Rhee goes, things are very chaotic in his government, which is pretty much run by policemen and some of the army units. With the war and all, they can't really tax the people here so they find other ways to raise money. Now the ROK government has come up with a new way to "draft" young men for the ROK Army. They set up a cordon of National Police that shuts off streets in a village or town and anyone who is of draft age (I think it's 18) is immediately served with his draft notice. To get out of joining the army, the new draftee has to pay the arresting officer a certain sum of money on the spot and they let him go. Those without money are pressed into service. There was only one thing wrong with their plan: they couldn't squeeze any money out of the houseboys that work for us soldiers because they are all under draft age—and they make about as much money as a business man in a little town. Up until now there was no legal or illegal way of separating them from their money.

Yesterday I discovered they had worked out a nifty squeeze play. The National Police used their influence with the U.S. Army to make it a policy that any houseboy whose name appears on a police blotter cannot work in the division any more. It's that simple.

Now, if a houseboy is caught when they close the draft-trap, he is immediately brought to the police station and offered an alternative - either pay or get booked for some minor offense, usually fabricated. If booked, his name is turned over to our civil affairs unit and he can no longer work as a houseboy. A nasty but clever little plan.

So the house boys who don't pay lose their jobs and this country is so desperate that many of them join the so-called guerilla bands. Since they know our ways so well, they become excellent thieves, stealing anything from heavy equipment to G.I.'s wallets and arms and ammunition. Our intelligence unit knows about all this but doesn't want to interfere with the ROK administration. Anyway, right now the guys in our tent are keeping a close eye on Kim to protect him as best we can. Dad, do you have any legal advice or ideas about dealing with this?

I've also been spending some time with the UN Regiments from Thailand and Ethiopia and it's a real learning experience. There's a bit of a language barrier but we are all soldiers and that goes a long way. The black soldiers from Ethiopia are all over six feet tall and scary as hell. The Chinese run when they see them! I'll tell you more about this in my next letter.

It's getting late, so I will close here; it's as good a place as any.

My love to you all - Wylie

CHAPTER 14
REPORT TO JUDY

❖ ❖ ❖

BY FREE AIR MAIL
22 April 1953

My Dearest One,

I'm gloriously happy tonight because more than a week without mail from you ended with the arrival of three letters which must have been delayed by some customary Army screw up. All the stuff you're doing at Montclair State sounds a lot different from the things I did in my freshman year, but then we didn't have a girl's lacrosse team at Princeton that I knew about! It's good that you are enjoying your courses. I remember that Elizabethan poetry can be kind of confusing at first, but I really liked John Donne and his metaphysical approach. But I know you will make a terrific teacher. It was nice of you to visit my Mom the last time you were home.

You probably noticed from the return address that I picked up an extra stripe last week, and thereby hangs a tale, but you have to promise you won't mention a word of what I'm going to tell you to either of our families because they would probably get upset. But I need to tell someone and you are my dearest one and my best buddy, too. The thing is I had my first experience with honest to God combat and the guys around here don't make a big deal about it, sort of like it's an initiation into a fraternity or secret society or something. But I thought it was awesome and I need to tell you about it. The first thing is that I'm fine - not a scratch - so there is nothing to worry about at all. Also, I haven't turned into a combat junkie like some of the hard cases here. The idea of returning to you as soon as possible calls for a high degree of self-preservation, so I'm not about to take crazy chances.

It was, as they say here, an isolated instance where my buddy Scott and I had a chance to hang out together while I was doing a story about a couple of guys who met at the front lines. Things didn't work out as planned and instead of returning the same day we had to stay overnight at the CP. About 2100 we were in the bunker listening to some wild conversation the "jive asses" were tossing about when the bugles started to blow and all hell broke loose. I was lucky (not really) enough to be in the spot the Chinks decided to occupy that night. I was scared, as our Captain likes to say, beyond the point of defecation.

Anyway, Scott and I teamed up with this real warrior named Tully McGregor and pretty soon we were in the thick of it. What I remember most was the incredible noise all around and the feeling that things were all moving in slow motion. But most of all I got the answer to the question we all used to ask ourselves in basic training, which was how were we going to react if we got into real fighting. I heard that a lot of guys unexpectedly sort of gave up and that you can never tell who will be the hero or the pussy. As it turned out, I was a bit of both, but it was nothing to be ashamed of.

The way it worked was that Scott and I kind of stared at each other at first and gradually absorbed that this was really happening, that there were people out there who wanted to kill us. Once that sank in we followed Tully who had been through this before; he was so calm and organized we settled down quickly and let our training kick in. It was like baseball practice where you learn by rote how to make a double play when the short stop snags the ball. We concentrated on using our weapons and worked as fast and as accurately as we could. After a while it was just doing a job, emptying my clip at the enemy, replacing the clip and doing it again.

Even though it happened all in slow motion, the time moved very fast. After a while, the kid was on a high. I don't know how it happened, but Scott and Tully and I were screaming every curse word we knew at the Chinks, telling them to keep coming so we could shoot more of them. It was a great feeling, like we were immortal, and we were laughing and crying at the same time, shooting like crazy. It's hard to explain, but it was almost like we were getting addicted to combat! We almost didn't notice it when they started coming toward us with their hands over their heads, ready to surrender. I never felt like that before but, now that I've considered what could have happened to us on that hill, I'm in no big rush to try it again. Anyway, now I know what the guys mean when they talk about the "rush of combat."

So that was it, and I guess that was why Scott and I were promoted to Corporal a few days later. It's a hell of a way to make grade!

Other than that, things have been fairly calm lately and I've been pretty busy with the correspondent stuff. There are always things going on worthy of a story in the Division.

Now it's getting pretty late, the time of night I always think of you, my darling. I'm so sorry we can't get any closer that these damn letters, but I want you to know that you are always in my thoughts and that I love you very much.

Your Wylie

CHAPTER 15

KOJE ISLAND

◆ ◆ ◆

"YOU ARE A LACKEY OF these motherless Yankee pig bastards who are raping our women with bayonets, sucking the blood out of our sisters and children, and destroying our beloved homeland with their bombs and napalm," whispered Lon Song-Il to the back of Kim's head as they stood in line for their evening meal of rice, squash and a gray conglomerate of expired K rations.

Kim had been listening to these accusations for weeks, uncertain why this virulent communist sympathizer had singled him out. Lon stood barely five feet tall, whippet thin with acne scars on his face and chest. He was Kim's age and proudly encouraged the eight or nine hairs growing from his chin into the semblance of a goatee. His almond eyes had an upward tilt at the corners, giving him a look of constant puzzlement. Like a baby rabbit, thought Kim, he certainly does not have the physical presence or look to suggest intimidation.

Kim stood half a foot taller than Lon, had now recovered from his injuries, and was exercising daily. He could have swatted Lon away, but chose to avoid confrontation since there was no way of knowing who Lon's supporters were. Someone had stabbed a prisoner in the adjoining barracks last week and he nearly bled to death.

"You are mistaken. I am a faithful soldier and flew my aircraft for almost two years against Rhee's army and Yankee invaders. I stopped only when my cursed aircraft crashed and I was captured against my will. We are now both prisoners." Kim paused to consider, then asked, "And how is it you are here, Shorty?"

Kim had observed that Lon easily became apoplectic. He knew that rage disabled the little communist and calculated his question accordingly. Lon stiffened; his cocked eyes bulged and his face grew red, emphasizing his purple acne scars. Some moments passed as he sucked air into his thin chest, exclaimed Sheikkeh! [2], and feebly pushed him. Kim ignored him and moved on.

His loathing fueled by Kim's refusal to be intimidated, Lon plotted revenge. Honor, combined with a fervent sense of superiority based on his party membership, demanded no less than Kim's death. It was a mission he would undertake unaided. The camp's communist ringleaders had never considered him as more than an obnoxious adherent to the cause and most of them had been moved to other locations during the past year. Those who remained were chastened and ignored Lon's personal vendetta.

Kim, meanwhile, ignored or avoided Lon and adjusted to life in the prison camp, making new acquaintances and learning the rules of survival. Any sense of allegiance to communist principles evaporated, as did any desire to return to the north at the war's conclusion.

Lon accepted the challenge of meting out justice on his own. Stabbing Kim in the back seemed the safest and most appropriate approach to the problem. He thought he knew where the human heart was located; that would be his target.

Although the POW compound remained overcrowded, the Army engineers who designed the facility provided for mess buildings that could be expanded to accommodate such an overflow. The engineers, universally renowned for either over or under engineering, and for using their genius to create systems easily misunderstood by ordinary soldiers, got it right on Koje Island.

They housed cooking facilities in a central Quonset hut with adequate ventilation surrounded by satellite tents. Proper refrigeration

---

2 Loosely translated from Korean as "Fucking Bastard"

was available and bins of coal stood neatly arrayed to fuel the iron cook stoves. The crowning achievement was the integrated system for grease and food waste disposal. Large sunken concrete vats topped by steel grates contained left-over waste that, by an ingenious system of baffles aided by gravity, segregated and consolidated the material. A monstrous tank for grease, accessible by a steel grate and ladder from the top, or from a steel valve at its base, awaited bi-monthly deposition in a tanker truck that hauled it away for reuse in soap and munitions.

One of the most undesirable jobs required to be done by the prisoners was to clean the walls of the tank with long handled scrapers when the stench became overwhelming, which meant daily. The grease quickly became black and viscous and, once contacted, required pumice and kerosene to remove it. Their peers rewarded those prisoners who willingly volunteered for such work with cigarettes, extra food, and deference.

Kim, who lost his sense of smell after the plane crash, was glad to accept the responsibility of cleaning the grease trap every few days in exchange for the numerous perquisites.

Lon worked in a shop in the compound that constructed garden tools and farm implements from two types of hardwood found in the local area. The prisoners made rake, hoe and scythe handles, buckets, carts, and similar items used by farmers around Pusan. Lon managed to steal a hoe handle almost a meter long that he intended to sharpen to a fine point. He planned to do this while alone, so he hid the implement in his pants leg while leaving the carpentry shack. This gave him a limp, but he looked so peculiar in any case than no one noticed, certainly not the ROK guards.

Lon gradually shaped his weapon with a piece of shale he found and practiced lunging with it, using it as a spear. After some days, it seemed ready, its splinter-like point hurtful to his palm. "Yankee sympathizer bastard, impure thinking collaborator with nose like a shriveled penis, this is for you!" he muttered as he thrust toward his imagined nemesis. Tomorrow, he knew, Kim would be behind the mess tent cleaning the grease traps, alone, awaiting his fate.

Kim walked toward the opening of the huge grease trap early the following morning, preparing to scrape the sides of the almost full vessel. It was a clear day and spring was coming. However, Kim could not smell the scents of the season or the odors wafting from below the steel grate. Lon, on the other hand, who approached Kim from behind, the spear in his right hand, was almost overcome by the unaccustomed stench surrounding his target.

Not breathing, Lon walked quickly, closing the distance between himself and his victim, gaining speed and momentum. Eyeing a point below Kim's left shoulder blade, he thrust his spear with both hands held high toward Kim's heart. He felt elated, powerful, unaware that his left foot contacted a puddle of grease atop the concrete vat that caused both feet to slide out from beneath him. He made a little shriek, which alerted Kim that he was under attack.

Propelled by his forward momentum, Lon skidded past Kim, bent at the waist with both feet a foot in the air, descending rapidly from the force of his intended attack. Trying to break his fall, he reached both hands toward the concrete. The spear fell from his hands, skidded across the concrete, and lodged in a grease-filled crack, point upward. In the last split second of his fall, Lon spied the sharp point of his spear poised to penetrate his belly. He twisted his body sharply as he fell, but the spear still punctured his abdomen, through and through, like a skewer restraining stuffing in a roast chicken. The sharpened stick encountered no vital organs, and the wound was not immediately painful, but Lon gasped when he saw the bloody point protruding through the jagged wound on his left side and fainted.

It took a moment or two before Kim appreciated the peril avoided. He looked at the scrawny body of his unconscious attacker impaled with a nasty looking spear and understood that the weapon was intended for him. The instinctive behavior of self-preservation asserted itself. Enough, he thought, is enough. I'm not going to give this little pest another chance.

He looked around the top of the facility to confirm he was alone and dragged the limp would be assassin to the edge of a large opening. Kim carefully raised the steel grate and dumped Lon in. He saw him sink slowly but completely to the bottom of the black, slimy grease. Lon had no epitaph other than the few oily, multi-hued bubbles that rose to mark his descent to his anonymous grave.

Few, if any, noticed Lon was missing. Kim, however, felt guilty about his reflex action and feared that his crime would be discovered. As the days wore on, however, he justified his conduct as being in his own defense and it weighed less heavily on his mind. He started a rumor that Lon had been transferred to one of the compounds reserved for hard-core communist sympathizers. As one of over a hundred thousand prisoners, his absence was soon forgotten.

Kim's belief that he had avoided the consequences of his actions was shattered one evening a month later when a ROK officer barged into his barracks one evening, clipboard in hand. He strode to Kim's cot, checked the number, and demanded Kim's name. It matched the information in his hand and he barked, "Get your things together. You are coming with me. You have five minutes."

Blackness surrounded Kim's myopic vision. Had Lon resurfaced? Did his bones clog the dispenser? Had someone seen? Based on his three years of military experience Kim volunteered nothing, swallowed his fear, quickly tucked his things into a blanket, and stood ready to leave.

"All right," said the officer," You are being transferred to a new mainland POW camp. You have a good attitude and it's getting too crowded here."

CHAPTER 16

JESUS

◆ ◆ ◆

JESUS MARTINEZ, WYLIE'S FORMER DRILL instructor, now a Sergeant and in North Korea, surveyed the little valley extending from the gully where he and nine of his platoon members hid. The grass was green and short, shrubs had leafed out, and the hills on either side sustained good cover — if they could reach them unobserved. Slanting early morning light created a mirage of water just past the encampment of a company of Chinese soldiers a quarter mile to the west. There seemed to be no enemy activity other than that. However, his quick count indicated they were greatly outnumbered. No element of surprise could overcome those odds.

Action the night before in the Punch Bowl area had been furious and confusing with poor communication among the UN forces. The Chinese and NK troops targeted the ROK battalion Martinez and his Company supported. They attacked through heavy rain about midnight. Air support was unavailable and artillery was ineffective because the commo wire that allowed the exchange of target information either shorted in the rain or was cut by infiltrators.

At 0300 a strategic withdrawal was ordered, and Martinez and the remains of his platoon headed southwest through the mud and rain, only to discover that their position had been outflanked. They moved through a rapidly closing corridor between enemy troops until, exhausted, they holed up in the gully where Martinez now considered their prospects.

"Gentlemen, we are in a difficult situation," the Sergeant said. "It appears that, although we have not been noticed, we are surrounded, have little food and water, and are low on ammunition. Also, there seems no way we can contact our Company, and we are unsure where our lines are. Of course, if it was easy, anyone could do this job. For a real infantryman it just doesn't get any better than this."

His men muttered unenthusiastic Hoorahs.

Martinez ordered, "I need you to space yourselves about twenty feet apart along the gully and find whatever cover you can. Don't dig fox holes and keep the noise down. If you haven't done it already, tape your dog tags together.

"Holloway, get a count of how many ammo clips there are and try to even them out. Same thing with water. We can live on our fat for days, but we'll need water tonight when we move out. Get a rest, ladies."

At midafternoon, a squad of about fifteen Chinese soldiers approached the gully. They had removed their uniforms. They were naked or wore underpants that looked like diapers. Martinez watched from the cover of thick shrubs, his eyes at ground level. Holy mother, he thought, these guys look like little kids. They're all skin and bones.

However, they carried large caliber submachine guns the G.I.'s called grease guns and Russian rifles. They were skinny but no less deadly. Apparently, there was a stream out of view beyond the gully and they were going to bathe there. They passed fifty yards in front of Martinez' position. The next hour he and his men listened to the enemy at play. Thanks for showing us where water is you miserable, mother-loving slope heads.

Before moonrise, in preparation for their departure from the gully, Martinez dispatched Holloway and Crandall to fill canteens with water from the stream.

"We may get parasites and the shits but we won't be dehydrated," said Martinez.

"Yeah, that's real encouraging, Hay-soos," offered Holloway as he and his companion began to crawl toward the water.

They returned, and the men drank thirstily, preparing for expected exertions. They were eager to move from the gully.

Cradling their rifles, they moved like snakes along the grass, slow, silent, zigging and zagging on their bellies, until they reached the tree line at the base of the westerly hills. Martinez took direction from the stars and headed his men up the hill, southward. It was time, he felt, to adopt his Geronimo persona, after his ancestor, the Indian warrior, indefatigable, unconquerable. He touched his leather bracelet, the amulet given by his mother, to make the connection.

On cresting the hill, they literally stumbled into a NK forward infantry position of about eighty men listening for and guarding against a UN counterattack. They were in a bunker and trenches recently occupied by Belgian troops. The North Korean soldiers discovered some hastily abandoned Belgian cigarettes, and the stench of the Gitanes and the sound of coughing warned Martinez and his men of unexpected company.

Determining his next steps was easy. Immediately behind them were large numbers of enemy soldiers; ahead lay their own lines with access impeded by diaper wearing little people, unaware of their presence and happily filling their lungs with acrid smoke. They were well armed but their weapons all pointed away from Martinez' squad.

With practiced hand signals, the Sergeant choreographed the next few minutes' activity. He ordered his squad to do the following: toss four grenades, two from each side, into the bunker, two seconds after releasing the handle—then throw the remaining grenades in rapid fire into the trenches. As soon as the grenades exploded, his men would fire their carbines and rifles for no more than a minute from the back of their line. While the enemy was disoriented by grenade and small arms fire from the rear, his squad would run with amazing swiftness around the enemy position, pausing to fire every ten steps, and descend the hill toward what he believed were their own lines. Martinez' men nodded confirmation of his strategy, accepting it as the best way out of a seriously bad situation, and took positions above the enemy trench.

Illumination from the crescent moon was just enough to disclose an opening at the rear of the bunker. Four squad members crawled toward the opening, waited two seconds after the clip sprang from their grenades, and threw them quickly as far as they could into the bunker. They stayed motionless for what seemed like an hour, as the fuses blazed toward the composition B explosive in the fragmentation grenades. Finally, there were shouts of alarm from the bunker just before the Americans heard the dull roar of four explosions and saw flames pouring from the back entrance and forward observation holes.

As those fireballs turned the night a bright reddish hue, the grenades thrown into the trenches exploded, and the Americans heard the sound of steel shards penetrating the flesh and bone of confused enemy soldiers. High-pitched screams filled the heated air. More explosions and small arms fire followed, as Martinez loped behind the trench, spraying it with rounds from his carbine. The others followed and, as the remaining North Koreans turned toward their rear, the squad members sprinted around their flank at the end of the trench and began running, zigzag fashion, down the hill.

As the enemy realized that their attackers were now to their front, Martinez paused in his descent to make certain all his squad members were heading down the hill. The dying flames from the guttered bunker provided enough light for him to see that his men were on their way, one soldier dragged by two other men. As he turned to follow them, he discovered that his right leg refused to hold him. He sank awkwardly to his knees, a dull ache rising from his right buttock. Pressing one hand there, he discovered a pulpy opening and smelled the iron rich odor of blood.

Two members of his squad rushed toward him, reached under each arm, and dragged him down the hill. They did not release him until they were out of small arms range, across the valley and beside an ancient quarry.

Corporal Crandall eased Martinez to the ground after the squad reached a protected place and worked on the Sergeant's wounds, difficult in the dim light. He applied pressure bandages and fashioned a splint from entrenching tools for Martinez' leg.

"How does it look?" asked Martinez.

"It's kinda dark, but it looks like you got hit in the leg and the ass. Through and through, Sarge, and not much blood," said Crandall.

Another squad member crawled toward Martinez to report.

"Carson didn't make it and Holloway took a round in the shoulder and I think maybe got something in the lung. He's coughing blood a little," he said.

Martinez gritted his teeth against the pain, put on his Geronimo face, tried walking using his carbine as a crutch, and stumbled around their position, checking in with each squad member. Their spirits were high after their successful attack on the NK soldiers. Everyone, including Martinez and Holloway, could walk. At first, neither wounded man accepted morphine. Pain, Martinez counseled, is our friend.

Three men dug a shallow grave for Carson, marked its location on a map as best they could, and hoped the graves registration people would find him later. Martínez saved one of Carson's dog tags, leaving the other one around Carson's neck.

Their Sergeant led the squad south, navigating by compass since the sky was starless, dark and cloudy. On high alert, the squad moved clumsily through the night. After a few hours, Holloway muttered "fuck me" with every other step, and Crandall hit him in the thigh with a morphine ampoule just to shut him up. Finally, at dawn's early light, they rested.

For an eternal three days and nights, Martinez led his squad southward toward their own lines, hiding during the day and moving at night. Sporadic sightings of enemy patrols and dysentery from available water slowed their progress. Holloway, functioning with the help of morphine, coughed dark blood, needed help walking, and vacillated between groggy silence and muttered curses. Martinez' leg darkened and swelled, but he pushed his squad on.

"Like they say," he said, "it's gonna be home for Christmas and steak and eggs for breakfast every day. Our battalion is just around the next bend. Don't complain that you're hungry; assholes. You ate yesterday. Time to move out!"

He hobbled forward. His men saw the swollen leg, the blood soaked pressure bandage on his rear, and his sweat-drenched fatigues in the cool evening air, and they followed, carrying Holloway with them.

Near midnight, on the fourth night after their attack on the NK troops, the squad cautiously approached an embankment near the top of an unnamed hill. A voice rang out ahead of them.

"Password!"

"Don't know the fucking password!"

"Who the bloody hell are you?"

"Third platoon, seventeenth infantry...you fucking Limeys?"

"You fucking Yanks?"

"Bet your ass, we are!"

"Come ahead. Slowly. Hands where we can see them."

The British troops welcomed them warmly and called medics for Martinez and Holloway. They passed out cigarettes and hot tea. Tiredly, the Americans told of their encounters and accepted rum rations with the tea. Half-tracks soon arrived to carry them to the rear, to a field hospital, to warmth and safety.

Sergeant Martinez' planning and execution of the attack on the enemy-held bunker later became part of the curriculum at West Point. It was taught as a classic example of an infantry squad maneuver that resulted in the elimination of at least thirty-five enemy combatants with the loss of only one man.

Martinez' leadership, while severely wounded during a four-day ordeal, was extraordinarily heroic. However, the actions of other soldiers during the Korean War raised the bar for heroism so high that his valor did not qualify for the Medal of Honor. The Army promoted

Sergeant Martinez one grade in rank and awarded him the Silver Star, the nation's third highest award. He received it as he recuperated in the ambulatory unit of the 53rd Infantry Division's MASH.

CHAPTER 17

ROMANCE IN THE AIR

◆ ◆ ◆

WYLIE, SCOTT, AND SHIT DAD were enjoying their second beers in the Headquarters Enlisted Men's Club and the two Corporals listened appreciatively to Shit Dad's tall tales about gigging alligators in the bayou.

"Ah was wrestling him so hard and squeezing his middle wit my legs that he belched up a whole arm he had eat the day before. It had my fren's wristwatch still attached, and it was keeping good time. We fried up alligator cutlets and gave my fren his watch back. Oh yeah, lessez les bon temps rollez!"

Later, prompted by Wylie, he explained that his request for a second tour in Korea was financially motivated.

"As a Private with combat pay ah git hunnert twenny dollahs a month," he said. "You know I like to drink good whiskey, which I would do either here or there, but here I get a fifth for one dollah. Ah don always have time to drink a whole bottle a day so I average about twenny dollah per month on essentials. Shit dad, the Army takes care of evathin else, so I have a whole hunnert dollah to send home to my momma eva month. No way I do that stateside!"

"Momma," Scott determined, was Shit Dad's actual mother and not a euphemism for wife, girlfriend, fiancée, or pet bitch. Scott was glad to clear that up because he was a bit confused until Shit Dad explained that "Blue" was the female hound that played such an important role in his alligator stories

Shit Dad ended the evening by walking cheerfully from the club with a sealed bottle of Johnny Walker Red under his arm.

Wylie awakened just before reveille the next morning to see Shit Dad enter their tent through the rear flap, red circles under his eyes and dung covering his boots. As he lowered himself to his cot, Wylie asked what was going on.

"Been helping a farm family up the hill plant rice. They got lots a mouths to feed and a couple of really pretty daughters. I been helping them for a while."

After breakfast featuring the Mess Sergeant's idea of gourmet chipped beef ("It's got fresh parsley in it!"), Wylie refilled his mess kit cup with coffee and headed to the P.I.O. tent. Barry Sonnenfeld was talking on the telephone with someone at Regiment, and Lamar Trenchant stared past Wylie at the distant hills just changing from green to red, pink, and white as spring flowers began to bloom.

Flowers don't care about war, thought Lamar, a closet romantic. He looked silently at the flamboyant hills and considered ways to express this deep thought in the letter he was crafting for his adored girlfriend, Debbie Jaliskowski. He envisioned her pining for him in her parents' Bronx apartment. He wrote her at least twice a day, three and four page letters brimming with closely observed descriptions of the war at Headquarters, along with outpourings of his love for her.

Dick Heron stood in front of Captain Standrich's desk, listening to the officer's musings. Standrich used an oily facial lotion after shaving that caused his pink cheeks to glisten. They reflected morning sunlight pouring through a side window, nearly blinding Heron.

"You know, Sergeant," said the Captain, "I've always felt we needed more punch in describing the division, especially in our newspaper. 'The Fifty-Third Fighting Swedish Division' just seems pretty anemic underneath The Saber, which is such an aggressive, masculine kind of name."

"Yes, you've said that before."

"Well, I had a brain storm last night. Came up with sayings that will really make us stand out!"

"Yes, Sir."

"I boiled this down to two different slogans, *Peacekeepers Working for You* and *Defenders of the Doorsteps to Democracy*. What do you think?"

Both, thought Heron, were egregious, but in the seven months he had worked for the Captain, he created his own system for evaluating the Captain's writings, ideas, and idle musings. For the occasional worthy pronouncement, he said, "Splendid, Sir." Mediocrity was rewarded with "That should do it," the poor or half-assed— "Good" with the "oo" stretched out, and the word inflected so an astute listener might perceive it as a question. The truly awful generated "Good, but..."

"I think they're both good, but I like the second one better. It has that alliteration with the three Ds and the analogy to doorsteps suggests we are leading upward, which is always the right direction. If we really need to change the description in the heading, I'd go with that."

"All right. Pass that on to Sergeant Pike so he can use it in the paper next week."

That settled, the Captain asked," By the way, how is Private Rowe doing? I haven't had a chance to talk with him for a few days; he seems very busy."

"Doing fine," said Heron. "I understand he's involved in reaching out to an indigenous family."

His morning's work done, Captain Standrich left the office and walked to the officers' mess to scope out the rest of his day over a cup of coffee.

Sergeant Heron, obliged to follow orders, composed a telex to the Division paper's editor in Tokyo, hoping the message would get lost along the way.

Tongue in check, believing Heron was engaged in some sort of prank, Sergeant Jules Pike in Tokyo inserted the phrase under the Saber's Masthead the following week. Generally, the change went unnoticed, except for the division commander, General Black, who was in the habit of reading the paper when visiting the General's latrine. Irritated, returning to his office, he asked his adjutant, "Who writes this crap?" as he adjusted his suspenders.

Later that morning, Heron told Wylie, "Got a heads up last night that a Sergeant over at our MASH was awarded a Silver Star. Signal Corps already has his picture, but we need copy. Here's his citation that describes the action in glowing military jargon. It says he is a credit to the Tohono O'odam Nation and the State of Arizona, and his name is Martinez I'd like you to go over and talk with him, cut through the bullshit, and see what really happened."

Wylie always enjoyed visiting the MASH because it gave him the rare opportunity to visit with a round-eyed nurse or two. However, it made him long for Judy, offering moments of pleasure and pain.

Martinez refused an opportunity to recuperate in Japan, believing he would then not likely return to his unit in Korea. Though his wounds were painful, they would heal soon enough. The doctors had repaired his shattered fibula, cleansed the thirty-caliber hole in his buttock, and plied him with sufficient antibiotics to repel the most aggressive little organisms Korea could muster. Four weeks after his injuries, his leg was in a cast and he sat on a rubber donut in his wheel chair as Wylie entered the ambulatory ward in the MASH tent.

"Son of a bitch, it's the college boy!" exclaimed the Sergeant, who had a strong recollection of the marksman he shepherded through basic training. Throughout recorded history, no recruit has ever forgotten his drill instructor, and Wylie, no exception, was surprised and pleased to be reunited with the one who had made his life a living hell for many weeks. Now with two stripes on his arm, he felt emboldened to say, "You bet your ass, but it's Corporal college boy now."

"Ooh, you have touched a sore subject; my ass isn't in bettable condition right now."

The two young men went through a familiar military ritual of breaking balls, intermittently exchanging information about their current situations and their activity in Korea. The Sergeant described in a self-effacing manner the details of events that led to receiving his citation, and Wylie scribbled pages of notes. Looking for "color" he asked if the Sergeant had received any revelations during the ordeal.

Martinez showed his leather amulet and said, "My Mom gave me this to protect me and keep me safe. So, before we began the attack I sort of touched it to connect with the ancestors. Turns out it has only limited power. It does keep you from getting killed but not from getting your ass shot off."

Not quite what Wylie was looking for. He would save that for later.

CHAPTER 18

LIEUTENANT BUTZ

◆ ◆ ◆

DURING THE SAME ACTION IN which Sergeant Martinez was separated from his battalion, First Lieutenant Randolph Butz, formerly of Wylie's Infantry Company at Fort Dix, was ordered to advance to the rear, saving as many of his troops as possible. Unfortunately, there was no "rear" available at the time, since both NK and Chinese soldiers surrounded the position he was holding. Before sunrise, he and his men had tumbled from their hillside position to the valley below where the terrain was flat and cover was nonexistent. At first light, he and Second Lieutenant Andy Bierce surveyed their situation.

Of their original one hundred and fifty-five men, about ninety remained, ten of them wounded. After almost two days of constant combat, they were exhausted, filthy, and hungry. Hundreds of NK soldiers were moving toward them from the end of the valley and they knew the enemy also occupied the hilltops around them. A stream, swollen by spring runoff, blocked the other end of the valley. Both Lieutenants agreed they had no choice but to surrender and ordered the men to lay down their arms.

A short, stout, angry Major who advanced pointing his pistol at the two young officers led the NK troops. Enemy artillery had decimated his troops and he was not in a charitable mood. His soldiers gathered abandoned weapons and formed their prisoners into a column. Three badly wounded men were dragged to their feet and shoved into line, where two crumpled to the ground before being propped up by their fellows. Bierce complained bitterly to the Major about their mistreatment, moving toward him. The Major placed the barrel of his pistol against Bierce's forehead, said, "I have the authority," and pulled the trigger.

Bierce's body was placed with two others who had died during the evening, and the Major made it clear that Lieutenant Butz was to lead the straggling column north.

Butz and his men were prodded north for three days, passing Chinese and North Korean units on their journey. The more fit helped the wounded and the worn, and Butz, who had good reason to believe stragglers would be bayoneted or shot, did his best to encourage onward movement. They stopped at burned out farms or warehouses and received small quantities of rice and spring crops like peas, burdock, and radishes. No medical treatment was provided and pressure bandages, morphine, and other medicinal supplies were gone after two days. The prisoners spent nights in the open and their misery increased with the attack of spring bugs and rampant dysentery.

Their captors recognized this sorry column of American soldiers could not continue to the prison camp on their own and, on the morning of their fourth day, trucks arrived to take them on their trip north. They were packed into the vehicles and began a two-day ride punctuated by choking dust and a constant jolting which raised bruises almost everywhere. Lieutenant Butz rejected the officer's passenger seat of the truck and rode in the back with his men. Those still lively enough to appreciate a joke commented on their sore Butz.

By the spring of 1953, the northern armies were concerned with the lopsided ratio of POWs in the South versus those in the North. Of the almost half million American troops engaged in the conflict, about seven thousand were Prisoners of War. North Korea sent about the same number of its sons to war, but over one hundred thousand became POWs. With the possibility of an Armistice on the horizon and the ultimate obligation to exchange prisoners, saving face required the North to collect of as many POWs as possible. Further, Chinese techniques of interrogation were producing confessions of war crimes on the part of American officers, considered valuable in their attempts to influence world opinion. Lieutenant Butz and his men were, therefore, valuable to the communist war effort and treated as such. The NK Major was reprimanded severely for killing such a potentially valuable prisoner as Lieutenant Bierce.

When Butz and his men arrived at their reeducation center, a cadre of guards who spoke at least rudimentary English greeted them. They gave the sore and filthy Americans hot potato soup and cold water for washing.

Their guards advised them at every opportunity there were no ill feelings that they had mistakenly taken up arms against the North Koreans. They understood that leaders who were lackeys of imperialist hegemony deluded them. The Americans were the unwitting collaborators of the illegitimate puppet regime of Syngman Rhee. At this center, they would have an opportunity to improve their education and understand why they had taken the wrong path. There would be lectures, written materials to complete and healthful physical activity. Of course, as in any military organization, failure to follow rules would result in punishment.

A few of the guards less fluent in English required translations of the colloquial comments offered by the newly arrived troops in response to this offer of reeducation. They were puzzled by "Bullshit, up yours, in a pig's ass, fuck yo moma, and no fuckin' way." They did understand the sounds of flatulence made by hands cupped under armpits.

Their captors assigned enlisted men to mud huts arranged in the prison compound, but Butz was marched to a shabby wood building that was designated as officers' quarters. The shack held a primitive wooden table, a handful of stools and spaces on the floor for mats. Two bare electric bulbs protruding from the ceiling provided enough light for the officers to record their thoughts and write their confessions. The guard handed him a straw mat, a tin cup, and a spoon. Butz introduced himself to the four other men in the room.

There were two American officers, a Major and Captain, an Australian Captain, and an Ethiopian Light Colonel, or so Butz thought, since he was uncertain about the gold pips on the black officer's lapel. The other officers had been captured within the past four weeks and were held, they believed, for deployment deeper into enemy territory. The Major was in the Artillery and the Captain came from the Signal Corps. The American officers reported that they received little food and were occasionally abused by the guards, but their spirits were high.

Their camp was a few miles north of the Yalu, under the care and tutelage of Captain Dong, the camp commander. Dong spoke excellent English, they said, but with an occasional lisp. Among themselves, the officers referred to him as "Ding."

Ding Dong concentrated on interviewing the white officers, avoiding the Ethiopian, who stood well over six feet tall and was, in Butz' view, black as an eight ball. Butz soon learned that the black officer was educated at Cambridge, had a bawdy sense of humor, and had the fastest reflexes he had ever seen. Matt Quigley, the Aussie, explained Captain Dong's deference to the Ethiopian officer.

"Haile Selassie, Ethiopia's Emperor, decided that each of his troops sent over here would be at least six feet tall; quite a few are close to seven feet. They like to charge the enemy, fully armed, waving swords, and screaming they are the lions of Judah."

He let that image sink in before continuing, "Too right, mate! The sight of those huge black buggers charging and screaming scared these wogs shitless and most of them just ran away. Someone started the rumor that the big black soldiers collected enemy heads to keep track of their kills, but storage and transport became a problem, so they began keeping just the ears. I think that little slant eyed prick,

Dong, heard about it. Just watch him. He checks his ears every time he sees Gabremeskal in the compound."

Butz kept that picture in mind as his interviews with the Chinese Captain became more intense.

Initially, Dong was solicitous, explaining it was his responsibility and pleasure to care for all the troops in his camp. In contrast to members of the NK army, he understood that the enemy officers had no choice but to do the bidding of their corrupt leaders and could not be held personally responsible for whatever war crimes they had committed.

"Yeth, as you know," he said, "many American officers have confethed their war crimes and accepted rethonthobility for their actions. I am sure their minds are at easthe now that the truth hath come out. We will be working together to help you and the other offithers review your hithtory and make your confethions."

Butz explained that he had certainly committed no war crimes and that his conscience was clear. Nevertheless, Dong provided paper and pencil and ordered Butz to write down his life history. He worked on it for two days but, when the Captain sat down to review it, he saw a single page containing Butz' name, rank and serial number.

"Thith ith not acceptable!" he fumed. "You must not insult the Chinese People's Volunteers who are representatives of all peace-loving peoples in the world. You must write down your life history and then we will begin with your confession. These are the rules. Please underthand that failure to obey our rules will result in punishment."

CHAPTER 19
P.I.O. DEVELOPMENTS

◆ ◆ ◆

RESPLENDENT IN A SPARKLING WHITE flowing Korean hanbok and little rubber boots, Shit Dad burst into the tent where the P.I.O. members slept and staggered to his cot. He sank slowly onto his air mattress, dangling a foot over the side, and announced to no one in particular, "Shit Dad, I finally did it. Got myself married, Korean style. Been helping that Korean family up on the hill and decided which one of the two daughters I liked best. Turned out to be the pregnant one and the papa-san figured that would be the one I should marry." He expelled a happy sigh that enveloped his corner of the tent in the unmistakable odor of kimchi.

Dick and Wylie, just returning from their morning visit to the piss tube, said, almost in unison, "Married?"

"It's a real nice affair with smoke and gongs and all the relatives dressed up and passing around the veggies and rice and that sour kraut with the dog meat in it. And my fiancée who is now my wife had on this real pretty kimono, what they call the hanbok here, all embroidered and you couldn't tell she was pregnant or anything. The girls were all giggling and silly and got me all dressed up in this costume. So the papa-san says some stuff and puts our hands together and I get the general impression we are married, Korean style. My wife and I had ourselves a short honeymoon just before I needed to get back to base."

Shit Dad rose from his cot to display his embroidered finery to the gawkers in the tent, adding, "I like this outfit so much I just wore it back here. I got my fatigues underneath."

"Shit, Shit Dad," said Sergeant Heron, "You know damn well you can't just go off and get married without approval. And you know damn well you can't get approval even if every chaplain on base gave you a blessing. It's against Army regulations! There is no doodoo deeper than what you are in. It's my ass if I don't report this to the Captain."

Unperturbed, Shit Dad said, "That Captain, he a nice feller. I don't doubt he will understand."

As Wylie entered the office tent after chow, Boomer and Phil Nordman were editing interview tapes on two Army reel recorders. They traveled up the line to interview troops defending the doorsteps to democracy and, with a recorder hooked up to a Jeep battery, interviewed assorted machine gunners, platoon leaders, riflemen, and unit medics. The script for the interviews was routine; name, hometown, rank and position, when were they expecting to return and was there anything they wanted to say to the folks at home. The interviewers edited the tapes and sent them to a central P.I.O. office in Tokyo, which forwarded them to radio stations near the soldier's home.

Phil was usually the announcer and he lowered his voice a tone or two to sound like someone extolling cigarettes or bath products. A typical interview went like this:

"This is combat correspondent Phil Nordman of the 53rd Fighting Swedish Infantry Division talking with Private Melvin Humptulips of Specter, Oregon here in Dog Company somewhere in Korea. Private, what's your job here?"

Humptulips answered, "Hey man, I'm a machine gunner. I shoot a machine gun, this BAR here."

"And how do you like your job?"

"It's itchie bon."[3]

"What do you like most about it?"

"A chance to blow shit up and waste some slope heads."

"Anything else?"

"Well, I like the guys I'm serving with. HooRah!"

---

3 Fractured Korean for "number one."

"You come from Specter, Oregon, it that right?"

"Yeah. Specter.'

'And is that where you'll be going when your tour is up?'

'Yeah. I'm a short timer. Just two months and four days to go.'

"Is there anyone special you'd like to say something to?"

"Yeah."

"And who is that?"

"My mom."

"What would you like to say?"

"Hey mom, I'm good. I'm gonna be home mo skochie.[4] I love you mom."

"Thanks, Private Humptulips."

It was not riveting journalism, and the more challenging aspect of the work was to edit the interviews to eliminate objectionable language or the disclosure of the soldier's geographic location. It was clear that Private Humptulips' reference to "shit" and "slope heads" would be replaced with his liking the guys he served with. Considering travel and set up time, they managed to complete fifteen interviews a day. The complicated process of editing the fifteen also took a day.

This morning the two radio correspondents were adding to their personal tape of outtakes from the interviews, principally answers to the question about saying something to someone special. Wylie listened in on the recent crop.

"Listen, Mom, you tell that brother of mine, he fucks with my car, I'm gonna break his head."

"Sweetie, the second thing I do when I come home is take off my pack."

"You tell that recruiting Sergeant when I get back I'm gonna hunt him down like a dog and mess him up!"

"Army makes a man outta me? That judge don't know jack shit."

---

4 Fractured Korean for "soon."

"Maybe he was kidding, but the Mess Sergeant said the S.O.S. (Chipped beef on toast respectfully referred to as shit on a shingle) today really was. I couldn't tell."

"Mona, don't you go near that Harry Maldonado. What they say about him and his sister is all true."

"Jack, you're full of it. Pussy ain't slanted over here."

"Of all the things bad over here, the coffee is the worst."

Ah, thought Wylie, Army journalism at its best.

The word about Shit Dad's wedding travelled fast as a jackrabbit from a prairie fire. When he entered the office in his fatigues still wearing the little rubber boots and ambled over to Sergeant's Heron's desk, attempting a feeble salute, all attention turned there.

In a lowered voice Heron said, "Sorry, man, but I told you. The Captain needs to see you now."

Captain Standrich had no desire to discuss Shit Dad's situation in public, so Heron directed the Private to meet the officer in an empty day room near the P.I.O. tent.

Shit Dad ambled there, walked into the day room, and attempted standing at attention before the Captain. He wobbled slightly in his little white rubber boots.

Standrich sighed, deeply concerned about the Private's immortal soul.

He began, "Pierre (Pie-air), it has been brought to my attention that you may be engaged in inappropriate behavior with a Korean woman. I hear that you have been leaving the camp to work on a Korean farm and that, quite recently, you claim to have married a local girl you previously referred to as your fiancée. You know, as every man here does, that marriage to a local girl is not permitted without military approval that must come all the way from Tokyo. Now, I understand that young men have needs, but you don't have to resort to marriage to fill them. Please, Pierre, tell me what's going on here."

"Shit dad, Captain, sir, is that all that's on your mind? I have done everthin' legal and proper here. No doubt about it. I have not gone AWOL to work on the farm because it was part of our camp program to help the indigenous, and I did not take any time away from workin' in the motor pool or drivin' you and the other P.I.O. folks. I admit I been a bit short of sleep but that's the fortunes of war, right?"

"Well, all right, that's a relief, but what about your parading around in that white get-up and saying you are married."

"I suppose I am sort of, but not in the military way, the way it was explained."

"Explained?"

"By the chaplain. Those lectures they give. About how marriage is a heavenly sacrament and we shouldn't let our peckers lead us on and all that. The point I took was that, if the Army didn't approve it, you couldn't get married."

Shit Dad relaxed his position and leaned in toward the Captain to emphasize his understanding.

"So," he said, "even if I did that little Korean ceremony, with the smoke and gongs and whatnot, it was definitely not approved by the Army. If I unnerstand it right, as far as the Army is concerned, I'm not married. If that's so, I can't be breakin' any regulations."

Captain Standrich digested that Cajun logic for a moment or two. There must be flaws in Shit Dad's argument and he felt certain that, somehow, a regulation or two had been bent, twisted, or broken. However, he put aside further analysis to ask his next question.

"Pierre, I need you to tell me the truth. Is there anything to the rumor that you have gotten that woman with child?"

"I do believe there is, Captain. There were two really pretty girls on that farm and they were both real kind and sporting to me, what with all the work I was doing up there with the planting and cutting and all. So one or the other would sort of slip into the rack with me on occasion to play with little Pierre. But the one who said she was pregnant, which I have no reason to doubt, she was the one I stood up with. Which was the honorable thing to do, I expect."

It seemed to the Captain that Pierre was doing the upstanding thing, even though he had lapsed into serial fornication and displayed questionable judgment. Considering the temptations offered, the vicissitudes of combat, and the fact that Shit Dad had saved his life, the Captain was not inclined to judge him now. He accepted Shit Dad's arguments. He decided to monitor developments in Pierre's life and pray for him.

"All right, Private," he said, "that's all for now."

"Thank you, Captain, sir." He paused at the door.

"There is this one other little thing I was meanin' to ask, Captain. You know, my new sister-in-law she doesn't really appreciate working on the farm so very much, and I was going to bring her over to G-2 to see if she could help with cleaning and laundry and such. That should not be a problem, should it Captain?"

CHAPTER 20

LIEUTENANT BUTZ II

◆ ◆ ◆

CAPTAIN DONG DID NOT HAVE facilities at his compound for interrogation as sophisticated as those of his peers in Manchuria did, so he improvised. He created a hole in the ground with sides about a meter wide and two and a half meters deep. The cover was made of wood lath secured by concrete blocks that permitted the elements and various insects free access to its inhabitant. Lieutenant Butz had been in the hole for most of a week.

He had not prepared his life history but acceded to Captain Dong's alternative request to write out a confession. After a few days he presented "I confess that I am very sorry to be here without any toilet paper," and plead guilty to a number of similar transgressions. Mild beatings had not improved his writing, so the camp commander dropped him in the hole where a guard lowered a small bowl of rice and water each afternoon. There were no other amenities.

For a few days, Butz amused himself with hoarse choruses of the Army Artillery song. On day four, after a downpour had eroded the sides of the hole, leaving Butz standing in revolting muck up to his calves, Captain Dong peered down and asked if his mind was clearer yet. He wanted him to recall how his unit had used germ warfare during its brief occupation of a North Korean village.

It didn't come to mind said Butz weakly, but he was ready to think about it for a while. The next day Butz developed shuddering coughs and the Captain decided continuation of this treatment would serve no further purpose. He was mindful of the common knowledge that the Korean Major who shot Lieutenant Bierce abruptly disappeared. Butz was pulled from the hole and carried to his straw mat, where he recovered for the next few days.

The other officers were treated to the same demands for life histories and prompted to remember war crimes they must have committed. The officers responded in various ways.

Gabremeskal Terrekon confessed that it was a crime that he had not been able to kill more of the enemy. During his interview, attended by three guards, the black officer leaned in closer and glowered at the small Chinese Captain, who nervously checked his earlobes. Even on short rations and in a filthy, torn uniform, Terrekon was an intimidating presence. Captain Dong never subjected the Ethiopian officer to the hole.

Quigley, the Australian, was a bit of an auteur who concocted outlandish fantasies about his life history, including many pages about his torrid love affair with Lana Turner. The writing included a chapter about how he saved Southern Australia by keeping his finger in a dyke. He was working on memoirs about his prior service in the Foreign Legion when Captain Dong realized that no twenty-five-year-old had lived that much history. He demanded that Quigley begin writing about his war crimes immediately. He was beginning an essay about germ warfare when Butz returned from the hole.

Both of the other American officers were beaten in an effort to refresh their memories about their war crimes. A handful of captured American flyers had broken under Chinese torture and admitted, in language obviously dictated by their captors, to engaging in "germ warfare." The Chinese circulated those confessions to the world press — a propaganda coup for the communists. Though only very few prisoners succumbed to torture and their statements were obviously fabricated, all prison camp commanders were ordered to obtain similar confessions from their charges. Captain Dong was doing his best to comply, but his prisoners refused to cooperate.

Matt Quigley, like the others, suspected the intensified attempt to obtain "confessions" was related to the Armistice negotiations, which were probably close to resolution. So, he played for time and labored with his pencil and pad to explain in great detail the history and nature of germs. He explained to Dong that the reader must understand germs in general before actually setting out the process by which they were deployed.

Fortunately, Captain Dong's knowledge of germs and their use in warfare was even more limited than Quigley's, although he was dubious about Quigley's sketches of magnified germs that bore an uncanny resemblance to communist leaders. The Stalin virus with a bushy moustache was Quigley's favorite. Some of the germs had raised middle digits and were found, according to Quigley, in remote areas of South America where they were cultured to increase their potency. He was capable of producing page after page of nonsense, and Captain Dong became impatient for the time when he could dictate Quigley's confession.

Butz offered absolutely no cooperation with the Captain. Even though not fully recovered from his time in the hole and weighing twenty-two pounds less than when he arrived at the POW camp, he stoically withstood any "punishment" he received from his frustrated tormentor.

In late June, guards marched Butz to the Captain's office where Dong handed him a confession to sign. Standing at attention in front of Dong's desk, he refused, and the two guards smashed their batons into his calves, forcing him to his knees. Further blows to his back and shoulders produced no cooperation. Finally, he was forced to stand at attention in the corner of Dong's office through that night and into the next day. If he tried to shift his position or slide to the floor, the guards administered punches or blows.

Butz remained resolute and, when Dong returned to his office the next day, it was clear that the Lieutenant would never sign a confession. Dong dismissed him with a wave of his hand and the guards dragged him back to his shabby quarters.

There were no further attempts to extort confessions, and harassment of both officers and enlisted men in the POW camp ceased. Food was scarce, but the guards occasionally distributed Red Cross rations and the prisoners managed to survive. On the last day of July, their guards passed on the news that the Armistice had been signed a few days earlier and they would soon be returned to their units.

It was time for jubilation.

Butz had almost healed by then.

CHAPTER 21
KIM KY YOUNG

◆ ◆ ◆

KIM FOUND THAT POW CAMP 9, north of Pusan, was a significant improvement over Koje Island, primarily because it housed none of the diehard communist agitators who challenged their keepers and less fanatical fellow prisoners. The prison huts were constructed of wood with thatched roofs and had wooden floors. Bunks were arrayed along the sides and each prisoner was issued a straw mat that was refreshed monthly. Food, though not abundant, was sufficient and the six or seven thousand prisoners were allowed free reign of the camp.

Fences and guard towers surrounded the compound but the forbidding nature of the camp was softened by the prisoners' laundry drying on the fences and idle chatter between guards and guarded. For most of the prisoners, life in Camp 9 was an improvement over their service in the NK army. There was no fear of combat or punishment by their superiors; they could associate with whom they wished; the food was adequate; Red Cross parcels were distributed; and, most of all, visitors were allowed.

The artificial division of the Korean peninsula occurred in an almost off hand fashion in 1945 when President Truman agreed with "Uncle Joe" Stalin to let Russia control Korea north of the 38th Parallel while American troops would support South Korea. Before 1945, all Koreans had been united in hatred of their Japanese occupiers and family ties extended throughout the undivided country. Consequently, in 1953, many of the prisoners in Camp 9 had relatives living south of the combat areas. Informal communication was excellent, and POWs and their relatives knew where their family members were located. So, when Auntie Soo arrived to visit Kim at Camp 9 he was overjoyed but not completely surprised.

She was his father's younger sister, middle aged and dressed in a nondescript Korean gown with a bandana wrapped around her graying hair. She was plump and full faced, but with sharp eyes and an air of being in charge. Auntie Soo had a reputation for shepherding her family through the miseries of the war and protecting them whenever she could. It was said she had business interests throughout South Korea and, possibly, some in the north.

Auntie Soo had a reputation for speaking her mind. She had splendid business sense and a personality that allowed her to cultivate strong friendships in high and low places. She used bribery effectively and had a very flexible view of ethical behavior. However, she was warm, giving, and fiercely protective of her family, and Kim loved her.

She smiled at her nephew sitting across from her at a table in the small meeting room and took his hand, looking carefully into his face. She began their conversation with a litany of complaints.

"Will our miseries never end!" she exclaimed. "First our families are burdened with the cruelty and oppression of the revolting Japanese pirates who cut off our noses and ears and sent our sisters into prostitution as comfort women. Now our families in the north are plagued by the demands of the Chinese Mao lovers and are either so stupid or cowardly that they fight their own kind who serve under the equally deplorable Syngman Rhee. It is almost too much to bear!"

She wiped her eyes with a large handkerchief.

Then she turned her thoughts to the subject at hand—nephew Kim.

""What has it been, seven years since we last saw you? And look at you! So big and strong. But still the problem with your eyes, no? I am so proud that you fly airplanes! So much has happened, I don't know where to begin. How did you come here? Are they treating you well?"

And on it went, with Kim interjecting an answer or comment when he could, like pushing chop sticks into a communal rice bowl. She had heard of Kim's imprisonment through another of Kim's aunts and journeyed to the camp by railway, ox cart and on foot. The main purpose of her visit to Pusan was to persuade Kim to stay in the south and take advantage of support from his relatives when prisoner exchanges occurred. Since Kim had arrived at that conclusion earlier, he did not require persuasion. Auntie Soo was pleased when he agreed to follow her wishes.

She explained in detail her location in still devastated Seoul and wrote down the addresses of nearby relatives, of which there were many. Kim took careful note. She promised to return the next day with fish paste delicacies and other favorites, but explained she must then leave since business affairs in Seoul required her attention.

The next day, she pressed a large wad of money, including GI script, into Kim's hand. She further surprised him, as she bustled away, by chatting with the American guards in an advanced Pidgin English, which Kim was beginning to understand. This was definitely not the Auntie Soo he recalled from his teen-age years.

Kim's injuries from the plane crash had now fully healed and his sense of smell had almost completely returned. His eyesight, however, was as bad as ever and he determined to acquire glasses that would improve his vision.

Kim was slightly older than many of the NK recruits in camp and bore the cachet of a pilot. Other POWs treated him with respect. Prisoners sought his opinion on personal and policy matters, and small tokens of gratitude and appreciation, cigarettes, wool socks, sturdy sandals, and the like found their way to his locker. He discovered an ability to resolve personal quarrels or dilemmas and his stature grew. By the end of May, he was known, in his corner of the camp, as a bona fide fixer, a revered position in any military organization, even a POW camp.

The camp had particularly porous borders since guards and commandants correctly believed there was little likelihood that their charges would attempt an escape to the north. Like osmosis, there was an interchange of goods and materials between the camp and the surrounding countryside, with gratuities smoothing the process. As Kim added the distribution of favors and needed items to his repertoire of leadership, a fine pair of glasses that corrected his fuzzy distant vision appeared on his bunk. He marveled at his crisp new view of trees, buildings, even clouds in the sky. He could see things as never before.

Now, after two years of halting negotiations between north and south, an armistice was at hand. South Korean President Syngman Rhee, however, remained opposed to an armistice since it thwarted his goal of presiding over a unified Korea. Americans were exhausted by the loss of treasure and the lives of tens of thousands of its young warriors so soon after World War II. The United States was more than willing to end the gory conflict, even if it meant not winning. President Eisenhower assured the Korean President he would have America's full support after the armistice—with financial help to rebuild the south as well as the continuing presence of US forces.

Even if Rhee were to accede to the armistice, he could not tolerate sending any NK POWs across the demilitarized line to the north. He wanted them to remain in the south as his political constituents, believing that many if not most of them had been pressed unwillingly to serve the communist regime. Therefore, Rhee developed a secret plan to free the North Korean prisoners — completely contrary to the needs and desires of the UN forces protecting the south.

At midnight, June 18, a task force of Korean MPs led by a ROK Colonel loyal to Rhee disarmed two American guards at Camp 9 and cut twenty-meter swatches through the four wire fences surrounding the compound. The prisoners gathered on the parade ground, and the Colonel announced that he was under orders to occupy the camp and release all anti-communist prisoners. Whatever their political leanings, all those within earshot determined that, for the moment, they were anti-communist and more than willing to be released.

All lights in the camp were extinguished and over four thousand POWs marched out of the camp and into the countryside. Rhee's followers made similar release attempts at more than ten other POW camps nearby but, once UN forces learned of Rhee's plan, reinforcements were provided and the escapes were thwarted. However, over twenty- seven thousand prisoners escaped from the southern prison camps that night. Only a thousand prisoners were recaptured and a handful killed. All the rest disappeared into the countryside and found asylum in the homes of friendly families.

Kim escaped with the first group from Camp 9 and, with his improved vision, began to follow the handle of the big dipper north. Auntie Soo's cash eased his almost three hundred-mile journey to Seoul where he arrived wearing new clothes and good leather shoes. As he walked down the dirt alley toward Auntie Soo's home, polishing his glasses with a clean square of white cotton, he resolved to help her in any way possible. He fingered the remaining wad of money in his breast pocket, grateful for her abundant help. He was puzzled, though. It was almost, he thought, as though Auntie Soo had advance knowledge of the prisoner release.

CHAPTER 22

A REPORT AWAY FROM THE FRONT

◆ ◆ ◆

BY FREE AIRMAIL
May 16 1953

My Dearest One:

I guess the torrential rain we've been having wrought havoc with the mail and I didn't have any word from you for almost a week, which was mighty disturbing. But today the kid is ecstatic —two letters from you and you even had time to write during final exams. So, before filling you in on what's been going on here I thought I'd comment on some of the things in your letters.

It must be a great relief to the family that your uncle's abscess has finally been cured. I'm sure your aunt must be happy about it, considering the weird place it was located. Please send them both my best wishes. That you've had an early spring must be nice. I don't think there are any daffodils around here because they have probably been blown away with mortar or artillery fire, but we do still have some of the pink and red azaleas up on the hills. At the moment it's not safe to wander up there because of the snipers, but they do make the hills look colorful.

I'm really glad your studies are going well. I know you'll remember that my first year at college wasn't such a great success, but, if I get the chance to go back, I guarantee it will be nose to the grindstone time.

Anyway, I'm sure you'll cream your tests and be well on the way to being an outstanding teacher. You know, my love, you could teach me anything!

So, Fred Schmidt's parents gave him a yellow MG for graduation. It must be great to be a complete doofus and have rich parents. When you go for a ride with him be extra careful because he's not too tightly wrapped and those little cars can be dangerous. Heck, it's dangerous riding around in Jeeps over here and they are more stable. Anyway, say Hi to Fred and his sister for me.

We've been so busy here the past few days that I almost (repeat ALMOST) forgot how much I missed and love you. What's going on is that there is a lot of talk of an armistice and the military Brass at I Corps Headquarters and in Tokyo are reorganizing troop dispositions to put more of the ROK Divisions on the line. That means the 53rd Division just pulled back to new Headquarters about fifteen miles south of here and one of the ROK Divisions near Seoul took over our positions. Our engineers have been working for about a month setting up our new operations and last week we packed up all our stuff and bugged out.

Like everything in the Army, it was hurry up and wait and we packed up our stuff and all the stuff in the P.I.O. office like typewriters, desks, all the recording gear, our weapons and so on, slept in our bags and prepared to move out the next morning at 0400. Well, there was a foobar or two and we didn't get rolling in our trucks till after 0800. We did get a cup of cold coffee, though, ha-ha. When we left it hadn't rained for a week so the roads were choked with dust which, of course, settled all over us till we all turned a fine shade of bisque, like my mom's refrigerator. It's a good thing there was no ambush because our rifles would probably have exploded what will all the dirt in them. Anyway, that was the longest fifteen miles I've ever traveled. However, we were pretty excited with our new quarters when we arrived.

First of all, I'm writing this from our new office, which is a Quonset hut that has solid walls with no water stains on them and a concrete floor. The rain is coming down hard now but we are cozy in our new home and there are outlets on the walls with fluorescent lights above that make typing this letter much easier. Lots of other buildings here have metal walls and roofs, like the EM Club, the dining hall and, believe it or not, a movie theater. Our sleeping tent is about the same as where we left but they issued us new air mattresses that don't have that musty smell and Kim, our house boy, is happy about that. Kim came with us, by the way; there was no way he was going to work for the ROK troops. He's discriminating in our favor.

So, it didn't take us long to get our gear stowed in the new sleeping tent, which was nice too because there was no soot covered winter tent liner over our heads. The tough part was to get the dust off us because there were no showers for a few days. I guess we were slaphappy because we just threw pans of water at each other while running around naked behind the tent till gravity got most of the dirt to ground level. Then Captain Standrich sent word it would be our asses if we didn't show up to square away the office area. After I completed the herculean task of placing a typewriter on my desk, I helped Phil and Boomer set up the recording studio that was located in its own little glassed off space like a "real" studio according to Phil. The thing was that we couldn't quite remember how all those wires and cords went together, but it was late and we were able to quaff down some illegal cans of 3.2 near beer to help our deliberations. Everything worked out OK because the Captain liked the setup and slipped us a bottle of Jack Daniels for future consumption. The Captain is a bible thumper, but he is a good judge of liquor. We figure we could do a lot worse than our Capt.

We lost a couple of days' work during the move and also had to dig out files and things that got jumbled together with some from G-4, so it's been very hectic catching up. That's where I am now, pretty much caught up and very comfortable working at this desk. We set up some speakers and can listen to classical music after hours which, at the moment, is Debussy's Claire de Lune. Kind of spoils the image of a tough Army combat correspondent, doesn't it?

There's been a lot of scuttlebutt about how negotiations for an armistice are moving ahead, and then everything comes to a screeching halt. As I said, they are deploying a number (can't say more) of the ROK divisions along the line and it looks like the Chinese are making one last big push to knock the Koreans back further south. Seems they've been listening to our own side, which is always handing out this Gung Ho rhetoric about how we're not going to be pushed around just before an armistice. I guess they think they will be able to keep whatever territory they hold whenever that happens. But I've been on the line now and saw some guys get it, and I'm pretty sure there is no way taking a hill back is worth it. Meanwhile, we're all hoping there's a decision to end the fighting soon, and there's this gallows humor going around about who will be the last guy to get shot before they ring the bell.

Dearest one, it's late but before signing off I want to add just two more things.

Sergeant Heron spoke with me yesterday and reminded me that he was getting to be a short timer and wondered if I had any idea who his replacement would be. Modesty forbids repetition of the things he said about me, but it looks as though I'll be the enlisted guy in charge of the P.I.O. so long as I don't screw up and stay healthy. That's pretty nice, but another good thing is that I get temporary duty in Tokyo in a month or so to work at the Stars and Stripes to learn their style, teletyping, etc.

Finally, Darling, I'm in a sort of sentimental mood tonight and that, of course, means all sorts of words and thoughts of endearment. But, they've already been said many times and I won't repeat them. Just know that I love you very much and, as close as a few thousand miles allow, belong to you. Good night and sweet dreams, fair one —Wylie

CHAPTER 23

A RIDE NORTH

◆ ◆ ◆

ALISTAIR BENCHLEY GINGERLY LOWERED HIS formidable bulk to the rear seat of the Jeep, like a hen descending on her clutch of eggs. Wylie squeezed in beside him and Shit Dad slid the Jeep into gear. Dick Heron was in the shotgun seat, holding his carbine and alert for potential guerilla attacks. The July afternoon was hot, dusty, and unrelieved by breezes except for clouds of ochre dust raised by passing Army vehicles. Alistair wore large tanker goggles that he wiped from time to time with a huge red bandanna, sighing mightily with the exertion of raising his hand to his eyes.

"Panmunjom, Panmunjom," he intoned. "They say that war is the ultimate extension of diplomacy and for two years both sides of this abysmal war have been playing at diplomacy and trying to rack up bargaining chips by marching up one hill after another and then falling down again. It's like a crazed exercise from Jack and Jill!

"So, here we are, on our way to the UN front lines to see if their cobbled up armistice will work. It will be intensely memorable if it does. July 27th, 1953 - almost exactly three years since the NK invaded the south. This will be the biggest story since the summer of 1945."

"I have my doubts," offered Dick Heron. "The UP guys told me yesterday that the Goonies launched a balls against the wall attack against three ROK Divisions in the east two days ago. Why would they do that with a cease-fire just around the corner?"

"Inscrutable Orientals or, as my forebears would say, WOGs," said Alistair.

"WOGs?" asked Wylie.

"Worthy Oriental Gentlemen, dear boy."

At approximately ten that morning the peace negotiators had signed the definitive armistice agreement and, sometime after noon, General Matt Clark confirmed the agreement by signing it eighteen times in front of TV cameras and hot lights. His comments were subdued and he expressed gratitude that the killing was finally over. There was no exultation; he considered it a time for prayer and called for unrelaxed vigilance and effort to maintain the fragile accord. The Chinese and North Korean armies did not have robust communication, so the negotiators decided to delay the cease-fire until 2000 hours that evening.

As soon as Heron and Alistair Benchley, who was at 53rd Headquarters that morning, heard of the armistice they arranged transportation to the front line Regiment in which Tully McGregor served. As Tully's friend, they invited Wylie along, and Shit Dad was recruited for his superior driving. None of them wanted to miss the long awaited moment, assuming it actually occurred.

Dust continued to collect on them as the Jeep rolled on. All four were lost in their own thoughts till Dick Heron asked, "You were up with the 7th Division at the T-Bone complex last January when they put on that big show, weren't you? The thing called Operation Smack."

Alistair nodded. ""I was indeed; and I hope what we will experience tonight will not be a repetition of that fiasco."

"I wasn't there," Heron added for Wylie, "but I talked with the wire service reporters who were. It was a lesson in, would you call it hubris, Al?"

"If it still means arrogance and a certain loss of touch with reality" said the Australian, "I would agree completely. In my experience, it is an ailment to which the military and politicians are most susceptible. Let me tell you about it, young Cypher."

Alistair and Heron recalled the details of Operation Smack for Wylie, with the Australian offering local color since he was there throughout the operation and its aftermath. G-2 advised General James Van Fleet, Eighth Army Commander, that Navy and Air Force aviators had hit the wrong targets sixty-three times during their sorties in 1952. He decided to validate bombing techniques and ground tactics in a grand operation designed to take a single hill occupied by the enemy. The target was called Spud Hill and a Company of the 7th Division was assigned the honor of taking it. The company had practiced in similar terrain in friendly territory nine times.

"My God, the softening up for that one hill was ferocious," said Alistair. "First they sent in fighter bombers, followed by medium and light bomber sorties to bomb the hell out of the whole T Bone area. They dropped over seventy tons of bombs and eight tanks of napalm the day before the attack. It didn't seem that anything larger or more durable than a cockroach would have survived.

"The next morning the Thunder jets arrived and they attacked Spud Hill with their half ton bombs in four waves. Then the artillery took over and blasted the position while a dozen or so supporting tanks rumbled into position at the base of the hill. It seemed as though all that firepower had almost reduced the hill to rubble and they might just as well have gone home then."

Heron reminded Alistair about the brochures.

"Oh my God, yes," he recalled, "those lovely three-colour brochures provided by the Army that highlighted the coming events. The sponsors were the Brass who organized the entertainment. Sort of like a program for a concert, but things went badly wrong during the third movement."

The last item before the attack was for eight Marine Corsairs to drop smoke screens in front of the tanks and infantry, but they either dropped their bombs too soon or failed to hit their targets. That foreshadowed an inglorious ending to the exercise. The event lingered in Alistair's memory.

"Foreshadowed, adumbrated, yes, yes. I foretold the fiasco to come to anyone who would listen, of which there were few. And I didn't make many friends up there when I reported about the Brass poring over those lovely three-colour programs."

Without smoke, the artillery, mortars, and even tanks concentrated fire on Spud Hill while a platoon prepared for the attack. They were ordered to begin on word from the Battalion commander, but his radio failed. The platoon, broken into four squads, began its ascent fifteen minutes late. They rushed the hill from north and south and, upon reaching the first outcrop, saw that the Chinese defenders, hardly the worse for wear, were rolling grenades down on them.

Within minutes, the enemy cut down the platoon commander and his replacement. The platoon and its relief platoon were overwhelmed. A third platoon went to their rescue but was repulsed and fell back with many casualties. Before midday, the regimental commander aborted the attack. Except for Alistair's reporting, Spud Hill would have become an unnoticed footnote to the conflict. However, reports of the battle for Spud Hill reached the U.S. Congress within a day, and the military was severely criticized for wasting lives and money on a "show." That was, of course, denied.

"Hubris," repeated Alistair. "Let us hope the fuck that doesn't revisit us tonight. It's time for me to move on."

"I kinda expected you deadbeats would show up. And who is this over-fed character with the funny hat? I don't see any rank, so I won't salute you. But I will give you a hand out of the Jeep," said Tully as he assisted Alistair in reassembling his bulk on the ground in front of a CP that offered a wide view of the Punchbowl complex.

The Chinese had been attacking that area with heavy artillery and mortars for over a week, descending from their caves and bunkers by night to inflict as much damage as possible on the UN forces. The troops on the line had a hard time believing those attacks would cease. They had no reason to trust the enemy. There was no slacking in their vigilance or preparedness.

Tully shook Heron's hand and gave Wylie a modified man hug that involved fancy hand maneuvers before the quick embrace. He turned to the driver. "You gotta be Shit Dad; Wylie's told me about you. Welcome aboard, man." Alistair introduced himself and required quick passage to the latrine. Once reunited, Tully directed them to a nearby bunker visible in the bright light of the full moon rise.

"Whatever's gonna happen," he said "we will see it all from here. It's all supposed to stop in about two hours and, as you can tell, it's dead quiet out there right now and has been since about 1800 hours."

They ate their rations and waited. Heron was reflecting on the irony of this all ending, as T.S. Eliot anticipated, with a whimper and not a bang. At 1900 hours, a bright green flare arose above the Punchbowl and a horrendous barrage of artillery and tank fire thudded into their positions. Everything the Chinese could muster: high explosives, white phosphorous, small arms fire, artillery, and mortar rounds liquefied the night into a river of noise, light, and hot metal. By the time it ended, half an hour later, the correspondents' hearing had dulled to the point where they communicated by hand signals.

Suddenly an eerie silence engulfed them, but it was a while before they recognized it. Then the Americans launched a cluster of white phosphorus flares, followed by a huge artillery barrage aimed at the Chinese. Wylie and Dick Heron were able to observe enemy soldiers scurrying to their trenches and bunkers, but it never occurred to them to fire on them. At exactly fifteen minutes before the appointed hour, all was quiet.

In the stillness, soldiers all along the line stood on ridgelines, clambered to the tops of bunkers, and exposed themselves to what would have been deadly fire minutes before. Positions on the enemy lines looked abandoned.

At exactly 2200 hours, a cluster of white flares illuminated the entire battlefield and the clink of bottles and singing from both warring camps broke the silence.

"It's a hell of a war that you fight by the clock," muttered a grizzled Sergeant who had been at the Chosin Reservoir. He joined the P.I.O. team and others in taking a pull from the bottle being passed through the bunker. Now confident the cease-fire would hold at least temporarily, troops all along the line exposed themselves and their positions to watch enemy activity. There was raucous laughter, loud singing, and movement across the valley. Some of the Chinese soldiers were dancing. They were, after all, undefeated. Some enemy soldiers walked to the base of the hill below Tully and Wylie and left gifts of candy and handkerchiefs.

"Well, if that don't beat all! Them Goonies are leaving presents for us," offered Shit Dad. Alistair, scribbling furiously in his notebook, raised his head. "It may be they are honoring a worthy adversary or just relieved this bloody mess is over. In any case, it's the first foreign war the Yanks haven't won. There may be a message in that."

Tully and his men were ordered to prepare the CP for withdrawal, organize equipment, police the brass, and load the trucks. Less than two hours after the armistice, they proceeded down the winding road to their rearward position.

The P.I.O. team's Jeep joined the convoy south. Wylie looked back at the abandoned CP, still visible in the moonlight. An evening breeze caught scraps of cardboard and paper that scudded across the hilltop like autumn leaves. No one in the Jeep said anything.

CHAPTER 24

A LETTER HOME

◆ ◆ ◆

BY FREE AIRMAIL
August 2, 1953

Dear Mom and Dad, Betty, and Ellie,

I know, I know, it's been over two weeks since I last wrote and I know you tend to worry now that Korea has really been in the news with the Armistice and all the editorials either praising or complaining about the fact that it has finally happened. I'm just fine and somewhat in awe of all the chances I've had here to actually see up close and in detail the historic events as they unfold. But before I go into all that, thanks for your letters and, girls, don't worry about spelling and grammar. I really like reading your lovely letters and some of the other guys here do, too! Maybe I can fix you up with some dates when I return to the home front!

Yes, I was up at the lines the night the Armistice went into effect and, let me tell you, neither side was reluctant to let all hell break loose right up until fifteen minutes before the deadline. It was really strange—you couldn't hear yourself think for almost two hours and then there was dead silence. At exactly 2200, whistles blew on both sides and flares went up and you could almost hear a universal sigh of relief that this damn war was over, or at least it was over for a while. No one really trusts the other side, what we now refer to as the "Goonies," and certainly Rhee's government has done all it can to delay or even ruin the Armistice talks.

Now, I haven't personally met South Korea's exalted leader (I hear that's how he sees himself) but I do spend time with the wire service correspondents down at the press billets in Seoul and last week there were a bunch of TV reporters who flew in for the latest news. Honestly, the wire service guys really seem to know what's going on and the TV reporters spend as much time on makeup and finding "sexy" military outfits as they do in digging out the news. But the TV guys have "producers" who do a lot of work for them. However, I digress.

You may or may not have read about Rhee's secret plan to release all Korean POWs a month or so ago to make sure these people wouldn't be sent to the North. He carried it out very effectively and thousands of prisoners escaped before the Americans got wise to it. It really put a crimp in negotiations for a while and Rhee got his way — again. Even though his authoritarian rule has already embarrassed the brass and Washington politicians, he is our man here and there's not much anyone can do about it.

Dad, am I just being naïve or is something wrong when the local leader essentially tells us to pound sand and we not only go along with him but pledge our continuing support? Maybe someday I'll be able to understand politics but I guess right now it boils down to trying to make the best of a lousy situation.

Anyway, in spite of Rhee's secret moves, the Armistice seems to be holding and there have been a lot of troop movements to accommodate the new DMZ area. I expect Division Headquarters will be changing its location pretty soon because they want more ROK Divisions on the line. Rest assured that, with the combat over, I won't be getting into risky situations, although there are lots of stories to work on, and there is a rumor I will be assigned to the Stars and Stripes in Tokyo for a while to do some special training. That would be really interesting but, for now, it's just a rumor. More about that later.

From your letters it appears all is well and the vacation to Hilton Head in the Lincoln sounds as though it was a great success. Again, it's getting late and I will close.

My love to all of you – Wylie

CHAPTER 25

NEWS TO JUDY

◆ ◆ ◆

BY FREE AIRMAIL
August 3, 1953

My Dearest Darling,

I've really been bouncing all over the place for the past few days and the kid assumes that lack of mail from his most favorite distaff person is caused by military snafus and not a lack of interest by said distaff person. This probably is going to be kind of a short letter because it is already late and I spent most of the day writing "color" articles about how the troops are adjusting to the Armistice. The interviews are pretty interesting and they range from guys who don't trust the "Slopes" for a second and are keeping their weapons ready for action, guys who are relieved because it looks like combat is over and their chances of getting killed have lowered dramatically, and gung ho new arrivals who are pissed that they won't have a chance to earn the Combat Infantry Badge right away. My reaction is that I'm completely relieved that there's not much now that stands in the way of my getting back to you, my love.

As you know, I was at the front when the fighting officially ended and I've got to admit I got belated goose bumps once I got past the awe of the event itself and watched the way the moment sank in with our troops. Sure, there was all sorts of celebrating and tremendous relief for everyone when the last whistle blew, but there was also a kind of

sadness. I guess it was anti-climactic when all was said and done, especially for the guys who had lost friends along the way or were on their
second tour and had experienced some of the awful things that went
on here. What got me thinking were some comments my Aussie correspondent friend, Alistair, and Dick Heron (he's my boss) made when
we were returning from the line. First of all, nobody has actually been
calling this a war; it's a "police action" or combat or engagement by
UN forces. We were thinking this might be a propaganda thing (since
that's what we do!) so that no one has to admit this is the first WAR
that Americans have LOST (except maybe the civil war).

Alistair is more fine-tuned to political things (I get lost just trying to figure out who New Jersey senators are!) and he anticipates
Eisenhower will take credit for ending the war and blame his predecessor for the over thirty-six thousand of our men who were killed
here, to say nothing of the guesstimated two million people from all
sides who were killed. What I'm trying to wrap my head around is
why so many people were killed after we beat the commies back up
north and the Chinese created a bloody stalemate and both sides were
TALKING about it for two years.

That......Whoah. Boomer just walked in the door with two letters
from you that arrived this afternoon while I was up at Battalion. Which
I have just now read. Which make me extremely happy and permit me
to discard this maudlin stuff, which is probably just sophomoric ram-
bling anyway. I just know that if I ever get to be an old man responsible
for sending young men into battle, that would be the absolutely last
thing I would do!

Anyway, my dearest one, I reciprocate all your sweet thoughts and
I wish more than you can know that I was with you right now. I will answer your three questions when I've had a chance to think about them
with a clear head tomorrow, but it may be a couple of days before I'm
near a typewriter. There's a big prisoner exchange I've been assigned
to cover, and we hope a number of Division soldiers will be coming

back from the prison camps up north. I hear it was pretty grim for them and I want to talk with them if they'll let me.

As always, you have all the love this lonely trooper has to offer. A sweet kiss goodnight with no holds barred - Wylie

CHAPTER 26

BUTZ RETURNS

◆ ◆ ◆

THERE ARE NUMEROUS WAYS TO use a rifle butt. A sharp blow to the head causes instant immobilization while a swift jab to the stomach results in temporary incapacity. A rap to the kidneys is a fine attention getter while a determined thrust in that area may cause the recipient to piss blood for a week. There were Chinese soldiers in Captain Dong's prison camp who were maestros of the rifle butt. They could coerce unarmed prisoners in numerous ways by varying the bodily location and force of application, bruising, tearing, or breaking as the situation required. The soldier assigned to arouse Lieutenant Butz early that September morning was instructed to leave no marks so he simply jabbed the sleeping officer in the ribs and motioned him to collect his meager belongings in a filthy pillowcase and wait in front of his shack.

The other two American officers in his shack had departed the day before and he stood with Gabremeskal, the Ethiopian officer, and his Australian friend, Matt Quigley. In the slanting morning light, he noted how worn Matt appeared and that he had lost weight in the seven months of Captain Dong's tender care. Butz' clothes were loose on his frame and he realized Matt was not the only one who lost weight.

Two Russian made trucks pulled up to the camp entrance and the three waiting officers were prodded to the back of the first truck where they were greeted by a group of emaciated and dirty American enlisted men seated on wooden slats. They helped the new arrivals on board, expressing considerable interest in the Ethiopian officer.

"Man, where do you come from?"

"Christ, you always been that black?"

Emphasizing his plummy British accent, Gabremeskal cheerfully explained that he led an Ethiopian Company and had been captured while storming a Chinese occupied hill. He noted that his black skin deflected communist bullets and that he had caused a number of enemy soldiers to meet their ancestors by the skillful application of his sword that, unfortunately and sadly, had gone missing. He finished his response by asking if the men had ever seen a lion of Judah. Answered in the negative, he expanded his chest as best he could in the crowded truck and roared, "But now you have, for I am one!" Silence, but for the rumble of tires and the diesel exhaust, ensued. It was some moments before the passengers continued to review the scuttlebutt about their destination.

If enough misinformation and rumor are exchanged among a critical mass of soldiers, nuggets of truth are eventually uncovered, if one or two are astute enough to listen well. Of the eighteen or so soldiers crammed in the back of the truck there was a listener, a scrawny Corporal with large ears supporting misshapen Army issue eyeglasses. His capabilities were apparently appreciated by other noncoms in the truck and he was asked," So, Sherm, waddaya think? What's going on?"

"Okay, so we know that an Armistice was signed a few days ago and that prisoner exchanges are going to begin right away," said Sherm. "The Army calls it Operation Big Snatch or Big Switch, according to one of the Gook guards at our camp. We know that the wounded prisoner exchange was called 'Little Switch' and I guess the Army isn't creative enough to change it much, so I'm thinking we are all on our way to the Big Switch. Whatever, we're heading south."

Sherm, weaker than he appeared, slumped in his seat after the exertion of his deductions. A buddy passed him water in a dented canteen, which Sherm drank as those around him considered his observations. There had been so many dashed expectations since their capture that the prospect of freedom was difficult to grasp. Some of the men avoided the thought itself, fearing the crushing disappointment should it not happen.

"Well, my guess is that we aren't more than about forty-five miles north of Panmunjom. It shouldn't take this piece of shit truck more than three hours to get there," added Sherm.

It was a very long three hours, and Randolph Butz was sweating profusely as the truck lumbered into the outskirts of Panmunjom. He, Matt Quigley, and a few of the noncoms in the truck were suffering from nausea caused by the lurching movement and the claustrophobic crowding under the dirty canvas covering, not to mention air that was thick with heavy motes of Korean dirt.

The truck entered a main thoroughfare lined with shell pocked buildings and ruined vehicles and turned sharply to the left, stopping in a parking area adjacent to the famous Peace Pagoda at Panmunjom. A guard and one of the interpreters from Captain Dong's camp scurried to the back of the truck and dropped the gate, allowing the soldiers to lower themselves carefully to the ground. Unsure why they had stopped, many of them believed it was a piss stop until Butz, leaning on a fender and, catching his breath, saw a huge Marine Major surrounded by other Marines approach the truck. Lieutenant Lee, Dong's adjutant, who held a typewritten list containing names of the prisoners in the truck, met the Major some yards from the truck.

"I must call out the names; it is the pro-toe-call."

Snatching the list from Lee's hand, the Major said," Fuck your protocol. These men belong to me now!"

Very carefully, the Marines assisted each of the returning prisoners, offering them a hand or shoulder and welcoming them back to freedom. Helicopters were standing by to take the seriously ill to immediate medical care, and ambulances waited to transport the men to a newly established Freedom Village fifteen miles south in Munsan for medical examination and further processing. Butz gratefully accepted support from the young Marine who held him at the waist, surprised at the man's expression, a combination of tenderness, anger, and concern, as he moved to help Butz. Christ, Butz thought, I must look pretty awful. He knew he had lost weight and hadn't shaved in over a month and suspected he looked a bit worse than Robinson Crusoe on a bad day. Those other guys in the truck didn't look so hot either, but they had enough strength to join Butz and Quigley in presenting their middle fingers to the retreating Russian truck.

As Butz' group was waiting for assignment to ambulances, a convoy of three open Army deuce and a half trucks appeared on the highway heading north. They were laden with returning North Korean troops. As they approached the Peace Pagoda area, they stripped off their issued clothing and threw shirts, trousers, boots, underwear, and anything else associated with the hated enemy to the ground. They made obscene gestures learned from their guards to the Marines and screamed their version of insults, as in "Fork you plicks" and "Eat sticks you sons of mothers."

The Marines reciprocated with gestures of their own. As the prisoners returning north slowed for transfer to waiting Russian trucks, they sang patriotic songs at the top of their lungs, ecstatic with the thought of returning to their communist homeland. Observing this, Butz considered the contrast between the two homecomings.

Quigley, sitting at his side on a bench next to the ambulances said, "I guess those motherless slant eyed pricks didn't have access to the tender ministrations of a Captain Dong. Too bad."

Wylie arrived in Musan the night before with a team of Signal Coops photographers and reporters from the Associated Press. Excited by the prospect of meeting returning prisoners and hearing their stories, he left the press billet before dawn to stand next to the entrance gate with other reporters. The early morning air was cool but heavy. It would be a hot day.

The prisoners began arriving in Musan at 0900. Wylie was shocked at their emaciated condition, their bedraggled clothing and how many of them seemed overwhelmed with the process of repatriation. By late morning, he had not yet mustered the courage to intrude on any of the soldiers with an interview. Signal Corps photographers were capturing the event on film and Wylie felt the returnees' unshaven faces and haunted eyes were more eloquent than any words he could put on paper. Silently, he bore compassionate witness.

At noon, Wylie was standing near the door of the MASH receiving area designed to process returning prisoners when he recognized the disheveled Lieutenant Butz shuffling toward him with the help of a MASH orderly. The Lieutenant was engraved in his memory because he believed Butz had conned him into taking eight more weeks of advanced infantry training— dooming him to service in Korea instead of the training for which he had enlisted. Although Wylie understood Butz' motives in persuading him to continue his infantry training, he had no fondness for him.

As Butz hesitantly approached the MASH tent, Wylie noted patches of gray in the full beard covering his chin and cheeks, and saw deep lines around his eyes and mouth. Jesus, he thought, Butz is maybe five years older than I am but he looks like he's fifty. Wylie had heard stories about the horrors of Communist prison camps and Butz' condition seemed to bear them out. He hoped his former company adjutant would be willing to explain what his experience was like during the months he was a prisoner.

Butz had no idea who the Corporal coming toward him with outstretched hand was. The young soldier seemed familiar but time and his recent ordeals had dulled many edges. He steadied himself and weakly accepted the handshake.

"Lieutenant, you probably don't remember me. I'm Private Cypher from your platoon in Company C at Fort Dix. I was..."

Recognition dawned. It was the college kid marksman he and Sergeant Branch had encouraged to continue infantry training. He had left Fort Dix shortly before Butz received his orders to command a platoon on the line. What, he wondered, is he doing here with a notebook and a sidearm?

"I'm with the 53rd Division P.I.O. and I am interviewing returning POWs. Would it be okay if I asked you a few questions?" Wylie offered to help him into the MASH tent.

"I don't have anything to say."

"But aren't you glad to be back?"

"Of course. You didn't ask dumb questions like that when you were in my Company!"

"Sorry. I'm just trying to get a sense of what it feels like for you to be out of the POW camp and back here with the Army again. How were conditions in the camp?"

"Tell you what," said Butz. "The Commies showed us copies of the Stars and Stripes with pictures of other POWs gathering boxes of apples, taking showers, chowing down with what looked like meat and vegetables and playing games in the snow. It was pure propaganda bullshit and I don't feel inclined to talk with any reporter who might be responsible for that kind of crap. Like I said, I have nothing to say. I got to get on with my processing."

Wylie had the good sense to wish Butz well and leave to find others to interview. "No comment" was the main response to his questions.

The rotund Colonel who examined Butz had an unfortunate habit of sucking air through his large front teeth as he applied the stethoscope and prodded him here and there. He ordered X-rays of the Lieutenant's legs that he reviewed as Butz reclined on a folding chair in the doctor's office. "You have any accidents or injuries to your right leg while you were up North?"

"The guards tuned me up every once in a while," replied Butz. "They may have had a fondness for that leg."

"Well, the thing is that you seem to have osteomyelitis in your right fibula. It's a bone infection that is caused by bacteria and made worse by trauma. You're going to need to spend some time in a hospital and rehab to get that fixed. You need to go to rehab anyway to get rid of parasites and get some good Army food in you. Looks as though you've lost about forty or so pounds. Anyway, we'll get you fixed up. Otherwise everything looks okay."

With that encouraging outlook, Butz was ushered from the medical tent to the Personnel office so his records could be brought up to date. A Sergeant asked him to sit and wait a few minutes while his medical report was added to his file. Then the Sergeant ushered him into a Major's office where the officer returned Butz' salute and asked him to make himself comfortable while he reviewed his 201 file that he selected from the top of a stack of similar folders.

"Looks like you'll be on one of the next helicopters to Kimpo and then on your way to the 8167th Army hospital in Tokyo," said the Major. "Many guys are coming back with nasty diseases we don't even have in the states, but the staff in Tokyo has lots of experience, God bless 'em, in taking care of all that stuff. You'll be fine. Now, it will just take a couple of minutes to get all your information up to date."

The Major confirmed the time Butz had been a POW and checked the papers in his folder. He questioned him about time in service and whether Butz had any personal items kept in another location. The Lieutenant's answers were precise and polite, but the Major could tell he was tiring quickly.

"Well, that does it. Two items of good news for you: you've been a Captain for three months and your back pay, including basic, combat and other allowances is enough to pay for a Cadillac Eldorado and a couple of weeks at the Top of the Mark in San Francisco. If you want, I can authorize the pay master to give you two hundred in cash right now."

The new Captain had not thought about money in months, but the prospect of cash in his pocket was attractive. "Sure," he said, "that would be fine."

In Tokyo, surgeons cleaned and debrided Butz' leg wound and pumped in intravenous antibiotics and worm medicine. After a week, he was able to keep down solid food and hobble around the ward with a walker. His doctors told him that the wooziness caused by taking painkillers would soon wear off.

Eleven days after his arrival, clearheaded and six pounds heavier, Butz was awakened from a nightmare, disoriented, and covered in sweat. With blinding clarity, he had relived his fourth day in Captain Dong's hole, struggling to lift his legs above the stinking muck that stuck to his calves like black leeches. Searing pain shot up from his right ankle to his hip, causing him to search for relief by changing his position in bed. Movement only intensified his agony. A nurse, alarmed by his screams, stood beside his bed, rubbing his shoulders gently, offering pain pills and soothing words. She replaced his pillow, sodden with tears.

That was the beginning of Butz' unending nights of misery and despair.

A DAY IN THE LIFE

◆ ◆ ◆

ON ENTERING THE P.I.O. OFFICE, Wylie saw Captain Standrich by his desk in the far corner of the office talking with a short, slender Corporal he had not seen before. Lamar Trenchant and Armand Backstrup were typing busily, unusual for this early in the morning, and Dick Heron was speaking on the field telephone. Phil, Boomer, and their equipment were gone and Barry Sonnenfeld was near the supply closet brewing what he referred to as coffee. Unusual, thought Wiley, the Captain is already here; he normally doesn't arrive till after 1000 hours – and he customarily makes up for arriving late by leaving early. As Wiley hung his sidearm on the peg near his desk, Captain Standrich motioned him over.

"Wiley, say hello to Oscar Furbish. He's been on sick leave for, what was it now, almost seven months? He was one of our Regimental reporters until he took sick. He'll be going back to Regiment in a couple days and sending his stuff to you till he rotates. He's a really good sports reporter, I can tell you."

Wylie and Oscar Furbish exchanged greetings and the Captain cheerfully waved them away. Wylie suggested they try to find some coffee at the mess tent, thereby avoiding Barry and his poisonous brew. They arrived moments before the huge coffee urn was to be drained and recharged for the noon meal and settled at a corner table before thick, white ceramic mugs containing a warm black liquid that smelled vaguely of coffee.

"So, Oscar, sick leave for seven months? Is that something you can talk about?"

"Sure. It was no big deal except for the minor fact that I almost died – a couple of times."

"Man that sounds rough. Were you in combat?"

"Only in a manner of speaking," Oscar said. "I was filing stories about routine stuff happening at Regiment and rewriting basketball and baseball items from the wires. The thing is, I'd look down at my Combat Correspondent badge and figure it was pretty much a sham. It bothered me that I was taking credit for combat experience I never had. Captain Standrich said the Regiment guys loved what I was doing, but I persuaded him to let me do a bit on a combat patrol, you know, actually report what going on patrol was like. This was last April when the Goonies were busy every night sending out their patrols and probing the ROK regiments with night attacks and artillery.

"A platoon Lieutenant in Dog Company said I could tag along on a moonlight foray where they were trying to collect prisoners. They handed me a carbine and I just got in line and went with the squad. I took a rasher of shit from the guys for being a co-ree-spondent and not a real soldier but we got along okay. It was a quiet patrol at first."

Oscar and Wylie grimaced as each took a slug of coffee and Oscar continued.

"We were well below a ridge line but I guess there was enough light to tell we were moving around. We took a couple mortar rounds but no one got hurt except me when a piece of shrapnel sliced through my boot and surgically removed about half my big toe. It hurt like a mother."

"And that got you seven months of sick leave?"

"No, that wasn't it. I was bleeding a lot from my foot, so they hustled me back from patrol to the aid station. They had to cut off my pants and the doc noticed that my balls were really swollen, you know, like tennis balls. I hadn't really noticed. Doc, he asked me if I had headaches or was throwing up or was sore all over. Stuff like that. I was feeling kind of crappy since I'd been on R & R in southern Japan a couple weeks before, and it turned out I had a case of brain inflammation, what they call Japanese encephalitis.

"So, the toe was a minor problem. I got this high fever and they sent me to a hospital in Pusan, but I don't remember much about all that because my brain decided I should be in a coma for about a month. That's when I almost died."

"Jesus! We're here worrying about getting shot and you almost die from what, a mosquito bite," asked Wylie.

"Yeah. Once I finally opened my eyes it took almost four months to get me back in shape, but I lost some hearing in my right ear. The good news is that I made it back and can never get it again. And they credited my hospital time to Korea service which makes me a short timer. Just a little over two months to go."

There was a long pause as both grappled with thoughts about irony, mortality and the direction in which the fickle finger of fate might next be pointing. They returned to the office, leaving two white mugs almost full of chilled Army coffee.

Wylie noted that Lamar was typing furiously, but it was not another copy of a press release. Rather, it was one of his daily outpourings of observations, philosophical insights, and declarations of eternal love to Debbie Jaliskowski.

A new photo of an attractive young blonde woman in a revealing peasant blouse and generous smile was taped above his desk, and Lamar's lips moved to echo the words flowing from his typewriter as he gazed at Debbie's picture. The night before, at an office bull session, Barry and Phil had discussed poetry, an art form Lamar had not tried. How hard can it be, he thought, to tantalize his loved one with new ways of communication. The flow of typing paused as Lamar pursed his lips to compose his first lines of verse to Debbie.

When I look into your eyes
All I see I idolize.
Your nose, your teeth, your lips, your breast
Are all outstanding from the rest.
Debbie you are so awful nice
With you I am in paradise.

The meter infected him, enthralled him as he composed twenty, no thirty, lines of slightly demented doggerel intended for the young woman of his dreams. Some of the words did not exactly fit, but he knew Debbie would take them to heart anyway. The letter totaled seven pages, which he folded carefully into an airmail envelope for dispatch the next day. He boasted to Izzy and Barry of his new skill and continued to extol Debbie's virtues to those who cared to listen, lavishly praising her surprisingly dusky areolas and blonde pubic hair. Much as they enjoyed these salacious descriptions, his office mates eventually tired of the far off wonders of Debbie Jaliskowski.

Shit Dad's arrival offered respite. Since he had been lubricating, cleaning and polishing the office Jeep with clear shoe polish, he was in his customary and unmilitary disheveled appearance: shirttail out, pants unbloused, and generous stubble on his chin.

"Shit dad, Dick," he said, "lemme use your phone to call Rado O'Brien at the motor pool."

Dick Heron graciously obliged.

"Rado! Hey, man, you doin' arrite? Good. Good. Listen, you still got that mess kit you had chromed in Seoul. Yeah, that's the one. Listen, man, how about I borrow it for a little bit. Help me out some with the new Lootenat who's doin inspections up here. That's good. I come get it very soon. See you Rado, man."

Shit Dad saluted by flourishing his cap from head to ground and back again, and left the Quonset hut. Unanswered questions lingered in the air, and Dick Heron decided to stroll over to the Headquarters office for a chat with the top[5], Master Sergeant Stanley Wrinkle.

Sergeant Wrinkle was old, at least forty, and his face echoed his name. It was weather-beaten and furrowed, although frequently lightened by a one hundred and fifty-watt smile. Wrinkle was all Army, knew every pertinent regulation, and loved his job. He was also kindhearted and fair, which endeared him to the headquarters' troops. He flashed his smile at Dick Heron and responded to his question.

"Ah, well, we got a new silver bar on the reservation that looks a bit like General Custer. You know, blonde hair and a little yellow moustache, kinda short and strutty. Funny built—put a helmet on his skinny head, he resembles a toadstool. Name's Lieutenant Bland and he is of the belief that military discipline has been too lax here after the armistice. The Colonel just wants him out of his hair so he sent him around to help with inspections. You haven't seen him yet because he's working his way up from the motor pool. He had an interaction that included Shit Dad this morning."

It happened at the monthly barracks inspection during which foot lockers, cots, personal articles and mess gear were examined. Although Shit Dad bunked with the P.I.O. staff because he wanted to, his "official" residence was in the motor pool where he kept most of his military equipment. It was there that he stood inspections. The men displayed their mess gear at the foot of each cot. Certainly, in a combat zone, no one was expected to polish those everyday utensils that were used mainly in the field, but they were expected to be modestly clean and sanitary.

All went well until Lieutenant Bland focused on Private Rowe and his cot. His canteen cup blazed up like a green neon beacon for it was, in fact, green, with tinges of black, brown and yellow. It was as one would have guessed, knowing it was used as a retainer for drained oil, battery acid, shaving water, soap, various local alcoholic beverages, kimchee, and as a footbath. Shit Dad never had even a twinge of

---

5 Highest ranking non-commissioned officer at Headquarters

discomfort because of his mess cup's multiple uses and considered its color a well-earned patina that added luster and dignity to the implement.

Lieutenant Bland, an adherent to strict military discipline rooted in academic studies and eighteen months of experience at Fort Devens, Massachusetts felt differently.

"Private, that is the most disgustingly offensive piece of military hardware it has even been my," he paused, searching for the word, "DISPLEASURE to inspect. You will have that revolting thing on my desk this afternoon at 1500 hours scrupulously clean, polished, and gleaming. There WILL be NO excuses."

Shit Dad humbly and simply said, "Yes, Sir!"

He decided to work on his Jeep for an hour or so and then he trudged over to the office and placed his call to Rado O'Brien.

Before entering Lieutenant's Bland's cubicle in the Headquarters office, he rubbed a smudge of green motor oil on the bottom of the gleaming chrome cup and tucked in his shirt. He found Bland's office, entered, offered his interpretation of a salute, and placed the cup on the officer's desk.

"There it is, Sir. Ain't it amazing how some elbow grease, pumice, and super fine grit sand paper can make that Army issue cup shine?"

"You trying to bullshit me, Private? That's not the cup I saw this morning!"

"Well Sir, it surely is. I kinda thought that myself, so I left a little part of it the way it was."

He turned the cup over to display the green discoloration, righted it, and replaced it on the desk. The interchange had attracted onlookers. A Major, Sergeant Wrinkle and two enlisted men witnessed the little drama playing out in the cubicle. Lieutenant Bland knew it was a different cup, but proof was missing. This damn Private had showed up with a cup, gleaming and identical to millions found in Army issue kits. The next time, he thought, I'll mark the thing or have this Cajun son of a bitch guarded while he cleans it. Meanwhile, best to retreat to fight another day.

"All right. Make sure you keep it that way. Now, get the hell out of here and, know this, Private, I've got my eye on you."

"Yes Sir," said Shit Dad as he scooped up the cup and moved smartly to the door. He had long since stopped counting all the eyes on him.

Sergeant Wrinkle visited the Enlisted Men's' club that evening as he did every few weeks. Although he honored the military chain of command, he also believed it important to mingle with the lower ranks since when orders rolled down' the "buck" usually stopped in front of Privates and Corporals. In his experience, the lower ranks always received the dirtiest details and he wanted to be sure he could count on their cooperation, however grudging. The liberal application of rounds of beer, at ten cents a glass, for the nightly denizens of the EM club helped provide that assurance.

Wrinkle put down a glass and joined Wylie at the table where he was transcribing notes. He had a bemused look, completely occupied with his task. He flinched when the Sergeant nudged him with a pitcher of beer and poured him a glass.

"So, Wylie, looks like Dick Heron is a real short timer. The word is you're going to take his job." It was just conversation. Wrinkle knew for a certainty that Wylie would be the next NCO of Public Information. He was responsible for managing the Corporal's promotion to the proper grade for the job.

Wylie smiled and raised his glass. "I've heard rumors to that effect."

Dick Heron and Captain Standrich had confirmed his pending promotion two days ago, but Wylie was learning to hold his cards close to the vest.

Wrinkle kept his poker face and changed the subject. "That's a mess of writing there. Anything interesting going on?"

"You know, there really is. This is one of the weirdest stories I've ever come across. I've been talking about it with my contacts in Pusan for most of the afternoon, and my friend, Petey Flasher, with IPS at the Seoul press billets. It's like it is a Halloween joke but everyone confirms it is true."

Sergeant Wrinkle betrayed his interest with a slightly furrowed brow and refilled Wylie's glass.

"Since the armistice the engineers have been dismantling the prison compounds at Koje Island for some other form of local development, and two days ago they began bulldozing one of the mess area sites. Apparently, they were busting up this monstrous grease trap after they drained all the nasty stuff out of it, and they discovered a body. Now, that isn't so surprising; stranger things have turned up down there. But it seems that being suspended in all that grease preserved that little body intact and also turned everything inside, including the bones, into, they're telling me, a sort of jelly. That poor bugger is kind of like a Silly Putty rag doll. I'll have some pictures of it tomorrow. With combat over I guess it doesn't take much to get some attention from the press. But, man, what a way to go."

"Amen to that," said the Sergeant and poured two more glasses of beer.

About a week later, Debbie Jaliskowski had finished work and was sitting on the couch in her parents' apartment. Lamar's seven-page letter lay on her lap and she riffled its pages. She had read it three times, once that morning and twice while she sat on the couch. The corners of her mouth were turned down and she gazed vacantly at the opposite wall. That dumb bastard, she thought, has gone nuts over there.

CHAPTER 28

CAPTAIN STANDRICH

◆ ◆ ◆

AT REVEILLE, THE HEAD THAT first appeared above the blanket on Shit Dad's cot was not his. Instead of the anticipated auburn thatch, glossy black hair protruded from the blanket, followed by equally dark and shining eyes, rosy lips and a robustly female upper body clad in a rumpled white blouse. As she stretched her arms, she pulled the blanket aside, revealing Shit Dad in worn skivvies. His companion pushed dainty feet toward a pair of rubber booties under the cot and stood in blouse and dark trousers, surveying the other occupants of the tent.

Dick Heron was brushing his teeth near the tent's entrance and was the first to see the new occupant. Normally, Shit Dad's adventures and exploits did not faze him, but this was definitely a potentially threatening event; as senior NCO in the tent, this flagrant fraternization by one of his charges could well bite him in the ass.

"What the fuck is going on?"

"Shit dad, Dick, this here is my sister-in-law, Mai Lee. She's gonna be visiting the Captain today for a job interview. It was kinda late last night when she showed up and I didn't want to send her back all in the dark. We made room on the cot. She's not that big."

Wylie awakened to this interchange. Though somewhat inured to the Shit Dad's life vision, he, too, recognized problems with the discovery of a very attractive Korean girl, freshly released from the warmth of Shit Dad's cot. The other occupants of the tent, now awake, were also trying to sort out what was going on and awaited developments.

Wylie asked, "You been sleeping with that girl?"

"Man, you got eyes or what? She needed a place to stay last night."

"Yeah, but were you SLEEPING with her?" Wylie still had trouble in expressing the customary military expression for intercourse.

"Well, you know my wife is pretty pregnant right now. Could be that a thing or two slipped into the crack last night, just for old time's sake, you know."

Dick Heron and his intended successor fully recognized the gravity of the situation. Should an authority figure discover that Shit Dad was playing hide the sausage in his tent with an indigenous person he would become persona non grata with prejudice. Not only would the office be deprived of his valuable services, but also countless soldiers who lived vicariously through his outrageous shenanigans would be disappointed. Priority one, they resolved, was to make the young woman disappear.

Wylie called upon Kim, their houseboy, for assistance. For a carton of cigarettes, split between Mai Lee and Kim, the Korean girl agreed to disguise herself as a bag of laundry and slipped adroitly into the canvas sack Kim used for that purpose. He shouldered the bag and jauntily carried his new cargo from the tent in the direction of the rocks by the stream where local women did the GI's laundry. As the bundle departed, Dick and Wylie exchanged glances of relief at disaster averted.

Myles Standrich was no longer a highly motivated warrior. He was a short timer whose commission would expire two months after rotating back to the United States and he did not intend to extend his military service. Because of his age, Myles escaped the draft in 1946, the year he graduated from high school. That spring a smooth talking Army recruiting Sergeant visited his senior high school class to extol the virtues of a peacetime Army. In a private meeting, the recruiter touted the virtually free education offered by the military and whispered confidentially that, in the snappy uniform he would be wearing to ROTC classes, he would attract more ass than a toilet seat.

"You just can't imagine how those Midwestern girls love a uniform," he explained. Myles, whose romantic repertoire was limited to heavy petting in the loge seats of the Rivoli Theater, gladly accepted the bait.

At Urbana University, there was no evidence that his uniform attracted members of the opposite sex. If it did, it must have been limited to the two hundred or so other young men who paraded twice a week in their khaki outfits. Nevertheless, during his sophomore and junior years Myles twice fell deeply in love, only to be rebuffed, humiliated, and cast aside like a stray dog by the object of his affection each time. Unfortunately, it occurred with the same person.

Blonde and buxom Gloria Vandevere, Social Vice President of the Omega Nu sorority, enthralled and devastated Myles twice. Gloria suffered from Wick's syndrome, an ocular/neurological disorder that caused a love interest to appear progressively uglier as her ardor increased. Unfortunately, during the two times she was attracted to Myles, the fonder she became of him the more he resembled Quasimodo. The moment revulsion overpowered passion, she tearfully bade him farewell. Unaware of her devastating ailment, Myles woefully accepted her rejection. However, he demonstrated resilience, stamina, and dunderheaded fortitude as his amorous pursuits advanced and retreated like a South American glacier.

During his senior year, Myles began a relationship with Anastasia Farquhar, a generously constructed anthropology major primed for romance by studies of sexuality in primitive cultures. After three steamy months of passionate experimentation that involved, among other things, large rubber bands; plums and kiwis; three varieties of baby lotion; clothespins; and a pair of oversized galoshes, Ana ran off with one of her married anthropology professors, purportedly to search for a lost tribe at the headwaters of the Amazon River in Ecuador.

Myles had little time to dwell on this turn of events because Ana disappeared but days before graduation. Searching for solace, he wholeheartedly reaffirmed his Baptist faith, feeling newborn in Christ. He graduated in a uniform decorated with gold Second Lieutenant's bars, enjoyed a brief leave with his parents, and departed for advanced training to become an artillery officer. It was about six weeks before the invasion of South Korea.

At Fort Sill in Norman, Oklahoma, Myles demonstrated a quick mathematical capacity that fostered the brisk annihilation of defenseless trucks, Jeeps, and tanks. His superiors recommended him for early promotion and continuing service in training recruits funneled into the Army's artillery. There he remained until his battalion received orders to support the 53rd Infantry Division in Korea. On arriving in Korea, he was urgently assigned as a forward observer responsible for identifying enemy positions suitable for artillery and fighter targets.

This was not an enviable assignment, since FOs were highly desirable targets for enemy snipers or, for that matter, any enemy combatant with a rifle, mortar, bazooka, flamethrower, or artillery. For three weeks, he beat the odds, adroitly using camouflage and changing positions until he came under small arms fire and hastily evacuated his hiding place. Three bullets found him, destroying his azimuth, slicing a three-inch crease on the right side of his helmet, and puncturing his right shoulder. Stitches at the aid station resolved the shoulder wound and fresh orders to join his newly arrived battalion ended the dangers of FO duties.

During the snowy January of 1953, Myles prepared to move his unit and its heavy artillery to a new position designed to thwart the anticipated movement of Chinese volunteers around the division's right flank. The corrugated mountain range in front of their position challenged fighter-bombers whose attacks frequently were off the mark and detonated harmlessly in the wrong valley or mountainside. Artillery was more reliable, with experienced gunners penetrating bunkers miles away. However, the artillery units were required to relocate rapidly, and the need for such flexibility sometimes led to confusion. A SNAFU[6] occurred the afternoon Myles moved his group westward through axle deep mud toward its newly assigned location.

As the scant wintry light faded, a burned-out troop carrier obscured the left arm of a fork in the treacherous highway. Missing the turn, the unit moved forward as quickly as possible in the wrong direction, toward the enemy. Terrain and weather hindered radio communications, and the column's first sign of their error was a barrage of mortar rounds that cratered their route and covered men and machines with ice and mud.

Myles took cover near boulders beside the road and tried to assess the enemy's position and strength. Enemy mortars came from behind a ridgeline two hundred yards ahead. Myles' men returned fire with small arms and worked feverishly to turn their trucks around in the narrow roadway. Myles ran to the rear of the column to direct traffic and organize the needed retreat. In twilight, he completed the maneuver and the column moved slowly toward safety.

As Myles swung aboard the last truck, a tattoo of small arms fire echoed from the roadside, striking the door, the front tire, and his exposed thigh, twice. The truck churned helplessly in the muck and Myles fell to the road as two soldiers with BARs gradually eliminated the squad of Chinese troops who suddenly appeared along the roadside.

At this moment, Shit Dad rounded the side of the immobile truck in his battered Jeep and came to rest beside the wounded Lieutenant.

"Shit dad, Sir, looks like the Goonies perforated you a little bit. You better let me help you get in this here Jeep so we can get to an aid station. Take my hand."

As he reached for the wounded officer, a palpable "ping" rang out as one of the remaining enemy soldier's bullets struck the Jeep's radiator. With one of its tires already flat and a geyser of steam spouting from the radiator, Shit Dad decided on prompt action.

---

6 Situation Normal, All Fucked Up

He deposited Myles unceremoniously in the rear of the Jeep, skillfully maneuvered it to the shoulder of the roadway, and sped toward the Y Battalion aid station. Both Myles' wounds were through the fleshy part of the thigh and had avoided the bone. He would heal and be ready for duty once again, now with two Purple Hearts.

His two combat wounds in three months prompted the recuperating Myles to ponder on his mortality. Enlightened self-preservation lessened his appetite for continuing active combat. Two weeks after surgery, he hobbled on his crutches to Headquarters G-2 to see if any positions involving lighter duty might be available.

The adjutant advised him of his promotion to Captain, a fortunate happenstance since the newly available posting as Officer in Charge of P.I.O. required that rank. The personnel officer assured Myles that four years of a liberal education at Urbana, his military training, and combat experience were more than sufficient qualification for the post. Sergeant Dick Heron, an experienced journalist, would be on hand for any needed guidance.

Within two weeks, Captain Standrich met Sergeant Heron on four occasions, located Private Rowe and arranged his semi-permanent assignment as P.I.O. driver, identified two other officers interested in skeet shooting, and traded his crutches for a cane that later metamorphosed into a swagger stick tipped with a thirty caliber round.

Despite his affection for the private, his demonstrated flaunting of military regulations and moral flexibility caused Captain Standrich to be wary in dealing with Shit Dad. Now, as he stood in front of his desk with a shy Korean girl at his side, Myles was alert for chicanery.

"Captain, this here is Mai Lee, the indigenous lady I been telling you about," said Shit Dad. "She is sort of my sister-in-law."

The Captain winced.

"She is the one I thought could help out with keeping the office clean, running errands, and such. I already talked to Captain Anastos over at Special Services who says she can do that for them."

Captain Anastos was to be Shit Dad's next visit, but he was following Cajun time. Did it really matter who said "yes" first? He was sure neither Captain actually cared.

He nodded toward the young woman. "She's a real hard worker, she knows some English, and she's learning fast. You should talk with her."

Captain Standrich was aware of the Division's policy of making work available to the local people that was supported by a modest budget for his office. He beckoned the young woman to approach his desk. She was dressed in a spotless white blouse, black pantaloons resembling pajama pants and rubber booties. Her black hair gleamed in the office lights that outlined her petite but well-rounded figure. Her demure smile showed strong white teeth and her round face was unlined and pleasant. She bowed slightly as she approached the desk.

"I pleased to meet you, Captain."

"How old are you, Mai Lee?"

"Twenny, maybe nineteen."

"Have you worked for the Army before?"

"I do washing, cleaning, sewing on soldiers' patches. All things."

"How far away do you live?"

"Up in Quanchi-ni, not so far, maybe four miles."

"Your English is good. Did you learn in school?"

"G.I. talk to me when I work. Pierre," she said, pointing toward Shit Dad, "he talk English to whole family. No school here for long time."

The unflappable Shit Dad moved from foot to foot during this colloquy, concerned that the Captain would ask a question he had not rehearsed with his protégé. The Captain pushed the chair away from his desk and stood to observe the girl more closely. She returned his gaze and bowed again, demonstrating her modesty and subservience. However, when she raised her head she looked at him boldly and smiled.

Sweet girl, he thought.

"Well, if Anastos says it's OK with him, then I guess it's OK with me. You work it out and see that she's properly registered. See if she can begin working next Monday."

He bowed slightly toward the girl. "Very nice to meet you, Mai Lee. See you soon."

As expected, Captain Anastos followed Lieutenant Standrich in granting approval for Mai Lee's employment and Shit Dad obtained her work permit and identification card from the friendly clerk at GQ.

That evening the couple prepared to leave the headquarters compound. Captain Standrich noticed them as he exited the nearby Officers' Mess and called Shit Dad to his side.

"Pie-air, are you sending that girl home alone in the dark?"

"Shit dad, she does that all the time. Not a problem."

"Does she live near the military highway?"

"Just close."

"In that case, why don't you and I drive her home?"

CHAPTER 29

SEOUL

◆ ◆ ◆

WYLIE HOPED HIS TRIP TO the press billets in Seoul would be in a Jeep or the front of a truck, but the only transport available that Saturday morning was on a wooden bench in the back of a deuce and a half truck. He was close to the cab but fine dust seeped in around the canvas and he felt gritty after fifteen minutes on the dusty highway that carried American and Korean soldiers to the capitol city. The ROK soldiers assembled toward the back of the truck shared a bottle of "Lucky Seven." Wylie heard that the locally manufactured rotgut whiskey, possibly flavored with antifreeze, killed parasites before inducing blindness. It was inexpensive, contained from 45 to 60 per cent alcohol (not necessarily grain), and helped counteract the fierce breath caused by daily consumption of the fiery kimchee loved by the ROK soldiers.

By about 1000 hours the first bottle of Lucky Seven was finished and the Korean soldiers were attacking bottle number two, their numbers occasionally diminished as one or another fell out of the back of the truck. Since the truck was traveling at the speed of a fast walk, those who could climbed back aboard. The handful of American soldiers in the truck enjoyed this entertainment but politely refused the offered pulls on the bottle. They intended to remain sober until they reached I Corps where the weekend would include visits to the new Enlisted Men's club, scrounging for clean clothes and showers, and the pursuit of female companionship in the back alleys of the city.

The trip took about two hours from the 53rd Division and their passes would expire Sunday at midnight.

Wylie had visited the Seoul press billets briefly with Dick Heron some weeks before. Heron introduced him to some of the wire service reporters living there as well as the visiting editor of the division newspaper. Sergeant Jules Pike, editor of The Saber, worked in Tokyo and visited Division headquarters every month or so and renewed acquaintance with the residents of the press billets in Seoul while there. Pike would be editing releases Wylie sent to The Saber once he replaced Dick Heron, and Heron wanted the two young men to become acquainted before he left for home.

Pike had been an editor of the Yale Daily News before being drafted and received rapid promotions in Korea before his Tokyo assignment. He and Wylie bonded over whisky, which Wylie was learning to tolerate quite well, and Pike assured him they would soon repeat the experience in Tokyo.

Dust dwindled and the semblance of a macadam road appeared when the truck reached the outskirts of Seoul. By this time, the Korean soldiers in the truck were subdued, glassy eyed, and clinging to the sides of the vehicle. They departed unsteadily when the truck reached a ROK army compound and filed through the gates.

Wylie concluded they were ending a short leave, visited their families in the 53rd Infantry area, and acquired Lucky Seven as departing gifts. He knew they received miniscule pay and few amenities for their service, which in many cases was forced on them. ROK discipline was harsh, bordering on cruel, and most of the soldiers couldn't wait to leave Syngman Rhee's army. Poor Goonies, thought Wylie, might as well get smashed on a Saturday morning.

Wylie asked the driver to drop him off near the press billets and he swung his mussette bag over the tailgate on a main thoroughfare, not far from the ancient Chang-Duk Palace in the center of the city. Blocky, four stories high gray buildings pockmarked with scars of combat surrounded him. He recognized holes from small arms fire, the saucer like craters of 50 caliber rounds, and the caverns created by rockets and artillery. Even though friendly forces had occupied the city for almost three years, little had been done to eradicate the signs of war. Patches of scrap lumber, drab sheet metal from G.I. canisters and rags filled spaces exposed to the elements.

In late summer no green grass, shrubs, or trees were visible, though yellow and red flowers peeked from flowerpots decorating a few residences. Seoul's citizens scurried along the streets or tended little stores offering food and services to their fellows. Piles of cabbages flowed along the sidewalks with other vegetables Wylie could not identify. Wylie was startled as a man shook kernels of corn in a wire cage above an open flame, where they exploded like rifle fire, transformed into a cylinder full of gleaming popcorn. Colorful paper kites occupied a corner of the road and mothers in pastel outfits haggled over the price of garlic cloves and hot red peppers braided together like gargantuan scarlet necklaces. This area of the city was far from United Nations military posts and almost three miles from I Corps headquarters, and Wylie was pleased to note there were no hawkers, trinket sellers, beggars or ragged children offering their virgin sisters for the pleasure of G.I.s.

Wylie was enthralled. This, he felt, was the exotic Far East, the unadulterated real thing, something out of a Somerset Maugham novel. He enjoyed that thought for a few moments. Then three small boys carrying school notebooks crowded around him, chattering and holding up their notebooks as though wanting him to read something. One boy deftly removed a recently purchased Parker ballpoint pen protruding from his fatigue pocket with the edge of a notebook cover. They scrambled away before Wylie discovered the theft. In a less charitable frame of mind, he turned the corner and walked to the entrance of the press billets.

The building Wylie entered was a hotel constructed by Japanese developers during their thirty-five-year occupation of Korea, which ended when Japan surrendered to the allies in 1945. Koreans detested anything relating to the Japanese, and the Seoul elders and Syngman Rhee's government were very glad to lease the building to the American forces to accommodate representatives of the press. It was gray and box-shaped like the adjoining buildings, with two sooty columns bracketing the entrance and ornate wooden doors carved with Japanese characters.

The building was three stories high, containing mostly single rooms and some small two and three room suites. Visiting photographers had converted some of the rooms into darkrooms, so some corners of the building had the acrid smell of shortstop and fixer. A large kitchen led to a dining room on the first floor, which opened on to a lobby featuring wood paneled walls in need of refinishing, a tall counter backed by pigeon holes for mail, and gray overstuffed chairs arranged haphazardly on tired carpets struggling to cover the dark floor.

An elderly Korean man presided over the lobby and rose from behind the counter to inquire about Wylie's needs. A brass nameplate on the counter spelled out "Wee." Hotel residents called him "Uncle Wee" and chipped in to pay his weekly salary.

Wee glanced at Wylie's correspondent badge and asked, "What want kind sir?"

"I think you have a room for me tonight, for a Corporal Cypher."

"Syfa, Syfa? Oh, yes. Pleasant room waits on second floor. Want hot watah?"

"Uh yes, hot water. Plenty of hot water."

"Maybe tomollo."

"Tomollo?"

"Nex day."

"Not now? Not today?"

"Tomollo."

Wylie was getting the hang of the conversation so, to satisfy his curiosity, he asked, "Is hot water included?"

"Always included. Always tomollo."

As Uncle Wee reached for a room key appended to a 50 mm shell casing he asked, "Want beer?"

"Today?"

"Yes, ri-now."

"Yes, I'd like that." Though it was just noon, a beer certainly would help cut the taste of dust in his mouth. Reflecting on the substance of the conversation so far Wylie asked, "Cold beer?"

"Cold like Pyongyang in winter!" Uncle Wee was beginning to enjoy himself with the young Corporal.

Wylie was unable to resist. "And where is the beer?"

"Sergeant Snipes got. One buck, two beer. Over in dining room." He pointed to the room across from his counter.

"Later," said Wylie and shouldered his bag. "Let's see the room."

Uncle Wee ceremoniously preceded Wylie and climbed the stairs to the next floor. The predominant color scheme was mottled shades of gray. Wylie's room, echoing that color scheme, featured a double bed, a sink, a generous sitting area with a chair and couch, two large windows, and flamboyant yellow curtains festooned with generic red flowers. The room had an attached bath, a freestanding tub with a showerhead on a pipe tucked into an alcove of the sitting area. With fresh sheets and towels, it was the finest accommodation Wylie had seen in months. Moreover, it was private, a truly unaccustomed luxury.

The first tepid stream of water from the shower, warmed by the ambient temperature of the building, quickly turned cold, causing Wylie to yelp as he scrubbed the dust of the road from the nooks and crannies of his form. Christ, he thought, I hope the beer is as cold as this shower. A brisk rub down and the pleasure of climbing into fresh clothing rejuvenated his spirits. He wandered down the stairs to the dining room where some of the guests gathered for lunch. They seemed a scruffy bunch, dressed in field jackets and denim jeans with colored shirts. Wylie recognized them as reporters for some of the wire services and a photographer for Universal newsreels. One of the reporters he had met weeks before motioned him to the table.

"Fred Able with INS. You're Wylie, right, from the 53rd?"

Wylie was impressed that the reporter remembered him and returned the greeting, joining the other four men at the table.

"Hey, Bo. Bring this man a beer," shouted Fred Able in the direction of the kitchen. Soon a large, curly haired man with an amiable expression and a brass badge with Sergeant's stripes pinned to a white beret appeared caressing a bottle of beer that he placed ceremoniously on the table in front of Wylie.

"Meet Sergeant Beauregard Snipes, the best mess Sergeant in the Far East Command," offered Able.

Snipes shook Wylie's hand, which disappeared between the Sergeant's thumb and fourth finger. Sergeant Snipes examined Wylie as though measuring him for a suit and made it clear that Wylie was welcome any time. It was Snipes' opinion that he could use a little more meat on his bones. Wylie risked mentioning he already had a mother and didn't need another, causing the Sergeant to guffaw and give a friendly slap to Wylie's back before retreating to the kitchen.

The conversation turned to the dearth of significant news and the recent departure of reporters who worked for major newspapers and television networks.

As ham and cheese sandwiches arrived, they agreed that this meant more opportunity for the wire service reporters who could now act as "stringers" and expand their audience and, they hoped, income. Since Wylie was on a low fixed Army income, much of this was of little interest and he was relieved when the talk turned to him.

"So, Wylie, what brings you here?"

"I just wanted to get a closer look at the city, walk around, maybe relax for a while. I've been to I Corps a few times but never had a chance to be on my own in Seoul itself. I guess I'm trying to get a feel for the city, the people, you know."

"Yeah, just be a little careful. These people are friendly, but they've lost a lot and there are all sorts of scams working to relieve G.I.s of their money. And it's not just paying to get laid."

"This is a new one," said the reporter for UP. "One of our guys got nailed with a shoe shine scam yesterday. You're walking along the street and suddenly a white blob of what looks like bird shit lands on your boot and, like magic, some cute little kid with a shoe shine kit shows up and offers to clean it up. You stand on the sidewalk, he fusses with the boot, gets it clean again, and he reaches up for some money. You take your money out of a pocket and get ready to peel off a small bill. Then he grabs the wad and pushes you back so you'll fall over the other cute little kid who is kneeling behind you. By the time you get back to your feet, the kids are gone and you've got some shoe polish and a rag instead of your money."

"Right," Fred Able chimed in," then there's always the bunch of kids who come fluttering around you with the notebooks and lift your pen."

Wylie remained silent, but he reddened a bit.

"Maybe we better introduce you to Kim," said Fred. "He's our fac-totum, jack of all trades. He drives, finds stuff we need, is a local guide and generally gets things done through unofficial channels. Every once in a while, he provides a hot lead of a political nature, but not very often. Mainly, he helps us in ways we haven't yet figured out. I think he's in the back."

Kim Ky Yong, former North Korean pilot and prisoner at Koje Island, was sitting on a shaded bench behind the hotel, reading a local paper and smoking a cigarette. He wore a brown suit, white shirt with black tie, and stylish tinted glasses. His thick hair, graying slightly at the temples, was brushed back and held in place through the liberal application of Vitalis. He looked like a middle class Korean business-man that, with the assistance of Auntie Soo, he, in fact, was.

Kim responded to Fred Able's call and joined the reporters in the dining room, bowing slightly as he shook Wylie's hand. In the five months he had been employed by the press billet reporters he worked hard at learning English and, though some idioms escaped him, he was conversant, especially in military terms and profanities.

"Kim, Wylie here would like to take a look around the city and we think you would be a great guide. You know, like you did for that lard ass from ABC last month. You got any free time today or tomorrow?"

"Yes, sir. You bet your ass."

Wylie arranged guided tours for that afternoon and the following morning with Kim. He decided he would like to shop for some civilian clothes, visit the Palace and one of the local parks that afternoon, and government buildings and the river front the next morning.

Kim had access to a 1939 Buick sedan, formerly owned by a Japanese Colonel during the occupation, that was liberated and re-paired by Auntie Soo and her friends. It would be available Sunday for the visit to the Han riverside, which Wylie recalled vividly from his troop train trip north. A walking tour was planned for that afternoon. Kim thought a fee of five dollars in Army script would cover the excursions. A few packs of Luckies would be a very acceptable tip. At about 1400 hours the pair left the hotel.

CHAPTER 30

TRAVEL REPORT

◆ ◆ ◆

BY FREE AIRMAIL
Army Press Billets, Seoul
August 23 1953

My Dearest One:

You'll have to put up with my hen scratches this Sunday afternoon because the nearest typewriter is a floor below me nestled among teletype machines and I don't want to leave the luxury of this private room to write you from where the wire reporters are hanging out. My, that's a long winded sentence that violates all the principles of story writing. What happened is that I took a weekend pass to Seoul to visit the Army press billets (that I wrote you about a few weeks ago) and look around the city more closely because I've only visited I Corps Headquarters and traveled around here by Jeep before. It's been so busy that I almost didn't think about you for a half hour at a time! I think the best thing of all is that I'm sitting in my own room in this old Japanese hotel. I can actually order what I want to eat here and am not at the mercy of whatever the mess Sergeant in Headquarters Company decides to throw at us!

I met a lot of new guys and had a really interesting time visiting the city yesterday and today. I have to catch a truck heading north that the Sergeant here arranged for me and there's a lot going on tomorrow so I'll fill you in this afternoon. First, though, I want to congratulate you on becoming an aunt and I'm glad your sister had such an easy time in labor. At least you'll be able to babysit for her till you go back to college which I guess won't be that long. I may be sort of old fashioned, because it's kind of hard to understand why her boyfriend joined the Marines instead of getting married. I can thoroughly understand why your family is upset! Anyway, please remember me to your mom and dad.

I'm sitting here looking out the window at a kind of bombed out building across the street that is really the way Seoul still looks in most places. When the Japanese were here for so many years they purposely let most of the Korean parks and palaces go to ruin. Then, when the North Koreans invaded three years ago, they blew up just about anything standing over four feet high. The ROK government was back in control of the city late in 1950 but they haven't done much to fix things up. There just isn't enough money around to repair buildings because they are still concentrating on defense. Nobody really trusts the North Koreans, even after the Armistice.

Anyway, I caught a truck down here yesterday morning and went over to the billets and, sure enough, there was a room reserved for me, just like my friend, Alistair, promised. They've got this old Korean here named Uncle Wee (There's a lot of "uncles" in this town) who takes care of the rooms and a great dining room. It would be an insult to call it a mess hall because the civilian reporters pay real money to get what they want here. So there the kid was, hobnobbing with the wire service guys with a cold beer. They were complaining how dull it was after the Armistice, but I don't think any of them except maybe the Universal News photographer ever had bullets buzzing around their ears.

I wrote to you earlier about the happenings at I Corps Headquarters, and I found being away from the military much more interesting. ~~The first thing I did was~~. Oh, I forgot to mention this Korean who was my guide yesterday and today. Like almost every Korean I've met here, his name is Kim and he works as a gofer and driver for the guys in the billets. His English is pretty good and he's only been in Seoul for about nine months. He worked down south during the war and I think he was too old for the Army or he had connections. But he certainly was a great guide and we even went around Seoul in a Buick today! Anyway, the first thing I did with Kim was buy a sport shirt and pants that weren't olive drab or khaki. We were kind of far from the military bases so it took a few stores to find something that was big enough. This one shop made up a pair of dark blue pants while we went to look at the palace area and they were just fine. It's been a while since I've been in civvies.

I don't think my new outfit disguised the fact that I am a soldier because all the Korean kids on the streets came up to me calling me GI and asking for anything they could think of like money or gum or chocolate. Kim shooed them away. Not too far from the hotel was this area of ancient palaces built over 500 years ago that is called Doksugung if I understood Kim correctly. But time and the Japanese destroyed a few of the original five palaces, and the one left that still looks good is called Chang-Duk. It's not a big deal by our standards but it is really old and very oriental with what looks like a double roof that protrudes from the sides. I took a couple of pictures that I'll send along when I get them back.

So for most of yesterday afternoon I was a culture vulture, except that I did spend a lot of time people watching. The city is really a mess. There are broken sewers and dirt streets and destroyed buildings everywhere. This morning we drove by the shacks set up right by the Han River. They are made of scraps of lumber and hammered out tin cans and sit on poles that make it look as though the shacks can slide into the river any time. Kim says they do almost every day and they just build them back up again. But you see the people, from the little kids to the really old mama and papa sans, going about their business and smiling and bowing when they meet and looking as though they are happy with their lives. Yesterday afternoon we went to one of the parks where there is green grass and a little pond and families were having picnics, flying kites, and buying soft candies. I tried one of the candies, which are like salt-water taffy, but so sweet, it feels like your teeth are rotting in an instant.

I've got to wind this up soon but I want to tell you about the ride in the Buick this morning. Kim showed up in this prewar dark blue Buick with red trimmed upholstery that had a huge back seat. It had whitewall tires and ran smooth as silk. I felt like a king or a general while Kim drove from the press billets south right through the center of Seoul down to the Han River. Except for military vehicles, almost everything else was bicycles and ox carts with a few horses thrown in. The smell was pretty bad but Kim says you get used to it. There were no new buildings, just ones from well before the war. Everything was dusty and drab and the Buick was covered in dirt after about a half hour. Between the Japanese and the North Koreans, the destruction was almost as bad as those pictures of Berlin we saw after the war. There were a lot of police around though, and Kim says they are always looking to arrest communists or sympathizers who would have to be pretty dumb to be wandering around streets full of police.

The most discouraging thing was driving along the river looking at the shacks I told you about and seeing all of the ruined bridges across the Han. Between the ROK army blowing them up when they retreated, and the North blowing them up when they retreated north again, hardly a single bridge remains intact. There were rusting iron bridges sticking up out of the water for over a mile. The engineers had replaced only a few of them so getting to the other side was a problem. It was kind of funny watching ox carts going over the new bridges, though.

Kim brought me back to the hotel a little after noon and I had a nice lunch (with a cold beer) with a couple of the wire service guys. The kid has to resist feeling self-important because what I'm doing and who I'm hanging out with is a far cry from being the callow infantry leader who arrived here those months ago. The Korean girls are not my cup of tea (Ha) so any thoughts in the female companion area – which I confess occur a lot – bring me only to you, especially since you sent me that photo of yourself in the black bathing suit a couple of weeks ago. I think of you more than you can imagine and I love you that much too.

Sleep tight my dearest - Wylie

CHAPTER 31

THE ARMY WAY

◆ ◆ ◆

AFTER MORE THAN SIX MONTHS in Korea, Wylie modified his initial impression, formed during basic training, of how the Army operated. He decided it was not by adherence to a rigid table of organization, military discipline, and thorough instruction. Rather, the character and personality of the troops themselves were as important as their military training and equipment. After numerous visits to foreign United Nations units, Wylie suspected the classic American need to overcome obstacles and "git her done" contributed to most of the successes during combat and peace keeping operations. Certainly, the infallibility of orders from "top brass" was a myth.

Beyond that, he tried to understand the elusive factors that actually supported military effectiveness. He thought he might have an answer after some conversations with Sergeant Beauregard Snipes at the press billets in Seoul and Beauregard's asshole buddy, Sergeant Zeke Potts, whom Wylie met during one of his visits to the press billets.

Beauregard and Zeke Potts were as unlike as two staff Sergeants could be.

Beauregard was a large, beefy, outgoing extrovert from Charleston, South Carolina who found his home in the Army as a Mess Sergeant. Although some suspected he failed his final exam from the Army's cooking college referred to as the "Cordon Noir," he believed in the restorative value of beans, butter and beef. Under trying circumstances, he delivered life-sustaining comestibles to uncounted numbers of soldiers during the Pacific Campaign of World War II.

From an NCO mess in Naha, Okinawa, the Army assigned him duty in Korea, to preside over the kitchen of the Army's press corps billets.

There he fed civilian and military members of the fourth estate. A corporal and two privates assisted in his culinary demands, and three Korean workers kept busy cleaning, scrubbing, and scouring Beauregard's beloved utensils. As his signature dish, he offered breakfast of powdered egg omelets fortified with hot peppers and orange peel, including a side of crisp potatoes fried in lard. Toast was optional. His coffee was better than average (not the highest possible recommendation), but he shone in that he offered cold beer on demand and could provide a rare rib eye steak any time between noon and 3 a.m. for a dollar. He was a well-loved legend among the press corps.

Beauregard told Wylie that, in his experience, slavish adherence to Army regulations, orders and other bureaucratic mandates ultimately caused operations to come to a grinding halt. Conflicts in language and interpretation, and the sheer volume of unexpurgated written material encouraged talented military entrepreneurs to elude or avoid the unreasonable or unreasoned, and try to get the job done. No one ever filled out a form in triplicate before leaping from a foxhole to confront the enemy. So, Beauregard and others, officers and enlisted alike, chose to interpret the rules as suggestions or guidelines so as not to delay or abort their missions. The continuing availability of rib eye steaks for his clients was a case in point.

The supply Lieutenant responsible for distribution of meat products from chipped beef to pork chops to filet mignon in the I Corps area loved a young Korean teacher who lived and taught some miles from his I Corps billet. Since his job did not require personal transportation, paper work to acquire it was fierce.

The Captain running the Motor Pool was an avid fisherman and tied his own flies, but was unable to find needed feathers and threads in Korea. The Sergeant in charge of C-124 cargo planes ferrying supplies in from Japan at the Kimpo air base had a great fondness for chocolate pound cake, unavailable in either Korea or Japan. Beauregard's Corporal was a budding genius as a pastry chef.

Consequently, the Mess Sergeant provided the cocoa, butter, eggs, white flour, and other needed ingredients to the Corporal who created the crew chief's pound cake who, in turn, located the feathers and thread in Tokyo for the Captain who made a Jeep and driver available to the Lieutenant who, in gratitude, provided Sergeant Snipes with an inexhaustible supply of rib eye steaks. The system worked flawlessly.

Zeke Potts was short, wiry, and bald, and his face showed hints of the wintry excesses of his hometown, Bangor, Maine. His approach to conversation was to say nothing unless it improved on silence. He compensated for lack of verbal dexterity by using his hands and head to figure out how to fix things with whatever was at hand. He was an expert machine cannibal and demonstrated this ability in removing and combining various parts of vehicles that were no longer moving — to support Patton's truncated thrust toward Berlin during World War II.

Zeke was also a talented instructor who trained mechanics in vehicle repair at Army bases in Georgia and California after the war, where he developed an interest in rail movement of military materiel, fascinated by the intricacies of railroad logistics. This interest culminated in an assignment as senior NCO in charge of rail transport at the Seoul rail yards.

Arriving soon after the Inchon invasion, his first duty was to oversee repairing and replacing the damaged infrastructure. So involved was he with his rail yard that he extended his tour of duty indefinitely to coordinate movements of personnel and needed materials. He reported to Colonel Lucas Pastorfield and his officers, and his main responsibility was keeping the trains running on time. This he fulfilled admirably; the rail yard hummed like the tuning fork in a fine Swiss watch.

Like his friend Bo, Zeke considered military regulations as suggestions and guidelines, which should not interfere unduly with the accomplishment of his assigned tasks. He also believed in friendly teamwork among the various branches of the service. He prided himself on fostering such cooperation, whether the other party was aware of it or not. The recent acquisition of a needed compressor exemplified this technique.

Potts was aware that the taxpayers of the United States had provided a large, rarely used, air compressor to the Marine base a stone's throw from the entrance to the rail yard. It was clear to the Sergeant that the highest, most effective, use of that compressor was powering the large tools used in the rail yard maintenance shop. Under normal circumstances, replacing the failing unit in the shop would require yards of red tape and weeks of time.

Potts dispatched two of his assistants, one outfitted with a clipboard containing sheets of official appearing military documents, to drive one of their trucks onto the Marine base and up to the compressor. The Private with the clipboard made a big show of examining the compressor, checking its serial number, and nodding confirmation to the driver. The two hitched the compressor to their truck and drove away. Potts anticipated that the Marines at the gate would assume the paperwork was in order mainly because it was inconceivable that GIs would have the balls to steal from the Marines and, if they did, they wouldn't be intelligent enough carry it off.

The Marine guard at the gate waved the truck through. The maintenance shop crew quickly painted the compressor olive drab and stenciled on a counterfeit serial number. The Marines never found it.

The two Sergeants met by chance in the I Corps NCO club in January, 1953 and quickly recognized in each other a kindred quality without which the military could not function. They were each natural born, dyed-in-the-wool dedicated scroungers. From that day forward, they collaborated, whenever possible, in facilitating, smoothing over, and advancing their needs and desires and those of their friends, all within the spirit of military collaboration.

During his most recent visit to the press billets, Beauregard continued tutoring the lanky Corporal in his understanding of the way the Army worked. He told Wylie that there was the "right way, the wrong way, and the Army way" of doing things. As an example, he told Wylie how it was that he could sit down, right now, to a lobster dinner in the dining room of the press billets.

It happened that the chocoholic crew chief noted a container marked "Perishable" lashed to a pallet at the rear of his C-124 and checked his manifest for additional information. It was two hundred pounds of frozen lobster packed in dry ice destined for the mess of General Arthur P. Dodger, commanding officer of a military intelligence unit located south of Seoul. The pallet was scheduled to be transferred from the aircraft to travel by rail to its final destination, placing it under Sergeant Potts' jurisdiction. The crew chief decided this unusual cargo and its destination would be of interest to Beauregard.

General Dodger had a reputation throughout the theater for his arrogance, self-interest, willingness to sacrifice his troops, and ability to espouse conflicting opinions at the same time. Consequently, however situations in which he was involved were resolved, he could claim he was right. He never missed an opportunity to declare that 1) it was shameful how Harry Truman had sacked McArthur and 2) he would welcome an opportunity to blast Manchuria to hell and back with an atom bomb. The Army Times circulated these opinions, and thoughtful members of the ranks recognized that obliteration of Manchuria would have an adverse effect on their longevity. It would be a gross understatement to say that General Dodger was not well liked.

Sergeant Potts was among those who did not regard the general with affection. Lobsters for that bastardly, cold-hearted, asshole warmonger? No way! Not deserved!

Nevertheless, Potts prepared the necessary copies of flawless paper work to direct the container to its proper destination. He observed the team that loaded it on to the correct rail car heading south.

Later, he made his usual inspection of the yard and, moments before the lobster train was to depart, unobtrusively switched the track ahead from south to east. It was dark and the engineer did not notice this change of direction for some time. When he did, more time would pass before the train could be redirected to the Seoul rail yard for rerouting south.

The next afternoon, an assistant told Sergeant Potts that a container marked "Perishable" had returned to the rail yard and all the dry ice surrounding it had evaporated. Close inspection showed a mass of pink, thawing crustaceans beginning to smell ever so slightly. What could be done?

As Potts later explained to General Dodger's aide, the choice was to use it or lose it, and he decided, with Colonel Pastorfield's approval, to make portions available to the Officers Mess and other deserving units in the Seoul area— I Corps Headquarters, Special Services, G-4, the Transportation Company, and the press billets, among others.

"Will two lobster tails be enough, Wylie?" asked Beauregard. "We had a little windfall here."

"Beauregard, this tops it all. You are a legend in your own time."

"Just takin care of bidniss."

That evening, Wylie added some comments to his personal spiral notebook.

"The Army Way—objectives achieved by the wise interpretation of military rules and regulations by fair-minded and experienced NCOs. Be sure they are given the authority to reach goals through analysis, wit, guile, creativity, and a sense of justice."

Wylie thought about three sergeants—Tully McGregor, Beauregard Snipes, and Zeke Potts. Admirable men all. He sighed and flipped the page in his notebook.

He scribbled in the date and wrote "Best lobster ever today. The Army provides!"

CHAPTER 32

STARS AND STRIPES

◆ ◆ ◆

WYLIE HAD NEVER BEEN ON an airplane before the tortuous trip between McGuire Air Force Base and Fort Lewis, and felt some trepidation walking toward the blunt nose of the C-124 cargo plane parked on the Kimpo Airbase tarmac. Glistening puddles reflected the blue sky and the throaty roar of departing aircraft assaulted his ears and stirred miniature whitecaps on the water. Mimeographed orders fluttered in his hand— three weeks' temporary duty with the Stars and Stripes in Tokyo billeted at the Hardy Barracks.

The Corporal in the transportation office found a seat for him in the next cargo plane returning to Haneda Army Airbase and told him to hustle to the aircraft with the smoke popping from its starboard engine. He threw his duffle bag through the opening and clambered up the short ladder to the interior, where Wylie found a bucket seat along one wall and stowed his gear.

The Sergeant in charge of cargo, being the plane's passengers, greeted them.

"Good morning. I'm Sergeant Winger and I will be your steward on the Tachikawa Limited, your flight to the bustling metropolis of Tokyo." Pointing to the cockpit where a major was reviewing his flight schedules, Winger added, "Unfortunately, all our first class seats have been taken, but there is ample room in the tourist section." He gestured to the bucket seats that lined both sides of the aircraft, most of them filled by soldiers going on R & R (Rest and Recreation) or rotating home to CONUS.

The Sergeant continued, "A light snack will be served on this flight. There are out of date K rations in the cardboard boxes in the rear of the aircraft and we have a jerry can of water over here. For those of you who have weak tummies and feel you may lose your breakfast as we cruise over the Sea of Japan, please notice the paper sacks stuck in the bulwarks near your seats. Should you fail to use them, your onward voyage will be delayed since you will be swabbing out your barf until the interior of my aircraft is clean and pure as a virgin's heart."

Sergeant Winger enjoyed giving his speech since it relieved the monotony of the one or two round trip flights he made each working day. The cargo plane usually was loaded with supplies on its way to Kimpo and with soldiers and odd military items on its seven hundred and thirty-mile return flight to Tokyo. Wylie settled in as the engines revved and initiated the loud drone that would stifle conversation for the next two and a half hours. As the airplane lifted off and turned to the East, Wylie glimpsed Seoul and the Han River through the port-hole opposite his seat. Otherwise, the view was of clouds, ocean, and sky until it touched down at Haneda.

The Private at the Haneda reception area surveyed Wylie's orders and issued new Class A uniforms since he was assigned to the Stars and Stripes office. His worn fatigues would be acceptable in barracks but certainly not, sniffed the Private, in the rarified reaches of the official newspaper for troops in the Far East Command. A Japanese seamstress affixed his Corporal stripes, his combat correspondent patch, and Division insignia and, in a few moments, he returned to the airfield walking clumsily in new low quarters, his boots in the duffel slung over his shoulder. He boarded a military bus, an olive drab version of the vehicle that once carried him to high school, and began the trip to Hardy Barracks.

While the airfield was reminiscent of other military installations he had visited, Wylie was unprepared for his first views of Tokyo. Unlike the gray crumbling structures in Seoul, Tokyo offered well-paved roads, landscaped vistas, and new high-rise buildings. There were bicycles, motor scooters, and cars instead of ox carts and horses, and the sidewalks were crowded with men and women wearing flowing gowns with wide belts, walking on high shoes that looked like sandals. Many of the women wore traditional dresses with colorful backpacks contrasting, Wylie thought, with the drab outfits worn by Korean women. Some pedestrians were in Western dress, mostly children or men in dark suits, white shirts and dark ties, and many of them covered their faces with things that looked like surgical masks.

It was easy to spot the few G.I.s walking on the streets; they stood head and shoulders above the crowds around them. The bus driver detoured through the downtown area so his passengers could glimpse the Ginza, Tokyo's answer to Broadway and 42nd Street in New York City. Though it was midafternoon, its lights glowed brightly, flashing Japanese characters whose meaning Wylie could only guess at, but the billboards picturing dancing showgirls were clear as crystal.

Leaving the Ginza, the bus climbed a small hill to the Akasaka-Roppongi District and stopped in front of the barracks. This exclusive billet, located next to the Stars and Stripes building, had been the Japanese West Point before World War II. Now it was the major Army building in Tokyo's downtown area, named after Corporal Elmer E. Hardy who died bravely early in the Korean War. Wylie looked up at the brick walls and cream-colored columns and reflected on the green tent with the plywood floor and potbellied stove he had left that morning. I'm probably not entitled to this, he thought, but I'll take it till somebody figures that out.

The Sergeant in the reception area said, "Okay, I checked out your orders and you've been assigned TDY to the Stars and Stripes personnel section. You'll be bunking with Don Lambinus in E 4 on the second floor. He's the only scrawny Corporal up there. Take it easy tonight. Tomorrow morning you report over to the Stripes office at 0900. Welcome to FECOM and the best damn garrison in the Army."

Concrete sidewalks, mowed grass, trimmed hedges, linoleum hallways, painted walls, mullioned windows, painted doors, light and airy spaces swept past Wiley in a pleasing haze as he found the E 4 entrance and climbed the stairs to the long corridor above. There were doors every fifteen or so feet on either side of the hallway and, as he started down, a head poked from one of the rooms, followed by a thin form awash in khaki.

"Hey, you Wylie?" said the head.

Wylie confirmed he was.

"Desk Sergeant said you were on the way. Jules Pike said you'd be here today. You're sharing with me because my bunkie just rotated and because I'm such an endearing person. I'm also the best proof reader in Tokyo."

A small hand protruded from the khaki: "Don Lambinus here."

Wylie shook the hand, returned the greeting, and considered his new roommate. Lambinus was slightly over five feet tall and thin enough to cast no shadow if he stood sideways. Wylie wondered how he had passed an Army physical, but his grip was strong and he seemed well muscled. His hair was prematurely gray and he had the air of a much older person. Wylie visualized him in a charcoal black suit and striped tie sitting behind a banker's desk in the First National Savings and Trust in Hope's Crossing. There was also a patrician quality to Lambinus. He spoke softly and with a self-assured tidewater drawl, as though he was about to order a mint julep from the trusted family retainer. He exuded good breeding and another quality Wylie had noticed among some Princeton friends, the effortless grace of old money.

Wylie observed that the room contained two beds with springs and mattresses covered with white sheets and GI blankets. Two dressers, footlockers, and chairs were near the wide window, and a wooden armoire for gear and clothing stood near the door. The plaster walls were painted a creamy yellow and Venetian blinds shielded the window. He quickly stowed clothing and gear as Lambinus smoked a small cigar with an ivory tip. As he rose from the footlocker, his elbow brushed a framed photograph on one of the dressers, but he caught it before it fell to the floor. It was the picture of a pretty blonde girl, head tilted upward, and shoulders exposed above a ball gown.

"That's Haynie, my fiancé, pining away the hours until my return to the bosom of our families in Charleston," said Lambinus, carefully stubbing out his cigar on an ashtray emblazoned with the Stars and Stripes logo. "Come on; let's get to the mess hall for supper."

Wylie decided that evening chow, although tasty and much better than the meal he had the night before, was not up to Sergeant Snipe's standards. However, he was hungry and enjoyed Lambinus' comments about life in Tokyo and work at the military newspaper. It was after 2100 hours when they left the mess hall, and Wylie was tired. He was sound asleep before Lambinus turned off the light in their room.

The following morning Lambinus accompanied Wylie across the barracks compound to the Stars and Stripes building. During the Pacific War, it had been headquarters of the Third Imperial Guard of the Imperial Japanese Army and, though damaged during the bombing of Tokyo, it retained its original grandeur. It was certainly more impressive than the press billets in Seoul. Lambinus nonchalantly entered the lobby where a short, beaming Japanese man presided over a kiosk where beverages, souvenirs, snacks and other items were available for the military residents.

"Hai Dozo, Hai Dozo," said Lambinus to the attendant who smiled more furiously before replying, "Hai Dozo!"

As they walked upstairs, Wylie inquired about the peculiar exchange.

Lambinus said, "Ever since I've worked here that little guy says 'Hai Dozo' to everyone who comes in. It's sort of a greeting that means 'here you are' or something like that. So we all just call him 'Hai Dozo' as though it was his name and say the greeting before he can get to it. We all think it's a big joke and no one ever gets tired of it. The new guys either think that's his name or it's some Japanese custom so everyone walks in saying 'Hai Dozo.' I guess we're easily amused."

They stopped in front of a pair of frosted glass doors and Lambinus said, "Here's where you'll be working for the next couple of weeks. It's where most of the editorial staff works, and also the editors of the weekly papers in Korea. Jules Pike is in there; he'll look out for you. I'll catch up with you later; my desk is upstairs."

Wylie pressed through the doors and gazed across the large room. It seemed to be an industrial space, supported by cream-colored square columns and crowded with desks, typewriters, and a preponderance of young men with a few women in various military uniforms. They were chewing on pencils, staring out windows, or banging forcefully on typewriter keys, attacking sandwiches of dun colored paper and carbon pages. Some of them spoke on telephones, gesticulating wildly with their chewed pencils, or puffed on cigarettes as they jammed telephone receivers between shoulder and ear and hammered their typewriter keys furiously. A bank of teletype machines lined a far wall, adding staccato bursts of racket to the clattering cacophony that filled the editorial room. Japanese runners carried sheets of paper back and forth through the large office and the papers, like salmon returning to their origins, ultimately flowed to glass partitioned offices opposite the teletype machines.

Worried looking men with furrowed brows accepted the papers and defaced them with red or blue crayons; some of the papers were simply crumpled and thrown vigorously in the direction of overflowing wastebaskets. In the farthest corner was an office with a raised floor, also enclosed with glass, which bore a sign with a single word, "Editor." As Wylie tried to see the occupant of that office, Pike touched his shoulder and shook his hand.

"They told me you were here. The editor, Bill Mullin, asked me to be your guide and familiarize you with how things work here. You'll need to know all this when you're running the P.I.O. But, actually, no one will be looking for you till Thursday so, after we look around here, you can go explore the Roppongi district for a day or two."

Wylie returned the greeting, and Pike showed him to the desks of other editors of weekly papers destined for units in Korea. The editor then introduced Wylie to a score of local luminaries who had sports columns, wrote editorials, or routinely had front-page bylines. They all seemed bright, cordial, and busy and, it seemed to Wylie, slightly dismissive of the new boy from Korea. Wylie accepted the attitude without enmity. None of them looked as though they had been in combat; he knew he was in a more exclusive fraternity.

Pike explained that all editions of the paper were created, edited, and printed in Tokyo, except for the Korean edition that was printed in Seoul. Pike told Wylie he would visit the Tokyo printing facility during his stay to familiarize himself with the intricacies of the process.

Pike noticed that Bill Mullin had left his office and was speaking with one of the reporters. Mullin was a man in his early forties, a civilian and experienced newspaper editor. Mullin, in a button down white shirt, rep tie, and gray flannel trousers, Noticed the Corporal in stiff khakis speaking with The Saber editor and guessed that he was was on temporary duty from Korea. He welcomed Wylie to the newspaper offices and explained that he would be expected to learn the teletype process, digest the newspaper's style requirements, rub shoulders with the editorial staff, and learn the rudiments of the printing process. When he returned to the 53rd Division, he might be sent specific story requests from the feature editors, and it wouldn't hurt if he became familiar with the new 35 millimeter cameras the Japanese were producing. Their photographers liked the cameras similar to the German Leica that a company called Nikon manufactured. Mullin was quite genial and it pleased Wylie that he took the trouble to welcome him.

After Mullin excused himself, Pike said, "There's just one more guy you should meet today and he's over in that corner by the drafting table. That's our cartoonist, Myron Goldstein."

Wylie was quite familiar with the cartoonist's work, which appeared almost daily in the newspaper. The troops who read and enjoyed Myron's work believed he understood their problems and aspirations and they frequently turned to the cartoon page of the paper first. Without offending the high command, Goldstein managed to poke fun at all aspects of military life and champion the travails of the lower ranks, though he focused on the army of occupation in Japan. As far as Wylie knew, he had never been to Korea.

Goldstein was tall and pudgy with dark thinning hair and a permanent five o'clock shadow splayed across a generous jaw. His dominant facial characteristic was a bushy black eyebrow that ran, uninterrupted by intervals of skin, from his right to his left temple. When he became excited, which was often, the eyebrow developed a life of its own, careering over his eyes like a demented giant leopard moth caterpillar. So fascinating was the eyebrow that it took some time for Wylie to realize that the whole person strongly resembled a character frequently seen in Myron's cartoons, the one on whom the manifest indignities of military life were frequently visited.

Myron graciously acknowledged Wylie's appreciation of his artistry and suggested he and Pike join him and a few other newspaper regulars at the Sakura bar and steak house the following evening.

Myron said, "I want to know what is going on in Korea right now. We hear a lot of stories about the communist guerillas, and Rhee's thugs, and corruption in high places. And then there are sports stories, the New York Philharmonic playing for the troops and what a great job we're doing on the Korean economy. Can you be my filter and help me sort out what's really going on there?"

"Myron, I'll give it my best shot."

"Mazel tov."

That evening Wylie wandered along the Ginza with Lambinus and sampled Tokyo nightlife. A faint buzz permeated the area, the product of hundreds of neon bulbs lighting billboards and marquees along the broad avenue. The lights pursued two complementary objectives— to create the gaudiest and largest combination of contrasting colors, and find the most ways to inform passersby, generally American military personnel, that girls, girls, girls wait within the theaters, bars, and ca-fes along the Ginza.

Almost every other entrance along the street led to a Pachinko parlor where players stood before what looked like upright pinball ma-chines and coached chrome balls into desired openings, contorting body and face to encourage the ball to trip the loud gongs, whistles and bangs emanating from the machines. Japanese couples in western dress dominated the sidewalks, along with members of the military easily spotted because of their height. Most of the soldiers, thought Wylie wistfully, seemed to have pretty Japanese girls on their arms.

"When you're finished gawking at the bright lights," Lambinus said, "we can see what's on at the Marunuchi Theater and get a drink at one of the bars. This stuff will all be here for you during the next couple of weeks, so you'd better pace yourself."

Wylie followed Lambinus toward the blazing marquee on the cor-ner ahead for his first taste of modern Japanese culture—topless danc-ers and warm sake.

CHAPTER 33
NEW FRIENDS

◆ ◆ ◆

THE NEXT MORNING WYLIE DECIDED to explore the Roppongi area on his own. Pike provided a carefully drawn map that showed the location of Myron's favorite bar near the Shinbashi Station just south of the Ginza, and Lambinus marked another location on the map to identify the Tokyo Onsen, the famous bathhouse that catered to locals and military alike.

"I guarantee those little girls there will get the Korean dust off you," Lambinus said to an intrigued Wylie. He spent the best part of the morning breaking in his low quarters, and walked from Hardy Barracks to the Imperial palace, circumvented its moat and turned to Hibiya Park where he enjoyed the asters, chrysanthemums and other fall flowers blazing from the borders of the well-tended gardens.

Just after noon, he settled into a small restaurant where a friendly waitress whose English was on a par with Wylie's Japanese displayed a menu with pictures of the dishes. Wylie ordered boldly and received the seafood special. He attacked a steaming platter of octopus and eel surrounded by glistening green vegetables and white rice with a pair of wooden chopsticks. I guess this is going native, he thought, as he fumbled his way through the unknown morsels before him. As the only round-eyed person in the restaurant, he was the subject of surreptitious surveillance, and the owner, a tiny woman perched on a high stool near the entrance, paid for the entertainment of observing him by sending an Asahi beer to his table. "Domo arigato," said Wylie, exhausting his Japanese vocabulary.

Two giggling waitresses cleared the table and Wylie paid the bill. Everyone in the restaurant bowed in his direction as he left the café. He was surprised at his cordial and friendly treatment. After all, he thought, we dropped two atomic bombs on these people just eight years ago.

By midafternoon, he located the Onsen and stood in the western waiting line with a number of other soldiers. As the line crept forward, a young Japanese man moved toward the back of the line, addressing each soldier in turn. One or two left the line and were led off by one of the man's companions. Soon the man reached Wylie and asked,

"Want to see a show?"

"I saw a show last night. Very nice. But not now."

"No. No. Personal show. Boy-girl show!"

Wylie was getting the drift. "No, not interested."

"Ooooh. No boy-girl show. How about girl-girl show?"

"No."

"Aaaah. Maybe girl-donkey show?"

"No."

"Dog?"

"Leave me alone."

Consternation was evident in the man's face. He appeared pained that he could not close a deal with customary perversions. Desperately, he asked,

"Yes. So. You want boy-boy show?" More a statement than a question.

Wylie made a motion to strike the man. He stepped back and squinted at Wylie as though the limited view would provide inspiration. Then his eyes popped open and he began to grin. Insight was his. He leaned toward the soldier.

"Aahaa. YOU be the show!"

Wylie threatened to kick him. He moved away in a wide circle and approached the next man in line. Then Wylie arrived at the entrance to the Onsen, paid the entrance fee, and began another Asian adventure.

He placed his clothes in a locker, covered himself with a towel, entered into the first of many rooms containing sunken bath tubs. American visitors to the baths referred affectionately to the imperious Japanese woman who directed him from one location to the next, as the "dragon lady." Wylie thought she resembled the girls' gym instructor at his high school since she wore a white polo shirt and white bloomers. There was, however, no whistle. Instead, she demanded, in shrill, loud, and incomprehensible Japanese that her charges move from location to location. There was no mercy for cowards or malingerers; they were prodded forward by her sharp and unintelligible tongue. As Wylie lounged in the hottest bath, he experienced a form of euphoria and felt that he was looking down on his parboiled body. That, he supposed, was what that body found at Koje Island must have resembled.

The dragon lady propelled him from the bath to another room where he was placed on a stool and young women used dippers to pour cool water on him. He had no ideas whether the water was hot or cold and simply enjoyed the sensation of the liquid coursing over his bright red skin. In another moment, they prodded him into a steam cabinet with a towel wrapped around his neck. Wet heat engulfed him and he decided this was just the right time for a nap. A young woman prodded him awake.

"Beeru?"

"Whaaat?"

"Beeru?!"

Wylie focused on the girl standing in front of the cabinet with a quart bottle of Kirin beer. She made the motion of pouring.

Ultimate he recalled the word for "yes."

"Yes, Hai, Hai, Yes."

The girl poured the beer into a slender glass, held it to Wylie's lips, and began to restore his body's liquid balance. Wylie nodded when he wanted more and soon consumed almost two quarts of beer. It was bliss. When the dragon lady determined he had been steamed enough, she rudely opened his cabinet and half carried the grinning soldier to the next and final station, the massage room.

It was brilliantly white, occupied by a waist high padded table and a petite but muscular Japanese girl dressed in pink bra and panties. She directed him to the table, turned him on his back, and began kneading his skin and muscles, beginning with his earlobes and scalp and working her way to his fingers and toes.

His was afraid her practiced fingers on his body would result in embarrassing stiffening, but his body, exhausted by the heat, remained dishrag limp in all extremities. He did not dwell on that condition, however, since he was concentrating on the powerful tingling sensation that arose in the wake of the girl's fleet and probing fingers. Apparently, she used an astringent lotion as she manipulated his body. The girl turned him on his stomach and the fingers carried on their assigned tasks. When she had digitally blessed every centimeter of his frame, she removed her dainty slippers and seemed to disappear, until Wylie realized she had ascended the table and stood at its end.

She stepped delicately on his calves and continued the massage with her feet, moving forward from buttocks to spine to neck, digging her toes into each vertebra. Then she straddled his torso and used her elbows on shoulders, neck, and upper arms, giving new meaning to exquisite pain. She vaulted from the table and bowed deeply to Wylie who remained immobile on the table, afraid that something might fall off if he moved too quickly. His clothes, carefully pressed and folded, lay on a chair in the corner of the room. The girl waited patiently for Wylie to reconnect mind and body, then assisted him from the table and helped him dress. She bowed again as he offered her some extra money and graciously escorted him from the room. As he stood on the sidewalk near the entrance to the Onsen, he felt as though he had gained a few inches in height and that his feet were not actually touching the ground. It was a very bearable lightness of being.

His feet, reacquainted with the sidewalk, carried him to the bar frequented by Myron and other members of the editorial group. Myron, Pike, Lambinus, and a corporal named Phlemly with the doleful face of a basset hound awaited him at a large table. The table stood against a wall from which a gas jet attached to a large burner protruded. Two attendants saw to braziers placed on the burner that bubbled with delicacies of various sorts. As Wylie took his place at the table, two other attendants moved down the table placing food on little plates or, upon request, in a waiting mouth. Having left the remains of earlier beers at the Onsen, Wylie ordered another large Kirin beer as others in the group worked their way through the cocktail of the hour – rye and ginger. There was animated talk of the day's events, gossip about news that would never be printed in the military paper, and salacious talk about coming visits of female entertainers to Japan and Korea.

"So," said Phlemly to Myron "is it okay to move back into the apartment?"

Myron fixed him with a doleful gaze. "Yes. My heart is broken. Michiko has moved back in with her parents. I thought it was the real thing this time, but my beautiful little bird has flown the coop."

"Christ, you say that every time you fall madly in love with one of them." said Phlemly. "By my count, and I know it's accurate because that's how many days I've been sleeping in the barracks, your latest romance lasted eleven days."

"What can I say? Such is life."

"OK. I'll move back into the apartment tomorrow."

Pike joined Wylie at the next visit to the toilet and explained the cryptic exchange between the two friends. Some months before, they had rented a shared apartment in the outskirts of the Roppongi district, partly because Myron wanted to escape what little regimentation the Hardy Barracks demanded, but mainly because the apartment had a tree growing up through it. He was ecstatic about the tree.

Phlemly and Myron arrived at the Stars and Stripes at the same time. Phlemly, with a prodigious memory and an encyclopedic store of trivia, served as a fact checker. He loved Myron's cartoons and frequently passed on tidbits of military nonsense that Myron would convert into hilarious cartoons. They enjoyed their teamwork and were comfortable with each other. It made perfect sense to Phlemly that they would share a Japanese style apartment and, of course, the tree.

Everything went well for a few months, until Myron acquired traditional Japanese clothing that he planned to wear while strolling down the Ginza or through the local parks on days off. He purchased a cream-colored outfit, embroidered with dragons in gold, red, and blue from a tailor who specialized in sumo wrestler garb.

Myron often left the apartment on a Sunday afternoon wearing kimono and hakama, walking stiffly in his tabi socks and platform getta, and carrying a large black fan. His size and incongruous attire never failed to attract attention, especially from the military police, but regulations allowed soldiers to fraternize in civilian clothing and they did not distinguish between stateside or local clothing.

Myron customarily meandered through the Roppongi district, turning heads in his wake, blissfully aware of the affect he was having on passersby. His eyebrow, however, caused problems.

Japanese shop girls, waitresses, trolley token-takers, and virtually any Tokyo girl between the ages of fifteen and thirty who devoured popular magazines believed the black caterpillar stretching above Myron's eyes was the ultimate aphrodisiac. "It so saxy," they would giggle to each other as they repositioned themselves for a better view of the balding samurai sashaying down the street.

Unsurprisingly, Myron soon discovered a palpable weakness for Asian girls and honestly and truly fell in love, albeit briefly, with the Bachikos, Katsukos, Michikos, and Sukis who crossed his path. With the speed of a striking cobra, the new couple took up housekeeping in the shared apartment, and Myron ruefully displaced Phlemly each time. Hence, the reference to his most recent broken heart and Phlemly's relief that he could return to their apartment once again.

As they continued drinking and devouring the morsels of food passed around the table, their voices grew louder and the jokes and comments more ribald.

"Watch out for Lambinus. It looks like he's close to the morbid moment."

"Yeah, Lambinus, no more rye and ginger for you!"

"Fuck off, you guys," said Lambinus and ordered another drink.

"I think it's too late," whispered Phlemly to Wylie, mystified by the exchange. "Just a few more minutes and he'll start to cry."

Wylie watched Lambinus as he sipped his new drink. As Phlemly predicted, his eyes began to redden and water. Soon large tears began to roll down his cheeks, splashing into the little plates below, the plinking sounds echoing his little sobs.

"Okay, Lambinus, let it out," said Myron, "You always feel better when you let it out. And you got a new audience with Wylie here. And we all want to know why you're crying, yet again."

Lambinus blew his nose on a convenient napkin and sniffed mightily.

"I'm sorry. I just get so sad thinking about it. It's ruined the rest of my life. And you all share the responsibility."

His words slurred a bit, but the emotion was genuine. He was heartbreakingly sad. "I am hoist by the law of unintended consequences," he declared, mixing metaphors grandly.

"See, Wylie, these so-called good friends here decided to give me a real birthday treat a couple of months ago—an all-expenses paid visit to Mama-san Mitsuko's gourmet whorehouse. The feature of the establishment is that you eat all these Japanese delicacies before, during, and after visiting the girls. So, you know, first it was a hot bath which was just large enough for two naked little darlings and me, followed by dishes of mushrooms and sashimi, followed by cute games where we guessed ages by looking at various body parts. Then we went into a private room with a big soft bed and the two girls opened a box on the floor and picked out these weird toys. One of them was a bunch of smallish chrome balls on a string. There were big rubber bands and back scratchers. They just pushed me on my back and went to work."

He then launched into a graphic description of motions and actions that Wylie had never before heard described. Lambinus' sobbing grew more pronounced as he continued the narration and finished with, "It was, unquestionably, the most intense sexual experience I could ever imagine and they made it happen three times!" He glared accusingly at his listeners. The table was silent.

To break the silence Wylie asked, "So, how could that possibly be bad?"

"Don't you get it?" asked Lambinus. "In less than three months I'll be getting married to Haynie who is a beautiful southern belle and, as far as I can tell, chaste. If I spend a lifetime with her, I'll never come close to experiencing the amazing pleasure that I did with those two girls at Mama-san Mitsuko's. I've been ruined by the best sex I'll ever have!"

Another deep draught of his rye and ginger refreshed his weeping, and Pike raised him gently from the table and helped him to the door. "You'll be fine tomorrow; it'll be okay," he said as he and Lambinus climbed into a tiny taxi and sped away to the barracks.

Wylie thoughtfully considered the impact of unintended consequences on his own life. He had no idea that splendid sex could be burdensome, but he was undiscouraged from its pursuit. The twenty-year old virgin simply hoped it would happen soon.

CHAPTER 34

THE TOKYO REPORT

◆ ◆ ◆

BY FREE AIRMAIL
September 12, 1953
Hardy Barracks, Tokyo

Most Adored One –

It must be sort of a shock to get a real live longhand letter for a change, but it's sort of late in the evening and here I sit in the room – pen in hand – scribbling on the back of the Stars and Stripes style book. My only companions are a sleeping Corporal, a stale bag of popcorn, a theater ticket stub, and a bottle of beer.

Must apologize for lack of letters this week but, to be real frank, most of my "free time" has been spent whooping it up in the town and hanging out with some of the more colorful members of the Stripes' staff. It's been nothing short of fabulous but most of my ready cash has now been spent on the inevitable souvenirs and the "better" clip joints, so I'm spending the next few nights here in the Hardy Barracks which is not all bad if you consider what awaits back at the 53rd.

I've formed a very positive impression of this city during the past week. All of the people are terribly friendly, and if you look a little bit lost at times, about five of them will come over to help you out. Also, it's a great relief from Seoul and Pusan and the other cities in Korea where little sawed-off gangsters are constantly pestering you about women and selling hwan and the like. And it's clean and doesn't smell here. It's just about like a slant-eyed New York City, except there's no round-eyed girl here named Judy who would sit across the table from me and laugh at my bad jokes. Even in this fascinating city, I always think of you.

Restrictions are nil for your lad – all I do is my job (I've mastered the art of the teletype now and have just about learned the style book so they just HAVE to send me out on some real stories!) and then the rest of the time is my own. As a refugee from Korea who is destined to return there (to the front lines, as it were) they seem to be extremely nice to me. That ticket stub is from the new show at the Daijo Inn I reviewed tonight, and I've had drinks and dinner with others of the editorial staff here quite a few times. The most interesting character is Myron (Call me "Ron") Goldstein who draws the cartoons for the paper (a couple of them are enclosed). He has given new meaning to "going native" that I'll explain another time.

Anyway, forget what I said about my staying here in Tokyo. The initial glitter and charm of the city have worn off a bit and an assignment here would, I think, be kind of dull. No question that the living quarters are much nicer here and it would be living in the big city. But I'd rather have the thrill of the boondocks where guerilla actions, pipeline explosions, floods, political tensions, and being a soldier change the pace of living and make life seem an iota more worthwhile. I'll miss the temples, shrines and parks, I'm sure, but it looks as though there will be fairly frequent visits to Tokyo. And, of course, there are other great places to see out here so long as I have leave and can hitch a ride on cargo planes. But for right now it looks as though I'll be in Seoul and Tongduchon-ni "for the duration."

I wish I could write more, darling, but the writin' arm is near wore out – it's been so long since I actually used a pen. You're lucky if you can read this!

To say that I love you, darling, falls into the understatement of the year dept. No matter where I am or what I'm doing, you're constantly before my eyes, dearest. And my tour here is half over so I'm on the down-grade now!

My love always in the extra-large economy size - Wylie

CHAPTER 35
THE INEVITABLE

◆ ◆ ◆

THERE IS NO GOOD DEAR John letter. No matter how the message is delivered, its sodden impact ranges from demoralizing to devastating. The three most popular themes of the letter revolve around the "it's not you, it's me" conceit where the writer confesses that

1) although she tried to be faithful during the many months John was away, she was waylaid by her desires and the good-looking guy who sat behind her in their high school class, and she was really sorry;

2) she had given a lot of thought to their relationship and felt, from the tenor of his letters and the fact that she needed to move on with her life, that it would be best if they drew apart. They would always be friends, and she was really sorry; and

3) though she appreciated the sacrifices he was making in guarding the door steps to democracy, the money he sent back wasn't sufficient to maintain the life style that she felt she deserved and that her new friend was willing to provide. She would be married by the time he received the letter. It was for the best. And she was really sorry.

Debbie Jaliskowski found the daily arrival of increasingly bizarre letters from Lamar more and more disturbing. She concluded that his Korean service had somehow affected him mentally and that he was weirder than she remembered. After he left for overseas, she thought it was her noble obligation to keep his morale up and write to him occasionally. Now, however, it was time to kick this weirdo to the curb.

She selected reason number 2 to convey a classical Dear John message to Lamar. She purchased a get-well card from Hallmark at the corner drug store and, inscribing it with her best penmanship, explained that it was time for her to move on with her life, that she wished him only the best and a safe return home, and that she was really sorry. She signed the card "Your friend — Debbie Jaliskowski."

Debbie sighed with relief as the bitter missive descended to the bottom of the mailbox on the corner. A weight had been lifted. Although no other local male replacement was in the picture now, and there were at least two possibilities where she worked, only one of whom was married.

Lamar ascribed the lack of correspondence from Debbie to a postal SNAFU and was pleasantly surprised to find her card on his desk early one evening. It had a lavender envelope and Lamar guessed she had decided to send him an early birthday wish, though it was two months away. He glanced at Wylie and Boomer at their desks as he carefully opened the envelope. He was confused when he saw a cartoon character with crosses instead of eyes and a large thermometer protruding from his mouth lying on a hospital bed. Not one for subtlety, Debbie had chosen a card that demanded "Get Well Soon!", which Lamar did not understand until well after he began to recover from the impact of the message inscribed in the card.

Though he understood Debbie's words, he was psychologically unable to accept their meaning. They were like dots on a page that only became a picture when held far from the eye. He stiffened in his chair. The card fell from his fingers as the blood drained from his face and nausea rose. Wylie and Boomer were alarmed as he rose unsteadily from his desk, stumbled to the door, and emptied his dinner into the butt can by the entrance. His retching continued for some minutes, causing Wylie and Boomer to rub his back and comfort him.

They thought a little ptomaine in the evening's mystery meat caused Lamar's condition.

It soon became clear to all that Lamar had received a Dear John letter. The aroma of self- pity wafted from him like decaying lilies and his red-rimmed eyes continued to well damp gobbets. He presented the classic picture of unalloyed grief, punctuated by musings of the "why me?" variety. Wylie, Boomer and the recently arrived Izzy, Phil and Barry tried to console Lamar from the depths of their inexperience. The idea was to get him drunk to deaden the pain of rejection, but Lamar seemed to want to savor it, to prolong the experience as though he intended to dissect its facets and report on each one. He was expounding on the unfairness of it all when Shit Dad and Sergeant Pangluss arrived, looking for drinking companions after a trying evening at the motor pool.

Phil mouthed "Dear John" and glanced at Lamar to advise the new arrivals of the situation. Pangluss, the oldest one present, removed the omnipresent cigarette holder from his mouth and placed it in his shirt pocket. Uncharacteristically, the burly motor pool NCO walked to Lamar and embraced him in a bear hug then stroked his hair and rubbed his back soothingly. As Lamar relaxed in the Sergeant's arms, letting out a long sigh, Pangluss said, "C'mon Private Trenchant; it's time for a boiler maker or two. There's nothing like smooth bourbon to heal a broken heart. And we've all had one somewhere along the line."

As though he were following a pied piper, Lamar paused in his lamentations and left the office with Pangluss. Shit Dad had hoped to find Captain Standrich there and Boomer told him he thought the Captain was still at the Officers' Club. Shit Dad left on his mission.

As Pangluss and Lamar walked to the Enlisted men's club, the Sergeant drew him to a secluded spot behind the MASH tent and embraced him again, raising his chin so he could kiss him firmly on the mouth. Lamar pulled away in confusion and Pangluss lulled him with tender words and gentle caresses. He accepted the next kiss from the motor pool Sergeant and took comfort in it.

He awakened the next morning at dawn in Pangluss' private quarters in a partition of the motor pool Quonset hut where vehicle repairs were made. He was on one of two cots in the strange room, the other occupied by Pangluss' sleeping form. As hazy golden light penetrated the room's single window, Lamar recalled the night's activities and bolted to an upright position on the cot. The noise awakened the Sergeant who slurred a "good morning" to Lamar.

"Want coffee? I got a percolator."

"No."

"You okay?"

"I'm not really sure."

"You feeling better than last night after you got the Dear John?"

"Yeah, I guess so.'

"Then you're probably okay."

There was a long pause as Lamar wakened fully and numerous revelations worked their way into sharper relief.

"Jesus Christ! Am I queer? Am I a queer? I don't believe it!"

The Sergeant swung his feet to the floor and looked steadily at Lamar.

"Now the fact of the matter is that I may be a queer, or a fairy or a homo, or maybe I just know what to do to comfort somebody who's had some girl kick him in the balls. Whatever, I don't think you're queer. Maybe your door swings both ways; maybe it was a onetime thing. I just think last night was good for both of us. Maybe it'll happen again sometime; maybe it won't. And maybe you'll find an acceptable piece of poontang around here and take your comfort in that. Just put the Dear John behind you, forget the bitch that sent it, and get on with your life."

"Yeah."

"So, how about some coffee?"

"Okay."

The evening before, Captain Standrich found Shit Dad waiting near the Officer's Club.

"Are you waiting for me, Pie-air?"

"Shit dad, yes. Wonderin' if we wanted to take another ride to the in-laws tonight. That Mai Lee surely is wanting to be with you again and my wife says papa-san is looking for some more of that pipe tobacco you gave him last time. It trades better than cigarettes. Jeep's all set to go."

"Let's see. It isn't that late. Let me pick up a couple things and then we'll go."

"Yes, sir, Captain."

CHAPTER 36
THE COLOR PURPLE

◆ ◆ ◆

CONTRARY TO POPULAR BELIEF, SLATS Morongo was not lazy. At the age
of twenty-one, he considered himself an eminently practical person
who evaluated the social necessity of tasks assigned to him and frequently decided that benign neglect was the best course. His mother
recognized this trait early, announcing to the relatives that young Slats
certainly wasn't afraid of hard work. Why, he could lie down right next
to it and go to sleep.

After high school in San Bernardino, California, he considered it
beneath him to complete applications for the junior college and chose
to work at a little restaurant that offered a "Speedy Service System."
His innate ability to discover the simplest and easiest way of doing
something, short of not doing it at all, served him in good stead and,
after a few months, he became assistant manager. He retained this
position at the little McDonalds restaurant for almost two years, when
he was drafted.

His trainers noted his aristocratic approach to work on various occasions during basic training. For example, when assigned to fireman
duty, he failed to stoke the barracks coal fires, causing pipes to freeze
and burst. He never cleaned his rifle properly and always forgot to
put a condom over the barrel when on guard duty in the rain. His approach to calisthenics during the daily dozen was so lackadaisical that
the little paunch he developed while working at McDonalds grew a bit.
The officers in his training company decided he was too unreliable for

assignment to an infantry company where his lack of work ethic could cause fatalities.

The personnel NCO at the Inchon repple depple saw the warning note in his personnel folder and assigned him to the engineer company that supported headquarters of the 53rd Infantry Division. His initial duties involved various forms of manual labor such as road repair, bridge construction, and putting up or taking down tents. Noncoms who demanded diligent toil closely supervised him and Slats had no opportunity to malinger or evade his duties. As time went on, he became accustomed to these requirements and, if not a model soldier, became a satisfactory one. But, like a dormant tectonic fault line awaiting release, Slats' basic lack of diligence simply slumbered.

After the armistice, the military was encouraged to support the South Korean economy by hiring Korean workers to undertake less skilled work performed by servicemen. Eager young Korean civilian men and women were grateful for the opportunity to earn a living in their war-torn country. Eventually they filled most manual labor positions and the engineer company decided to train Slats as a truck driver. It was an ideal position for him since it involved being seated most of the time, commanding heavy equipment with little exertion. He had found his niche in the Army and was soon promoted to Private First Class. A few months later, the Army decided he was sufficiently reliable to drive a shower truck, a more skilled pay grade, and he earned a second stripe.

With the cessation of hostilities, amenities for the troops gradually improved. Tents gave way to Quonset huts, fresh vegetables from local farms were added to the soldiers' diet, movies became more readily available, and sanitation improved. One improvement was the creation of shower tents. Engineers installed numerous showerheads on a central partition atop a concrete slab, all connected to an external valve destined to receive hot water from a shower truck. The truck had a large water tank heated by a gasoline boiler.

Regulations required that water pumped from a local stream be passed through filters that removed larger items like algae, minnows, leeches, frogs, shell casings, and indeterminate crud. The driver then fired the boiler to heat the filtered water to a temperature that would assure the destruction of all microbial malefactors. The super-heated water was kept at that temperature for at least ten minutes, and then allowed to cool to a comfortable shower temperature. After months of cleaning with the occasional basin of tepid water, hot showers were an intense morale booster for the troops, even if they were only available once or twice a month.

Wylie, his comrades at the P.I.O. and soldiers from Special Services, MASH, and various other Headquarters units waited with pleasant anticipation at their shower tent in skivvies and combat boots with newly issued khaki towels draped over their shoulders. It was to be their first hot shower in many weeks. Slats had parked his truck next to the tent and attached the hose to the main valve. In moments, water rushed from showerheads inside and happy horseplay ensued as the men lathered their bodies, exulting in the hot water splashing on their skin.

Slats regulated the pump to maintain a water pressure that would not empty his tank too quickly. He knew the temperature was correct since he had developed his own technique for delivering shower water, unbothered by requirements that he considered imperious and unnecessary. Once he drew the filtered water into the water tank, he warmed it to proper shower temperature and maintained the temperature with occasional bursts of heat. The filter, he believed, kept out any unpleasant items and boiling the water was just an unnecessary frill, imposed by overcautious officers. Once his tank was empty, he detached the hose and headed to repeat the process at the next assigned shower tent he was to visit.

A few mornings later, as Wylie made his visit to the piss tubes near his tent, he experienced a searing pain in his nether member that caused him to gulp in surprise. Boomer, standing next to him, also yelped and said "What the fuck?" Examination disclosed that their penile appendages seemed to be glowing at the tips and were extremely tender and painful. During the course of the morning, a distinct swelling set in and they hastily made their way to the MASH tent for a visit to the medic who usually presided over their monthly short arm inspections.

Ominous words from lectures they had received about horrible Asian venereal diseases echoed in their heads, though the virginal Wylie did not believe they could be contracted solely from self-abuse. Scott was in the line at the tent. They compared symptoms and discovered they were similarly afflicted.

"Christ, it's like I've got a hot poker between my legs and I haven't had pussy since we left Fort Lewis," said Scott. "That's got to be the slowest acting clap in the world!"

"It ain't the clap," said Corporal Diggins as he finished examining the bumper crop of penisses in the medical tent.

"What we got here is one of them nasty local funguses that come from water and soil. The docs call it non-venereal Balanitis or," he paused to emphasize his erudition, "Candidiasis. Don't worry, it's not serious, and your peckers won't fall off —for a while."

He laughed at the ashen faces. "You treat it by dipping your wicks in a solution of warm water with potassium permanganate a couple times a day. I recommend you use these paper cups with the pills I'm gonna give you instead of your mess kits. Come back in two and a half weeks and you should be all healed up."

After a week of dipping, the multi-hued members of Headquarters Company afflicted with the disease possessed semi-permanently stained purple love muscles. Their condition instantly identified them at public urinals and engendered a form of mock envy among the unaffected.

"Damn," said Barry Sonnenfeld, "will we always be discriminated against? You guys get these splendid purple peckers that look like cockscombs while we must be content with ordinary flesh colored, but large swizzle sticks. It ain't fair. No it's not." He almost doubled over with laughter as he returned to his tent.

Wylie was concerned that the deep maroon color to which his penis had matured would become permanent, as in Potassium Permanent. Purple was not his favorite color. How would he, some day, ever explain it to Judy?

During basic training, Hispanic recruits befriended Padriac O'Brian, from South Boston, because of his sunny disposition, flaming, spiky orange/red hair, and his ability to concoct mischievous detours around Army regulations. He was "simpatico," and the Newyorkians called him "Colorado." That was shortened to "Rado" (Rah-dough) and later, after basic training, it was corrupted to Ray-dough. That was how all in 53rd Headquarters Company called him.

All self-respecting Army posts require a cadre of scroungers, fixers, and hustlers to grease the unofficial wheels of commerce and smooth the way over regulations and chains of command. Rado was a hustler. His forte was poker, but he was equally at home creating sports pools involving Army teams, handicapping cockroach races, and organizing cock fights in nearby villages.

He had a following among young officers at Headquarters Company who slaked their gambling thirst on outrageous bets involving unpredictable future outcomes. For example, on a cloudless fall morning Rado would bet that it would rain on the parade ground between 1400 and 1500 hours, or he would bet that no less than five black goats would be grazing in the culvert behind the mess tent —a location where black goats had never before appeared— some time before noon. The young officers won a fair share of the time, and Rado earned a reputation for honest dealing. Certainly, there was no suspicion of cheating, but Rado managed to send home monthly money orders far exceeding his Private's pay.

Rado, another beneficiary of Slats' ineptitude, believed his empurpled appendage complemented the thatch from which it protruded.

Would it not be wasteful, he thought, to ignore creative use of what he hoped would be a temporary Technicolor event. Considering the lethargy settling on the base since the armistice, it might liven things up if a squad of amethyst toned male members could be transformed into a noteworthy and memorable event, something on the level of sighting an asteroid shower or winning the football lottery.

Rado proposed a midnight march on the nurses' barracks to Scott McIlvane who worked with him in the motor pool. Scott considered it an excellent suggestion and passed it on to Wylie and others in the company who were on the purple pill. They agreed and organized an incognito midnight march on the nurses' quarters by those sporting purple appendages.

Such an event cried out for exploitation, and Rado bet a select group of young officers that the nurses would appear in their bed-clothes at the designated hour. He kept the bets low, but word spread and a large turnout was expected. After all, there was little distraction available on the post and the troops were easily amused.

The squad with the fashionable appendages formed up behind the MASH tent under a full moon. The uniform of the night was un-laced combat boots, a web cartridge belt with canteen, colored scarf representing their military affiliation, a rifle, and a rice sack over their heads as a disguise. It was now almost two weeks since they initiated the required treatment, alleviating most discomfort, although the color of the affected members had intensified to a vibrant magenta tinged with copper, clearly visible in the moonlight.

The self-appointed noncom leading the group adjusted his cartridge belt, faced forward, and barked, "Order arms! Fowaaard march! Port arms at the half step."

The noncom frequently referred to his own squad affectionately as a bunch of swinging dicks. Now, in all their glory, were the actual items sent into synchronized motion by his call for port arms at the half step. That command produced maximum side-to-side motion and some excitement to the items on display. The thirty or so members of the squad were doing themselves proud in purple as they approached the nurses' tent by the light of the silvery moon.

Somehow, possibly through a slip of the lip on Rado's part, a large group of spectators, including some nurses who awaited the marchers outside, stood around the tent's entrance. By coincidence, a search light flickered on as the squad turned the corner, bringing into sharp relief the items on display. As the squad reached the tent, the noncom ordered the group to march in place, thereby shifting the side-to-side movement to an up and down motion. The crowd uttered a roar of approval.

By then all the nurses were standing in the company street joining the onlookers in laughter and catcalls.

"Hey, Rado, way to go. Not the greatest disguise, but you've never looked so good!"

"Standing tall except for that soft half inch in the middle!"

"Where did all these blonde guys come from?"

"We're going to need you to help color eggs at Easter time."

"But seriously, are they going to stay purple forever?"

"Never have so few done so much with so little."

"I don't know. It kinda looks like salami to me."

It was three or four days before the purple penis jokes diminished, but all agreed it was an event definitely on a par with watching an asteroid shower or a volcanic eruption. Rado added more winnings to his account.

Sometime later, a diligent Captain in the medical unit at I Corps headquarters was consolidating incident reports, a bureaucratic exercise he detested. He noticed a significant increase in Balanitis infections presenting at the same time in the same geographic area. Having seen this once before and suspecting a shower truck was involved, he provided a route map to the MPs. Slats soon came under suspicion and observation confirmed that his slovenly approach was probably responsible for the outbreak affecting the now notorious purple pecker platoon.

He was reduced in grade to Private and assigned to assist Uncle Ho, the venerable Korean contractor who came through the streets of Uijongbu with his oxcart every day to collect night soil from various military latrines. He consolidated the material in two large uncovered wooden barrels secured to his ox cart and ultimately used it to nourish the vegetables grown in the region.

Bitterly, Slats referred to his new job as honey pot duty.

CHAPTER 37

CIGARS

◆ ◆ ◆

IN THE 53ʳᴰ INFANTRY, WHEN a Sergeant received his first rocker, the upward curved chevron below his three stripes, tradition demanded that he hand out cigars to all within easy reach and submit to rough hazing on first arrival at the Sergeant's mess.

Sergeant Wrinkle delivered Wylie's designation of rank personally, saying, "Sergeant Cypher, it will be my pleasure to buy you a drink at the NCO Club tonight," loudly enough for all to overhear, and Dick Heron chimed in with his congratulations. Phil, who had been promoted to Sergeant two months before, handed Wylie a set of stripes and indicated he was looking forward to reaming him out that evening. Wylie tried to shrug off the congratulations with a smile although he had already proudly written Judy that, when his promotion came through, he would be the youngest sergeant in the Division. Captain Standrich, who had recently arranged to install a private office in their Quonset hut, poked his head out and added his good wishes on the occasion. He then returned to his office where Mai Lee was tidying up.

The Post Exchange was in another Quonset hut close to the mess tent and Wylie, whose finances had improved somewhat since his return from Japan, examined the display of cigars and selected a box of 25 Cuban La Glorias that cost more than forty cents each. This must be the good stuff, thought Wylie, since a carton of Luckies cost only a dollar. He had never smoked a cigar before, consuming only the occasional cigarette with hard liquor, but he looked forward to sharing a smoke with his friends on the post.

Thus provided, Wylie left for the NCO mess for his first official dinner as a Sergeant. He saw Shit Dad streaking toward him in customary disarray.

"Hey man, nice stripes. Wylie, you got some money?"

"Not much; I just bought some cigars."

"Cigars. Oh yeah, cigars. I need some of those."

"Not these."

"Shit dad, it's a celebration. I gotta have smokes and tobacco to hand out. Cigars would be good. Yes, really good."

Wylie sensed another fascinating episode in Shit Dad's life was about to be revealed. Nevertheless, he hesitated before asking the critical question, apprehensive of the answer.

"What celebration?"

"Man, I just was made a father! We got a little boy, looks sort of like a hairy walnut. We're gonna call him either Francois or Kim, or maybe both. It's my first baby, and that's what we all gonna celebrate. Now don't be stingy, Wylie. Cigars or money? Whatta you got?"

Wylie handed over ten dollars for which he had no immediate use and his friend ran into the PX, preparing to negotiate with the Corporal behind the counter.

A wave of indifference greeted Wylie as he entered the NCO mess for the first time. Even his friend, Sergeant Wrinkle, seemed aloof, as did others he knew well. A Korean bus boy showed him to a vacant table for two and, as he sat, an unknown voice said, "Christ, what is that smell? Does someone need a diaper change?"

From another corner, "Looks like any sorry ass Corporal can get an extra stripe if his nose gets brown enough."

"Bet he doesn't need a razor in his kit. I hear he still wears braces at night."

Further insults to his manhood, his intelligence, and his bowel habits ensued and Wylie continued to smile and pretend to appreciate the originality of the hazing. After a few more minutes of this, a tall MP Master Sergeant entered the mess hall, his helmet clamped on his head, and his steely eyes focused on Wylie.

He strode to the new NCO and said, "I'm here to arrest you for carnal knowledge of a teletype machine and other serious infractions of the military code of conduct. You're coming with me!" At that point, Tully McGregor could no longer keep a straight face and began laughing, as did most of the others in the room. He removed his helmet and gave Wylie a brotherly embrace, saying, "It's been a while, you sorry son of a bitch."

As Tully joined his friend, Sergeant Wrinkle and others offered congratulations to Wylie and arranged for quantities of his new favorite drink, rye and ginger, to arrive at respectable intervals. Wylie accepted the offerings with thanks, handed out cigars, and turned to Tully.

"So, looks like you got all your stripes back, but what's with the MP outfit? Last time I saw you, you were still on the line with a platoon."

"It turns out a Major at Battalion had a hard on for me because of what he considered my past insubordination, you know. Whatever the opposite of preferential treatment is, that's what I got. There is this light bird Colonel owed me a favor from before and he was adjutant for the MPs at I Corps. He found me a spot as top at the MP Company in Uijongbu a month or so ago and I've been managing the company since then. It's pretty quiet but I'm getting used to it and it's a good way to fill in the six months or so till I rotate. I was going to look for you up here a couple weeks ago, but Stan Wrinkle suggested I wait a while to help you graduate to NCO status. Looks like you're doing okay."

Wylie reached across the table, put his hand on Tully's shoulder, and said, "Step in it and come up smelling like a rose! I'm really glad to see you again, Tully, and I'm glad things are going well with you. I don't know much about all the things MPs do but maybe I can travel the eight miles to Uijongbu and do a feature on your outfit. Sort of a police story in deepest Orient, or something. Meanwhile, how about a rye and ginger?"

"It's not my usual drink, but who would I be to turn down free liquor."

Though interrupted by other NCOs from time to time, the two friends exchanged personal stories and information. Tully was quite interested in the Wylie's experiences in Tokyo. He had travelled to Bangkok for his R & R because he heard Thai girls were exceptionally beautiful, and was planning to visit Tokyo before his return stateside. After midnight they said goodbye and Wylie walked unsteadily to his tent.

Kim gently shook Wylie's shoulder to rouse him the next morning.

"It's been wevelly for ten minutes," he said. "Time to get up."

Only Barry and Shit Dad remained in the tent, Barry shaving and Shit Dad struggling with his boots. As Wylie rose to a sitting position, he sensed that ice tongs clamped his forehead and the base of his neck and something peculiar had happened to his eyes. His tongue seemed permanently glued to the roof of his mouth. He suffered from blurred vision, slurred speech, nausea, and a sense of impending doom. Also, the bladder attached to his now normal penis seemed to have expanded overnight and required urgent deflation.

"Shit dad, looks like you got one of them head banging morning after epizootics we used to call the Sunday penance. This'll help," said Shit Dad, and offered Wylie a pint bottle labeled Bayou Bourbon. He drank, slowly. It did help. He believed he would be able to walk. It was a bayou miracle. He managed to pull on his boots and stagger to the nearest piss tube where it took almost three minutes to empty his bladder.

Relieved, breathing fresh air on a sunny morning, the insistent knot of pain behind his eyes diminished and Wylie began to suspect he would survive the day aided by a steaming cup of coffee. He dressed and picked his way to the NCO mess, suddenly aware of the pride he took in his promotion to Sergeant and potential NCO of the Public Information office. Not bad for a twenty-year-old who almost flunked out of Princeton. Was that clanging sound he heard the concussion of his big brass balls? Could be, he thought, could be.

As he picked up his pace toward the mess, Shit Dad fell in step with him and confided, "Big party last night at papa-san's place. We truly celebrated Kim Francois' birthday. The Captain was there. He be a real sport and a generous man too. And I tell you I do believe we'll soon be relatives. That Mai Lee is closer to him than warts on a toad. No doubt about; he's gonna be my brother-in-law."

CHAPTER 38

GREEN BOTTLE FLIES

◆ ◆ ◆

ON A SEPTEMBER MORNING, WYLIE sat on the passenger seat of the Jeep that Shit Dad navigated along a dirt road slick with dew. Corporal James Beam of the Signal Corps reclined in the back, cradling his 4 x 5 Speed Graphic camera to cushion the jolts from the road. The air was warm and hazy, and Wylie gazed at the distant green mountains in the land of the morning calm wondering what wartime disasters the lush foliage concealed.

Shit Dad interrupted Wylie's thoughts by pointing toward Korean toddlers playing in the muddy ditch along the road. He said, "See them little buggahs with the blond hair and kinky black hair playin' with the gook kids. They're leftovers from when I was here before— G.I.s hookin' up with Korean girls."

As a tiny blond, mud spattered child urinated in the ditch, Shit Dad added, "The Koreans call them 'oeguk' because they're foreigners and they ain't got blood purity. My wife says that mostly they get ignored or worse. The poor little creatures don't really have a chance here. Mostly they always end up suckin' hind tit."

Wylie looked at five small children playing with makeshift boats of scrap wood in the muddy stream. He felt embarrassed that he had not noticed the racial differences among such children before. The oeguks certainly were unlike the Korean toddlers.

"Yeah," said Wylie, "Poor little buggers. Seems like a lot of them over there. Know why that is?"

"There's a mission for them orphans and such over by that creek, over where the trees are. I took some pictures for our files a couple weeks ago," Jim chimed in. "It's religious or something. They got some nun or something running it. The place is kinda run down, you know."

Wylie thought that might make a good story, and filed it away for a later time. He even wrote it down in his notebook that evening.

The Jeep sped on toward Y Battalion.

Considering the tenuous nature of the armistice and the proximity of the Division's regiments to the DMZ, leaders mounted war exercises regularly to maintain combat readiness. The mission they were to report on today had piqued Sergeant Heron's interest. In the hastily arranged temporary locations of the various battalion command posts, Y Battalion had been incorporated into an almost abandoned farming village. When the villagers returned, they lived as friendly cohabitants with the officers and men of the headquarters unit, separated by a burned-out farmhouse and a stone barn.

For some time, the villagers had been depositing manure from their animals, straw, and hay in the barn as preparation for planting winter crops. Recently, this pile achieved the critical mass required to attract a huge colony of green bottle fly larvae that, in those languid September days, voraciously consumed the available droppings and multiplied geometrically into a fearsome squadron of biting flies, marauding in constant attack formation.

The villagers were the first to experience the brunt of the airborne attacks, but the bold green insects soon developed a taste for white meat and became a pure nuisance for the battalion headquarters personnel. Mosquito netting laced with insecticide had no effect on the green bugs and repeated attacks with aerosol insect bombs simply emboldened them further. Scratching and itching became the main activity of the headquarters troops and there was concern it was affecting their fighting capability. The headquarters commander placed an emergency call to the division chemical company, commanded by Major Phil Smatter.

Major Smatter, a warrior through and through, believed in attacking any enemy with overwhelming force to assure glorious victory. Therefore, the exercise on which Wylie was to report featured a squad of chemical corpsmen individually armed with flamethrowers. They planned to attack the barn, the piles of manure within, and the masses of green bottle flies with the goal of total incineration and complete elimination of the biting horde. To provide a training aspect to the exercise, the team would also start a fire to simulate a threat to the Battalion CP. A team of trained fire fighters would complete the program by extinguishing the burning barn and surrounding vegetation.

As Wylie's Jeep arrived, chemical corpsmen with flamethrowers were approaching the infested barn. Wylie and James introduced themselves to the Major, and selected positions where Wylie could observe the unfolding conflagration and Jim could record the activity on film.

Major Smatter led his troops into action, pointing out vulnerable areas for attack with a chrome-plated bayonet he wielded like a conductor's baton. As the advancing soldiers ignited the blue flames at the tips of their flamethrower nozzles, a shimmering cloud rose to meet the attack. Soon the whooshing sound of soaring napalm and kamikaze flies in their death throes filled the air.

The Major directed the flamethrowers with assured swift motions, resolved that no fly would live to bite again. The troops arched their nozzles higher to incinerate the flies in flight. Major Smatter roared curses at the enemy and screamed encouragement to his troops. The piles of manure and what little wood remained in the stone barn ignited and that, with the crackling corpses of demolished flies, created a most unpleasant stench. Some soldiers in the surrounding audience withdrew.

Jim hoisted his speed graphic to capture the impressive inferno on film. It looked as though the liquid from the flamethrowers was attacking the fire itself as the blaze rose higher.

Soon after the flamethrowers ran out, Wylie interviewed Major Smatter and his chemical corpsmen, making certain he had names spelled properly and hometowns identified. He then worked with Jim to be sure all the soldiers photographed were fully visible so the photos could appear in their local papers, with the Division's name prominently displayed in the captions.

Wylie hoped for colorful comments or stories to add to his copy. He quickly wrote down some of the imprecations Major Smatters had flung at the flies. "Green bellied commie bastards" and "You motherless baby raping fiends" had a certain ring to them, though they probably wouldn't get past the censors.

As the combat photographer and correspondent went about their business, the Major told the team with flamethrowers to withdraw so the firefighters could take over. The barn and hillside were cheerily ablaze and Jim stationed himself to picture the G.I.s holding the fire hoses in heroic poses. Joe Rosenberg's iconic photo of the flag raisers of Iwo Jima was in his mind's eye.

The heavy-duty pumps siphoning water from the stream adjoining the CP were humming and pushing high-pressure water through the hoses held by the firefighting team. A strong spray pulsed from the hoses as the fighters raised their levers and shoved forward. The fire was almost under control when, one by one, the hoses lost pressure, the spray weakened to a trickle, and stopped.

The Corporal operating the pumps ran swiftly to each one, and, after a brief examination, shouted, "The cocksuckers stole the gas out of them all. They were full this morning. And they left just enough to run the pumps for a few minutes. The Cocksuckers!"

The cocksuckers were probably local black marketers, known as slicky boys, who stole all manner of military items and sold them as needed to the local populace.

The unhindered flames were now approaching the storage tent behind the MASH unit, known to contain ether and other highly combustible materials. Instead of an orderly training exercise, a whiff of chaos engulfed the hillside as waterless fire fighters fought to keep their hoses from being singed and various ranks were cursing unknown and unseen cocksuckers.

As senior officer in the area, Major Smatter hastily established a water brigade with all liquid bearing containers available and ordered gas for the pumps. He and two members of his flamethrower team ran to the MASH tent and beat the edges of the fire with hastily commandeered blankets. A squad of junior officers and enlisted men, including Wylie and Shit Dad, formed a line with washbasins to carry water from the water tower at the CP. Their efforts kept the flames at bay until the pumps warbled to life and the trained firefighters once again took command.

The fire was soon extinguished and Major Smatter congratulated his men. As the team members prepared to leave, Shit Dad discovered himself next to a chemical corpsman who was a friend during his last Korean tour, and the two happily renewed their acquaintance.

He introduced the man to Wylie. "This here Corporal is Harry Bonaventura. He's been working with all this nasty stuff a long while. Knew him back in fifty-two. He fried a lotta gooks back then. He got war stories up the gazoo. You should talk to him some time."

Bonaventura shook Wylie's hand and grinned. "This crazy Cajun thinks he saved my ass a couple times. Actually, it was the other way around."

The three walked toward the barn to examine the smoldering remains. Shit Dad and Bonaventura took turns hitting each other in the arm, a manly form of greeting that left them both sore the next morning. "Looka that," said the Corporal, observing the smoldering mass. "No way no fly is gonna stand up to a good old Army flamethrower; no way."

One hell of a training exercise, reflected Wylie. We probably destroyed thousands of green bottle flies but damn near blew up the MASH unit along with a bunch of soldiers and fricasseed the CP.

From Major Smatter's perspective, the mission was a complete success. Not a single green bottle fly survived the attack. No consideration was made of the fact that the farmers' barn was ruined and the fertilizer and soil amendments needed for the winter crop were useless.

Returning to headquarters, Wylie made notes about Corporal Bonaventura in his steno pad. He intended to interview him soon and hoped that the Corporal could supply solutions to some of Shit Dad's remaining mysteries. And, yes, there was that religious orphanage to check into.

CHAPTER 39

AMELIA

◆ ◆ ◆

SOON AFTER THE BATTLE OF the green bottle flies, it occurred to Wylie
to revisit the area where so many biracial urchins had appeared. He
hoped to report on a story that would shed pleasing light on relations between big-hearted G.I.s and Korean orphans. Perhaps there
was something to Jim's reported religious angle and he could create a
"Twofer," a single story with two or more markets.

The orphanage was less than a mile from Headquarters Company,
so he walked there. He discovered a long, gray, many-windowed building with a typical thatched roof beside a slowly flowing, suspiciously
dark stream. On its south side, someone had made an attempt at a
garden, and some cabbages, leeks, and other fall crops grew among
weeds. Someone had suspended a worn Jeep tire from a tree limb by a
frayed rope, and two small children of distinctly non-Korean heritage
happily pushed the tire back and forth, uttering high-pitched squeals.
Wylie heard other children inside as he noticed a white painted wood-
en cross nailed above an entrance door.

A tall, middle aged man dressed in a flowing Hawaiian shirt, blue
jeans, and sandals came through the door way and blinked at Wylie.
He noticed his combat correspondent badge and said, "I'm Father
Chapel. You must be looking for my daughter, Amelia. She's just inside. Please go on in."

Father Chapel hastened around the corner and Wylie moved
through the door to search for the woman named Amelia.

Sunlight penetrated the trees surrounding the building and gave the brightly colored walls of the anteroom a warm glow. The space was crowded with crudely constructed rocking horses, stools, toys, a slide, and even a sandbox in a corner. Seven toddlers in various stages of undress crowded around the playthings, rocking, digging, laughing, and falling. Three young Korean women in traditional dress moved among the children, offering guidance and solace as needed. One little boy with tan features and curly black hair sat on a ceramic chamber pot cheerfully emitting happy grunts.

Amelia Chapel was on her knees, scrubbing part of the concrete floor furiously with a rag. From Wylie's perspective, her rounded behind dominated his field of view and he needed a moment to understand what he saw. It was as though time and space were disjointed, like seeing a familiar person in an unfamiliar place and not recognizing him. A well- rounded posterior in dingy tennis shorts was an unexpected sight in a Korean orphanage or, for that matter, in the entire village of Tongdudong-ni, where the Chapel enterprise was located.

Should he say "Hello" or "Good Morning" or clear his throat, wondered Wylie? "Good Morning" in an overly loud voice prevailed.

Amelia dropped the rag in the bucket, rose, and turned toward the stranger in the doorway.

"I hope to hell you're bringing the powdered milk and eggs we asked for three days ago," she said angrily.

It was not, thought Wylie, an auspicious beginning to an interview. Under ordinary circumstances that would not have bothered him, but Amelia was instantly impressive, an attractive young woman about Wylie's age that any young soldier would have liked to know better.

Tall, red haired, well-constructed, and well favored in the looks department, she wore tennis shorts, frayed canvas sneakers, and a faded gray Wellesley sweatshirt. Dirt smudged her left cheek and her hands were red from scrubbing. She secured her hair with a bright green bandana that complimented her eyes. Altogether, thought Wylie,

Amelia Chapel was a real dish, but she seemed, at that moment, to be pissed at him.

"I don't know about powdered milk and eggs," confessed Wylie. "I'm from Division P.I.O. and I wanted to see about doing a story about your work here and giving you some publicity."

"Shistle Pistle," said Amelia, "I thought you were delivering stuff we needed that some guys down in I Corps promised a few days ago. Sorry about that."

She glanced at Wylie's sleeve and asked, "So, Sergeant, what do you need to know about what we do here that isn't obvious?"

It was at this point that the bare-bottomed little boy, having completed his efforts on the ceramic pot, decided to share its contents with Wylie. He strode resolutely to his side and emptying the pot on his left boot.

"Dammit Kim, you've got to stop doing that!" said Amelia as she snatched the pot from his little hands. "I spend half my time cleaning up after you. Get over to Mama-san." Completely unconcerned, little Kim scampered, giggling, to the side of his Korean foster mother.

That's one way to break the ice, thought Wylie. However, being shat upon did not seem an auspicious beginning to any relationship.

"Well, we don't usually greet guests that way," said Amelia. "Let me wipe that up for you and we'll go outside to talk."

Amelia extracted the rag from the bucket and swabbed the soiled area. Wow, thought Wylie, this girl is really something.

They sat on a wide bench under a pine tree, Amelia watching the children playing with the tire, Wylie watching Amelia. He unfolded his notebook and waited for her to answer his first question.

Amelia stretched her arms before her and shook her head, as though to clear it and gather her thoughts.

"Dad had a congregation in Marble Head, Massachusetts for about fifteen years. That's where I grew up. Last year one of Dad's friends, a Marine Chaplain here, wrote about how badly the biracial kids are treated. The babies and mothers are ostracized and treated like lepers. The Korean culture has strong requirements of blood purity and powerful sanctions against people considered impure. Sometimes they just take the babies and kill them."

As Wylie listened and took notes, Amelia continued, "So Dad worked with several congregations in the Boston area and got out-reach funding for an orphanage for those babies. Last year he got approval from I Corps to acquire a building and came over here to set the whole thing up. The orphanage started around Pusan, but after the armistice, it moved here because that's where the need is. Dad and some Korean helpers cleaned this place out and helped with the kids."

"But, how is it that you're working here?" asked Wylie.

"Well, you know, I graduated from Wellesley in May with an art major and the only way I would be able to get a job was to go to Katy Gibbs for a year to learn to be a secretary or something. Dad said he could use my help here, so this is my Katy Gibbs program in Korea. I came over here a few months ago and it has been intensive on the job training. The pay's not very good and there's always a chance we could get shot at but it makes me feel good to give these little kids a chance— and I spend more time with my Dad than ever before. Also, I have this great title. I'm Executive Director of the orphanage, which lets me clean up baby poop and scrounge stuff from I Corps."

Wylie, impressed with this redheaded life force, noted additional details about the number of children in residence, the cadre of Korean helpers working there, and past help from surrounding military units. He was certain he could orchestrate additional support through Division and Regiment headquarters with the publication of appropri-ate stories in The Saber. He knew Pike was a sucker for human-interest stories of this nature. Wylie carefully interspersed items of his own history as the interview progressed; a year at Princeton might help in his attempt to impress the first round-eyed girl he had seen in months.

"I can't promise anything, of course," said Wylie, "but what you are doing here is so necessary and helpful that it will appeal to lots of edi-tors. I'll look over the pictures already taken here and maybe ask for more that fit with the story about what you are accomplishing. Is it all right if I come back if I have any more questions?"

"Of course," she said. "We do get help from the Army and Marines every once in a while, but if you can promote more help from them, that would be wonderful for the orphans. Thanks."

Not able to think of anything more to delay his leaving, Wylie shook her slightly chapped hand and took his leave, returning to Headquarters on foot.

She is so pretty and smart, he thought, beginning to develop unsupported romantic notions quickly dampened by pangs of yearning for Judy. Where was he going with this? It was stupid! She was an older woman by at least two years and, based on his high school experience, that seemed an overwhelming hurdle. Yet, hurdles are there to be surmounted, aren't they?

As he walked back to camp, he was chastened by the irony of having a pair of clanging brass Sergeant's balls while, as Scott McIlvane frequently reminded him, remaining pussy whipped. However, if an association with Miss Chapel developed, he intended to be more forward and assertive. Maybe, he thought, his experiences in Korea had changed the old Wylie.

The next morning, he contacted Corporal Beam at the Signal Corps tent and asked for copies of his photos of the children at the orphanage, along with, incidentally, general pictures of the operation that might include a shot of the young woman who worked there. The pictures arrived the next day, and Wylie began to cobble together a warm human-interest story about the soldiers of the 53rd Infantry, the kids at the orphanage at Tongdudong-ni, and a special young woman who was the Executive Director.

RECLAMATION

◆ ◆ ◆

GENERAL BLACK HAD CAPTAIN STANDRICH'S full attention. He called him over while both were witnessing a parade honoring departing division cadre who received various medals and awards. Without any introductory comments or greeting, he said, "You know it's a damn fine thing our chemical corpsmen and infantry are doing to clear up all the mines those Chinese bastards plastered throughout the countryside just before the armistice. And it's not just to protect the U.N. Forces; it's basically to prepare the farmland so the indigenous can be self-sufficient again. I think this is a splendid example of how our troops are helping the Korean people and you P.I.O. people ought to get in front of it and publicize the hell out of it!"

"Of course, sir, that's a splendid idea," said the Captain who had but a vague notion of the activities the general was describing. "But," the Captain added as he recalled certain aspects of protocol, "don't we need clearance from military intelligence? The subject might be a bit touchy."

"It's already been reviewed. I Corps G-2 gave me a heads up this morning. No reason at all to delay, especially during this fine weather. Got it?"

"Got it, sir."

Two days later Jim Beam, Shit Dad, and Wylie found themselves looking down over a waterlogged terrace of rice paddies near the same CP where the epic battle against the green bottle flies had occurred.

Major Smatter stood a few yards away observing a squad of chemical corpsmen assisted by soldiers from the engineer battalion and infantrymen from Y Battalion. Wylie was surprised to see the chemical corpsmen strip to their skivvies under a warming sun and begin to walk, single file, into the knee-deep water of the paddy.

Corporal Bonaventura was in charge of the detail. Wylie had been so busy taking notes during the green bottle fly campaign that he had not taken a careful look at the Corporal. He had a compact, well-muscled body resulting, Wylie guessed, from working out with weights. Dark haired and skinned, he must have avoided Army dentists since one of his front teeth was missing, making some of his consonants whistle as he spoke. Bonaventura's sunny disposition resulted in numerous gap-toothed smiles.

Standing next to the division journalists, he explained what was going on.

"Just before the armistice, there was a lot of last minute shit going on with the NKs. They wanted to make it as tough as possible on the indigenous so they blew stuff up, burned homes, and tossed land mines all over the place. They didn't keep any records of the mines so they didn't have to turn anything over when they pulled back from this place."

He gestured to the paddies below and the little farming village farther down the valley.

"Anyway, we've been deactivating mines ever since then, and the Major got the word couple days ago that a farmer and his ox each lost a leg to antipersonnel mines right in this here vicinity."

Bonaventura reached into a bag on the ground and picked up a peculiar dun-colored object. It was cylindrical with a protruding mushroom top, which had four metal straws pointing upward at oblique angles.

He held it toward Wylie and said, "This one's deactivated. See, they bury the base in the ground and let these triggers stick up. Then they put some brush or straw over the triggers so it's not easy to see. It's activated by pulling this little pin here. You come along and step on a trigger, you're okay. It's getting off that's the problem. Once the pressure is off, she blows and there goes your leg, if you're lucky. If you're a kid, that's usually all she wrote."

Bonaventura handed the mine to Wylie who depressed one of the spring-loaded triggers gingerly. It pushed back. This was one shitty war, thought Wylie, before recalling that all wars are shitty.

Jim Beam was positioning himself to obtain low angle photos of the detail wading through the paddy.

"I thought you looked for mines with those metal disks on the end of a wand, or something," he said to Bonaventura.

"That'd be nice, but they don't work when the mines are under water. We cleared the fields over there that way and waited for a warmer day to get after the paddies. As it is, we're gonna freeze our gonads anyway. Listen, I gotta set an example and get in the water with the guys. We should have this whole thing cleared in an hour or so. Aside from freezing though, we gotta keep an eye out for the flotables. That's the little chunks of shit that get loose from the night soil that they use to feed the seedlings. But, what the hey, I love my home in the Army!"

He moved to join the others, pulling off his fatigue shirt, displaying his taught muscles.

Shit Dad decided there was nothing he would rather do that morning than wade through noxious water and hunt for explosives buried in a rice paddy. He walked to his friend, removing his fatigues as he went.

Wylie joined Major Smatter who was collecting captured mines and placing them in a pile for later disposal. The Major disarmed them before adding them to the growing pile. Wylie took notes as the Major described the process.

"We've found that the most effective way to locate these particular antipersonnel mines is to feel for them along the surface of the ground under water, sweeping a hand in front. When we feel a trigger, we dig around the mine in the wet dirt and expose the entire device.

Then the men hand the mine back along the single file line until it gets to me."

The Major showed Wylie a small opening at the edge of the mine he held.

"I disarm it by placing this little bar in here and it goes on the pile. To be fair, the point man is rotated every hour or so – at least once a day. Now, this isn't for attribution, but we haven't had any fatalities yet, though Private Dumbrowski did lose his hand and forearm a month ago. These guys all get special combat pay, though."

Wylie wondered how much that was. The Major thought it was twenty dollars or so a month.

Shit Dad had now positioned himself behind Corporal Bonaventura who seemed to be finding a mine every twenty yards or so. He carefully passed each active mine to the man behind him. They had worked their way more than half way down the terraces when the Corporal stopped, a frown on his face.

"Major, I found something funny here. It's kind of like a metal plate. It sure as hell ain't no land mine. It's BIG."

Major Smatter waded through the cleared area to the Corporal and reached into the slimy water. Soon he was on his knees in the water, liquid up to his waist, scooping mud from the object.

"Pass down a bayonet," he called to one of the infantrymen. Using the blade as a trowel, he exposed more of the device, feeling it carefully with his hands. He uncovered two large fins set at right angles and attached to a large metal cylinder.

"Sonovabitch!" he exclaimed. "It's one of ours. It's a damn five hundred pounder that never exploded, and it's half buried in this rice paddy. God knows what target they missed for this thing to end up here. We're not about to haul it out of here; it must be disposed of it right where it is. Corporal you stay here with me. The rest of you get up to the ridge line."

The squad hastily waded from the paddy and climbed to the top of the hill. Bonaventura reached into the slime and examined the bomb too. He agreed with the Major that they must explode the bomb in place.

The Corporal made his way up the hill, retrieved two large metal containers of C-4 plastic explosive, blasting caps, and detonation wire from their supply truck, and returned to the Major. The two carefully packed the exposed surfaces of the large bomb with C-4 until the Major decided there was enough. Bonaventura pushed a blasting cap into the explosive, attached the detonation wire, and slowly unwound the wire as he and the Major waded back up the hill.

The other members of the team agreed among themselves that it was one big mother-hunching bomb and scurried for cover behind the hill. Wylie and Shit Dad joined the engineers and other soldiers who also took cover in the lee of the ridgeline.

Jim Beam lay full length just at the top of the ridge, pointing his Speed Graphic at the unexploded bomb half way down the slope below. The Major attached the ends of the wire to the detonator, cranked the handle a few times, and raised the plunger.

"Okay men, it's fire in the hole. We'll be safe here, but you may want to cover your ears." He depressed the plunger, which made a little swishing sound. For a brief half second, nothing happened.

The electrical charge coursed along the wire and fired the blasting cap that ignited the plastic explosive. The Major had been over generous with the C-4. The ear-shattering explosion raised the bomb from its reclining state to rise tail-first into the air. The detonation removed substantial quantities of dirt, forming a crater into which the bomb slowly descended. The dirt flew skyward, cresting the ridgeline, descending on the troops gathered there, covering them with a foul smelling dark brown chunky paste of detritus.

As the five hundred pounder struck its nose on the bottom of the crater, its internal clock reactivated. The time delay fuse ignited and, moments later, the huge bomb exploded. Compared with the enormity of the bomb's detonation, the C-4 blast was like a hiccup. Fire and smoke obliterated the entire paddy, sending a crimson crescent of vast quantities of real estate into the sky. Eardrums shattered and quaking earth sent soldiers still standing to their knees in a shower of muck. The stunned troops saw the results of their efforts through a brown cloud still clinging to the ridgeline. The rice paddy was obliterated, replaced by a deep muddy crater that included a good portion of the surrounding countryside.

Jim Beam managed to take a single picture before the first wave of silt hit, cleaned his lens, and replaced his film pack just in time to capture the monster explosion that lifted the entire hillside, seemingly above his head. Being closest to the center of the explosion, he was buried in muck as bits of metal pinged against his helmet, which he thankfully had not removed. The second photograph was spectacular, but Army censors classified it as "Secret" for obvious reasons.

Wylie and Shit Dad recovered their balance and slithered back up the hill, joined by Corporal Bonaventura, to help extract the photographer and view the immense crater that had been the hillside rice paddies.

"Looks like we can pack up and go home," said the Corporal. "No mines left here. Now where the hell are my damn boots?"

Oily muck covered unattached boots or other items of personal clothing or equipment left on the ground. The troops salvaged what they could, but Bonaventura found only one boot. Other than being covered with disgusting crud, the supply truck had escaped injury, and four infantrymen righted the Major's Jeep, which had been blown on its side. As its wheels struck solid ground again, the field telephone in the Jeep rang insistently. Bonaventura answered.

"What the fiddledee fuck are you up to?" shouted Colonel Highman, commander of Y Battalion.

"Let me get the Major for you, sir," said Bonaventura.

"Major Smatter, here," he said, scraping mud from cheeks and nose.

"Smatter, what the fiddledee fuck is going on over there? We're five miles away from your operation and that explosion knocked over our water tower! What the fuck are you up to? Do I need to send troops?"

"Not necessary, sir. It's just a routine operation" lied Smatter. "We are just taking care of some mines and had a minor glitch. Everything is just fine now. We'll be clearing out in fifteen minutes. The operation is completed."

"Okay" grumbled the Colonel and replaced the handset. He stood at his office door and watched engineers surveying the toppled water tower.

Major Smatter looked at the vast depression created by the exploded bomb. Water from the remains of the rice paddies began to seep toward its bottom and little rivulets of mud formed on its sides. The Major wiped his glasses on his sleeve and turned toward the supply truck.

Wylie and Shit Dad stood at the crest of the hill, saw the muddy pond forming at the bottom of the fresh depression, and noticed a group of Korean farmers in soiled white clothing and straw hats at the opposite side of the crater. Heads bowed, they stared in disbelief at the depression in front of them. Centuries of labor in creating the terraces, their water supply, their livelihood, food from the next harvest, all vanished in the blink of a thundering god's eye.

Wylie saw the sadness and pain on their faces. The poor farmers didn't have a choice, he thought, and wondered if they might eventually take solace in the fact that there were no more land mines. That meant no more lost legs or death to careless children. But at such a price. Such a price.

Wylie joined Shit Dad who was helping Jim Beam back to their Jeep, which was parked in a sludge free zone. Jim kept shaking his head, as though that would restore the hearing he had lost. Shit Dad placed his muddy and battered camera case in the back of the Jeep and helped Jim find comfort in the seat. They sped back to Headquarters.

CHAPTER 41
WARFINGER ARRIVES

◆ ◆ ◆

THE AROMA OF CORONA SUPREMOS wafted toward the ventilator in Major General Bart B. Black's trailer as he poured a generous dollop of whiskey for Colonel Chuck Warfinger who sat comfortably across from the General in a padded campaign chair.

"I'm really pleased you're joining the Division, Chuck. It's like old times. Plowing north from Anzio, kicking the Wehrmacht in the ass. The show over here was really different; more political, you know, but our boys in the 53rd were magnificent. It's a shame you missed it, but you were holding your own in Fort Dix. Ice?"

"Thank you, no."

More reminiscences as Warfinger probed his friend's mood, waiting for an appropriate moment to review his pressing concern. As the General paused in his description of activities in the Division during the past few months, Warfinger seized the opportunity to change the subject.

"With all due respect, Bart, I was surprised, you might say disappointed, to find that I've been assigned to run Special Services here. You know I like to think of myself as a warrior, and I think I proved that in the Big One. I was hoping to be given an infantry regiment, not run a GED school for enlisted types and be an impresario for third rate musical combos who some lame brain in D.C. sends over here to entertain the troops."

"I respect that, Chuck, and I know you are a seasoned warrior, but I'm really thinking about your future. You'll have to admit you have some rough edges that certainly weren't smoothed over with the wire brush of combat. It's my thinking that you could use a tour where your organization ability and diplomacy are required."

"But, besides that," the General leaned closer to the Colonel, "I need someone I can trust not to screw things up. Some people I thought were good have let me down."

The General sighed and inhaled the smoke from a quarter inch of his glowing Corona.

"Even though combat has ended," he went on, "we still have many reporters popping up looking for stories. Apparently, visiting entertainers and their interaction with the troops make for good copy. When DeeDee Vaughn and her twinkling starlets toured two months ago my former adjutant was photographed at the Generals' mess with his hand firmly planted on Miss Nebraska's ass and staring down the front of her blouse. Thank God Hank Walnut knew the photographer and worked out a deal to suppress the photo."

"Chuck, the division needs a seasoned officer to avoid that sort of embarrassment," he added.

"You make good points and, as they say, I serve at your pleasure. I'll do the job as best I can," said a somewhat glum Warfinger.

"Excellent. I think you'll be in good hands. You've got Major Buck Adder for adjutant and he's been at the job for half a year. Transferred over from the Adjutant General's office and is a real detail man. Captain, what's his name, Anastos was a school teacher somewhere and does a nice job with the training. I think most of the enlisted have some college, so you're not going to have a bunch of grunts."

"Bart, I'm relieved to hear it."

The General motioned to whiskey bottle.

"How about a dividend, Chuck?"

Wylie was chatting with Corporal Milo Natter from Special Services over a beer and peanuts. Since he was buying he felt entitled to quiz the Corporal about any special events on the horizon since, among other things, Natter's outfit was responsible for special events, shows for the troops and coordinating visits from non-military dignitaries.

"Not a whole hell of a lot," said Natter. "We're shepherding Mr. P. Pibul Songgram, the Prime Minister of Thailand, on a tour of the DMZ and a meeting with our top brass. He will be reviewing the Thai troops stationed just north of here and then there will be a parade with us, members of the ROK army, and a couple of Thai companies. Come to think of it, it probably makes a good story, what with Thailand being the first Asian nation to send troops to help the South Koreans. Those little guys are tough as nails and not afraid to fight. They had a casualty rate of almost twenty per cent."

"You're pretty well informed about all that, Milo."

"Yeah, well, I started up with a Thai girlfriend on my last R & R in Bangkok. Maybe it sinks in by osmosis," said Milo. "Anyway, what do you think? Good material?"

"Of course," agreed Wylie. "Good international relations, comrades in arms, excellent photos if it's a good day, all that. It should be even more powerful than my story about how well the Turks and Greeks are getting along in the land of the morning calm."

Milo snickered appropriately. "And then, in about six weeks, we're going to have Charlie, also known as "Smudge" Jackson, and some of the original members of his R & B band here for a few weeks. He was drafted and took infantry basic. But he's on TDY here to entertain the brave men of the 53rd."

"I'm about to display a shocking level of ignorance. What is R & B?"

"Didn't get much Rhythm and Blues at Princeton? Concentrating on Mozart and Beethoven? Smudge Jackson is right up there with Little Richard and Fats Domino. He's had four or five bestselling records. Little Richard had "Tutti Frutti" and Smudge had "Mazie got the Blues.""

"Yeah, I guess I heard of them," lied Wylie.

"Well, you'll have a chance to hear more in a few weeks."

After another beer and Milo's joking about Wylie's shallow cultural outlook, the subject turned to the new head of Special Services, Colonel Warfinger.

"He's a bit more relaxed than Major Adder, but I sense that he would rather be heading an infantry or armor outfit than sitting in an office at Division headquarters. He's a quick study, though. Only been here a couple of weeks and has absorbed all our training schedules, knows who the instructors are and is working on a division talent show with the Red Cross. He's all over the thing with Smudge Jackson. I get the feeling he wants to make life more interesting for the troops."

"We'll have to consider doing a feature on you guys. Maybe we can combine it with an article about this R & B guy."

Colonel Warfinger was warming to the tasks involved in his new assignment. He considered himself a "big picture guy" and was pleased that Major Adder had an accountant's eye for detail. He set aside half an hour each morning for Adder's reports that detailed with minute precision the number of hours dedicated to the numerous and various projects undertaken by the group. There were cross references to similar projects completed in the past and comparisons that highlighted time expended and projected efficiencies.

After these preliminaries, Adder focused on his favorite report — the budget. Neatly inscribed columns of numbers paraded across Warfinger's desk as his adjutant explained disbursements and trends affecting the amounts allocated by the military to support the unit's activities. The Colonel suspected the review of numbers had an erotic effect on the Major since his voice rose in pitch and his breathing quickened as he reached the bottom line each morning. Getting off on numbers, thought Warfinger, is just weird.

The Colonel, still on the sunny side of fifty, was a bachelor. This was a social asset in the military since he could be counted on to escort single women to various military affairs. This, in turn, led to numerous brief affairs, none of which, however, resulted in marriage.

As commander of Special Services, he had frequent contact with the leader of the Red Cross women assigned to the 53^{rd,} and he enjoyed a bantering relationship with the sturdy Sonja Applebaum. He found the meeting and greeting of visiting dignitaries more agreeable than expected, especially since his staff managed the niceties of such events with grace and aplomb. He found also that he could indulge his hobby of reading military histories fully since there were frequent periods when his command presence was not required.

During his idle moments, he thought about ways to enhance and expand the work of his unit. Its mission, according to the statement in the Division's TO&E was "to increase morale by providing recreational activities, including crafts, theatrical productions, and parties to troops stationed in Korea."

A classmate stationed at I Corps sent him some classified material about the Japanese occupation of Korea that he found fascinating. It reminded him of the ways major powers had subjugated and colonized areas in the past. There were echoes of the Spanish in Peru and Mexico, the British Empire in India and "manifest destiny" in the United States.

"Buck," he said as Major Adder was completing his morning briefing, "did you know the Japanese drafted Korean women to act as "comfort women" for their troops? They believed it was an important part of keeping up morale and I guess that was so. Terrible thing, though, to kidnap all those women and turn them into sex slaves. A lot of them are back in Korea right now."

"No, sir, I didn't know that. But I do know there are a lot of Korean "comfort women" ready and willing to service our guys right now, for a reasonable price, and they are just down the road from the main gate." His expression and tone of voice suggested strong disapproval of the customary services available near any military post.

"Well I don't guess there's much anyone can do about that," Adder added.

The next afternoon Warfinger found himself with Colonel Cutter at the headquarters MASH unit. The doctor had relieved the pain of a pesky hangnail on a big toe. As the Colonel inhaled a cigarette and his patient replaced his trousers and boots, Warfinger inquired about the prevalence of VD in the division.

"Well, you know we give them all the lectures and warn them to use protection and give them a short arm inspection as often as possible but there's been a real increase in infections since the armistice. There's just more opportunity these days. I'd say one man in twenty gets gonorrhea and one in fifty comes down with syphilis. Thank God for penicillin."

"Thanks, doc; the toe feels a lot better already. I owe you a drink. See you at the club tonight?"

CHAPTER 42
THE WRONG WORD

◆ ◆ ◆

CAPTAIN STANDRICH WAS NOT HIS customary cherubic self as Wylie entered the Public Information office. For one thing, he was not in his cubicle; for another, he was in the office a few hours before his customary time of arrival. And he seemed to be waiting for Wylie. His expression was decidedly unfriendly.

"Sergeant (not 'Wylie') the shit has hit the fan, and it is rolling downhill looking for you!"

Never before had the laid-back officer addressed his noncom in anger and Wylie realized serious matters were at hand. He placed his coffee mug on his desk and stood to attention before the Captain, all the while inventorying any actions that might have prompted his superior's irritation. He had no idea what he might have done.

"Colonel Warfinger gave me a royal and undeserved once over with a wire brush this morning, "said Standrich. "It's all about that disrespectful article YOU wrote about the Thai Prime Minister when he reviewed the troops a couple weeks ago. That all happened when I was on leave; I never reviewed it before you sent it to the Saber, and I refuse to accept responsibility for your screw up!"

"But, sir, that was just a boilerplate feature about his visit and reviewing the troops and all," said Wylie. "There was absolutely nothing controversial about it."

"Hah! Think so? It seems that you wrote the Prime Minister was the leader of his COUNTRY when, in truth, he is leader of his

PARLIAMENT. They have a KING, you should know, who is the leader of their country. It appears that the Thai military and government take intense umbrage at such disrespect of their king."

"Well, sure, they have a king but, for chrissake, it's only one word – and an honest mistake," offered Wylie.

"Be that as it may, General Walnut has taken a personal interest in this screw up. Report to his chief of staff right away. Dismissed!"

Shaken, Wylie left the office to walk along the path outlined in whitewashed stones to the office of General's Black's second in command. He adjusted his uniform and checked his boots for dirt on the way.

Colonel Harsh, the General's assistant, glowered at Wylie from time to time as he sat waiting in General Walnut's anteroom. His nervousness and anxiety intensified as he sat, awaiting impending doom, for almost two hours. Finally, the Colonel pointed toward him and motioned him to the General's closed door. He passed through and stood at attention ten feet from Hank Walnut's campaign desk.

The General scribbled on a yellow legal pad for a few moments before acknowledging Wylie's presence. With a weathered brown face topped by brilliant white hair and eyebrows, he somewhat resembled a walnut dredged through marshmallow fluff. The look in his eye as he focused on the Sergeant before him belied any softness, however.

"Remain at attention, you sorry fuckup."

"Yes, sir," said Wylie, believing that the General's glare was dissecting pieces of his internal organs and moving them en masse to his descending colon.

"Your ignorance of Thai politics, you miserable, tit-sucking excuse for a reporter, is exceeded only by your inability to engage in the most rudimentary fact checking," began the General.

"Your article in our division newspaper (and thank God it was never picked up by other media) was supposed to be complimentary of our Thai allies. Instead, it has caused what amounts to an international incident."

General Walnut pushed up from his chair and thrust his marsh-mallow-topped head aggressively toward Wylie.

"The commander of the Thai battalion suggested that we in the 53rd are either incredibly stupid or purposely disrespectful of Thai royalty. The Prime Minister has sent a note of disapproval to our ambassador in Seoul."

Wylie's palms were moist and droplets of perspiration clung to his cheeks. It took all his concentration to remain at attention. He focused on Walnut's fierce snowy eyebrows, then flinched, and stared morosely at his feet, hoping the floor would open so he could more quickly begin his descent into hell. No such luck.

"On top of that," the General, now standing upright behind his desk, continued, "On top of that, I've been messaged by one of our CIA operatives in Seoul that your article is thwarting their campaign to show how communism is threatening the Thai monarchy. It seems the most beloved people in the whole country are the king and queen. And you, you four star peckerhead, decided the PRIME MINISTER was in charge."

The General paused. Ominously, Wylie thought.

"If the Thai Colonel had his way he'd take you out behind the motor pool and have you shot. Unfortunately, and to my eternal regret, I don't have that authority. You will, however, get your ass in front of that Colonel and offer him your most profuse abject apology. Is that understood?"

Wylie croaked, "Yes, Sir!"

"Okay. Get your miserable butt out of here. And don't get too comfortable with those Sergeant stripes."

Wylie didn't know this was an empty threat since the General had already been informed there was no other likely replacement for him on Captain Standrich's team. However, it seemed to the General an appropriate ending to a mild ass chewing.

Colonel Harsh accosted Wylie as he walked numbly back into the anteroom.

"Oh eight hundred."

"Sir?"

"Tomorrow."

"Yes, sir, tomorrow." A pregnant pause. "And where would that be tomorrow?"

Exasperated, the Colonel confirmed, "Colonel Kasem Sanitwong's office at the Thai Expeditionary Forces Headquarters. And you better show up in your Class A uniform."

The Thai headquarters were less than a mile from the 53rd Infantry location and Wylie decided to walk there the following morning, practicing various forms of abject apology. His interview with General Walnut was the first time in his life he had been so rudely excoriated, if one didn't count the numerous times recruits were demeaned during basic training. Coming from a General, however, it had much greater impact than insults from a drill instructor.

The residual effects from the interview were still apparent. A certain threatening looseness in his bowels remained. He was convinced this could be the end of what was a promising, but brief, military career. On the other hand, he felt perversely honored that a one-star General had taken time from his busy schedule to personally chew him, a mere enlisted man, out. That's me, he thought; dumb enough to find a silver lining in this seriously ominous cloud.

The Thai Colonel was a short, weather-beaten officer whose decorations declared that he had seen combat. He had a scar on his left cheek that slightly elongated that side of his mouth but he spoke quite clearly. He surprised Wylie by motioning him to a chair beside his desk and offering a cigarette.

"Sergeant, it appears you have made a stupid mistake."

"Oh, yes, sir, and I appreciate the seriousness of it and offer my most sincere apology. This incident has…"

The Colonel interrupted by raising his hand to cut Wylie off.

"Yes, I believe you know you have made an error but I doubt you do understand how insulting it was to me personally and our soldiers here. And, if it had happened in my country, consequences to you would be extremely severe."

"I am truly sorry, and…"

"I will explain and you will listen."

Wylie adopted his very best listening posture.

"For centuries the Kings of Siam have been considered the fathers of the nation. They are revered by their subjects and the King and Queen are beloved by us all. King Bhumibol has reigned in our country since June, 1946 and was crowned King in May of 1950, just a month before the war broke out here. He married our Queen just two months before his coronation."

All of this was news to Wylie. He listened carefully.

"In reverence to the monarchy, we have enacted "lèse-majesté" laws that make the King inviolable," said the Colonel.

"Any insults or criticism can result in three to fifteen years in jail. So, Sergeant, if you were in my country right now and had stated the Prime Minister was the leader of our country it would have been considered a severe insult to the King. There is no question you would already be languishing in a Bangkok jail right now. Perhaps you begin to understand the very serious nature of your stupid error."

"I do, sir. I do. If there was any way I could take it back, I would. What can I do to make amends?"

The Colonel reached into a drawer and pulled forth a very official looking document, typed in Thai script underneath the regimental crest. There was a single line at the bottom of the document. His name was spelled out underneath it.

"This is for your signature. It is your humble request for a pardon by the office of King Bhumibol. The document describes you as a repentant peasant supplicant seeking royal forgiveness, and it mentions in complete detail your thoughtlessness and stupidity. My adjutant who drafted it confirms this document has an excellent chance of resolving the matter and resulting in a pardon. This is very important if you should ever wish to visit our beautiful country in future."

There was no hesitation; Wylie signed his name on the paper, thinking all the while how disappointed his father would be that he signed without understanding. Sometimes, he thought, you don't have a choice.

The next day Wylie concluded there was some merit to the proverb that bad things happen in threes. Colonel Harsh informed him he was under orders to report to a Mr. Joshua Brittle at the Embassy Compound in Seoul ASAP. Two hours later he arrived at the reception desk of the gray pillared Embassy building not far from the I Corps Headquarters. A grimly silent Marine Corporal in dress blues escorted him to the office of Mr. Brittle and told him to wait there.

As Joshua Brittle entered the office, he removed his blue suit jacket and loosened his tie. In the process, he displayed a chrome plated 32-caliber automatic tucked into a holster on his belt. He was in his mid-thirties, tall with close-cropped sandy hair, and he eyed Wylie as though he had just discovered a scorpion in his boot.

"You Psyfor, the communist sympathizer?" he asked.

"What!"

"I don't have enough trouble with the cockamamie Rhee regime I gotta worry about card carrying commie sympathizers in our own midst? How'd you ever get a secret clearance?"

Wylie was dumbfounded. What was this hotshot talking about?

"We've combed your background and discovered you've been very clever in disguising your political leanings, but we know that you have a cousin who was in the International League of Students and that's good enough for me."

Brittle reached into a drawer and pulled out a folder that looked suspiciously like Wylie's 201 file.

"Very cute, getting yourself assigned to a propaganda unit. That's what I call infiltration, all right. You didn't arouse suspicion until you wrote that article about the Thai Prime Minister. Then it was clear as a crack of lightening. Who put you up to this? How did you know about our operation in Thailand?"

"I don't know what you're talking about. I've already eaten a rasher of crap over that stupid mistake, but you're nuts if you think it's some kind of communist conspiracy," said Wylie, bristling.

Brittle slowly rolled up his shirtsleeves, sat on the edge of his desk and looked down at Wylie.

"I know you're not dumb enough to think you can get away with this. Why don't we get the ball rolling by your telling me who suggested you give the U.S. Military a black eye by insulting the King?"

Brittle was a CIA agent with considerable experience in Thailand and Korea. He believed there was little likelihood that the Sergeant squirming before him had done anything other than make a foolish error. But that error had slightly upset a campaign the CIA and the U.S. Information Service had begun in 1952 in Thailand to show how Communism opposed the people, their religion and their King. They had even created forged communist pamphlets in Thai that attacked the monarchy.

Though Wylie's mistake in a feature article was not taken very seriously within the political constituency (they suspected it was just a typical error from an outsider who did not understand their culture) it was an event the CIA could not simply overlook. Consequently, Brittle had been assigned to massage the offender with a half-inch wire brush to see if a slight flaying produced anything other than sincere indignation.

Brittle's accusations continued for another half hour, heightening Wylie's confusion and irritation. The thing which kept Wylie from striking his interviewer and leaving the office was that little pistol winking from Brittle's waistband.

Finally, the interview was over. The CIA officer dismissed him with the admonition to keep his nose clean and that they would keep an eye on him. Wylie wondered if Brittle had any other facial clichés up his sleeve and left the building, guided by the Marine Corporal. On the way back to Headquarters he fantasized he would be met by a firing squad.

That evening Master Sergeant Stan Wrinkle joined Wylie in the NCO Club for a boilermaker.

"Stan, know anything about the laws of unintended consequences?"

"Only that I've suffered some of them. I'm married, you know."

He appreciated the Sergeant's leavening of humor. There had been little of that the past few days.

Though it was probably common knowledge by now, Wylie described his recent run of interactions with hostile officers.

With admiration, the Master Sergeant acknowledged the quality of the reamings Wylie had recently received.

"Yeah, General Walnut has a reputation for masterful ass-chewings. They say, in fact, that it really isn't that. I've been told he just sort of chews all around the ass and then steps back to watch it fall off."

Wylie had to laugh. "That description seems fair; you'll get no argument from me."

They continued their conversation and quickly consumed two more shots of Jack Daniels. Wylie was beginning to feel as though he might ultimately survive the recent debacle. Sergeant Wrinkle patted him on the shoulder.

"Tell you what. It is unlikely that such expert practitioners of the art will ever again chew you out in such a short period of time. Whatever future ass-chewings come your way will pale by comparison to what you've already experienced. You've been hardened, Wylie, against all upcoming ass-chewings. It's like insurance. It's character building."

The best part about thinking of it that way, decided Wylie, was that it implied he actually had a future.

CHAPTER 43
PUBLIC AND PRIVATE RELATIONS

◆ ◆ ◆

I WISH SHE WERE CLOSER to some military unit, thought Wylie. Then I could get in touch by phone to see if she was there. Although the trip by Jeep to the orphanage took less than ten minutes, he couldn't be sure Amelia would be there.

Although she had not been overly sociable to him during his last visit, he was surprisingly eager to meet her again, to know her better. What, he wondered, would prompt a highly educated young woman from an elite Seven Sisters school to care for unwanted orphans in a village just slightly removed from the Stone Age? He hoped the packet of press clippings and photographs he carried would help unseal the mystery.

Stepping through a small dust cloud raised as the Jeep came to a halt, he was relieved to see Amelia. She was pushing a little African Asian girl on the tire suspended to the tree in front of the orphanage. The child screamed with delight each time the tire reached its apex and Amelia pretended to cover her ears as the child returned for another push. Two young Korean women were also in the yard, supervising other small children playing in the sand box and hiding in surrounding bushes.

Amelia had exchanged her tennis shorts for faded blue jeans and wore a tattered fatigue sweater over her Wellesley sweatshirt. She had covered her red hair with a navy-blue bandana. As she turned toward Wylie, he gulped, almost overwhelmed by her beauty. She exuded buoyant good health and athleticism, combined with an expression of candor and a hint of impishness.

As before, Wylie inwardly said "Wow." He felt a sensation similar to when he saw Judy after an absence, but it was sharper, more pronounced as he looked at Amelia. It must be, he thought, that I just haven't seen that many round-eyed women my age for a long while.

She paused at the swing and the little girl peered at Wylie with curious eyes. Amelia moved toward him.

"Well, Sergeant, here you are again. Do you still need more information about the Chapel project? May I offer you some water or lemonade?"

"No, no more information. I just wanted you to see some of the press clippings about your project. And lemonade would be great!"

He glanced around the yard in front of the dormitory. "It looks as though you have had some help here. Everything looks more squared away. Is that a new play area over there?"

She gestured toward the brightly painted sand box and jungle gym. "Yes, some engineers from Y Battalion came by with some "leftover" lumber and put that up last week. But I can't figure out where "leftover" red and yellow paint came from. They are dear fellows and they played with the kids a lot. Could be you and your stories might have had something to do with that?"

"Could be," acknowledged Wylie, eager to take credit whether or not due.

They were seated side by side on a bench in an area of the entrance lobby that she called her office and Wylie placed the contents of an envelope on her desk, the top of a packing crate. He showed her the feature article Jules Pike had included in The Saber and a similar but abbreviated article in the Stars and Stripes. Her photograph was in both pieces, and little Kim of the loaded chamber pot appeared as well. She read the articles and other clippings included carefully.

"This is very nice work, Sergeant," she said while patting his shoulder. "It explains why we've received baby clothes from the Red Cross and a used ice box from X Battalion. There has even been some talk about finding a "leftover" generator somewhere so we can put away our kerosene lamps."

He agreed that was all heartening news and then placed his most prized accomplishment on the desk in front of Amelia, a page from the Wellesley Alumna Magazine, which featured a photograph of the Chapel orphanage and explained in detail what their recent graduate was doing.

"That is embarrassing," she exclaimed, secretly pleased that her classmates would read about her endeavors.

"I know dad will be very happy to see all this. We owe you a debt of gratitude, young Sergeant." And she kissed him on the cheek.

Now that, thought Wylie, is a marked improvement over the last visit.

Carrying his lemonade (and where had she found lemons?), he followed her through the orphanage building to see several improvements that suggested a distinct military origin. In the dormitory for the Korean helpers and housekeepers, he discovered some of the air mattresses recently replaced by spring mattresses in division had been recycled, as had G.I. cots and kitchen utensils. Two slightly chipped enamel washtubs now stood near the inside water pump, ready to receive diapers and soiled children's clothes. He was unsure how much his efforts had contributed to the changes, but improvements definitely had occurred since his visit almost six weeks before.

His nursed his lemonade as long as possible, and when it was finished, there was an awkward moment when he handed the glass to Amelia and muttered something about getting back to division. She gazed at him carefully with her clear emerald eyes.

"Oh, that's too bad. I thought maybe we could take a little walk together through the village."

Wylie certainly could make time for that.

Tongdudong-ni was a farming village with some large outbuildings used to warehouse produce. The family homes were thatched roofed adobe structures raised a few feet above ground. The open spaces below houses allowed floodwaters to pass harmlessly through during the rainy season. During the winter, tenants filled the spaces with straw that they burned to provide heat against the bitter cold.

Since it was the nearest village to the 53rd Division headquarters it now featured two bars, a tailor who customized military clothing to eliminate its sack-like qualities, and an embroidery shop that produced baseball jackets with "Korea," dragons, fanciful Korean characters, division emblems, and given names emblazoned in garish threads. A cobbler burnished standard brown boots to patent leather sheen and installed zippers in the instep side to eliminate the need to tie laces. Merchants sold all manner of souvenirs created from discarded brass shells in shops along the hard-packed dirt main street. Between the bars was a "massage parlor" operated by an enterprising mama-san where soldiers went to forget the girl or girls left behind. That establishment guaranteed keeping Colonel Cutter and his medics in need of fresh supplies of penicillin.

Wylie had passed through the little village many times before, but it seemed different as he and Amelia strolled down the main road toward the fields of rice and sorghum turning golden brown in the crisp fall air. He suspected that enjoying an animated conversation with a lovely young woman in this out of the way place enhanced his appreciation of the place.

As they reached the fields at the end of the village, they were forced to detour around a cart drawn by two ancient oxen moving at a stately pace, pulling the cart on which Uncle Ho slept peacefully, rocked by the to and fro of the beasts' plodding steps.

"Whew!" exclaimed Wylie as they passed the two sloshing barrels mounted on the cart's bed, their lids precariously askew.

"Night soil," said Amelia. "Uncle Ho is a fixture around here. He collects the stuff for the fields outside the village. He usually has some G.I. who helps him, but he doesn't seem to be around today."

As they wandered through golden fields, the couple exchanged details about the towns where they grew up, compared favorite things, including movies, books, and music, and discussed their college experiences. Neither of them would later recall the exact content of their conversation, but would remember how interesting it was, how coincidental their tastes, how well they agreed on the many important issues they considered.

Wylie felt doubly blessed. Here he was carrying on a lively conversation with one of the prettiest round-eyed girls he had ever seen. To his surprise, their age difference of almost three years seemed to matter not at all. He could not recall being happier—even with Judy. He pushed aside the pangs of guilt caused by remembrance of his first love.

"So, getting back to your job at the orphanage and all, is it working out the way you thought it would?" he asked.

She turned thoughtfully to Wylie, slanting late afternoon light burnishing her russet hair.

"You must be reading my mind. The experience is very different from what I expected. Different but more rewarding. Dad helps a lot, but I find I have to be very self-reliant and assertive to keep things moving. I have found qualities in myself that I didn't know were there. That is a pleasant surprise."

She reached for a stalk of grain and rubbed off the seeds between her fingers.

"But the best thing of all" she said, "is when one or two of those little munchkins run to me laughing and hugs me, so pure, so giving, despite being hurt by this ugly war. That's a reward I don't think I could find back in Boston... But I'm rattling on."

She gestured toward the setting sun. "Look how late it's become. I need to get back and I'm sure you must be on your way too."

Wylie reluctantly agreed, although he would have given up a month of three-day passes to remain with her just fifteen minutes longer.

As they returned to Tongdudong-ni, Amelia took Wylie's hand in hers and held it until they parted.

As Wylie climbed into his Jeep, Amelia suggested it would be nice to see him again and asked, as an afterthought, if he knew a Sergeant Pangluss, a Corporal McIlvane, and a Private Rowe, the one, you know, they call "Shit Dad."

Of course he did! Scott McIlvane was one of his best friends. Why did she ask?

They had been by a few days ago and had left some metal tanks and other surplus items behind the orphanage. They would return, they said, amid winks and laughter, with a surprise. It had certainly aroused her curiosity.

Wylie assured her that they were all good men and that Shit Dad, as a new father, was highly motivated in caring for the orphans. What they had planned, though, he couldn't say. But he would certainly return soon to see what they were up to.

And what were they up to, he wondered as he headed the Jeep back to Headquarters Company.

CHAPTER 44
A PROJECT DEVELOPS

◆ ◆ ◆

COLONEL WARFINGER STOOD IN THE center of the empty warehouse storage area and surveyed his surroundings. The solidly made building was of beam and post construction and had a fifteen-foot-high corrugated roof. It had been used to store grain during the winter months and ice packed in sawdust through the summer. Unused during the war, many local farmers now worked for the UN forces or had been taken by the ROK army. Since other local warehouses held the reduced local grain crop, this building stood empty.

The structure stood a few blocks from the center of the village, adjacent to a field on its north side and next to a small mill and tannery on the south. It smelled of the decades of ripe grain that has passed through its portals, earthy and sweet. Warfinger believed the space would do. It just needed work.

As the Colonel continued his examination of the Tongdudong-ni warehouse, a vehicle pulled to a stop outside the large sliding doors. A dark blue 1939 Buick sedan settled to a stop and a Korean man in a blue serge suite left the driver's seat and opened the rear door for a short, portly Korean woman who descended from the car carrying a large rattan handbag. She was dressed in white shirt and navy blue slacks and daintily spat out tobacco-tinged spittle into the dusty road beneath her feet.

This was Warfinger's first meeting with Auntie Soo. He had not expected a dumpy, gray haired Korean woman who looked as though she should be frying noodles on a street corner in Seoul. He began to doubt the recommendations of his friend in I Corps and the commander of the Criminal Investigation Division in Seoul. They told him that she had her fingers in many pies, was well connected with the Rhee government, and was involved with the Kkangpae, gangsters and thugs in Seoul and Pusan. She was wealthy and had the reputation of being an astute businesswoman. By reputation, he thought, she would be a perfect business partner.

Given her reputation, Warfinger expected a Dragon Lady—svelte, beautiful, perhaps smoking a cigarette in a long holder, exuding danger. Watching this middle-aged, frumpy, tobacco chewing woman move toward him on the arm of her driver, he was disappointed. However, she had arrived as promised to discuss a vaguely described business arrangement relayed by a mutual friend. It was time to talk business.

Two weeks earlier, Warfinger experienced a Eureka moment when a series of ideas, impressions, and incidents coalesced in his mind and the "plan" sprang forth, fully formed and iridescent, in the gloomy confines of his cubicle in the officers' latrine. It was simplicity itself, and offered solutions to a multitude of problems that plagued the division. It would certainly boost troop morale, reduce the incidence of VD, provide a form of recreation along the lines of "theater and parties," and enhance the budget for other projects that might otherwise be out of reach of Special Services. How straightforward! How elemental!

Special Services would sponsor a house of prostitution, which would be run to the highest standards of cleanliness and hygiene.

"That, Buck, in a nutshell, is the idea," he told Major Adder. "Not only will it eliminate several local problems, it can be used as an incentive for the troops. The more you consider it, the sky's the limit."

Buck Adder was on board immediately. He was tallying both the business aspects and the financial prospects as Warfinger expanded on his plan.

When Warfinger finished, Adder said, "You know, the F.B.I. counted towels and sheets and customers who visited Al Capone's houses of ill repute in Chicago to convict him of tax evasion. I think I have a record of those calculations and could make up a business plan pretty quick. But just off the top of my head it seems an extremely sound venture. How were we planning to fund it?"

Warfinger was ready. "That's an interesting question and I thought about it in my head. I could advance some from my savings and I suppose Special Services could invest a little. I was considering making the investment available to other officers..."

"I suppose that's possible."

"Or we could get a local Korean partner to help with the money and management. What the hell, with a war just over and lots of dollars and hwan floating around, somebody's got to have a pile of money. That's what I plan to work on."

Adder agreed with the wisdom of that approach and promised to put a sharp pencil to paper, in strictest confidence of course. The next morning, after completing his usual daily report on the situation at Special Services, he unrolled a sheaf of papers and pointed excitedly to numbers in the bottom row. His voice was pitched toward falsetto range and his breathing was labored.

"The R.O.I. is spectacular. Based on extremely conservative estimates of customer servicing, employee costs plus benefits, and assuming a price level that would not put the competition out of business, thereby averting unpleasant repercussions, we recoup the investment in less than three months. And we would be creating excellent job opportunities for indigenous personnel. Sir, this is a project where everyone wins!"

Warfinger was pleased. "Let's go for it!"

The two Colonels sat across from each other on the veranda outside the Officers' Club. Each held a glass with a generous splash of whiskey and, in a momentary break in the conversation, they gazed across the olive drab tents in the headquarters compound to the surrounding hills that showed the first blush of fall colors. Warfinger had just exposed Cutter to the delicate aspects of his latest project and the doctor mulled it over while sipping his drink.

"There's no question we could arrange to test the employees at least weekly for contagious diseases," Cutter said. "We have the personnel and facilities readily available here. And I'm sure that the enlisted and young officers who presently perform short arm inspections would welcome a change from that duty. I also have in mind a nurse who could assist in examinations. Principally, I am interested in the welfare of the men and there is no doubt that the project you have in mind would further that objective. Have you considered ensuring that our men use proper protection?"

"It goes without saying that all employees would be trained in that area. There would be no exceptions in that regard."

Colonel Cutter finished his drink. "Certainly looks as though the project would significantly reduce the Division's incidence of disease. That wouldn't go unnoticed at I Corps. You know, we get rated in things like that."

"That certainly makes sense."

Cutter leaned across the table and confided, "There may be some hard cases who could object to this project because it is slightly unorthodox. I trust it will proceed in a confidential way."

"It will be strictly need to know, need to know."

"Then I believe we should proceed. You'll let me know when our services will be required."

Warfinger walked briskly through the warehouse door to greet the Korean woman.

"Mrs. Soo, thank you for coming all this way to meet with me. There are some chairs and a bench just inside the door where you could see the building and we could discuss the details of this project."

Auntie Soo joined the officer on a folding chair while Kim lingered by the Buick. She settled, moving her shoulders to test the most comfortable position and placed the handbag on her lap. From the bag, she extracted a lidded, silver cup that served, during their conversation, as a spittoon.

She rubbed the bridge of her nose and blinked before giving Warfinger an undisguised look of appraisal. She appeared satisfied. In careful English, she said, "These days it is not a long ride here from Seoul. The roads are much improved and the car is comfortable. Now, since it is becoming late, please tell me about your plans for this whorehouse."

The Colonel was slightly upset with her bold description of his project. In his mind, it was a much loftier endeavor, a place of succor for his troops organized in a proper military way. Nevertheless, he explained the fundamental aspects of the project. Auntie Soo nodded encouragingly as he spoke and reviewed most carefully the assumptions and numbers provided by Major Adder. She suggested the projections seemed slightly optimistic, but was in basic agreement with them.

"You have engaged my interest, Colonel. Exactly what sort of partnership were you offering?"

"We were planning to arrange the proper transport of potential customers and maintain order and discipline with our people. Of course, it is clear that we would manage all medical matters. We would also provide assistance with the construction and design of the facility and would help with reviewing the employees, both workers and support staff."

"That is all quite clear. And what would you expect from me?"

Warfinger shifted in his chair and summoned his most confiding expression.

"It would be awkward for the military to make a direct investment in the project. We were expecting the local investor to arrange for the lease of this building, absorb the cost of construction, help with the maintenance, and, of course, help hire and manage the personnel."

"I see. And how would income and disbursements be handled?" The silver cup received a donation.

"I guess there would be a cashier, and Major Adder, who worked up the project numbers, has volunteered to take care of disbursements. We can be flexible on that issue."

Damned inscrutable Asians, thought Warfinger, her expression hasn't changed one bit all though this discussion. Auntie Soo leaned back in her chair and asked, "What did you have in mind about the ownership arrangement? What would my share be?"

"Major Adder and I thought a sixty/forty split, with forty for you, would be quite fair." He was prepared to accept an even split but he considered himself a sharp trader and wanted to leave room for negotiation.

"Thank you. I believe I now understand the project fully. Let me consider it for a few moments and I will give you my response."

She left the Colonel and walked slowly to the car where Kim awaited with a bottle of beer he had removed from a cooler in the trunk. Auntie Soo climbed into the back seat and allowed Kim to pour her a drink. She looked at the ceiling of the car as she drank. After some moments, she pulled herself together and rejoined Warfinger.

Calmly she said, "You are proposing an extremely risky project. Should your generals ever learn of it, it will be shut down immediately and all involved will be considered criminals, military and Korean alike. You are planning to abuse young Korean women and endanger their future. Security will probably be as porous as an old sponge and white envelopes must be sent to many of our officials. And I am expected to trust the words of a waegukin whom I have never met before, even though your friends in Seoul speak highly of you as a man of substance. For these reasons, I tell you this is a very hazardous business proposition."

Warfinger had allowed these aspects of his project to filter to the back of his mind where they lingered unconsidered, like an old college text gathering dust on a shelf. Now that Mrs. Soo had highlighted them, his main concern was that he might have to search for another partner.

"I'm sorry that you feel that way about it," he offered.

"Fortunately, I have some experience in this business and I would be willing to participate and make my contacts and know-how available, but not for the paltry share you propose. After all, you will really need my help in attracting and managing the girls and dealing with our country's officials. That is much more difficult than military maneuvers."

She spat delicately into the silver cup.

"I would consider joining this project for an eighty percent share and would have one of my people work as the cashier."

Much relieved, Warfinger realized that haggling was afoot. After cordial but protracted negotiation, they settled share ownership. Auntie Soo would own sixty-one and a half per cent and joint oversight of the money coming in.

As his new partner departed in the Buick, Warfinger congratulated himself on his astute business acumen. From a simple thought in the officers' latrine he had generated the beginnings of a venture that promised wonderful things for all concerned. He felt sure of its success, its potential as a business model to be copied throughout the peninsula. He was eager to report to the others interested in the venture. The thing is moving ahead!

Auntie Soo was wasting no time, either. She promised that she and her team would return in a few days to begin converting the dusty warehouse into a classy pleasure palace.

CHAPTER 45

MIDNIGHT
REQUISITIONS

♦ ♦ ♦

THE FIRST THING TO COME off the back of the truck parked in the orphanage courtyard was a Herman Nelson heater that Scott and Shit
Dad carefully maneuvered to the ground. It had seen better days, but
Sergeant Pangluss had tested it and was sure it would be suitable for its
intended purpose. Lamar Trenchant pulled odd lengths of galvanized
pipe from the bed of the truck and Sergeant Pangluss carried a canvas
bag of plumbing tools to the foyer of the orphanage where Amelia
Chapel observed their activities.

"Okay, beautiful lady," said Scott in his best bedroom manner,
"Show me where the Sergeant left the stuff the last time he was here."

Amelia laughed at the "beautiful lady" line and directed Scott to
a vacant room in the back of the orphanage. It had been selected,
said Sergeant Pangluss, for its proximity to the stream and because it,
like most construction in the village, provided easy access to the open
space beneath. Shit Dad and the Sergeant had deposited a number
of "surplus" items there during the previous week, and the two now
examined the materials and agreed that had everything needed. Scott
trundled up two tanks of welding gas to prepare for the work ahead.

Amelia divided her time that Saturday morning between supervising the orphans' mama sans and watching the G.I.s on their mysterious mission. By about noon, when the soldiers had placed a siphon

and filter in an underwater cage in the stream and converted an aircraft fuel tank into a boiler, Amelia knew they were doing what American soldiers do so well. They were converting an unlikely array of scrounged, "found," and "surplus" items into whatever was needed. They were using the improbable to create the impossible, as the commander of the Engineering Battalion was fond of saying.

Amelia guessed that, after months of hand pumping water and heating it on a kerosene burner, the good Samaritans in olive fatigues were creating hot running water for the orphanage. She had not believed it could be possible and joined the work crew to express her deep thanks.

"You're completely welcome, Amelia," said Sergeant Pangluss. "In one of his write-ups, Wylie said you could use a lot of things, including hot water, and I took that as a personal challenge. Scott and Shit Dad are around most times and I sort of infected them with the idea. Lamar, he's just kind of mopey lately and needed something to fill his time off. Also he's turned out to be a pretty fair scrounger."

The team accepted the coffee Amelia offered, along with some Korean sweet cakes prepared by the orphanage cook. It was the best coffee they had tasted in weeks, principally because it had been brewed in a percolator Amelia had found in Seoul, not in a fifteen-gallon drum.

"Now, it looks like we're not going to get this all done today, but we should have it buttoned up tomorrow," said the Sergeant as the work continued.

They modified the Herman Nelson to heat water in the aircraft tank. Pieces of galvanized pipe bristled from the tank and snaked to locations under the orphanage, to the kitchen, bathrooms, and Pangluss' secret pride, a shower featuring a stainless steel head he had liberated from the Engineer Battalion.

Late in the day, they tested the pumping system created with three truck water pumps running on belts attached to a North Korean motorcycle engine. Scott had almost completed a relay to coordinate the pump and heater functions. Shit Dad and Lamar concerned themselves with the niceties of wastewater disposal, creating an outflow downstream. As they left, Amelia waved them good-bye with complete admiration for all they had accomplished.

The next morning, the four plus Wylie returned. He was recognized as an expert marksman, but plumbing and similar trades were not his strong point. However, he contributed by hauling pipe, cutting through flimsy walls and partitions and holding items and tools as required.

Pure altruism had not brought Wylie there that morning. He wanted Amelia to know he helped. It's fine to spread the word about the needs of the orphanage, he thought, but hands on participation feels like the manly thing to do. He did not yet feel confident enough to approach Amelia directly, even though he sensed that she was more than fond of him. His internal swagger evaporated as the Executive Director popped in and out, offering refreshment and words of praise.

Was she smiling at me, wondered Wylie? Did her hand linger over mine when she handed me the coffee?

Back at the truck, hauling pipe, he thought, what is this, sophomore year in high school? I'm a soldier, goddamit, and a Sergeant to boot. But, attracted as he was to the red-haired Amelia, he still felt awkward and confused when she came near.

"Now that you two knuckleheads have managed to haul this fine piece of Korean slate to the corner, you might think about turning it over so the right side is up," said Pangluss to Shit Dad and Wylie. Sheepishly, they did as bid. Scott and the motor pool Sergeant shaped and grooved the stone with an engine-grinding tool, creating a "mother hunchin first class piece of slate shower floor" according to Scott. Within an hour, the fixture was completed. It rivaled anything in the officers' showers at Headquarters and the stainless-steel showerhead reflected the noonday light in circular patterns around the room, dancing on Amelia's chin as she watched water descend for the first time.

"Awesome, absolutely fabulous," she enthused, and she ushered in the mama sans and some of the children to marvel at this glory of American ingenuity – indoor plumbing! Little Kim, grown steadier since Wylie last saw him, rushed into the water, screeching with delight and gargling warm water in his open mouth before racing after two other little boys with the intention of spraying them with its contents.

After testing the system, the men returned tools and the remaining surplus supplies to the truck. It was unlikely that items obtained through midnight requisition would be returned to their origins. Sergeant Pangluss believed that possession was eleven tenths of the law except, of course, for his materials that found their way into other's hands.

Lately, though, the advent of more rigorous accounting practices and the requirement that officers and noncoms actually sign receipts when items were moved in and out of their control challenged the freewheeling practices during combat. Bureaucracy always tried to stifle entrepreneurship, believed the Sergeant, and that's why God created the untraceable barter system he and other motor pool noncoms employed.

Pangluss had almost an acre of used vehicles and other parts, which, accumulated during combat, had no paper trail and never existed. There was a lively trade among motor pools in nonexistent parts. Pangluss and Scott, with Lamar Trenchant's help, were building a souped up, one hundred and twenty-five horse power modified Jeep to race in the Pusan eighty-eight in the spring. Since they were building it from nonexistent parts, there was sincere concern whether it would run. Technically, they had created the Jeep out of nothing.

Amelia offered lunch as they were preparing to leave. She proved to be an artful scrounger herself, and the toothless mama san who was the orphanage cook made the most of the various comestibles she acquired. The cook's wizardry turned normally outdated and unpalatable K rations into enjoyable stews for the children, and she combined semi-crystallized jams into candy treats for the little ones. For the adult visitors she offered fresh caramelized sliced turnips, rice, K ration hamburger patties magically reconstituted into Swedish meat-balls, a salad of fresh greens, and warm bread. Amelia placed cold Cokes and Ballantine beer beside the aromatic dishes and the soldiers filled their plates more than once.

Shit Dad who, with the collusion of Captain Standrich, had been spending frequent nights with his Korean family, asked for a helping of kimchi from the pot in the corner. There were a number of unorigi-nal comments about sending the mess Sergeant over for cooking les-sons. Amelia continued her effusive praise of their work as she ate with them and the cook beamed at their compliments, showing a grand expanse of darkened gums.

"Did you have any more articles to show me, Sergeant?" she asked Wylie as the soldiers prepared to board the truck.

"Yes, as a matter of fact, I do. I almost forgot," lied Wylie who had searched unsuccessfully for an appropriate opening all morning. He retrieved the envelope he had placed in the truck.

"This may take a little while," he said to Pangluss with an expres-sion conveying the desire that they quickly evacuate the area.

"See you all later," said Shit Dad as the truck pulled away on its return trip to headquarters.

Wylie showed Amelia an article he had clipped from the Army Times that included one of Jim Beam's photos of her bathing an or-phan. She looked both disheveled and extremely pretty.

"That's very impressive, Wylie," she said. "I'm sure all your public relations have done much to improve the life of our little orphans. Thank you so much."

Though appreciative of Wylie's work, Amelia was still enthralled by the idea of running water in the orphanage. She looked over her shoulder toward the interior of the orphanage.

"I'm still blown away by the idea of hot running water here. That's awesome!"

Like a child with a new toy, she inspected the shiny pipes, wash-basins, and spigots bristling in newfound locations. He follower her through the building as she tested each one of the newly installed fixtures. He chuckled at her little grunts of satisfaction as she opened and closed handles and felt water flow over her fingers.

"This is really wonderful," she said, hugging his arm. "But I want to take another look at that shower."

They stood together in the anteroom to the shower, looking at the black slate base still glistening from its water test. Amelia seemed lost in thought, a little smile on her lips, holding Wylie's hand, her eyes fixed on an unknown distant point.

Trying to imagine her thoughts, Wylie guessed this had to be pretty neat, here in this Korean farm village and all, having comforts of home to care for her precious children. Yes, it was a big deal. He was glad that he helped make it happen.

Amelia turned toward Wylie, smiling, and placed a hand against his cheek.

"Wylie, would you like to take a shower with me?"

That unexpected question stunned Wylie. Amid the chaos of electrical impulses in his brain stimulated by her closeness, her hand on his cheek, her green eyes peering into his, her partially opened lips, sweet breath, the question fraught with unexpected promise, he froze. Briefly. Then, somewhere out of the muddled mass between his ears, an unexpectedly sophisticated signal allowed him to say, "Nothing would give me greater pleasure."

Amelia smiled, took his hand, and led him slowly to the bench in the anteroom of the new shower. Wylie, overwhelmed by her offer, unsure of what she expected of him, lost in virginal confusion, stood awkwardly next to her. Eliminating any uncertainty, she unbuckled his web belt and tugged down his fatigue pants. That was the encouragement Wylie needed. He stripped off his boots and clothes and stood naked, pink, and ready, in front of Amelia who, with equal alacrity, had removed her baggy clothes and revealed herself fully to Wylie. She was even more stunning than his fantasy images of her.

Wylie had a spiritual moment as he saw Amelia standing before him. Unclothed, three dimensional, self-assured, perfectly formed, vibrant, and reaching toward him, she seemed like a goddess. Checkerboard sunlight streaming through an adjacent window etched patterns on her fair skin, highlighting russet hair tumbling to her shoulders, her full lips, her breasts, luxurious amber pubic hair, an inner thigh. Joy and lust flushed his cheeks, and he reached for her, bent to kiss her, but she eluded him, laughing as she ran to the shower, tested the temperature of the water, splashing him as he followed. When they were both wet and slippery, she allowed his kiss, which she returned passionately, pressing herself to him.

Later, dozing next to Amelia, he struggled to understand his feelings of tenderness and gratitude toward this lovely young woman. The intensity of his emotions surprised him. He had never felt this way with Judy.

He rested his hand on her shoulder and Amelia turned to him with a sleepy smile. He wanted to hold her forever. No, he wanted more. He wanted to embed all of her in all his senses.

He tasted the skin beneath her chin and by her earlobe. It had a mild salty flavor that reminded him of plump oysters and ocean breezes. He closed his eyes and concentrated on the warmth rising from her body, feeling it on his cheeks, the backs of his hands. She smelled of peaches, lemons, and lobster.

Lightly stroking her thigh, brushing against the tightly curled triangle of hair, he listened to the soft slither of his palm gliding over her milky skin. He heard her quick intake of breath as he touched a tender spot. He focused on the shadows playing in the hollow of her neck, the soft tawny hairs on her forearm, sunlight playing on the silky skin of her lower back, the reddish freckles on her left breast, and the sweet, gentle curve along her thigh.

He wished he were talented enough to capture her as a sculptor or painter might—to preserve her for the ages, to make her eternal, his

Venus, his Giaconda. As he continued to take detailed inventory, she raised her arms and turned to him.

His Venus burrowed her face in the hairs of his chest and gently tugged at them with her teeth. Time for reflection had ended.

CHAPTER 46

TAKING CHARGE

◆ ◆ ◆

DICK HERON SENT A TELEGRAM to his wife that asked her to stop writing. He was coming home! He had completed his service in Korea and would rotate back to CONUS and discharge within days. In local parlance he was a "short short timer" who would be home "mo skochie."

The evening after Heron received his orders, Wylie toasted him at the NCO club and thanked him for his friendship and guidance. Wylie knew he would miss his friend and mentor and asked, after three rounds of drinks, for any final words of wisdom. After serious consideration, Heron leaned across their table and said, "I only have three little words for you: don't fuck up. No more mistakes like that Thailand thing."

Wylie accepted the sage advice without challenge. On leaving the club the two young men shook hands and exchanged an awkward hug, both pretending their feelings for each other resulted from too much alcohol.

On the day he left, Dick Heron said his farewells to all in the office and had words of encouragement for each of those he had worked with for many months. Everyone experienced a sense of loss for, though there were promises to look him up, get together, and keep in touch, no one truly expected that to happen. Once engulfed by life away from Korea, whether as a civilian or a soldier, service in the land of the morning calm soon became a faded memory.

Soon after Dick Heron heaved his duffel bag aboard a truck and headed toward Seoul on the first leg of his way to San Francisco, Sergeant Wrinkle presented Wylie with orders designating him a Staff Sergeant. Receiving his second "rocker" within days of his overpowering liaison with Amelia was, he thought, like hitting a homer with the bases loaded, or winning the football lottery twice in a row.

He was pleased with his new rank but realized that his heightened responsibility and visibility as a noncom offered greater opportunities to fuck up. He understood Dick Heron's advice. He would certainly have to be very careful and work harder to avoid mishaps. It was a sobering thought. On a brighter side, his base pay increased to over $150 a month— almost twice as much as when he arrived in Korea. He looked forward to sharing his newfound wealth with Amelia.

With Sergeant Heron's departure, Wylie's priority was to rebuild the P.I.O. staff. As Captain Standrich pointed out, normal rotation home had taken its toll. They were short at least three staffers and needed another regimental reporter. Wylie was responsible for recruiting but he was not sure how good he would be at that.

Shit Dad's nemesis, Lt. Myron Bland, had exhausted all opportunities to engage in military inspections, and his repeated requests for a new assignment tried his Colonel's patience. Since he seemed not to fit particularly well in any other division position, G-1 assigned him to assist Captain Standrich in the belief that he would not embarrass himself. The Public Information Office had a long-standing opening for this position that no other young officers seemed interested in pursuing. Bland, however, considered it an opportunity to advance his military career.

Belying an imperfect understanding of the P.I.O. mission, the Lieutenant reported dressed for action, and entered the office helmeted, with a sidearm, and a grenade clipped to the left pocket of his starched fatigue jacket. Captain Standrich, who was there briefly to welcome him, explained that grenades were unwelcome, much to the relief of the enlisted men. Disarmed, the Lieutenant took a desk toward the rear of the Quonset hut where he sulked for a while. In the following days, he spent considerable time on the telephone and made a show of glaring at Shit Dad whenever the Private entered the office.

Captain Standrich seemed to be dividing his duty hours between off base inspections with Shit Dad and working on his skeet range. Lieutenant Bland was very eager to get "hands on" experience in the world of public information and, since Captain Standrich was unavailable as a mentor, Wylie was obliged to answer many inquiries about office procedure.

After a few days of continuing interruptions, he ventured into the field of personal diplomacy to point Bland in other directions. First, he suggested Bland inhabit the Captain's office to review stacks of copy that Wylie managed to uncover. Second, he asked the Lieutenant to interview locally available women who worked at MASH or the Red Cross for a forthcoming feature story about *WOMEN IN COMBAT!*

Bland readily agreed with those suggestions. Hobnobbing with women under the guise of official business was, in his view, equivalent to a paid up hunting license. Wylie was thinking more in terms of fishing. Once the hook was set, he encouraged the Lieutenant to engage in research for the elusive *WOMEN IN COMBAT!* feature by reviewing background information available in issues of last years' Army Times. It was a painstaking process, but Bland felt equal to the task. Quiet reigned, for a while.

Sergeant Oppenheimer's replacement at the repple depple in Uijongbu was not as helpful as his predecessor was. Wylie hoped he could help identify potential candidates for the P.I.O. but the Corporal apparently expected Wylie to do the sorting himself.

The Corporal said, "See, Sergeant, those masterminds stateside send any young trooper with an infantry, artillery, armor, engineer or any other damn John Wayne type specialty over here. Those who have special skills and training end up in Japan, Germany or never leave the states. So you're gonna have to search through all these gung ho types for something that fits your public information world. I've got about four hundred and fifty personnel records in the tent over there if you want to look them over. And good luck with that."

"I think maybe I'll just talk to the guys who are here," said Wylie. "Some of them may admit they have talents beyond blowing things up."

The Corporal tapped on the PA microphone and called the men in the depot to assembly. Wylie stood on a raised platform in front of the office, looked at the fresh recruits from CONUS, and tried public speaking.

"I know you all are eager to get assigned to front line duty and spend the next sixteen months behind sand bags squinting across the DMZ at enemy troops squinting back at you. You must be looking forward to palling around with the ROK troops on your flank. You'll be treated to frequent inspections and will enjoy our beautiful Korean winter from the comfort of your bunkers, and you'll be the first to test out the new Mickey Mouse boots that are now supposed to actually keep your feet warm this winter. And, of course, you will be treated to all those Andy Hardy movies to watch in your spare time."

The assembled recruits looked confused. They wondered who was this big mouth asshole and what was he getting at. He talked like a non-com but the stuff he was saying, was it like, whatchamacallit, sarcasm?

Wylie had their attention, and he continued by introducing himself and explaining that he was looking for recruits who could write and were interested in sports, current events and history. He suggested that working at headquarters might be more pleasant than assignment to a line outfit.

Some of the recruits were intrigued by Wylie's pitch and his salesmanship. He concluded by saying he would be in the G-2 tent ready to interview anyone interested. As he left the parade ground, about a dozen recruits broke off and wandered to the G-2 tent.

By noon, Wylie had settled on four candidates, all draftees, and all with more journalistic experience than he had on arriving in Korea.

John Takei, a Nisei from Los Angeles had spent two years in UCLA working as a feature writer for the college paper. He was short and round.

John Orton was a hundred and forty-pound six-footer, prematurely bald, yet Wylie's age, who had edited his high school paper in Fargo, North Dakota. Orton had worked for a few years in construction before his draft number came up. He was a clerk typist and Wylie was impressed with his use of language.

Both recruits answered to the name of "Jack." For simplicity, the P.I.O. team referred to them as "High Jack" and "Low Jack."

Tiny Brewer was also a six-footer, but weighed twice as much as High Jack. He had played football at Duke and was a walking sports encyclopedia with a colorful vocabulary, full of "popped it in the keyhole, might ought to git that one, that dog won't hunt, tell you what, and kicked the leather off'n it" expressions. He would be a great replacement for Barry who was leaving in about six weeks. Wylie's hand disappeared as Tiny "shook on the deal." If Wylie ever needed a bodyguard, he thought, look no farther than Tiny!

Private First Class Jefferson W. Jefferson, a track star from the University of Texas at Austin, had the biggest feet Wylie had ever seen.

"Yeah, I know," said Jefferson. "Everything is big in Texas, including my feet. The Army had to search for days to find boots that fit me. But, I'll tell you what…. I'm a proud black clodhopper from the lone star state!"

What impressed Wylie, aside from Jefferson's easy manner, was that he had been an English major and published a story in the Saturday Evening Post about the origin of "Hook 'em horns," the UT battle cry.

Oppenheimer's replacement efficiently cut orders for the four recruits and, within an hour, he attached mimeographed papers to their personnel folders. The group gathered near a space heater to await the truck that would carry them and their gear to Division headquarters. Wylie noticed that Jefferson and Tiny were engaged in lively conversation while the two Jacks were reading letters. Low Jack was using

Army issue glasses that kept slipping down his nose. Well, here we go, thought Wylie, it's my first try as a recruiter, and I hope I've made good choices. As it turned out, three out of four were fine.

Shit Dad offered his Cajun congratulations to the new members of the staff and helped them settle in on their spring-loaded steel cots with real mattresses. His syrupy Louisiana accent and folksy expressions charmed the recruits. Kim, the houseboy, was happy with his new charges; he received five dollars a month from each tent resident and the recent departures had affected his monthly pay. He was particularly impressed with Jefferson's huge boots and joked about charging extra to keep them polished. Having someone who would look after their laundry, run errands, maintain the tent, and provide occasional illicit goods was a pleasant novelty for the replacements. Maybe service in Frozen Chosen wouldn't be so bad after all.

"We're family, now," Shit Dad told Wylie that evening as they walked toward the mess tents. "Me and the Captain, cuz we married sisters. Far as I know that makes us in-laws, wouldn't you say?"

"You bet," said Wylie as he waited for the complete story to unfold.

"The Captain, he's a good man, but a bit sheepish, you know? He's been fooling with Mai Lee for most five months now and I believe she finally told him he wasn't getting any more unless there was some ceremony involved and, I 'spect, some financial exchange. She wasn't pregrant or nothing, but she needed a Co-mit-ment. Last Sunday the Captain gives in, and they have the ceremony up on the hill, 'cept the Captain stays in his civvies, doesn't wear the classy white bath robe like I did, but he's sure as hell married Korean style. There was the smoke and the food and the funny dancing. Oh, yeah, we brothers now!"

This turn of events presented complications. Despite Shit Dad's protestations that he was only unofficially married and not in violation of military strictures, Wylie knew otherwise. If Captain Standrich was following Shit Dad along this slippery matrimonial path, its discovery could well affect the well-being of any recently promoted non-com who ignored or facilitated this gross infraction of regulations.

This potential Foo Bird, he reckoned, could drop a load of shit on me. Sergeant Heron left at a good time, he thought.

What was the worst that could happen? He might be reduced in grade, chewed out, reassigned to scut duty. He shrugged it off. Stan Wrinkle was right. Once you've been reamed by experts you are inoculated against serious concern about the risk of future screw ups. He quickly decided to support the questionable judgment of the two bridegrooms and do his best to keep their secrets. He was sure that would not be a problem as far as the Captain was concerned. The garrulous Shit Dad, on the other hand, might be more difficult.

As they turned away from each other to reach their respective mess halls, Shit Dad added, "It's a comfort to know the Captain will still be here when I'm supposed to rotate in a couple months. I need to figure out how to stay in Korea, man. What with baby Pierre and all. This Army has so many nonsense rules they make my head ache. But I know we'll figger it out. See you, man."

Wylie hoped he was not included among the "we" in Shit Dad's need to figure things out. Wylie foresaw fresh disasters ahead.

CHAPTER 47

REFUGE

◆ ◆ ◆

THANKSGIVING AT THE 53ᴿᴰ INFANTRY in 1953 ushered in cold winds and a
dusting of snow. It was time to break out the parkas and wool fatigues
freshly arrived from the United States. Wylie managed a barter arrangement with the supply Sergeant who issued the warm fatigues. He
exchanged a carton of Chesterfields, an acceptable form of currency
in Uijongbu, for a wool shirt in a size that could wrap around a certain
red-haired girl. He added cranberries, canned pumpkin pie filling,
and a bottle of California Chardonnay to his footlocker in anticipation of his next visit to the orphanage, scheduled for Thanksgiving
evening.

Early during Thanksgiving week, Lieutenant Bland had an interview with the head nurse of the MASH unit, Major Barbara Bernard,
who agreed to participate in the elusive WOMEN IN COMBAT!
feature. The Major was tall and angular, with penetrating eyes that
glared through thick- lensed glasses. She adopted an imperious manner to avoid the heartbreak of caring too much for her wounded patients. Eschewing rank, she asked her patients to call her "Barbara,"
but she seemed so formidable that all her patients called her Major
Barbara.

The head nurse enjoyed her conversations with the young
Lieutenant; she thought she recognized appealing insecurity under
his false bravado. This morning, she told him about harrowing medical emergencies that Bland might incorporate in the section that he

planned to call "grace under pressure." He originally hoped to find a nurse named "Grace" but, with Wylie's help, abandoned that idea.

"Fortunately we haven't had too many emergencies lately," said the Major. "We're grateful that there hasn't been that much excitement here since the armistice. These days we get a lot of patch jobs because of road accidents, and then there are the normal clusters of diseases, social and otherwise. Now that cold weather is here, we're expecting more chest infections."

Bland was clearly not excited about chest infections, so the Major tried to recall more interesting events.

"Come to think of it, we almost had a drowning here," she said. "Some loony tank driver drove a big ass Pershing tank into the river by Uijongbu when we had that heavy rain last week. It was stranded right in the middle, with rushing water up to the turret. The crew managed to swim to shore except that the current sucked the gunner under for a while. We took care of him and he was okay. But the thing was that the driver was dead certain he was driving an amphibious vehicle. I had to sedate him because he was telling me all about the colors he was hearing. Doctor Marcus thought he might be in shock, but he was good the next day and he and the gunner went back to their regiment. It was kinda strange, though."

Bland made note of this incident and asked Major Barbara what she did for recreation and if she had any hobbies. She confessed to being a darts player, having perfected her game while stationed in England. In fact, she was division champion in a not very crowded field. The Major offered to teach Bland the game at the Officers' Club that evening.

The following day Wylie conferred with Bland in office and the Lieutenant went over his notes, which included the peculiar tank incident. To both it seemed like just another screw up; the driver probably had too much to drink the night before.

Wylie put it out of his mind until later that day when he received a call from the INS correspondent at the Seoul press billet, Fred Able.

"Hey Wylie when you coming to Seoul? I believe you owe me a drink."

"And why would that be?"

"Heard you got another rocker. With all the bread you're earning now you can afford to buy me a dollop of good scotch."

"Too right, as Alistair would say."

"But aside from that," Fred added, "I was just calling to clue you in on some weird shit that's happening at I Corps. There's some new kind of jungle juice going around that causes hallucinations and other illnesses, and the Brass was worried the North Koreans are putting stuff in the water. But my reporting indicates it's connected to some civilians from Fort Detrick in Maryland who were interviewing North Korean sympathizers and some of our own POWs. I'm calling my friends in Public Information offices in some of the divisions to see whether this is just an I Corps thing or whether it's also in other places. I know you've got one ear on the railroad tracks up there so if you hear anything, I'd appreciate a call."

"Be glad to do it, Fred."

He hung up and was about to tackle an unruly mess of teletypes on his desk when he recalled part of his conversation with the Lieutenant that morning.

Did he say the tank driver was hearing colors?

That afternoon Wylie walked along the snow-covered road leading to the little shops outside the camp gates and stopped in front of the store that announced "KOREAN MARKETT" in bright red letters. The proprietor, Mrs. Park, planted herself firmly on a chair in front, absorbing as much of the afternoon sunlight as she could while wrapped in a black dyed G.I. overcoat. Wylie held out a wool fatigue shirt and indicated where he wanted words embroidered. Mrs. Park held out samples of embroidery that magically emerged from an inner pocket of her coat, and Wylie selected bold yellow letters encapsuled in a gold braid border. He had typed the desired words on a sheet of paper and the storekeeper promised completion that evening. Wylie glimpsed two women pumping rockers below ancient sewing machines in the back of the store and was amused; he remembered his grand-mother working such a machine when he was little.

The next day Wylie learned that, while combat may have ceased, physical danger had not. Soon after the armistice, Communist sym-pathizers in the south formed small bands to harass the ROK army, engage in terrorist tactics and steal anything of value. The U.S. Army referred to them generically as "guerillas" and formed special teams to identify and eradicate them. Mid-morning, Tully McGregor called to tell Wylie guerillas had staged coordinated attacks on a convoy of supply trucks heading from the Seoul area toward the 53rd and a warehouse for medical supplies. He reckoned that Shit Dad could drive Wylie to the site of the convoy attack in about half an hour, and gave directions. Wylie called the Signal Corps and requested a photographer.

Wylie and Jefferson piled into the P.I.O. Jeep and Shit Dad barely stopped for Corporal Beam at the Signal Corps tent before heading through Uijongbu to the site of the attack. The road was particularly treacherous that day as the shaded parts were slippery with ice and the sunny, open areas had thawed and become muddy. "Just slip slidin' along," sang the Shit Dad as he navigated from one slippery patch to the next until he stopped at the crest of a hill overlooking three crippled trucks on the road below.

The front truck, tipped on its side, slid part way down a ravine, and its cargo of olive drab boxes spilled from the back like broken pottery. The other two trucks were smoking, one from the engine compart-ment, and the other from the back. MPs were on the scene and Wylie noted two tarp-covered objects lying beside the road. An ambulance suddenly appeared behind them and Shit Dad pulled the Jeep to the side so it could pass. The large Red Cross in the white circle slid past, and medics jumped out to attend to a soldier crumpled in the front seat of one of the trucks.

"Try not to include those bodies in your shots," said Wylie, knowing that military censors would reject any photograph of death or serious injury. Beam understood the policy but planned to include them in the few films he would keep for himself. He hoisted his Speed Graphic and box of film slides to record the gruesome event.

The two reporters interviewed the MPs and the uninjured driver. An anti-tank mine immobilized the first truck, and a handful of guerillas armed with grease guns and army carbines attacked from a culvert across the road, killing a driver and his assistant. Another driver was severely wounded while the third driver and assistant returned fire with their carbines. They scrambled down the ravine and took cover among fir saplings. The remaining assistant driver had been resting in the back of the first truck and became unconscious as the vehicle tipped over. Apparently, the attackers thought he was dead and he did nothing to persuade them otherwise.

"Them little bastards was looking for medical supplies, all right. I could hear a couple of them yelling 'penecirrin' and ripping open the boxes with the red crosses on them," said the uninjured driver. "They didn't have anything but themselves to haul stuff away and they ended up grabbing a few boxes and carrying them away on their backs with those lines that go around their foreheads and to the back. They tossed these Molotov cocktail things in front and back but only a couple of them lit up. The damn thing was over in just a few minutes. And here I thought we were okay driving on these roads back here."

The MPs rerouted what little traffic there was and confirmed the substance of the driver's report. Engineers with tow trucks appeared and a crew gathered spilled contents and winched the wrecked truck upright. Jim Beam photographed the activity and, when the road was cleared, they returned to the Jeep and the 53rd.

Wylie did not believe some mastermind had orchestrated simultaneous attacks; the assault on the supply trucks, though deadly, seemed an amateur affair focused on obtaining medicines unavailable in the north. On the other hand, he learned that medical supplies like syringes, surgical kits and, of course, penicillin and other antibiotics had disappeared from the regimental warehouse. The guerillas had been busy, but the special teams charged with eliminating them were busy too.

On Thanksgiving, Wylie and the P.I.O. team chronicled the day's events. The Army determined to provide the best possible Thanksgiving dinner to the troops. Even those on the line received a turkey dinner with all the trimmings, in marked contrast to the previous year when vicious fighting had thwarted such efforts. Headquarters mess Sergeants drew on supplies of frozen turkeys, and heaped drumsticks, mashed potatoes, squash, stuffing, cranberry sauce, and pumpkin pie on mess trays for a staggering noontime dinner.

Wylie and the P.I.O. staffers busily interviewed soldiers throughout the division for "hometowners" and Wylie experimented with his new Nikon 35-millimeter camera to picture soldiers with crossed drumsticks and happy smiles. It had been a busy day and he looked forward to Amelia's company that evening. On his way to the orphanage, troubling thoughts about the "weird shit" at I Corps and the guerilla attacks briefly intruded. They vanished when he saw beckoning lights through the frosty panes of the orphanage windows. He approached the doorway with a little duffel bag under his arm.

As usual, little children played in the antechamber and complained when their caregivers pulled them away to get ready for bed. Amelia appeared, motioned Wylie to a hidden corner of her "office" and greeted him with a warm kiss. Then she watched as Wylie unpacked treasures from his bag, inventorying them as he spread them on her desk in the alcove.

"Here's a delicate California white wine to go with these purloined turkey parts," he said, "that will go very well with the tins of smoked oysters recently harvested from the briny waters off Japan. Delivering an entire pumpkin pie was beyond my pay grade, but I've discovered that the pumpkin pie filling doesn't really require the pie part. It's good just spooned from the can."

He delivered his monologue imitating a barker he had heard on the boardwalk in Asbury Park, New Jersey, complete with florid gesticulation, and held up an almost full half-gallon tin of cranberry sauce. "This sauce goes perfectly with the turkey...don't worry about the moldy stuff. It comes right off. And here are saltines carefully gleaned from our K rations. I somehow thought that cold mashed potato patties would spoil the mood."

Amelia's giggles bubbled up to laughter as he displayed the saltines on his sleeve like a sommelier showing off the label of a fine wine and she hugged him and stroked the back of his head.

"I have some freshly baked flat bread and some turnips from our winter garden that should go very well with this wonderful feast. Shall we sit by the kitchen fire and have our Thanksgiving?'

"Sure, but there's just one more thing," said Wylie and passed a package wrapped in brown paper to her.

She examined the wool fatigue shirt with the gold braid rectangle over the left front pocket containing, in bold yellow thread, the words "Executive Director." She laughed again, and then her eyes moistened.

"I don't know what to say, Wylie. It's absurdly military and very thoughtful, all at the same time. Thank you very much."

She offered her lips again, and they moved to the warmth of the kitchen to enjoy their holiday dinner. Later, when the wine bottle was empty and the fire had died to glowing embers she modeled her shirt and they practiced exciting new ways to ward off the chill of a Korean Thanksgiving night.

CHAPTER 48

REPORT TO NEW JERSEY

◆ ◆ ◆

BY FREE AIRMAIL
53rd Infantry P.O.I.
November 28, 1953

My Dearest Judy:

You've been so good about writing (three letters in the past week!) that I really feel guilty about not keeping up my end over here. It's really been hectic here this past week, what with the holiday and all, but I'll try to make up for it with a longer letter since it's Saturday afternoon and I have some time to myself. It's really good to hear how much you're enjoying your sophomore year and I think your idea of concentrating on health care subjects is a really good one. I think you dad's right that it wouldn't hurt to have a doctor in the family one day. Anyway, I'm sorry your uncle's abscess has returned. Maybe you can doctor him some day. Also, please congratulate your mom on winning the Sweet Adelines contest. I've always admired her singing voice.

Anyway, I mentioned that I got promoted to staff Sergeant in my last letter and that I took over from Dick Heron who was a nice guy and I will miss him. He taught me a lot. Since then I've been getting into the swing of running the office, even though it isn't as easy as Dick always made it look. The Captain isn't around very much these days but I have a new Lieutenant whose name, funnily enough, is Bland and he is around most of the time. It looks as though we've going to work pretty well together.

I wrote you before that I had my first taste of recruiting for some new staff and it appears I did pretty well, if you believe three out of four is a passing grade. This huge guy named Tiny is our new sports writer and he is terrific. He knows more sports clichés than anyone I've ever met and makes the stuff going on in our regiments sound like big league games. He and Boomer are doing interviews with our players that are very popular, and Tiny is going to I Corps for the "playoffs" this weekend to do what they call "the color." I'm not sure how long I'll get to keep him. Some member of the brass may take a shine to him and he'll be in Seoul or Tokyo. Which is where, Tokyo I mean, I'll be going the second week in January for another TDY. Jules Pike wants to go over things with me and it's more fun doing it in Tokyo than Seoul!

The colored guy from Texas with the huge feet is also working out. He's doing some features on life on the line and he fits right in with the "jive asses" up there. He has had one of his features published by the Army Times already so he's doing quite well. Low Jack is OK too. He's coordinating the stories we get from the regiments and writing about visits from dignitaries. The problem was with the guy we call High Jack, Jack Orton.

I was going to send him to Regiment but I thought he needed some time here to get used to how we operate. I should have suspected something when the first thing he did was buy three bottles of scotch whiskey and stow them in the safe in our supply closet. He told me scotch was the only thing he drank because it had the least fusel oil of all liquors and that it was the fusel oil that caused hangovers. He is totally against hangovers. What I didn't know was that he drank at least a bottle a day, and that he's not like Shit Dad who can really hold his liquor.

So, a couple of nights ago he left our tent to relieve himself at the "piss tube" and we sort of forgot that he never came back until Kim shook me some time after midnight and said he thought "Oton" was in trouble. So Boomer and I climbed into our parkas and boots and went out with flashlights. It was really cold and we found him bent over the piss tube at the waist completely passed out. I believe he would have been frozen stiff by morning if Kim hadn't worried about him. Anyway, he's back at the repple depple now waiting to become someone else's problem. I gave in to Lamar Trenchant and assigned him to the regiment "High Jack" was supposed to report from. So, I'm still short one guy.

There's been some guerilla activity around here lately that's worrisome. Basically, it's bad guys trying to steal supplies, but they managed to kill a couple of our people last week so we are all on alert, and even the P.I.O. staff is keeping weapons handy. I've been told I have to drill our staff, like I could even remember how to do that! I guess we were lulled into a false sense of security the past couple of months. The interesting thing is that a lot of medical supplies are disappearing and my friend, Tully, assumes they are all headed north. One of his jobs is to figure out how they get them there. Not to worry though. The closest I get to medical supplies is when we have short arm inspections. But I will not dwell on that!

The kid has also been helping out some friends at the motor pool with little projects over at an orphanage nearby for partly G.I. little kids. I wrote some stories about what they are doing there and took some pictures of the children with my new Nikon camera and I will send you some when my friend over at the Signal Corps gets around to making up some prints. I also got some photos of this local character named Uncle Ho who carries "honey buckets" or "night soil" (which are euphemisms for you know what!) in these two huge vats set in a cart pulled by a pair of oxen. He goes through the base every day behind those lumbering bulls and then takes the stuff on through Uijongbu. It's not very aromatic but it makes for a very interesting picture.

Frozen Chosen is beginning to live up to its name. We had snow before Thanksgiving and we are all in wool fatigues and parkas these days. Water in our jerry cans is beginning to freeze overnight but there are still Korean women down by the stream doing our wash. I haven't quite figured out how they manage that. But I have warm memories of that cold day we went skiing at Vernon Valley, and the clouds of steam when we talked. And how warm your cheeks were when we came into the lodge. So, cold as it is I still have that picture of you in my mind and warm, even torrid thoughts. I send you my love.

All the best - Wylie

CHAPTER 49

RHYTHM AND BLUES

◆ ◆ ◆

PRIVATE SMUDGE JACKSON AND HIS entourage arrived at 53rd Division headquarters about ten days before Christmas. Colonel Warfinger had persuaded his counterpart at I Corps that his division's soldiers, who were holding the line at the 38th Parallel, would benefit greatly from a Christmas concert by the Rhythm and Blues group. Smudge, like most of his band, was drafted and an astute young officer at Fort Benning, Georgia recognized the Detroit draftee and arranged to have him assigned to a Special Services unit in Japan after he completed eight weeks of basic training.

Except for Haggis O'Toole, Smudge found members of his band among the ranks in the Tokyo area. Leroy Larkin from Chicago played piano, and the properly named two hundred and sixty pound Fatboy Brown strummed the bass. The white member of the group, Honky Lewis from New York, lived for nothing other than playing drums while the cadaverous "mile high" Sergeant Ringle was on leave from the Army band to play sax with Smudge.

Haggis O'Toole managed the band. His anglophile Trinidadian father named him, thinking that Haggis was the proper name of a person. When Haggis was two years old, he and his mother immigrated to Detroit where he met Smudge in the fourth grade. They shared a strong friendship since then.

Less talented than virtuoso Smudge, Haggis nevertheless played guitar with his friend in their high school band. When his friend's musical abilities became better known and he began recording with Savoy Records in Newark, New Jersey, Haggis discovered he had solid business instincts and became Smudge's manager, agent, and best friend.

Haggis was short and slender and, as his mother said, blacker than a coal shovel. When Smudge was drafted and Haggis was not, he volunteered for three years in the regular army on the condition that he would serve with Smudge. The Army honored that condition and the two friends had been together in the army, in almost civilian roles, for a year when they arrived at the 53rd Infantry.

With a nod to Paul Williams and his Hucklebuckers, the group called itself the Tokyo Boogie Buckers and played throughout Japan to enthusiastic military audiences. Once word about the popular band reached other military bases in the Far East Command, they traveled to locations away from Japan. Divisions near the 38th parallel were favored for engagements during Christmas of 1953.

The band, amplifiers, music stands, instruments, and other paraphernalia easily filled an army truck. Haggis and Smudge monitored carefully the loading and unloading of two leather bound cases, one containing Smudge's favorite and backup guitars and the other holding his vintage Jim Walker "Fireball" model plane. Passionate as Smudge was about his guitars, he also enjoyed flying model planes with a control line.

If they found a parade ground or a field near one of their "gigs," Smudge and Haggis would send the balsa and tissue plane model into the air and put it through its paces, zooming gracefully through the air, buzzing like a thousand wasps. With the same dexterity he used to create arpeggios on his guitar, Smudge made the little model perform intricate maneuvers while Haggis tended to let it circle him as he rotated the handle. They always had enthusiastic onlookers as they put the little plane through its paces.

The Boogie Buckers planned to give concerts at each of the three regiments during the next few days before returning to the headquarters area. There they would perform a Christmas Eve concert in the recently completed "Swedish Meat Bowl," which was a large tent with a raised platform facing a gently sloping foothill of the surrounding mountain. A quartet of Herman Nelson heaters would keep the band warm, and VIP benches were in place for the Brass and Press. Powerful lights would illuminate the stage and a sound system would blast their music well beyond Uijongbu.

Wylie poked his head into the band's tent the morning after their arrival and noted a sweet yet acrid smell he had not sensed before. Wylie heard heavy breathing from the slumbering bodies facing the tent walls. The only one who seemed awake was Leroy Larkin sitting on the edge of his cot, rubbing sleep from his eyes. His slender arms looked out of place in the sleeveless "Muscle T" shirt he wore.

He mumbled some curses, noticed Wylie, and said apologetically "Musta toked a little heavy last night. Mouth's like the bottom of a birdcage."

Wylie nodded his head as though he understood and introduced himself. He offered to walk with Larkin to the mess hall for breakfast. Larkin accepted and, in slow motion, pulled on his fatigue shirt, field jacket, and gloves. To the waking figures on the cots he said, "Gonna chow down. See you cats later."

"Up yours, man," growled one body while another exhaled, "Sheeeit."

"The cats are always a little cranky in the morning," he noted, "but they'll be fine when they get their shit together. That's normal when you work at night, right?"

Wylie agreed and enjoyed chatting with Leroy as they walked slowly to breakfast. He discovered that Leroy was interesting, funny and well informed. He listed the places they had entertained since he was drafted, and exposed Wylie to an artist's perspective of army life. Leroy's main complaint was that the army tended to get in the way of making art or, in his case, music. He explained to Wylie that he lived to practice, play, jam with the group, eat, get laid, get high, sleep a little and do it all over again. Worrying about correct dress, saluting, weapons practice, curfews and the like was, like, a drag, man. Wylie was sympathetic, but Leroy's continued enumeration of ways in which the heartless Army interfered with his artistic life was interrupted by the arrival of Smudge and Haggis who entered the mess bleary eyed, thoroughly out of uniform, and in need of something stronger than coffee. However, they grudgingly accepted coffee from the admiring mess sergeant and settled beside Wylie and Leroy. Steam from their mugs of coffee rose to their red-rimmed eyes, which turned curiously to Wylie.

"He's a writer like it says on his shirt, Combat Correspondent," offered Leroy.

"Yes, I'm...."

"Not looking for any combat, bro. Been staying away from that! Louise doesn't like combat," said Smudge.

"Louise?" asked a confused Wylie.

"It's his GIT-ar, man," offered Haggis. "He's just playin' you."

"Yeah, man, it's early," said Smudge." I just be jerking your chain."

Fueled by hot coffee, the conversation among the three continued at a rapid pace, and Wylie realized that somewhere in the past few moments he had completely lost the thread. In preparation for his interview with Smudge, Wylie listened to his recording of "Mazie got the Blues" and Fats Domino's "Ain't that a Shame," involuntarily moving his feet, head and hands with the music. He listened again and decided that he enjoyed R & B. He had also read Smudge's biography on the record jacket, but that cursory research hardly prepared him for the musicians' chatter that included words he had never heard before and musical references he dimly understood. Smudge looked at Wylie's slightly dazed expression and decided the subtle hazing had lasted long enough. He turned his large body to Wylie and held out his hand.

"I'm Charlie Jackson. Everyone calls me 'Smudge.' I'm guessing you're here to interview us."

He admitted that he was, shook Smudge's hand, and introduced himself as "Wylie," which generated guffaws from Haggis.

"You got coyote blood? You catch any roadrunners today?"

Wylie had heard all possible references to the Road Runner cartoon character for the past five years but pretended to laugh at Haggis' originality. He turned toward Smudge to begin his interview, placing his notebook on the table in front of them. Though he had done it many times before, Smudge went over his Detroit background, talked about his first break, and modestly described the popularity of his bestselling records. In answering Wylie's question about hobbies, he waxed eloquent about the mystique of control line flying and promised to show him his Fireball.

"We got to break it off now, man. We have a clarinet player and guitarist we need to audition and go over our material. We like to have local talent play with us on these gigs and it's a boost for the audience to see a couple of their own guys up there with us. You'd be surprised what kind of talent gets drafted."

As they all moved to leave he added, "We'll be jamming in that big Quonset hut tonight. Come on over and we can finish talking. Give you a preview of the show."

He gladly accepted and sorted out his impressions after the big man left. Warm, well- spoken, confident, highly talented. He made Wylie feel as though he had been his friend for a long time. So, thought Wylie, that's what charisma is. I'd like to get some of that.

He returned to the office and reviewed progress of the various assignments posted on the board on the sloping wall of the Quonset hut. He reported items of interest to Lieutenant Bland since Captain Standrich was not available, and reviewed progress on the WOMEN IN COMBAT! feature. The Lieutenant was rapidly losing interest in that project and told Wylie he was thinking about an article on the game of darts in the military. Sure, said Wylie, sounds good. He had not yet mastered Dick Heron's approach to blunting half-assed ideas.

Since he had assigned Low Jack to cover Smudge's concerts at the three regiments, Wylie briefed him on the substance of the morning's interview. He then opened the envelope Jim Beam had left on his desk and sent photos of orphans playing and Uncle Ho driving his oxen to Judy along with a hasty note. He burrowed through teletypes scrolled across his desk and passing out assignments to the staffers. Jesus, he thought as he took a break for coffee and the piss tube, I'm turning into a boring bureaucrat. It's embarrassing. Charisma looks a long way off!

As Wylie opened the door to the rehearsal hall that evening, Smudge and the group were repeating the last bars of "Big Momma's Boogie," which he had composed just before leaving for Korea. Fatboy sweated profusely even in the chill of the hall as he coaxed a hypnotic backbeat from the bass. The new clarinet player riffed the lilting melody for a few bars and Smudge finished the piece with complicated chords that ended abruptly, surprising Wylie. Leroy continued to noodle on the piano even though the piece was over and Wylie noticed a cigarette in the ashtray on the piano. Wylie was not a smoker, but he recognized the unusual smell of the slowly burning cigarette. Leroy puffed deeply and said, "It's just some good weed. We got plenty. You want some?"

The question demanded serious consideration. Though he was on friendly terms with various forms of alcohol and was currently experimenting with rye and ginger, the idea of indulging in what the CID called a "controlled substance" seemed dangerous, though exciting. Curiosity fought with his sense of self-preservation, and curiosity was gaining the upper hand. He rationalized that 1) what the hell, he made it through combat, 2) these guys seemed to show no ill effects from smoking weed, 3) they would probably think he was a pussy if he refused, and 4) this would be a firm step on the path to CHARISMA. He looked at Leroy and said "Sure."

No one doubted Wylie was a pot virgin. They gathered around him like minnows attacking a fallen crumb, explaining proper technique.

He absorbed the advice provided and signaled Leroy he was ready to try it. As instructed, he blew on the glowing tip and sucked the aromatic smoke into his mouth preparing to draw it into his lungs. He gagged and coughed and the smoke streamed through his nose. He sneezed and coughed at the same time and his eyes watered. There was laughter from the band and Smudge said try it again, which he did once the tears left his eyes. This time he succeeded; the warm smoke invaded his lungs and he held it there until he felt near bursting. He exhaled and waited for the promised high, the mild euphoria, avidly watched by the members of the band. And he waited. And he waited some more. He felt exactly the same. Nothing happened.

"Bummer," said Fatso.

"Yeah, sometimes goes that way. It's like you got to build up a reverse resistance."

"It'll be better the next time. You'll see. Want to take another drag?"

Through watery eyes, Wylie shook his head "no." He thanked them for the opportunity but maintained that he needed to finish his interview with Smudge, and they sat together for a while as he added information to his notebook.

Whatever the future held for Wylie, being a pot head would not be in the scenario.

Low Jack reported that the Smudge Jackson concerts were a huge success at the regiments. There were standing ovations and loud demands for encores. The troops had fallen in love with rhythm and blues and Private Charles "Smudge" Jackson was a hero, along with the members of his band. The Stars and Stripes published some of the photos Wylie had taken with his Nikon, and Low Jack and Jeff Jefferson scored their first bylines in the Tokyo paper. The Swedish Meat Bowl was ready for the Boogie Buckers' Christmas Eve concert.

Everyone from the division headquarters area not on guard duty or involved in emergency operations awaited the concert that was to begin late in the afternoon of Christmas Eve. The helicopter group decorated the plastic bubble of one of its Bell H-13 helicopters as an airborne Santa Claus with a red cap, white eyebrows, beard, and button eyes. Haggis arranged with the pilot to pick up Smudge out of sight at the bottom of the valley and deliver him and his guitar to a clear area near the front of the stage to open the concert. Smudge and the band members were dressed for the occasion in light gray uniforms with red piping. When Smudge emerged from the helicopter through swirling dust and the racket of whirling blades, the crowd greeted him with loud cheers.

Smudge jumped to the stage and began the concert with a boogie version of Rudolph the Red Nosed Reindeer. Those who had heard Gene Autry's version sang along. Two Christmas carols and then three of Smudge's compositions: "C'mon, shake my hand," "Down and out Blues," and "Big Mamma's Boogie." followed. The troops shook their heads, clapped their hands, and tapped their feet. Colonel Warfinger, seated in the VIP section, followed along, delighted with the program, and pleased that he had prevailed in delivering this entertainment to the troops. General Black, not known as a fan of rhythm and blues, seemed to enjoy it as well.

Leroy's piano, abused by hauling it to each of the regiments and back to headquarters in Army trucks, required serious tuning the afternoon of the concert. As always, a touch of weed heightened his acoustic awareness and his red-rimmed eyes broadcast those beneficial effects as he plunked the last "C" chord and declared the piano in excellent tune. The wheels under the piano allowed him to push it easily to the side of the stage where it would be located for the concert. In his mildly elevated state, he overlooked depressing the silvery metal locking levers that immobilized the wheels. Solid as the piano appeared, it was ready for freewheeling.

Halfway through the concert, Smudge strummed the opening chords of "The Hucklebuck" and Smudge pointed to the musicians, one after the other, to begin their solo interpretations of the popular song. Fatboy enthusiastically stomped about the stage, brandishing his large instrument like a pogo stick, ending his set with his fingers almost below his knees as the bass wailed in falsetto.

Leroy began his digital aerobics without realizing that Fatboy's wild movements had dislodged his piano and sent it sliding slowly down the gently sloping stage toward the far end. Once discovered, Leroy had no choice but to abandon his bench, follow the piano on its course, continue his furious playing, and pray that the piano would somehow stop its precipitous course. Beads of sweat appeared on his brow in spite of the chill air.

The sight of Leroy moving crablike beside his sliding piano, playing frantically, skinny arms flailing like fan blades, electrified the audience. To a man, they rose and cheered, believing it was a part of the act. Leroy's world gyrated as the curtains behind the stage seemed to whizz by. His feet threatened to rebel against his squatting position and send him sprawling onto the stage, and part of his brain announced this was the coolest buzz he ever had experienced.

Leroy decided he had no choice but to make the ultimate sacrifice, continue playing his beloved ivories, and follow his piano off the edge of the stage into the dark unknown.

Fatboy, Honky, and Smudge dropped their instruments and intervened, shouldering the piano to a slow stop a few feet from the end of the stage. Safely arrested and greatly relieved, Leroy finished his set with a glistening arpeggio, rose from his crouched position, strode to center stage, and executed a florid bow. The crowd roared its approval.

The band choreographed all future concerts to include a sliding piano. It became Leroy's trademark for years.

The concert continued with songs by Johnny Otis, Fats Domino and Smudge's "Gee, How I Love You" and concluded with familiar Christmas carols ending with a soulful "Silent Night." Cheers and a standing ovation filled the evening until, finally, reluctantly, the audience broke up and soldiers returned to their tents and huts singing or whistling tunes from the performance. Most of them would recall the Boogie Buckers' concert on that frosty Christmas Eve as the best show ever.

Wylie, who watched from a seat in front of the stage, clambered up to congratulate the band as the crowd dispersed.

"That rolling piano was incredible, Leroy. Never seen anything like it."

"Glad you liked it man. Been saving it up."

"Hey Wylie," said Smudge," you want to see my Fireball in action, come on over in back of the MASH tent tomorrow morning. Haggis and I are gonna be flying in the morning."

"Be there," said Wylie.

The temperature was just below freezing and a light dusting of snow covered the ground of the playing field behind the MASH area. Smudge and Haggis were there when Wylie arrived with Jim Beam. Jules Pike had expressed interest in running photographs of the R & B star at play and Wylie hoped he would be given a turn at flying the Fireball. Corporal Beam photographed the two musicians fueling the thimble sized tank and spinning the propeller to start the engine. It popped to life and began to buzz as Haggis held the model and Smudge walked away with the line and handle. Haggis set the plane on the ground at Smudge's signal and the wheels plowed through the light snow as the plane lifted off and zipped through the air. Smudge adroitly sent the little craft through stalls, loop de loops, and dives until the engine sputtered off and he landed it perfectly at Wylie's feet.

Smudge said, "Give it a try, man. Just remember to keep the handle parallel to the ground till you get comfortable with it."

Refueled and started, Haggis held the model and Wylie took the handle from Smudge and prepared to guide the model airplane. He was surprised how dramatically small movements of his hand affected the plane's flight but he managed to guide it successfully until its fuel was gone. He enjoyed the sensation of controlling it and appreciated why it would be popular with young men. It was noisy and fun.

It was Haggis' turn, and Wylie helped Smudge fuel the little plane and crank its engine. Haggis was not as expert as Smudge but he managed a few dives and turns. On one of his backward moves, he encountered a patch of ice and slipped. As he put his hands back to cushion the fall, he dropped the handle and the plane buzzed away, dragging the handle behind it. Haggis recovered and began to run after the handle as it bounced along the snowy ground, causing the model to veer in its path.

A fast runner could have captured the handle but, although Haggis was swift for his size, the path was not clear. Directly before him was a clothes line on which laundry girls had hung Major Barbara's favorite embroidered pillow case and her unmentionables to freeze dry. Haggis had to maneuver under and around the laundry, frozen stiff as a tent pole, while the fly handle bounced along the corrugated side of the MASH Quonset hut and the Fireball continued on its escape route. The sharp frozen edge of an unmentionable cut the side of his cheek as he ducked under the line, but he forged valiantly forward.

Wylie and Smudge shook with laughter at Haggis' antics, though Smudge harbored concern for the future of his little plane. The handle almost in his grasp, Haggis leaped upward and missed. He collapsed beside the oil barrel next to the nurses' tent as, its fuel exhausted, the Fireball executed a perfect landing on the road in front of the tent. There it rested as Haggis collected himself and walked to retrieve it. He tried desperately to wave off a Marine truck laden with gifts for the children at Amelia's orphanage as it rounded the corner behind the tent. The driver couldn't change course and the truck's front wheel crushed the little airplane. When Haggis bent to retrieve it, only the tail section remained.

A few days later Wylie said goodbye to Smudge and his musicians as they prepared to return to Tokyo. Sensitive to Smudge's feelings, he changed a proposed headline about the Boogie Bucklers' "smashing" success to "resounding" triumph. Smudge had packed the plane's tail section in its large leather case, determined to acquire another Fireball.

The band gathered around the pot virgin and said their farewells. It was a brief acquaintance, but Wylie felt very comfortable with the band members. Smudge wrapped his big hand around Wylie's, pulled it away, and offered a fist bump. As their truck rolled away across the frozen roadway, Wylie thought, for a moment, that he had just received a slight dusting of charisma. How cool is that? he thought.

CHAPTER 50

OFF THE BOOKS

◆ ◆ ◆

MAJOR SMATTER UNROLLED A LARGE map of an area along the DMZ, polished his glasses with a handkerchief, and pointed with his bony finger. It was to a spot north of the 38th parallel, well into the demilitarized zone. That surprised Wylie, who understood incursions into the demilitarized zone were not only disallowed under rules of the armistice but also potentially fatal. He realized why he had been sworn to secrecy and had his security clearance checked yet again. He wondered if the prickly feeling along the back of his neck was a comment on his decision to join a clandestine mission.

Corporal Bonaventura had developed a fondness for Wylie. He suggested it would broaden Wylie's horizons and make him a better reporter if he participated in a slightly "off the books" mission, as he put it. Major Smatter approved, but only on the condition that Wylie took no notes and all information revealed would be considered as top secret. Such precautions served only to heighten Wylie's interest. Captain Standrich agreed and said "I don't need to know the details, Wylie; just be careful, okay."

In the command post, Major Smatter faced the dozen members of his team and said, "Ladies, it so happens that one of our jet fighters blew the hell out of a commie supply train a week or so before the armistice. We confirmed the hit. We now have intelligence there might be either explosive materials, poisonous chemicals like phosgene or corrosive gas or other kinds of nasty armaments still sitting in the box-cars. Here's the latest photo intel we have, from a couple days ago."

The Major passed out three large glossy pictures that showed a multi car freight train. The engine was twisted partially on its side, the front buried in a shallow berm along a warped track. Some of the cars rested upright while others tilted precariously. Boxes of some kind spilled from one of them. There was no sign of recent activity in or near the train. It was located in a densely wooded area with a single dirt road visible about half a kilometer away, to the south.

Once the team had absorbed the information on the photographs, the major went on, "Like a lot of our other missions, this is pretty touchy and we're going to go in heavily armed. We've got to check out each car and be sure there's nothing dangerous or useful to the enemy. It looks as though they haven't located the wreck yet. If we find anything of value, it's possible to get a truck up that dirt road, so we'll have one standing by. But most likely we'll just have to blow the mother up. We're going to have to hike about five miles to infiltrate the area properly, so put on your dancing shoes."

Corporal Bonaventura went over the map information carefully with a few members of his squad before they planned the route to approach the wreck. The Major, who would join the team, reviewed the plan and suggested some minor changes. Wylie was impressed with the collegial manner in which the team worked. They would leave in two hours, before the rise of an almost full moon and travel to their point of departure in three Jeeps and a truck. Wylie would ride in one of the Jeeps.

As instructed, Wylie carried a carbine he drew from the quartermaster that afternoon, and his .45 caliber semiautomatic pistol he kept holstered at his side. Bonaventura put a friendly hand on his shoulder and directed him to the supply room of the CP where other members of the team were gathering supplies.

The Corporal asked Wylie to loosen his belt and lower his fatigue pants. "Here's four thirty round clips for the carbine. You strap them to your legs below the knee, two on each leg. Use this gaffer tape; it won't pull out your leg hairs so much. And, let's see, yeah, you can carry these four grenades. Stuff them under your shirt and they won't show under the field jacket. I think the forty-five is okay, but keep it under the jacket, too."

Confusion showed on Wylie's face and Bonaventura said, "Just do it, man. You'll understand later."

He followed the Corporal's instructions and noted that many in the squad were also sequestering various forms of armaments and ammunition under their fatigues. The gaffer tape held the clips of ammunition tightly to his legs and, since the grenades seemed to roll around under his shirt, he used the tape to corral them as well. The clips of ammunition hampered walking slightly but he soon became used to that. In twenty minutes, the squad, lumpy under their fatigues, was ready for the night's assignment.

Their vehicles moved slowly from the CP and traveled with dimmed lights to the U.N. guard post on the southern side of the DMZ. Members of the British Expeditionary Forces were on duty that night and two soldiers approached their convoy to check orders and inspect weapons. The armistice agreement demanded that troops entering the zone carry no more than five rounds per weapon.

The team members, led by Major Smatter, innocently offered their weapons for inspection. They complied. The Tommies waved the convoy onward and the vehicles descended slowly down the narrow dirt road that led obliquely north.

With hooded flashlights, Bonaventura and the Major checked their location as they penetrated more deeply into neutral territory. They soon reached their departure point. Two men continued forward with the truck and the rest of the team bushwhacked, in tight formation, toward the place where the freight train was located. One of the men handed Wylie a heavy mussette bag, saying, "Be careful with that!" That warning added to his anxiety as he picked his way forward over irregular terrain with the others.

After an hour, the Major called a halt. They could see the ruined train through an opening in the brush beside the tracks. Wylie made his way to Corporal Bonaventura's side, intending to follow the veteran expert in operations of this kind. The Major indicated with his ever-present bayonet the disposition of the team and, two by two, they scrambled toward the boxcars. Wylie felt fear spread frigidly down his spine and his breathing quickened. This isn't like combat, he thought. What if this is an ambush? What if the cars are booby-trapped? As Bonaventura moved forward, Wylie hesitated briefly, then, more concerned about cowardice than mortality, quickly followed the Corporal toward the railroad tracks.

Moonlight glinted weakly from the tilting top of the car they approached, and the Corporal wrenched open the metal door canted forty-five degrees from the ground. As the door creaked open, a wooden box the size of a steamer trunk slid from the interior and crashed to the ground before their feet. Both soldiers froze, fearing the box might explode. After a few terrifying moments, they heard the sound of gurgling liquid. Bonaventura whispered, "Scared the shit outa me. Coulda been maybe nitro and we'd be sitting with the angels."

Wylie realized that his state of dread was fully justified.

"Let's get in here and take a look at this stuff," said the Corporal. From box cars behind them came the reassuring echo of "Clear!" whispered by other members of the team.

Inside, the Corporal shone a beam from his flashlight at the jumble of boxes stacked helter skelter inside the tipped boxcar. They were all the size of the box that fell out when he opened the door. There were stenciled markings on the boxes, but they were in unfamiliar letters that Wylie could not understand. Bonaventura looked at the repeated letters "водка" and began to laugh. "Wylie, my mom is Russian and that's Cyrillic. What we got here is a whole box car full of Russian vodka!"

The two jumped back to the ground as the Major walked along the tracks conferring with other members of the team. Bonaventura announced in a hushed voice, "Can't be sure, sir, but it looks like cases of nitro glycerin in there. Beats me how the stuff didn't explode during the attack and all. How do you want us to handle it?"

Recalling the fiasco at the rice paddy, the Major quickly replied, "Can't just leave it here, but we have to be careful with its disposal. Put in charges and make sure they're on at least an hour's delay. I want us long gone when this sucker goes up." Smatter then decided he had business elsewhere and he and one of the team left immediately to return to the rendezvous point.

The other members of the team, believing they needed to prepare for the immediate destruction of the boxcar, gathered around the Corporal and began to prepare tools of demolition.

"Not so fast, dickheads," warned the Corporal. "First thing you gotta do is empty your canteens."

There was consternation among the troops and delight for Wylie, who clearly saw where this was going.

"Like I said, empty your canteens right now." A deliberate pause. "We're gonna refill them with first class, grade A, super fucking good Russian vodka!"

He used his bayonet to pry off a side of the crate that had fallen from the car and pulled out an undamaged bottle, wet with vodka, smelling of juniper. The aroma quickly enveloped the squad and smiles glinted in the faint light. Water splashed from a dozen canteens and the squad gathered around the broken crate and harvested spoils of the night's work. Liquor burned a few throats as near empty bottles were consumed to avoid waste. Wylie participated with the rest, mainly, he reckoned, to reduce the double chill of subsiding fear and cold night air.

Two runners went to the waiting truck, which soon rumbled to a halt a few yards from the broken boxcar. With alcohol-inspired alacrity, the squad moved all the boxes of vodka it could hold to the back of truck. Additional bottles replaced explosives and arms the men carried to destroy the train. Sadly, a dozen or so crates could not be collected. They remained in the boxcar, to be consumed in an infernal funeral pyre when the detonation occurred.

With the truck safely on its way, Bonaventura and his team placed explosives throughout the train and created a redundant ignition system that would begin the conflagration about forty-five minutes after they left. The Corporal checked their handiwork and turned the switch. Wylie saw a little red light begin to glow on one of the detonators and joined the others as they worked their cumbersome way back to the waiting Jeeps. Shortly before their arrival, a series of distant explosions began and the men turned to observe a bright orange glow above the trees behind them.

"Normally, it's red," Bonaventura said to Wylie. "Must be the booze turns it orange. Crying Goddam shame."

The Major had left on one of the Jeeps and the squad gathered at the rendezvous point to address the problem of how to conserve their booty. After rejecting a few vodka-fueled bone headed suggestions, Bonaventura considered a proposal offered by a skinny PFC, their chemical specialist.

"We could bury them right next to those tanks of poison gas and chemicals we ain't supposed to have," he said. "Nobody's gonna go past all those skull and crossbones signs we plastered all over the place. Put them in the ground, cover them with a tarp. Who's gonna find them?"

Regulations concerning what visitors could take out of the DMZ were ambiguous. Consequently, the two Tommies guarding the team's exit road found themselves the new owners of a half case of fine Russian vodka as they waved the happy Yanks through the check point.

Smatter's team returned to Headquarters at midnight. Well before first light, they had interred the cases of vodka underground, guarded by chemical warning signs. Bonaventure gladly added rationing the spoils of war among their liberators to his management duties. Under his stewardship, the booty lasted for more than three months, depleted by the thirst of its rescuers and by its use in trade or commerce. As befitted a liberator, Wylie was granted access to the cache. He did not abuse the privilege and used his share mainly to trade for rare items Amelia needed at the orphanage. It was very good stuff, though, and the lovers did, on occasion, enjoy its properties as an aphrodisiac.

CHAPTER 51

MOVING FORWARD

◆ ◆ ◆

AUNTIE SOO'S BUICK WAS PARKED on a side street next to the warehouse and she sat on a folding chair wrapped in a blanket in the corner of the building, surveying the work going on around her. The leaking roof of the warehouse had been covered with flattened cardboard cartons secured with salvaged nails. Workmen applied handmade curved tiles to make the roof weather tight and the raw brick color of the new tiles distinguished the building among the gray brown roofs surrounding it.

Workers hired from the farms lying outside Uijongbu were separating and flattening NAAFI cartons liberated from the British Regiment's dumpsite and attaching them to the interior walls for insulation. Other villagers were applying a stucco mixture to the outside and smoothing it with trowels and hoes. Carpenters were building partitions atop chalk lines drawn on the concrete floor while an office crow's nest took shape near the eves. The manager would have an unobstructed view of the cubicles taking shape below.

Auntie Soo had deputized Kim Ky Young as construction overseer mainly because she knew he was completely trustworthy and thought the job not too demanding. Kim divided his time between the press billets in Seoul and working on the project in Uijongbu. He had driven his aunt there that morning so she could discuss important matters with local businesspeople and observe progress with her practiced eye. She planned to meet Buck Adder that afternoon to review construction costs. Major Adder intended to keep accurate records of all aspects of the operation, and Auntie Soo needed to explain to him how and why certain disbursements, customary in Korean business arrangements, should be handled.

One of the potential beneficiaries of such disbursements entered the building and walked toward her, bowing politely and asking after her health and family.

"As good as an old woman can expect. Thank you for honoring me with your company this morning. As you can see it will not be too many weeks before this enterprise will be opening its doors and I wanted to give you my assurance of full cooperation with your business."

Her companion was the owner of a bar two blocks away that catered mainly to ROK soldiers and a few G.I.s. He listened gravely and expressed his appreciation for her thoughtfulness.

"This building will become an entertainment center for American soldiers and as such will include two bars. If you look closely you can see, over there, how they will be situated."

The man could see a roughed-out platform of wooden beams, indicating a bar area four times as large as his.

"And how, dear Aunt, will we be cooperating, if I may ask?"

"You will explain that your establishment no longer serves American servicemen," she said, "and direct them to this place which will be called 'The Palace.' We will be watering the drinks just as you do but charge more because of the extra opportunities for entertainment available here. We will, of course, have girls encouraging the soldiers to drink."

"That is certainly an excellent arrangement," he said hoarsely, "but, you know, esteemed proprietor, that American soldiers in my bar pay ten to twenty times more than the ROK soldiers can. They provide the meager profit I need to support my family during these difficult times. I humbly await knowledge of how you intend to reward this form of cooperation."

Auntie Soo leaned forward in her chair. "You will receive three hundred hwan a week for the foreseeable future. But you realize, of course, that cannot go on forever, since it is inevitable that you will lose customers to this establishment. So you must be content to serve your own countrymen. Be assured, also, that our arrangement includes fire insurance for your establishment. A spark in this cold winter wind could be treacherous. And here," she handed six hundred hwan to the bar owner, "is an indication of my good faith."

On leaving, the man bowed again, unable to find words to cover his feelings of despair. I just begin to make a little money in this godforsaken village, he thought, and now, at best, I have four or five months left before that hag from Seoul nibbles it away. Time to consider working the black market with my brother in Pusan.

The idea of protesting or arguing with the Korean woman never occurred to him. Her reputation in such dealings in Seoul preceded her. Those who crossed her either were found floating in the Han River or had fatal "accidents' usually involving a sharp bladed knife. No, he had survived the war and was raising a family. Undoubtedly, that old crow represented bad luck. He would be wise and move on.

Auntie Soo sighed. She had three more locals to interview today and then there was the problem of recruiting staff. Here she was counting on Song Song Park, an old friend who had aided her when the Japanese jailed them both for defying their harsh domination in late 1938. Song Song was discreet, persuasive, and, even in his fifties, had a discerning eye for attractive young women who frequently found themselves playing capture the dragon in his bed.

He had accepted the pleasurable assignment of vetting potential staff members whose responsibility would be to capture dragons belonging to The Korean Palace's clientele. Youth, ardor, a willingness to learn, and a pleasing face and body were his criteria for employment, and hard cash with excellent medical benefits were Song Songs' selling points. This morning, he stopped by to report on the progress he had made in canvassing the town and the surrounding countryside, as well as potential candidates he had considered in Seoul.

Song Song was as affable and charming as ever. He exclaimed at Auntie Soo's youthful looks and inquired about the health and wellbeing of her entire family. Once the usual amenities were completed, he drew closer and reported.

"It is not going as well as I had hoped," he said. "The city girls turn up their noses at moving to a farming village and the local girls lack a certain, what would one call it… sophistication. They want to run away at the sight of a man stick such as the one I carry. However, it has not all been in vain. There are five candidates I can recommend, though two will require training on the job. If it is all right I will introduce them to you next week."

"Of course. But only five? This Major Adder insists we must have at least fourteen operators with significant additional support staff to, as he calls it, 'break even.' However, you have only been recruiting for a few weeks and it is still a month or so before operations will begin. Perhaps your standards are too high. Remember, we are dealing with young American soldiers who, I've been told, will make love to a knotty pine board."

"I am certain that I can do better than knotty pine boards."

Both considered that a very witty repartee and chuckled as Song Song bowed slightly and left his friend to reconsider the work in progress around her.

She watched as three men raised a lath partition in the area to be known as the honeymoon suite. In the back of the building, another team of workers was lining the earthen walls of a cellar with plates made from discarded fifty caliber ammunition boxes. The workers thought it was an odd place to install a root cellar but, as their leader said, they weren't being paid to think. Her nephew approached to confirm the location of bathrooms and laundry tubs and, after they talked, went outside to the Buick to locate plans and drawings he had collected the night before.

After leaving the truck that brought him to the checkpoint beside the division entrance, Wylie decided to walk to the orphanage. He enjoyed the satisfying crunch of snow beneath his boots. It was an invigorating preview to seeing Amelia again. The brisk walk made him feel the way he saw her— happy, full of life, strong, capable, fresh.

As he passed an old warehouse, he noticed a dark blue Buick parked on a side street. How many of those could be in this area, he wondered and walked toward the car hoping to see Kim, his guide in Seoul. Just then Kim emerged, preoccupied with locating missing papers in the car. He scarcely glanced at Wylie since almost all G.I.s looked the same to him and drew up short with his hand on the passenger door handle when Wylie called his name.

"Hey Kim! It's me, Wylie. You were my guide in Seoul of couple of months ago. From the press billets. You drove me around in this car. How are you doing?"

Kim realized there was no reason to be alarmed and smiled at the young soldier.

"Yes. Yes. You wanted to look at the bridges and houses at the river. Sure, I remember."

Wylie suppressed a smile at Kim's pronunciation. All the "r"s sounded like "l"s so it was "liver" and "lemembah." On the other hand, Wylie could barely find a bathroom or main road using the Korean language and he was thankful for Kim's improving English. They chatted on about the weather, Kim's work in Seoul, and how the Buick was running in the cold. Wylie finally asked about his being in Uijongbu.

"I do some work on the family business. We fix this building."

"Great," said Wylie. "I hope I'll see you here again soon."

They parted, and both men returned to interrupted business.

Amelia's welcoming hug clumsily encompassed him, his winter clothing, and parka. She rubbed her warm cheek against his cold one and smiled. It was no longer necessary for him to concoct excuses to visit; they simply wanted to enjoy each other's company whenever possible. She drew him to the kitchen, the warmest spot in the building, and took both his hands in hers. He saw she was wearing the

"Executive Director" wool shirt under a down jacket that might have come from a Chinese soldier.

They kissed, but Amelia reluctantly withdrew, explaining that she was awaiting the arrival of three new children, one a baby, from a village where severe flooding had occurred just after Christmas. Her father had visited the village after the disaster and discovered one or more of their parents had been lost.

"Sure; I can't stay very long either," said Wylie. "I've got to be in Seoul later this afternoon to meet with Fred Able and a couple of other guys. I have some information on a story we're working on. I just really wanted to see you, especially since I was tied up with the Boogie Buckers all Christmas."

He reddened, almost embarrassed to admit, "This may come as a surprise, but you're really important to me."

Amelia pressed a finger to his lips and smiled. "Likewise, Wylie. Likewise."

Soon a rickety pickup truck pulled into the courtyard and two young women Wylie recognized as workers at the orphanage left the truck with their new charges. A few of the little residents broke through the doors to see the new children and romp in the fresh snow. Wylie left with the sounds of their laughter ringing in his ears.

Fred Able and Wylie's friend Alistair introduced Henry Ponce III as a reporter for the Washington Eagle, and then they sat around a battered wooden table in the antechamber in the former Japanese hotel. They sipped their drinks as Wylie reported on his interview with the tank driver who thought he was in an amphibious vehicle.

"It took me a while to locate him, but once I figured out which armored group he was attached to, I covered their live fire exercises for a feature article in the stars and bars. That was my opening to get to know him better. His name's Waverly and he's a decent guy.

"After we had a couple brews, I just came right out and said I'd been told he heard colors and wondered if that was so. He kind of rolled his eyes as though it was a 'here we go, again' moment but he admitted it had happened more than once. He called it 'weird shit'—the same term you used, Fred."

The other men were very interested.

"It seemed to me that he was trying to validate his experience by repeating it to someone other than himself. He described lying on the hospital cot after his submarine tank maneuver feeling that he was out of his body looking down on himself. He was on a sunny beach looking out over the ocean and, as the waves were breaking, he saw streaks of beautiful colors in the sky. He is convinced he heard the colors."

Fred and Alistair nodded to each other as Wylie continued.

"Apparently, this happened again after he was discharged from the MASH, the hearing colors thing, and I caught him as he was getting very worried about the 'weird shit' going on in his head. When I asked him what he thought was going on, he confessed that one of his buddies assigned to CID at I Corps gave him a little square of blotter paper and told him to put it in his mouth if he wanted a cheap high. He was getting bored with tank exercises and he did that three or four hours before his Pershing tank turned into a rowboat. He made me promise not to get his buddy in trouble, which I will honor. That's what I have to report, and I hope you illustrious gentlemen can make some sense of it."

Alistair heaved himself closer to Wylie and patted his shoulder.

"Well done, Wylie. It fits with what we've learned from contacts in I Corps. Fred and I were nibbling around the edge of this little happening with our contacts but it was Harry, here, who sorted it out."

Harry was on temporary assignment in Seoul. Alistair had told Wylie privately that he believed Harry worked with OSS in World War II and still had ties to the major United States intelligence agencies.

Harry was in his early forties with a compact body, rugged features, and an air of authority. His sandy hair was thinning and he had the habit of running his hand over his head checking the bald spot. As Wylie spoke, he did that a few times.

"That's not a bad piece of reporting, kid," said Henry Ponce III. "I have pulled together some additional information that fits the scenario you describe, but this could be extremely sensitive stuff. If we can't get brassbound corroboration, we could be hung out to twist in the wind—at best."

Wylie was pleased to be complimented by a bona fide civilian hotshot reporter with a nationally recognized byline. It took the sting out of the "kid" reference. He had no illusions that he was an independent journalist. On many occasions, Captain Standrich bundled up potentially sensitive stories for review by the division's chief of staff and commanding officers. Some of the stories never returned.

Wylie understood that members of the civilian press also were constrained by their editors, a need to protect sources, and unwritten rules about ignoring harmless peccadilloes. However, working with reporters in the Seoul press billets, he began to yearn for more independence. Perhaps this story represented a chance to be part of some real investigative reporting.

"What kind of clearance do you have?" Henry asked.

"I have access to Secret documents, though I mainly see Confidential ones. You know, the daily password and things like that."

Henry considered Wylie's response.

"That's good. Fine. We need to think about this," he said "Maybe we'll talk to you later."

As though a curtain had descended, their conversation abruptly turned to sports, gossip about visiting commentators from the networks, and how soon they might return to their home offices. Wylie added what he could to the conversation but, feeling confused and disrespected, sensed that Henry Ponce III had already assigned him to twist in the wind. He was relieved when Sergeant Snipes bustled in and drew their attention to the four inches of snow collecting on the windowsill.

CHAPTER 52

FULL DISCLOSURE

SERGEANT SNIPES CONFIRMED A HEAVY storm was forecast that night.

"Be smart, Wylie," he said, "No sense heading back tonight. We got plenty of empty rooms and plenty of rib eyes steaks. Get Uncle Wee to fix you up for tonight and we'll work on getting you back to the 53rd tomorrow morning. I already told your driver to go sack out."

Wylie laughed. "Not giving me much of a choice, are you."

"That was my plan. I don't think they give you enough to eat at division. No lobster tonight, but we still have plum pudding."

After the cold shoulder from Henry Ponce III, Wylie appreciated Sergeant Snipes' good-natured cajoling.

"Listen, I told you before, I already have a mother."

Snipes offered Wylie his middle finger as he strode back to his kitchen.

Uncle Wee assigned him a large corner room with a double bed, which prompted thoughts of organizing a visit to the press billets with Amelia. As Wylie prepared for bed, Alistair knocked on his door. He stood in the hallway with Henry Ponce III.

They entered and Wylie sat on the end of the bed while his two visitors occupied the battered couch near the window. Alistair had gained more weight since Wylie last saw him; he covered over half the couch. Postwar poundage thought Wylie.

"Fred's sending out a story and has to pass on this visit," said the Australian. "Harry and I want to fill you in."

Henry Ponce III made an attempt at a conciliatory smile.

"No offense, kid, but I needed confirmation from your friends that you could reliably keep your mouth shut. Your secret clearance and good words from Fred and this wallaby bait here provided that. Also, you added to the story and I was concerned you might stumble into something else and expose us all to problems."

Crowded by Alistair, Henry Ponce III left the couch and stood by the window, glancing at drifting snow. Turning back to Wylie, he said, "So, want to hear a hypothetical story on background, off the record, and in confidence?"

Wylie swallowed the "kid" reference and nodded. Of course he did.

Harry nodded to the Australian, and Alistair began.

"Remember that Fred told you some weeks ago that his contacts in the MPs informed him about that damned peculiar behavior among prisoners and enlisted over at I Corps? Well, Fred and I were able to connect that with a visit by some civilians from Fort Detrick in Maryland and dark types from Langley. As we tried to learn more, all went exceptionally quiet."

At Alistair's request, Harry continued the narrative. Before the war, he explained, a Swiss chemist discovered a new drug that acted as a respiratory stimulant. But, since it was not very effective it was abandoned. Then, about five years ago, the manufacturer began marketing it as a psychiatric cure-all in the States under the name "Delysid."

"It was promoted as the second coming of Christ," he said. "The pharmaceutical company claimed it would effectively treat alcoholism, schizophrenia, criminal behavior, and possibly sexual aberrations. Naturally, the military and intelligence agencies were interested and began experimenting with it. Then the manufacturer discovered dangerous side effects and, to cover its ass, took the drug off the market.

"The government agency experiments continued, mainly by the Army at Fort Detrick. They were done in secret, not subject to public scrutiny, and the drug was easily created from lysergic acid. It became known by its chemical acronym, LSD."

Wylie said that he had never heard of it.

Not many people had, explained Harry. That appealed to the military experimenters. It was very easily consumed; a drop on a sugar cube guaranteed wild hallucinations. The first time Harry heard of the drug was from friends in military intelligence who explained it was being used to attempt a "reverse brainwash" on American prisoners who confessed to deploying biological weapons against North Korea.

"But," said Harry, "They went even crazier after they got the drug. Lost touch with reality. Poor bastards were fucked up worse than ever. Some of them committed suicide."

He went on. Military doctors believed there would be better results with men who had not succumbed to Chinese torture, so the experiments continued, sometimes on regular military personnel without their knowledge. Careful notes were taken about what were called "trips." The results were unpredictable and sometimes induced severe psychoses, but the experiments continued. Wylie's story about the tank driver and the blue blotter paper strongly suggested he had taken LSD

About half way through Harry's narrative, Wylie began to sense that he was being set up for some denigrating punch line at the end of this cock and bull story. He guessed it was good sport for two experienced journalists to make fun of his youth and naiveté. However, he felt hurt that his friend Alistair would join this game. How gullible do they think I am, he wondered? They are talking about Americans here. About doctors and scientists. We don't do that.

He rose from the bed and looked at the Washington Eagle reporter.

"Listen, okay I'm tired. I know you're having your fun, but cut to the chase. Give me the punch line so I can get some sleep!"

"Wylie, I know it's hard to believe, but you are wrong to think we are playing a prank or having you on. This is dead serious," said Alistair. "Sadly, Harry speaks the truth. Fred and I confirmed most of this from our own sources. We have validation that a young soldier thought he could fly off the roof of I Corps headquarters and broke both legs and an arm."

He shifted his weight on the couch and sighed. "Now you're beginning to understand why it's unlikely this story will ever be told."

Harry shrugged off Wylie's incredulity and continued.

Fred had contacted him in Washington about the connection to Fort Detrick and Harry began his investigation. When Fred explained the "weird shit" in Seoul, Harry promised his firstborn to his editor in exchange for a temporary assignment to Korea. On his arrival in Seoul, the three pooled their resources and contacts and concluded that LSD had been employed to help debrief leading communist sympathizers identified by Rhee's police, ranking North Korean prisoners, and military personnel suspected of important crimes.

No one was willing to discuss results, on or off the record. However, even with the highest security, word of the new drug escaped, along with an unknown quantity of LSD impregnated on numerous sheets of blotting paper. Prison guards, members of the intelligence community, and medical personnel who discovered outdated vials of Delysid in dusty corners fueled the small underground business for micrograms of the drug that guaranteed a cheap high.

Fortunately, Alistair added, it seemed no new supplies had become available and the "weird shit" seemed to be winding down. It would be just another uncorroborated story to add to others he had filed away for possible future use. Convinced what he had heard was probably true, Wylie recognized why Harry was so interested in the LSD story. Harry could use the threat of disclosure as a wedge for prying sensitive information from contacts in the future. Alistair and Fred were just good reporters following a juicy lead. Discovering the story, learning the truth were almost as satisfying as getting a great "scoop."

As distressing thoughts whirred through his head, he wished he had never learned of hearing colors or met Sergeant Waverly.

The two correspondents said goodbye and left Wylie alone in his room. He stared out the window at swirling snow and suddenly felt nausea, a churning in the pit of his stomach and gorge rising at the back of his throat, worse than when he drank too much whiskey. At the same time, he felt as though tiny insects were nibbling at the folds of his brain. He rushed to the sink in the corner and became desperately sick.

Miserable after suffering a succession of dry heaves, he sat on the floor next to the sink, fearful that his sickness might return. Fleeting questions and possible answers thrummed against his head like a blue bottle fly caught in a bell jar. Christ, he thought, I've been interviewing people, listening to their stories, and accepting most of what they say without challenge. What if most of it is bullshit and I'm too naïve, too dumb to recognize it?

He thought of grainy black and white images of ordinary looking men sitting in the dock at Nuremburg. If it's true that military intelligence is using mind altering drugs on prisoners and our own troops, how does that make them different from the doctors at the Nuremburg Trials? A recollection of pink clouds erupting from distant heads replaced the image of prisoners in the dock. Oh my God, he thought, just a few months ago I was in a place where I was killing people. How different is that? Does fighting for my life provide justification? What does that say about my values?

And just how many rotten things are going on out there that I've missed or don't know about?

The wind blowing snow across the courtyard penetrated the wall next to the sink, sending chill pangs across Wylie's shoulders and back. He dragged himself to the bed, pulled the covers to his chin, and stared at the ceiling above, vainly trying to close his eyes against the threatening darkness.

For the first time in his life, Wylie was overwhelmed with challenges to his beliefs, causing him to engage in serious introspection, and he was not good at it. He realized any knowledge he might have of the subjects raised that evening was superficial and uninformed. This was not something he could dismiss glibly or pass over with a joke. He had glimpsed a grown up world of deception, venality, and evil.

As the night wore on, he began to think of seemingly innocent encounters that might not have been so. He suspected the motives of people like Uncle Wee, Scott McIlvane, even Alistair. In despair, he concluded there was hardly anyone he could really trust. He would just have to be very careful in the future. He was awake most of the night. Even the soft sound of snowflakes falling on the windowsill bothered him.

Finally, he slept. At dawn, blushing light entering his room declared the end of the snowfall. Wylie rose from the bed and wandered to the window, looking at the reddened snow-covered rooftops surrounding his hotel. It promised to be a beautiful morning.

Fully awake, he recalled last night's revelations. He shook himself like a dog emerging from cold water, as though shedding damp fears, repelling unworthy thoughts. He opened the window and sucked in cold, fresh air that stung his throat and made his eyes water.

Fuck it, he thought, it's going to be a beautiful day. I'm an Army Sergeant in charge of a division P.I.O. office and I have a wonderful girlfriend. I have important responsibilities and large brass balls, and I can choose to hear all colors of the rainbow, not just dark ones.

He shaved, dressed, and went down for breakfast, preparing for another day of work. Beauregard offered him blueberry pancakes with honey.

CHAPTER 53

MARILYN!

◆ ◆ ◆

WYLIE FLATTENED THE UNUSUALLY CRYPTIC telex from Jules Pike curling across his desk with the palm of his hand.

"STORM*WARNING*MARILYN*MONROE*ARRIVING*SOON EST*WILLCALL*1800*PIKE."

Wylie, like every other G.I. serving on the peninsula, was keenly aware of the blonde movie star who had recently appeared in "Gentlemen Prefer Blondes." The troops in Korea had elected her Number One pinup girl. She was mentioned in scores of Boomer's "home towners" as the girl that artilleryman, machine gunner, or corpsman would most like to come home to. Tattered copies of the original Playboy magazine that included nude photos of the young star were worth their weight in gold and fueled many erotic fancies among lonely troopers.

The big news of the previous week had been her sudden marriage to another American icon, the Yankee Clipper, Joe DiMaggio. The Stars and Stripes showed pictures of the Yankee slugger and his beaming new bride as they boarded a Pan American Clipper for an unknown destination. Now Wylie's friend in Tokyo said that the actress was on her way to Korea.

The field phone rang a few minutes past the hour and Pike's scratchy voice echoed through the speaker. He explained the star couple had selected Tokyo as their honeymoon location since neither of them had previously visited this exotic place and Joe wanted to pursue some business dealings there. They were staying in Frank Lloyd Wright's Imperial Hotel in Tokyo where they attended a grand cocktail party and reception. In addition to ambassadors, business moguls, and artists, members of the military brass were invited. Pike wasn't sure how he managed it, but Myron Goldstein, the cartoonist, and his friend Lambinus were invited as members of the press.

Myron reported that one of the general officers there approached her and suggested that a visit to see the troops in Korea would be a tremendous morale booster for the soldiers. Since this was supposed to be their honeymoon, Joe was not pleased by the suggestion, and tried to discourage the proposal. He thought it would be too dangerous, but Marilyn said she was thrilled at the idea and that it was the least she could do. Plans for her visit were made that evening and Marilyn was to arrive in Seoul the day after tomorrow, February sixteenth.

Myron was already salivating over cartoon ideas featuring the movie star and horny soldiers. The civilian press attending her would generate more stories and pictures than Bill Mullin, the editor, could use. However, he was impressed with the candid and intimate close-up pictures Wylie was taking with his little Nikon, so Mullin arranged for Wylie to be part of her military entourage. Pike joked that meant the editor no longer considered Wylie's writing his strong point. He provided contact information and said he was telexing orders for Wylie's TDY to Captain Standrich that evening.

Now there's an unexpected development thought Wylie. One week I'm having my fundamental beliefs challenged by some bullshit LSD story and the next I'm hob nobbing with a famous movie star. I've found my home in the Army!

By the time Wylie arrived at Kimpo airport in Seoul two days later, the buzz associated with Marilyn's arrival had electrified the Allied command. Soldiers were taking three-day leave and stuffing C rations into their packs so they could claim the best viewing locations (there were no seats) in advance for her scheduled performances.

Enterprising motor pool Sergeants parked deuce and a half trucks near hastily constructed stages and sold mezzanine seats for her performances. USO administrators wrangled with base commanders about her schedule and managed, on short notice, to organize a program that entertained over one hundred thousand troops during her two-day visit.

At Kimpo that morning, it seemed to Wylie that every correspondent and photographer in the Far East Command and the entire civilian press corps in Seoul awaited Marilyn's arrival. The official greeting committee ranged from full bird Colonels to Privates driving Jeeps. Sharp creases, polished boots, and shining brass were everywhere and even the civilian press corps seemed less scruffy than usual. On Sergeant Pike's advice, Wylie wore his Stars and Stripes armband that, along with his correspondent's patch, was supposed to give him an official aura. However, in the excited throng, nobody noticed, and he found himself shouldered to the edge of the crowd near one of the helicopter hangars, still looking for the contact Sergeant Pike had identified.

As Marilyn's plane drifted into view through cloudy skies, he heard someone say "Hey, buster," and realized the burly Captain standing at the entrance to the hangar was calling him. "Sergeant Cypher, right?" he said, pointing to his name badge. "I'm told you have orders to accompany Miss Monroe." Wylie gladly admitted that he had such orders and offered to produce them.

Captain Wojahowski ("Woj" to ranks above and below him) wrapped a large, friendly arm around Wylie's shoulder and let him into the hangar.

"Yeah," said the Captain, "I got the request from Tokyo to liaise with you about Miss Monroe, which didn't mean jack shit but you, it turns out, have powerful friends. Bo Snipes and Smudge Jackson both been after me, so I'm assigning you temporarily to my helicopter crew. So happens that Lucky Lucy has been selected to ferry Miss Monroe to her concerts. Think you can handle opening and closing the bay door?"

Wylie valiantly attempted to sort out the contents of the Captain's soliloquy. The cryptic information about his contact at Kimpo on his temporary duty orders mentioned the Captain, but what was he saying about Bo and Smudge? And who was Lucky Lucy?

Sensing Wylie's confusion, the Captain explained that he had ferried the Boogie Buckers around South Korea for their concerts. A great fan of the rhythm and blues artist, Woj befriended Smudge who gave him autographed copies of his albums. Earlier that day, Woj met Smudge and two other members of his band when they arrived in Kimpo to join the Anything Goes Band of service members backing up Marilyn.

Word of Wylie's plum assignment reached friends at I Corps, division headquarters, and the press billets. In addition to Smudge, Bo Snipes put in a good word for Wylie.

Wylie wondered if there was anyone in South Korea Bo Snipes DIDN'T know.

He thanked the Captain for his offer and walked with him to the Sikorsky H-19 helicopter waiting a hundred yards from the hangar. A cartoon of a scantily clad blonde woman holding a horseshoe was painted under the cockpit. "Lucky Lucy" was emblazoned underneath. Woj introduced him to Lieutenant Cropper, his co-pilot, and the two enlisted crew members. Then the two officers clambered up to the cockpit for an instrument check.

Meanwhile, Marilyn's plane landed and Wylie looked across the field as soldiers pushed forward a mobile stairway and a squadron of shiny Jeeps surrounded the landing area. Moments later, she appeared in the doorway, dressed in olive military fatigues and leather pilot's jacket, her famous blonde hair caught in the cold wind gusting over the tarmac. The twenty-eight-year-old actress smiled and waved. Wylie was sure he could hear the sound of hearts melting among the cheers arising from the field.

The commanding officer of Kimpo welcomed her, and two young officers escorted her to a Jeep without embarrassing themselves. The

Jeep drove the one hundred and fifty yards to Lucky Lucy and two USO types appeared from nowhere to place a footstool below the helicopter doorway. Wylie held the door back as she descended from the Jeep and entered the helicopter, followed by the two USO types and two other officers.

For security, both officers carried side- arms and were accompanied by an enlisted man holding a Thompson submachine gun. He saluted and signed thumbs up to indicate he was ready for action.

Wylie closed the door and settled into a canvas seat across the aircraft from the movie star. Her face was flushed from the wind and cold and she was, in Wylie's opinion, completely adorable. She was excited about being in Korea and bubbled on about how much she looked forward to entertaining the troops. Her voice was almost exactly as it was in her movies though not quite as breathless. She looked up at Woj in the cockpit and asked everyone's name. Then the propeller and rotor began to turn and conversation halted as the aircraft lifted off and headed north. Wylie held up his camera and mouthed, "Is it okay?" Marilyn, who shared a mutual love affair with any photographic apparatus, nodded an enthusiastic yes.

The Sikorsky rose above the airport and turned north over the Han River and Seoul itself bound for the 3rd Infantry Division. Snowflakes began to fall and dust the hillsides above Seoul, revealing various military installations from the helicopter's windows. Marilyn asked Woj if he could please fly lower so she could wave to the soldiers below, then asked if the sliding door could be opened to provide better visibility. The officers overcame their legitimate concerns for her safety and Wylie carefully opened the door. Marilyn promptly lowered herself face down on the helicopter floor and, as she inched her body outside the door, Wylie and the submachine gunner grabbed her legs and held them down as she waved madly to the troops below.

The soldiers of the infantry regiment below the helicopter's path were stunned with the bizarre sight of the golden haired entertainer protruding from a helicopter waving and blowing kisses at them. Every tent and building disgorged its occupants and scores of cameras pointed skyward. Marilyn was enjoying herself immensely and persuaded Woj to retrace his flight path. Snowflakes blew in through the open door as she laughed and waved again. Wylie held down one of her legs and was relieved when one of the other enlisted men slid the door shut. Marilyn returned to her seat, laughing and brushing snow from the fur collar of the flight jacket and thanked her supporters. Wylie's inventory of amazing young women met in Korea increased by one. No one in Hope's Crossing, New Jersey, would believe what had just happened. He just hoped there was enough light for some of the pictures he had taken.

The excitement about Marilyn's arrival increased as news of her helicopter escapade on the trip north was broadcast through word of mouth, field phone, and telex, and the United Nations soldiers awaiting her performances greeted her with intense ardor.

There were riots at three of her performances as troops pushed toward the stage. Soldiers who had been trampled were removed by ambulance. Wylie, who attended her first two performances, reported the riots but that news was promptly censored. His photographs of her arrival and on the helicopter, especially the picture of her brushing snow from her collar, were not, and his byline now appeared below pictures of Marilyn.

After a brief rest and lunch at headquarters, Marilyn changed from her G.I. issue fatigues into a low cut plum-colored dress covered in sequins and prepared for her first event. The dress alone won the hearts of all the troops who stood in front of the amphitheater that afternoon. Snow began to fall lightly as she walked across the stage to the microphone and waved away a field jacket offered by an attendant to cover her bare shoulders. The troops roared, only to be silenced when she began to banter with some of the soldiers close to the stage and explained what an honor it was to perform for them. She singled out a few soldiers close to the stage and asked them questions about their service in Korea. Then the band began to play some of the tunes from her latest movie, Gentlemen Prefer Blondes, as she swayed across the stage, sequins in motion. Wylie, standing in the "wings" of the stage so he could photograph the audience, watched jaws drop as she performed a little dance from the movie before beginning the *Diamonds are a Girl's Best Friend* song. She kept the microphone close to her mouth as she began the song, giving it her best torch song attack, but as she reached the lyrics of the second verse

Square shape or pear shape
These rocks don't lose their shape

she thrust her arms apart on "rocks," causing her breasts to strain against the sequins, exposing more of her generous bosom. Pandemonium ensued. Wylie awaited this part of the show eagerly during subsequent performances.

After the show, Wylie chatted with Smudge, Fatboy, and Leroy and asked why there was no sliding piano. They refused to dignify his jest with an answer. Wylie thanked Smudge for having him assigned to the helicopter crew, which Smudge graciously accepted. There was no time for more chatter because the group had to rush to another performance a few miles away.

Wylie traveled with Marilyn's retinue, which seemed to grow larger every hour, and watched her charm another ten thousand troops that afternoon. He did not press his luck by attempting to join the movie star at the General's Mess for dinner, but found a typewriter to prepare copy about the event and write a quick letter to his sisters who would certainly appreciate his being so close to a MOVIE STAR. That night he slept in the 3rd Division P.I.O. tent, and rose early the next morning to continue with the tour.

"That Public Relations Colonel from Tokyo noticed that all the generals are pushing each other aside to be seen with Marilyn, so it's enlisted with the goddess from now on," confided Perry Sleeper from

UP as they boarded a school bus with other members of the star's retinue. "We're gonna see stripes and no stars for the next couple of days. Much more appealing photo ops for the fans back home. And it looks as though she's really enjoying the tour."

Wylie agreed. In his limited experience, dogfaces always produced better copy than brass. As they reached the next hastily organized open air theater, already filled with thousands of soldiers stamping their feet for warmth in the brisk morning cold, Marilyn left her military escort and walked up to soldiers waiting at the front of the stage. Her blonde head bobbing above fatigues and fur collar, she shook hands and addressed some of the soldiers as "Honey" and told a Private who pointed his camera at her, "You've got to take it off," meaning his lens cap. He immediately doffed his fatigue cap before a friend elbowed him and pointed to the camera. Wylie stood nearby, clicking his Nikon, completely besotted with the joyful star. She's a real trooper, he thought, as she arrived on stage in her purple dress and shimmied through her theme song. Here it comes, he said to himself, as she thrust apart her arms on "rocks" and the crowd roared approval.

The next performance required a short helicopter trip to Z Regiment where Marilyn was to have lunch with enlisted men while the musicians and her entourage arranged the stage for her performance. The star giggled at the gauntlet of young officers who offered to guide her to the aircraft, and Wylie walked alongside taking pictures as she approached the craft. Captain Woj, who seemed to have a Marilyn monopoly when it came to transport, noticed Wylie and beckoned him to the helicopter doorway.

"Hop on. Never know when she'll need someone to hold her legs again." he ordered and Wylie moved swiftly to the back of the Sikorsky.

A light bird Colonel from Z Regiment helped Marilyn aboard and the big blade began its "wop...wop...wop" to lift them to their new destination. Once settled in the bucket seat she glanced toward Wylie and the other enlisted man.

"Oh, Honey," she said recognizing them both, talking loudly above the sound of the blades, "You were so good. You held me, before." She reached toward Wylie, who was seated almost next to her, held his face, and firmly kissed his cheek. The other EM almost fell to the steel deck as he squeezed toward her for his reward. Engine racket prohibited conversation, but Wylie and Marilyn exchanged a few words as they debarked for her next concert. She was quickly engulfed by her entourage. As Wylie watched her board a Jeep, Captain Woj tapped him on the shoulder.

"She's something else."

"Yeah."

Very inadequate response, thought Wylie who was trying hard to maintain his noncommittal, somewhat cynical journalist persona while being thrilled at a movie star's kiss

"She's beautiful inside and out," he finally mustered.

"Yeah."

Marilyn remained near the front lines until the following day, and Wylie took pictures of the actress and her audience. His films were taken to Seoul each day and flown to Tokyo for processing. A few of his candid photographs, showing her in soft, flattering light at ease with groups of soldiers were published in the Stars and Stripes. Apparently, the editor preferred them to the harsh lighting of the Signal Corp's number 50 flash bulbs. Wylie also forwarded journal-like articles that were not published, although Myron Goldstein used his material to concoct cartoons featuring a tall, skinny Sergeant named "Wylie" whose eyes often reflected an image of the blonde actress.

Marilyn returned to Japan three days after she arrived, suffering from a slight case of pneumonia but completely enthusiastic about entertaining so many United Nations troops. In Japan, she visited wounded soldiers still in hospitals and expanded her cadre of fans. Then, finally, she continued her honeymoon with her new husband.

Wylie sent letters to his parents and Judy about his brush with Hollywood royalty, explaining that it really wasn't such a big deal. For his sisters, he enclosed photos of himself with the star, realizing that, in their eyes at least, it was a big deal. No pictures for Judy; he felt guilty about his unreported relationship with Amelia. If Judy saw a picture of him with Marilyn, who knows what conclusions she might draw about his continuing fidelity.

CHAPTER 54

BUSINESS
DEVELOPMENTS

◆ ◆ ◆

THE BUICK PULLED UP ON a side street beside the almost completed Palace. Kim strode to the passenger door and helped his disconcerted aunt to the pavement.

Auntie Soo's weekend was not going well. Among her many business interests were a group of thatched huts alongside the river in Bupyeong, a rural village not far from Seoul. She made the little homes available to workers who supported her numerous projects at appropriate rental prices, which she deducted from their wages. To eliminate unnecessary costs for plumbing, the toilets in the homes were contained in little thatched out houses that protruded over the river.

In another cost-saving move, she assigned certain workers to harvest their fair share of aviation fuel from the pipeline that supplied the base in Seoul. The line ran along the river and the preferred collection method was to drill a hole in the steel pipe and let the fuel flow into a bucket. The fuel, similar to kerosene, was excellent for stoves, lanterns and modified ancient automobiles. Once collected, the worker sealed the hole with a screw, ready to be unscrewed at the next collection time.

One-eyed Park was distracted while collecting fuel by 1) an attractive girl carrying a basket of winter turnips and 2) an extremely urgent and painful need to rid himself of fiery kimchi he had consumed the day before. He resolved this conflict by scurrying to the nearest used kimchi disposal location, the lavatory of the thatched home across the road. The girl with the turnips could wait. Once relieved, he carried the bucket of fuel to his uncle who poured it carefully into glass lanterns and bottles for use by the villagers of Bupyeong. One-eyed Park was blissfully unaware that he had failed to replace the screw in the hole of the pipeline.

Of the various directions the aviation fuel could have taken, the path of least resistance ran to the river, which moved sluggishly past Auntie Soo's company houses. It was too soon for the spring runoff, so the fuel tended to puddle on top of the water near the bank, and continued collecting there during the night.

One-eyed Park strolled past the riverbank the next morning enjoying deep drags on one of the Lucky Strike cigarettes provided by his uncle. He arched the glowing remains toward the water and a brief gust of wind deposited the ember atop the small rivulet of fuel cascading to the river. A blue flame expanded from the point of impact, coursing toward the river where it danced to the stagnant pool of high-octane liquid hugging the bank under Auntie Soo's tenements. Soon that segment of the river was ablaze.

Gold and crimson flames shot skyward, licking the frame homes and their protruding battlements. The golden inferno caught thatched roofs and burned brightly as the fuel on the river gradually exhausted itself. Along the row of houses, people ran out doors away from the river, some clutching their bottoms and uttering terrible curses. A local fire brigade quickly assembled and managed to extinguish most of the burning roofs, but two of the houses became smoking ruins. One-eyed Park observed the scene with wonder, not once suspecting his involvement.

The tenants of Bupyeong were inured to hardship, having experienced the terrors of separate armies crossing their village, the rigors of winters with scant food, and the confusion of post war occupation.

None of this had prepared them for the unique injuries caused by the flaming river.

Three elderly women had been taking their ease in their outhouses as the flames reached upward, as had two men preparing for their day's employment with Auntie Soo. Their most vulnerable areas had been, according to their claims, charred and singed. It was an unfortunate and ignominious conclusion to one of life's little pleasures and they were certain that, in some way, Auntie Soo caused their anguish. She, after all, had organized the liberation of the aviation fuel in the first place.

Auntie Soo had to deal with not only the reconstruction of damaged homes and the temporary relocation of their tenants, but also the medical treatment of the five who had occupied the substandard rest rooms above the water. She listened politely as each in turn described to her the details of the accident with emphasis on the smell of burned hair, the scorching of flesh, the unlikelihood of future sexual concert, and the pain and suffering expected to continue for months if not years. After the listing of physical impairments, the negotiations began and, following an exhausting afternoon, she provided each tenant with a bundle of Hwan to help soothe all ailments.

The next part of the process was to search for someone to blame, for, injuries to her people aside, this accident was costing her real money. She enlisted one-eyed Park to help in this endeavor, which produced no potential perpetrators. Fortunately, Park had identified the leaking pipe before Auntie Soo's arrival and replaced the screw.

His employer was still stewing about this costly accident as she took Kim's hand and stepped down to the pavement beside the Palace.

Her mood did not change when she saw that Colonel Warfinger awaited her. The Colonel visited the construction site that he and Major Adder called the "Palace project" frequently. The Colonel considered the Palace project his idea and enjoyed watching it come to fruition. He arrived early for his meeting with Auntie Soo to observe progress and take notes about possible improvements. Today, just a few days away from a "grand opening," the decorators were putting the final additions on the wall hangings and setting up the beds destined for the cubicles along the walls.

Auntie Soo had demanded that the chief decorator create an atmosphere that in no way referred to hated Japanese design. That was difficult since there were few distinctive Korean design elements, other than the country's written language. Japan had imposed its own tastes on its subjected citizens for thirty-five years.

The decorator was also charged with crafting an ambiance as far removed as possible from drab military surroundings. Auntie Soo wanted the Palace to look "classy" and Warfinger was in accord. As it happened, the decorator had recently seen the American movie "Moulin Rouge" in the segregated Korean section of an I Corps theater. The film, which chronicled the life of Toulouse-Lautrec, used fin de siècle sets throughout, and he thought that look was definitely "classy."

The owners approved his preliminary sketches and he employed a group of craftsmen to make his designs come to life – no small task since he worked almost exclusively with surplus or liberated military items. Thus, shell casings were converted to ornate brass lamps, winter fatigues were sanded and dyed to resemble red velvet upholstery, reams of paper were bleached and dyed shades of ochre, pink and cream before being applied to the walls. Used two by fours were converted into frames for couches, beds, chairs, dressers, and tables and piles of used ammo cans became almost any metal item that could be shaped, hammered, or welded. Basins for the cubicles had a former life as mess trays and recently issued khaki towels stocked the shelves of the little boudoirs.

Although many of these materials were "found" items, Auntie Soo had to pay the artisans and fund the bribes and gifts required to keep the project on track. As always, she pleaded poverty as she grudgingly extracted the required payments from the inner pockets of her clothes. Suppliers noted the seemingly inexhaustible supply of

Hwan sequestered in the folds of her clothing, thereby belying her statements that the payee was taking food from the mouths of her grandchildren. The work continued quickly, however, and most of her artisans and contractors would have been disappointed if she had not put on her poverty act.

Warfinger noted the astonishing combination of reds, creams, pinks, and deep blues that assailed the senses of anyone visiting his new bordello. Somehow, the Korean artisans had converted olive green paint into bright primary colors and splashed them onto furniture and walls. Bed sheets were now brocade, and swags of maroon velvet obscured the frames of false windows and entrances to cubicles. A long bar gleamed with brass fittings, including an elevated footrest which ran its length. Near the reception area were discreet drawings of about forty sexual positions so the clientele could communicate their requirements to partners not so fluent in English. Clearly, this was a classy French bordello from the turn of the century, so incongruous that its users must appreciate its audacity and availability. The Colonel was delighted and looked forward to the opening of the Palace project. It was unfortunate that discretion required his absence from that event.

"So nice to see you, Walfinger,"

"I hope you are well, Ma'am."

"I have my troubles, but thank you."

"It appears that you have done an outstanding job here."

"I think it will do," she sighed.

Their conversation continued until the Colonel came to the point, which was to confirm the arrangements for medical inspection of the "talent," a term Warfinger has learned from his recent association with stateside entertainers. Other euphemisms were employed to describe the duties of employees. Mountain Moe, who had been a Sumo wrestler during the Japanese occupation, was an "entertainment director" who would keep the "clients" in line. Office workers, servers, and the cleaning crew were "associates," while whoever observed the cubicles from the cat walk above was the "reviewer."

There was no euphemism for those who collected the money. Auntie Soo and Major Adder established an impressive collection system with checks and balances that would warm the heart of any accountant. The cash would flow in predetermined amounts to predetermined pockets and Special Services would be able to fund wonderful programs for the troops, once appropriate deductions had been made. The two Army officers might blather on about how the Palace project would help the troops, but Auntie Soo believed it was, as always, about money.

After she organized the times and places for medical examinations with Warfinger, she raised the issue of how much more to compensate the talent for engaging in other than normally prescribed positions and procedures. She mentioned, for example, leather, whips, and high-heeled boots. The Colonel vaguely understood such practices and promised to reply after discussing the matter with other investors, but he felt certain that services that were more sophisticated demanded greater reward. Auntie Soo said she was glad he appreciated her point, although she had secretly calculated how to divert any premium pay to her voluminous pockets.

The Colonel lovingly reexamined the décor of the Palace project before he left and Auntie Soo made her own inspection of the gaudy bordello. Everything seemed to be in order. She had dealt with potential competitors; she had squeezed contractors who offered the lowest bids a bit more; and Song Song Park had delivered all needed talent. The talent currently resided in three of Auntie Soo's homes, eager to offer their services to the expected inflow of clients. She was not particularly interested in the furnishings and décor other than that they seemed appropriate and were in no way reminiscent of the hated occupiers. It all seemed a bit garish for her frugal tastes, but she felt certain it would impress the clients. It pleased her, since this was the first time she had organized a high-class whorehouse.

After Warfinger's departure, Auntie Soo discussed final operating details with Kim and met with contractors who awaited incremental payments. For once, the needed cash was not available in her pockets and she signaled Kim to invade the cache kept in the Buick. These and other details settled, she went alone to the room toward the back of the building that was her private office. She knelt on the floor beside a fiber mat that she moved aside to reveal a door snugly set in the floor. Once opened, she gingerly descended a ladder to the room below. The kerosene lamp she found in a niche near the ladder illuminated the room, revealing cases of penicillin and Aureomycin, syringes, surgical kits and mundane drugs like the APC pills routinely given to GIs. Cases were marked in English, Korean, French, and Spanish indicating their sources, all taken by stealth, bribery or violence from the stores of United Nations forces stationed in Korea.

Well, she thought, at least something is going right for a change. You, my friends, will soon be on your way north, as soon as our Captain returns from his recent voyage to Nampo.

CHAPTER 55

EXPEDITIONARY FORCES

◆ ◆ ◆

AS HINTS OF SPRING DESCENDED on the Korean peninsula, Wylie received a dispatch from Bill Mullin, editor of the Stars and Stripes, suggesting he would like to see "color" articles about some of the United Nations troops stationed in Korea. He was interested in original stories about the foreign soldiers who had served in combat to defend the people living below the 38th parallel. The idea appealed to Wylie. Here was an opportunity to learn more about the activities of the soldiers in some of the foreign battalions near the 53rd Infantry.

His previous experience with Expeditionary Forces was buying items like Cadbury chocolates at the British and Australian NAAFI houses (recommended by Alistair), samples of pâté at the French Post Exchange, or inexpensive jewelry for his sisters at the Thai PX.

He planned two weeks of reporting that would permit visits to at least a handful of the twenty expeditionary force headquarters located in South Korea. Wylie told Capitan Standrich that he believed Jeff Jefferson and Tiny Brewer could certainly "hold down the fort," and the Captain agreed with his assessment. It was likely one of them would take his place after he rotated stateside.

He needed Alistair's advice about which of the Commonwealth outfits to contact. There were units of British, Canadian, Australian, New Zealand, and South African troops near the lines and, as far as he was concerned, they all had different accents and funny hats. France and the Benelux countries all had a presence in Korea, and the nearest was a Belgian regiment about fifteen miles east of division headquarters. He had bumped into numerous Ethiopian soldiers who guarded his division's right flank and enjoyed American movies. There were, of course, the Greek and Turkish units that maintained a respectful distance from each other, and Philippine and Colombian forces maintained a strong presence guarding the DMZ with ROK soldiers. He had no desire to revisit the Thai unit. His scalding interview with its commander remained fresh in his memory.

"Bloody good idea," exclaimed Alistair on his next visit that occurred while Wylie was planning his reporting trip.

"As an Australian I suggest you visit our lads. They're brave to the point of stupidity and won't quit till the job is done. In a lot of ways, they are like Americans – question authority, take the initiative and quickly invent new ways to solve problems. They're kind of raw, having been civilized only half as long as you Yanks, and they refer to the Brits as Pommy Bastids. The 'Pommy' stands for 'Prisoner of Mother England,' which is what most of us were when we arrived on that huge island."

Alistair paused to consume another of the beers Wylie provided and continued. "Now those same Pommy Bastids are nothing more or less than trained killers. That bulldog mascot aptly describes their approach to combat - grab the enemy and rip their throats out. They do it for sport. You will notice they all have hobnail boots. They're not for traction; they are to stomp an enemy when no other weapons are available. I tell you, lad, they are the ones you want with you in a fight. Also, they have the best stocked NAAFI house in this part of the country.

"Now the Kiwis are good soldiers, can't say anything bad about them, but you're got to remember there are twenty sheep for each one of them in their country. They're a caring bunch and have the advantage of starting their lives in New Zealand because they wanted to be there. So, to continue my pontification on stereotypes, they are slow to boil but, when they do, they'll drag you down to hell with them."

Wylie took a few notes as Alistair continued.

"I don't know much about the Canadians. There's an old joke about how they're either hockey players or prostitutes. One of my pals mentioned that to a new editor at his paper who was his boss and the boss said, icily, his wife was Canadian. My friend asked what team she played for. Anyway, the troops are all potential hockey players. They're rugged and tough and we lost a lot of them on this peninsula. Couldn't go wrong with them.

"Now those Yarpies (it's a very derogatory term, but I like to say it) from South Africa, they all seem to have had combat experience in their own country and they're very wary. In my experience they're cool headed and can shoot straight. Also very independent and reliable. They have to be persuaded that an officer has the real goods before they'll follow him. They're kind of loose that way.

"So, Wylie, which ones do you think you'll visit?'

"I'm going to try the Brits first. You persuaded me with the NAAFI, and they have the best whiskey," Wylie joked. "That they're relentless killers influenced me some too."

During the next few days, Wylie organized his visits, deciding to limit them to four and arranging routes that would return him to Headquarters Company so he could file stories for Bill Mullin. He planned to visit the Turkish, British, Belgian, and Greek units. They were located across the peninsula near the front lines. Sergeant Pangluss agreed to release Scott as Wylie's driver since Shit Dad was occupied more and more with Captain Standrich on undisclosed missions. Three of the locations Wylie intended to visit were within a half-day's drive, but the Greek regiment was almost a full day away by Jeep. The Colonel commanding the Greek regiment invited Wylie to visit during their Easter celebration, so that would be their final stop.

"Like old times," joked Scott. "Off into the boonies and facing the unknown, though there's not so big a chance we'll get shot at this time."

"Amen to that!" said Wylie as he tossed his duffel into the back of the Jeep and settled next to Scott. It was warm enough to ride without cover, but Scott kept the windscreen up and checked the security bar welded to the front of the Jeep. It was designed to deflect or cut communications wire strung neck high across roads by "guerillas." They both carried carbines and Wylie kept his recently issued side arm, a .45 caliber Colt service pistol, on his hip. He had just re-qualified with the pistol and retained his sharp shooter reputation. It was a favorite weapon because it would stop an enemy at close range even if he was hit in the earlobe. Secretly, it made him feel a bit like John Wayne. In his last letter to Judy, he had enclosed a picture of himself looking across the DMZ with the pistol at his side.

Corporal Jim Beam stowed his camera case and sprawled across the back seat, toying with Wylie's little Nikon camera. "It'll never replace the 4x5 Speed Graphic," he said, "but it's got a really fast lens. Probably get a good shot of a black cat in a coal bin." Wylie decided not to mention the pictures of Marilyn Monroe he had published in various stateside papers, all taken with his little camera.

There were good roads leading to the British compound and last night's frost kept the dust down. They arrived without incident just before noon and the guard at the gate directed the "Yank wankers" to a young public relations officer who was pleased to help them in any way. No units, it seemed, were averse to publicity.

They spent the afternoon interviewing the unit commander and photographing troop exercises that included rappelling from helicopters, extravagant use of flame throwers for Jim Beam's benefit, and hand-to-hand combat drills, all carried out with manly shouts and grunts. Wylie observed their combat boots. Alistair was right; they were definitely lethal weapons.

That evening they sampled "lager tops" in the EM Pub. Wylie found the mixture of lager beer with a splash of lemonade refreshing and a positive dust cutter, but Scott preferred the dark bitters that were miraculously available on draft. Corporal Beam began with whiskey and soon accompanied an impromptu singing group in his off-key tenor. As the three Americans left to make their winding way to their assigned tent, the British bar flies decided that they weren't the assholes they thought they would be, but were a bit of all right.

The following morning Jim Beam awoke with a blinding hangover that required Scott and Wylie to administer quantities of cold water to his face and head, followed by several swallows of whatever alcoholic beverage he prudently carried in a tin flask. It suddenly dawned on Wylie that the photographer did his best work while drunk. When he mentioned it to Scott, his friend laughed at his observation of the obvious. Beam's perennial condition was well known.

Sustained with the life giving elixir, Beam shouldered his camera case, squinted at the bright morning sunlight as one of the soldiers from the night before walked up, and asked "Tea up?" Beam staggered as though hit with rifle butt. "You Limeys don't have coffee?" But, fortunately they did.

Wyle and the photographer joined the young public relations officer on a tour of a nearby farming village "adopted" by the British regiment and observed soldiers using heavy equipment to supplement ox drawn plows in preparing the fields for sowing. Wylie interviewed the soldiers, obtaining quotations for home towner interviews and collecting name and rank for Beam's pictures. Wizened farmers showing gap-toothed smiles obliged the photographer who also followed some toddlers for surefire human-interest images. Before they left, the young officer distributed rakes and hoes for the elders and chocolates for the children. Heartwarming, thought Wylie, fucking heartwarming, and then recoiled at his own cynicism. Chastened, he wondered where such mean-spirited thoughts originated. He drew a blank until he recalled his desperation the night of his meeting with Alistair and Henry about LSD. Just one too many photo ops, one too many public shows of charity. It would pass.

The next morning the three departed to visit with Turkish soldiers located a two-hour drive west of the British Battalion. It was the first time Wylie met with soldiers who followed the Muslim faith and the first time he tried Turkish coffee. Both were a revelation. The officer in charge introduced himself as Captain Bulent Kudret and he spoke American, the result of three teenage years living with an aunt and uncle in Queens, New York. He had dark hair and a bristling mustache, but he was not tall and his eyes had a liquid softness. Wylie assessed his character as they walked to a canteen located in a Quonset hut; he just looks.... kind, not at all what he expected from Turks who defeated commonwealth troops at Gallipoli.

The Captain offered the three American soldiers biscuits and slender cups of coffee hardly larger than shot glasses. Jim Beam politely thanked the officer and, always in need of caffeine, consumed the drink in a single draught, only to turn red and sputter out the coffee grounds that filled half the cup. Wylie sipped slowly, enjoying the hot, sweet brew and managed to avoid most of the solid bits. After watching Beam, Scott concentrated on the biscuits. Wylie had spoken with Captain Kudret by telephone the week before, and the Captain suggested they report on a bivouac exercise and a promotion ceremony. The bivouac exercise was in progress when they arrived and included live fire, guaranteed to make Jim Beam happy with images of smoke and flame and soldiers in odd uniforms dashing through the trees.

Scott attended to refueling the Jeep and exchanging cigarettes with Turkish soldiers at their motor pool as Jim Beam focused his Speed Graphic on the activities beyond the encampment. Various soldiers engaged the Captain as he and Wylie walked to the knob of a hill overlooking the excitement below. The soldiers seemed extremely respectful of their officer, who frequently touched their arms or shoulders in a passing gesture. When Wylie asked about it, the Captain said, "In most of the forces in Korea there's an emphasis on rank and discipline and military order. We approach that in a different way, as though we were a family or clan. As far as I am concerned, the soldiers under my command are my sons, and I am their father. Our noncoms are like older brothers. In battle, our motivation is to support each other in any way possible. The loss of one diminishes us all."

Turkish combat troops were permitted to dispense with some of their religious obligations, but when exercises were halted for the day, the camp address system called them to prayer and, in the fading afternoon light, Wylie was able to photograph the large group of soldiers kneeling and in repose. It was one of his favorite pictures but was never published because it was unwarlike. However, the feature article with photos showing smoke, flames, and vaulting Turkish troops was very popular.

After the evening meal, Wylie and crew tried thick nonalcoholic grape juice while they watched Turkish soldiers entertain themselves with robust dancing challenges and hilarious imitations of belly dancing. Jim Beam decided it went a bit too far when a noncom with a huge belly kept trying to knock him off his chair with well-placed up thrusts. He excused himself and wandered off holding his half-full glass, soon to be reinforced with the contents of his tin flask. Scott and Wylie joined a fevered circular dance that involved jumping and shouting, and they happily yelled many Turkish words that they could not understand. Later, as they walked to their assigned tent Scott said, "Man, never had so much fun before standing up and sober. I'd go to war with these guys any day!"

Wylie spent more time with Captain Kudret the next morning, writing down his recollections of combat engagements and repatriation of the many Turkish soldiers who were interned in North Korean prison camps. Many Turkish prisoners never returned.

Out of habit, Wylie asked about his hometown, which was Antalia on the Mediterranean Sea. When Kudret finished describing the location and atmosphere of the ancient seaport, Wylie thought he could smell the salt air and hear waves lapping against the hulls of boats. As they departed, the Captain shook Wylie's hand and invited him to his home —someday. He had carefully written his name and home address on a card. Wylie kept it safe for a very long time.

By evening, they returned to 53rd Division Headquarters. Corporal Beam received orders to leave the others to cover an award ceremony the next day. Wylie drafted Tiny Brewer to travel with them to the Belgian unit. Tiny claimed to have studied French in college and Wylie hoped the Belgians would understand a North Carolina French accent. It did not occur to him the Belgians might speak Flemish. He clacked away for a few hours, filed two stories relating to the Brits and created caption sheets for Jim Beam's photos. He planned to delay the next day's departure so he could discuss urgent business with a red haired Executive Director.

CHAPTER 56

TROUBLE ALONG THE WAY

◆ ◆ ◆

As THE TOURS OF MANY of his people ended and they rotated home, Sergeant Pangluss had difficulty finding new talent for the motor pool. Eager to recruit from within division, he mistakenly believed that the Private recommended by the Engineers could be trained to complete routine preventative maintenance on the many vehicles in his care.

Slats Morongo had worn out his welcome with the Engineer Battalion and his superior noncom had no qualms about recommending him to Sergeant Pangluss who, in his opinion, had been just a bit too free and easy in midnight requisitions of engineering supplies. A large quantity of missing pipes came to mind.

Slats had undergone on-the-job training for a few weeks when Pangluss assigned him to changing oil and filters, greasing, and checking belts and fluids on Jeeps in the motor pool. Slats, now a short timer with just four months of service left in Korea, was not motivated toward excellence. As usual, good enough was his highest standard— a standard required to avoid returning to honey pot duty with Uncle Ho. Uncle Ho did not miss Slats. He could run his honey pot business better without him.

Slats drained the oil from nine Jeeps in the motor pool and replaced it in eight. The Jeep with the oil deprived Willys engine was assigned to Scott the afternoon he was to drive Wylie and Tiny to report on the Belgian unit.

Wylie planned to arrive at the Belgian company late in the afternoon, well before dusk. That permitted a morning consultation with Captain Standrich and Jeff Jefferson and a brief visit with Amelia during which he suggested a vacation together for a week or so in Japan. Amelia was delighted with the idea, but wondered about travel arrangements. Wylie was sure he could work something out.

The three soldiers boarded the Jeep at 1500 hours for the two-hour trip east, with Scott driving, Wylie riding "shotgun," and Tiny crammed in the back with their mussette bags trying to conjugate French verbs. Scott assured Wylie the route was well marked and there was no possible way the trip would take more than two and a half hours.

However, they encountered an unmapped fork along the way, marked only with ancient carvings in stone. The collective wisdom aboard the Jeep apparently did not apply to routing decisions and, as the blue shadows of dusk crept toward the distant hills, they found themselves churning down a single lane dirt road in the direction of the sunset. The chill of evening did not descend, however, as Scott and Wylie felt unaccustomed warmth from the engine compartment, prompting Scott to peer at the temperature gauge. As the needle strained past the 220 mark, the radiator cap suddenly released a geyser of steam and the engine stopped abruptly, relaxing as a molecular heat exchange fused glowing metal parts together.

"What?" asked Tiny.

"Oh shit!" said Wylie.

"Fuck me!" exclaimed Scott who was the first to realize they were immobile but for their feet on a dark Korean night devoid of signs of human habitation. After the luxury of liberal cursing and kicking the front of the Jeep by all involved, Wylie took command. They each had a canteen full of water and a spare blanket and Tiny admitted to having a handful of O'Henry bars in his bag. Candy and water were their evening meal and Wylie volunteered to take the first watch of the night as the other two contorted themselves to sleep on the Jeep's hard seats.

Wylie settled himself on the berm beside the dirt road and almost forgot their predicament as he looked toward the luminous Milky Way, an almost reachable band of light never seen so large and accessible before. Alone with his thoughts in the crisp night air, he reflected on the young women in his life, the robust and adorable Amelia and the distant, unattainable Judy. Irritating flickers of guilt troubled his mind as he conjured up images of Judy. There was no way around it. He was being as unfaithful as he could be to Judy, but he was afraid to admit it, to write her. He resolved to wait until he returned, when he could tell her in person. That was the fair and decent thing to do.

A shooting star crossed the horizon, and Wylie developed a new and painful concern. Maybe *she's* also found someone else; those references to her best friend's brother and his 1953 Ford Crestline might imply that. Might that excuse his duplicity? Was he conjuring up her possible romance with the Crestline guy to justify his relationship with Amelia? Why was this so fucking complicated? Maybe....

Scott jabbed him in the arm.

"My turn on watch yet? My back and this seat can't find no way but crossways."

Wylie returned to the Jeep and tried to assemble his body around the gearshift and hand brake. His attempts to find a comfortable position trumped further self-recriminations as weariness overcame him and he managed a few hours' sleep.

At first light two figures appeared on the road behind them, their long shadows preceding them. The three soldiers took cover beside the Jeep and held their carbines at the ready. It soon became clear that the swaybacked mare and the Korean farmer in the wide brimmed hat leading her did not represent present danger. In relief, they bowed slightly and said "Konichi-wa," which the farmer returned in greeting. The mare eyed them suspiciously. The farmer gestured toward the Jeep, looking quizzical. Scott drew his finger across his throat and turned his thumb down. With the same hand, he rubbed his stomach and pointed to his mouth. The farmer brightened and smiled, gesturing them to follow him down the road.

The three took their gear and plodded behind the mare, kicking up dust on the road for half a mile before the farmer turned to follow a well-worn path leading to his home, a little frame building with a thatched roof beside a chicken coop, a horse, three cows and goats. Two acres of brown stubble stretched behind the house; Wylie realized this was a man of substance.

With great ceremony, the farmer gestured them to enter his home and the three congregated on the hard dirt floor near a fire pit where two small children gazed at them with astonished eyes. A flustered woman tending the fire exchanged what seemed to be heated words with her husband, something along the lines, Wylie was sure, of "What do you mean bringing these smelly foreigners into my kitchen at the crack of dawn. You what? You want me to feed them? You want to take food from the mouths of your children for these pasty faced louts?"

But the farmer prevailed and his wife pulled the children to her side and gestured for the three soldiers to sit on the floor while she prepared food. She suppressed a smile as Tiny lowered himself cautiously to the floor and settled uncomfortably among pots and crockery.

The woman uncovered a pan warming by the fire and handed hunks of Korean bread made with red pepper powder to the three soldiers. Scott eagerly consumed his share and quickly doused his burning lips and tongue with water from his canteen. Watching Scott's reddening cheeks, Tiny and Wylie chewed small pieces slowly but also soon reached for their canteens. The inferno passed quickly, though, in time for them to receive the next item on the menu, earthen bowls of steaming liquid that appeared to be soup prepared with kimchi. The aroma of peppers, garlic and something vaguely familiar but not quite known rose agreeably from the bowls. The woman offered wooden spoons and Scott sampled the brew first. "Good," he said and plunged ahead, as Wylie examined his bowl in the dim light of the hut. It contained something unique.

In deference to his rank, the lady of the hut added to Wylie's portion a single delicacy remaining from a special meal the night before. A goat's eye peered malevolently from the center of the bowl, its rectangular pupil seemingly focused on Wylie's nose. The heat of cooking clouded the cornea but its goatish essence remained, causing Wylie to freeze with the bowl in one hand and the spoon in the other. There was not much opportunity to consort with goats in Hope's Crossing and Wylie's only intimate experience with goats was as a small child in a petting zoo. Yet some primitive synapses in the lower regions of his brain stem confirmed that the demonic presence in the bowl was of goat and, very briefly, he locked his eyes on it. It seemed to look back, balefully. Turning away, he noticed the husband and wife looking at him expectantly as a fevered stream of consciousness ricocheted between his ears:

Holy shit! That is the most repulsive thing I've ever seen but they're looking at me like it's some big deal do I really have to eat the thing I don't want to do that oh no I most certainly don't want to be near the disgusting thing if I don't I'll just be another ugly dumb American insensitive xenophobic it's scary what could it possibly taste like this guy he took us in he and his wife are my hosts manners… manners be polite clean your plate what the fuck how bad could it be?

He smiled weakly across the room at the farmer and his wife but hesitated before lifting the eye with its gold-fringed pupil and placing it in his mouth. It tasted musty and had stringy material protruding from the back. He did not think swallowing it whole was possible, so he squeezed it lightly between his back molars. It felt like a large grape, tight skin with a resilient interior. A little more pressure and something moved sluggishly under the taut exterior. That movement triggered a spontaneous reaction and he bit down forcefully.

That motion created sensual choreography that would remain fresh in his mind for years. Under the sixty-seven PSI bite pressure of his molars, the eye yielded quickly and burst creating an audible popping sound that caused Scott and Tiny to turn in his direction. A thick, viscous, oily saline solution flooded his mouth, invading all virgin crevices. It was so surprising that he swallowed most of the liquid before coughing, thereby dislodging the husk of the eye, which then lay expectantly on his tongue. With unnaturally heightened senses, he was sure he could feel the rectangular shape of the pupil within the limp husk. Something in the desiccated eyeball crunched. He raised the earthen bowl to his lips and drank desperately, sending all unwanted oral substances to find new homes in his innards. He took his first breath since placing the eye in his mouth and the Korean couple beside the fire beamed approvingly. Wylie put down the bowl and nodded to them, awaiting a possible upheaval that fortunately never came.

After capsicum burns on lips and mouth and the nourishing kimchi soup, the three soldiers were not inclined to try further courses in their breakfast adventure. They bowed politely to their Korean hosts, and Wylie murmured "kamsamnida," the word for "thank you" that Kim had taught him.

The promise of a clear day showed through the door to the hut and they moved outside, followed by the farmer. His wife stood in the doorway and smiled as the three considered their next steps.

"Okay. So we have a problem here. If that Jeep was a mule we'd of shot it between the eyes. It's going nowhere. What we have is shanks mare, but where, fearless leader, should we point our boots?" Tiny asked Wylie.

Before Wylie could respond, Scott pulled a map from his pack and spread it out on the ground. The Belgian unit location was marked with a penciled cross. As they studied the map with increasing anxiety the farmer joined them, fascinated by the detailed topographic information. After a moment, he placed his finger on the map indicating a spot not far from the penciled "x" and pointed vigorously to his feet. Met with incomprehension, he tried again, placing a finger on the map, moving it slowly toward the "x" and pointing to the south.

"Shit, man, he's showing us the way," exclaimed Scott. Wylie pointed in the same direction and asked "Belgian, Belgian?"

The farmer brightened. "Bel-jin, Bel-jin, ye,ye."

The farmer led them out the path to the road they had walked the evening before and pointed south. He traced crossroads in the dust and indicated a left turn some distance away.

As they rearranged their gear, Tiny removed his blanket and handed it to the farmer, indicating it was a gift for his children, and Wylie and Scott did the same. Two uneventful hours later, they approached the white painted posts delineating the entrance to the Belgian unit and reported the condition of their Jeep to the commander. His English was sparse, but the adjutant, a Captain, spoke Irish-accented English learned from a girl he courted while studying in Dublin for a year.

It took the American soldiers a few moments to decipher the English language spoken with combined Irish and Belgian accents through the bristling blonde moustache that drooped over his mouth. Captain Reumont dismissed the demise of their Jeep simply as "fortunes of war" and had his clerk call the 53rd Infantry motor pool to arrange for its retrieval, meanwhile offering to return the three to their headquarters when they had finished their assignment. The Captain led them to the mess hut and offered coffee and croissants, which Wylie, in particular, consumed eagerly as the memory if not the taste of the goat's eye lingered. Fortified, Wylie discussed the day's activities with the officer, and he and Tiny outlined how they intended to report on the joint infantry/armor exercise the Belgian unit was planning to undertake with elements of the 7th Infantry Division that afternoon.

By 1300 hours, tanks and personnel carriers roared toward dimly seen targets across the scrub covered plain extending from the Belgian unit to distant foothills. Wylie and Tiny ran through dusty indentations of armored vehicle treads with Belgian sappers whose primary responsibility seemed to involve pausing every few hundred yards to blow something up. The Belgian infantry simulated small arms discharges, but tanks fired live rounds and mortar teams pounded the hillsides with shells containing explosives and smoke. It's like a fine little war, thought Wylie, recalling his night of combat. All we need is darkness and some phosphorous flares to make me feel at home.

As they ran, Wylie paused to photograph the heavy vehicles plowing through dust-clogged sunlight and grimy Belgian soldiers moving on and along with the armor. From a ditch, he managed a low angle shot of approaching armor surrounded by troops that ultimately became the lead photograph in the story he and Tiny wrote about the joint exercise. Individual photographs of soldiers in action poses became Belgian hometowners, carried by newspapers in Antwerp and Brussels. AP and INS picked up the well-coordinated combined UN training program as well, and headlines like UN TROOPS ON ALERT AT DMZ appeared in stateside papers. But now, nine months after the armistice, that didn't sell many papers. People seemed to be more interested in all the communists Senator Joe McCarthy was rooting out in Washington and Hollywood.

After the attack on the defenseless foothills, the commanders looked at their watches and called a halt at 1500 hours. The Belgian equivalent of "smoke if you got 'em" rang out and the soldiers rested beside vehicles and hummocks lighting up noxious cigarettes that smelled like overheated brake drums. Partly to avoid that smell and partly because they hadn't been so physically active for a while, Wylie and Tiny returned to Belgian headquarters where they discovered Scott with two Belgian noncoms trading English and French curses and scatological definitions, complete with definitive gestures and noises. The major language exchange had apparently been completed, as Scott was working on "salope." He told Wylie he was pretty sure it meant "bitch" in French. Neither of his friends seemed to care.

The Belgians had no Sergeant Beauregard Snipes to tend their mess and the three Americans dined on pedestrian fare that evening, grateful that the garlic-laden vegetables and fried potatoes contained no frogs' legs or snails, as Scott had suggested. Captain Reumont found them as they left the mess hall and invited them for a drink in his office, cordially producing a bottle of Elixir d'Anvers that he explained was a digestive herbal liqueur – distinctively Belgian. The bittersweet taste appealed to them all, though the warmth in their bellies did not immediately translate into the desired alcoholic buzz.

By the time they had consumed most of the second bottle, however, they were on a first name basis with their host. He proceeded to outline the history of his unit during combat that, inexplicably, caused him to chuckle and guffaw and poke Tiny in the arm, saying, with his Irish/French accent "But you know what I mean, of course." They pretended they did as a courtesy and to foster good relations among UN forces. Soon they left the Captain chuckling to himself in his office and struggled through the pleasant haze of the Elixir d'Anvers to their bunks. Tiny fell asleep in a sitting position and Scott urinated in the washbasin. Wylie wasn't sure that was a terribly good idea as he fell to the bunk and slept instantly.

The next morning the three carefully seated themselves in the Belgian Light Utility Vehicle (which Scott thought looked suspiciously like a Jeep) and began their return trip to 53rd Infantry headquarters. Their driver bore a striking resemblance to Jack Palance, the evil villain in Shane, and scowled at them when they tried to converse. Tiny's comments about the fine weather in his version of French were ignored until the driver turned and spoke a few curt words over his shoulder. Scott laughed, relying on his recent language course in the Belgian idiom.

"Hey, Tiny, this guy is fearless," said Scott." He just called you a pig's asshole."

Tiny decided not to tangle with Jack Palance. The trip continued in silence, without incident, and they arrived back in division before noon.

They were invited to visit the Greek regiment the next morning to participate in their Easter celebration, so Wylie and Tiny tried to clear their desks that evening. As Wylie rushed to complete filing a story, a mournful Shit Dad pushed through the door and stood by Wylie's desk.

'Wylie, man, I got problems. You gotta help," said his friend." They gonna make me leave my family and rotate back to the states and the Captain he can't figure out how keep that from happening."

He produced a thick sheaf of official looking papers and placed them carefully on the desk.

"Shit dad, these here are the Regulations. You gotta read them and figure out how I can stay here, stay with my family. You can do it, man!"

CHAPTER 57
EASTER

◆ ◆ ◆

ANDY PAPADOPOULOS, COLUMBIA UNIVERSITY TRAINED adjutant of the Greek regiment, had almost completed his obligatory two years of active duty in the Greek army near the Albanian border when his unit was assigned to service in Korea. He reluctantly extended his service obligation by a year and accepted a promotion to Major. Fluency in English proved to be an asset and he served as liaison with the American and Commonwealth units serving in his sector. The assignment to host reporters from the Stars and Stripes at the regiment's Easter celebration was an opportunity to hone his public relations skills.

By March of that year, it seemed the armistice would hold, so the Greek regiment worked to make its operations more permanent and improved the structures and facilities used by the troops. Proud of their improved facilities, Andy intended to show them off to the reporters. After their arrival and appropriate introductions, he began their tour with a visit to a Quonset hut barracks for enlisted men, a luxury that impressed the two correspondents who were still living in tents at the 53rd Infantry.

Wylie blinked to help his eyes adjust from midafternoon sunlight outside to the dim interior of the Quonset hut. He saw steel cots arrayed on both sides of the arched room with dim light entering through eyebrow windows inserted along the hut's corrugated walls. He made out a group of Greek soldiers in T-shirts and fatigues surrounding a steel cot in the middle of the hut. One soldier was on all fours on the cot, his fatigue pants and skivvies bunched around his knees, his posterior pointed in the direction of the ceiling. The luxurious dark hair covering his body reminded Wylie of a wiry Airedale.

Curious, the visitors walked into the room to investigate, closing the door behind them, darkening the room further. As they moved toward the knot of Greek soldiers, one of them slid behind the man on the cot and fired up his Zippo lighter. Its yellow flame emphasized the faces of the encircling soldiers like a Rembrandt painting. The soldier on the cot stiffened, groaned, and delivered a mighty fart, immediately ignited by the Zippo's flame.

A long neon blue methane flare shot from the soldier's ass across the chamber, bathing it in brief, but ethereal light. The Greek soldiers expressed their awe and appreciation with cries of delight. The soldier on the bed, however, was not delighted, since the flare had burned the hair and singed the flesh on his most tender areas. He cursed, groaned, and cursed some more, rubbing his hands over charred buttocks, brushing off the ashy remains of body hair. Andy rushed to the injured man, examined the damage, and ordered the soldiers to cover him. His comrades carried him from the barracks, still cursing and moaning, for medical attention.

Shaking his head in disbelief, Andy said to Wylie, Tiny, and Scott, "That's the third time it's happened this month. Somebody tells them that farts ignite and they have to find out for themselves."

Andy looked back at the vacant cot. "That was pretty impressive, though. That flame must have been at least five feet long."

"Wow," said Tiny, "it gives new meaning to 'backfire.'"

That was the correspondents' introduction to the Greek regiment. This seems promising, thought Scott.

Wylie found the battalion's preparations for the holiday quite exotic, so he and Tiny reported on the numerous activities the soldiers pursued the Saturday before Easter. There were no military maneuvers;

the entire outfit concentrated on preparation of a traditional feast. Andy led them from one location to another, pointing out that Easter was the most important Greek holiday, normally a weeklong event, which, because of military necessity, was being shortened to the day celebrating Christ's resurrection.

In a large kitchen, chefs in rakish toques kneaded and braided dough to prepare Tsoureki, traditional Easter bread, and young Korean women dyed mountains of eggs a bright red color. Helpers stuffed grape vine leaves with rice and various fruits. Tiny recoiled as workers chopped squid caught off the coast of Japan into bite-sized morsels. Wylie was fascinated by the colorful hues of the food being prepared for the next day and wished there was enough light to capture the activity in the kitchen on Kodachrome film. He settled for black and white Tri-X film that was sensitive enough to make good photos in poor light. It was successful. Editor Bill Mullin loved his picture of a fat chef with a huge black moustache stirring a steaming kettle next to a pile of squid destined to become calamari.

Andy then directed them to an area of the parade ground beside regimental headquarters where soldiers wielding long sticks and tools that looked like tridents tended smoking trenches. What seemed like an entire flock of lambs lay fastened to spits, roasting in the trenches. Cooks adjusted glowing embers of charcoal with their long sticks and turned the lambs with the little tridents. Wylie took his pictures with smoky haze emphasizing the late afternoon shafts of light above the trenches. Glancing into the pits, he saw the lambs' eyes were open. He took no close ups of the roasting animals.

They joined Greek soldiers enjoying a light supper in the mess hall and, with Andy's help, interviewed a number of them in hopes of finding colorful comments to add to the article Wylie and Tiny planned to write. The comments were much the same as those of all soldiers, foreign and American, that they had interviewed over the past months. Touches of homesickness, pride in their outfits, say "hi" to the girl back home, unprompted declarations of the number of days left in Korea, and a smattering of Korean phrases punctuating their comments.

When Wylie closed his notebook, it was time for the religious services in the auditorium they had visited earlier. Its large doors were open and the gathering troops had unobstructed views of the Easter services. Large white candles flickered along the walls as a chaplain and his assistant began the services that Wylie thought were familiar even though he could not understand a word. Andy stood at his side and explained what was going on. At midnight, the priest announced "Christ is risen" and field artillery pieces near the hillside fired charges. All the troops responded with "Truly He is risen" and "True is the Lord."

The ceremony ended, Andy led his three companions toward the resurrection table. "Now," he said, "the real fun begins. Serious eating and drinking starts now and lasts all night. Then tomorrow we feast on the spiced lamb!"

The battalion commander was a burly man with what seemed a standard issue thick black moustache. He smiled broadly at the three Americans and motioned them toward a table covered with a white cloth and festooned with bottles of a clear liquid, a pitcher of water, and glasses. He spoke to them in Greek with words of warm welcome and pointed to the bottles on the table.

"The Colonel wants you to know he is very happy to have you here as his guests and he invites you to join him in a drink of our ouzo. I think you'll like it. It tastes like anise or licorice," said Andy.

The Colonel poured a clear oily liquid in a glass, added water and handed the glass, now turned a milky white, to Wylie. "Slick!" said Scott, impressed by the magic liquor. They all tasted the cloudy ouzo and decided it was delicious. As the night wore on, refills arrived often and unbidden. Just before dawn, Andy arranged to have them escorted to bunks in one of the Quonset huts.

Light poured in through the millimeter slit between Wylie's eyelids and attacked his retina like hurricane waves crashing against a rocky shore. Midmorning sunshine poured through the circular opening in the door of the Quonset hut, cruelly cutting across the floor and blazing on to his head resting on an air mattress. Turning his head away from the light somehow precipitated the sudden expansion of the knot in his stomach that resolved itself in a massive belch. The atmosphere around his head smelled of licorice tinged with something oddly sour. He decided to escape the odor and tried to stretch his legs.

The legs refused to move. They were paralyzed. My God! he thought, the ouzo has affected my nervous system. His muddled brain quickly conjured up the image of his return to Hope's Crossing in a wheel chair, learning to walk with crutches, fastening heavy leg braces. Every evil thing he had ever done passed before his eyes like toilet paper unrolling.

He was preparing for life as an invalid when Tiny shifted his thighs from Wylie's calves and rolled into a nearby washstand, upsetting a pan of cold water that spilled on them both. Scott, awakened by the ruckus, began to laugh at his sputtering friends until he realized someone had poured molten lead in the cavity between his ears and his mirth abruptly died. This fine example of American military might presented itself to Andy Papadopoulos as he entered the hut.

"The Colonel thinks you are the most amusing American he has ever met," Andy informed Wylie. "He wants you to sit next to him during the Easter meal today."

Wylie dimly recalled that the Colonel had laughed uproariously each time he thanked him for a glass of ouzo that morning, and he laughed with him without understanding the joke. Earlier, Wylie had asked the young officer sitting next to him how to say "thank you" in Greek. Lieutenant Coutsis, who had consumed a bottle of retsina earlier and who had only a rudimentary acquaintance with English, misunderstood Wylie's question and provided the Greek for "fuck you" in response. He and Wylie practiced proper pronunciation of the difficult opening "ch" consonant until Coutsis was satisfied.

The Colonel, also well lubricated with ouzo, was amused by the bold and iconoclastic American Sergeant who said "fuck you" with a gracious smile each time he received another beaker of cloudy ouzo. The Colonel seemed to think it became funnier each time Wylie said it. Wylie recalled none of it; he was focused on making a vow to avoid ouzo for the rest of his life, a promise to himself he almost kept.

Cleaned up and walking cautiously through unrelenting daggers of noonday sunlight to the dining tables set up near the resurrection table, the three Americans were subdued and respectful of the Greek troops who seemed clear headed and cheerful. The Colonel greeted Wylie warmly and ushered the three visitors to seats at the head table.

Wishing he had not forgotten his Ray-Ban® sunglasses, Wylie turned to Andy and said, "No more ouzo." Andy took it as a question, though it could have been interpreted as a request.

"After this morning we're pretty much out, but the traditional drink at our Easter feast is retsina, and we have barrels of that, thanks be to God."

The Colonel understood the reference to wine and ordered a few bottles of the golden nectar for the head table, exuding bonhomie, personally filling Wylie's glass. Wylie exuded in return and the two clinked their glasses. To Wylie's pleasant surprise, a few sips of the wine, with its faint taste of turpentine, quickly dulled the throbbing behind his left eye. He risked looking onto the sun washed field in front of the head table. The retsina seemed to have a healing effect on Scott and Tiny as well, and they brightened as the Easter feast unfolded.

Cooks extracted roasted lambs from their smoldering pits. They carved the meat and carried it to tables set up on the parade ground, joining platters of rice, vegetables, salads, and piles of braided bread. Andy led his American friends to one of the tables where they filled trays with the delicacies of the day. It was a splendid meal, full of novel and exotic tastes. The Colonel held his wine glass high and toasted them.

The celebration continued through the afternoon and Wylie did his best to moderate his consumption of food and alcohol. Scott, still in recovery from the morning's excesses, sipped judiciously from retsina and noted the gradual lessening of the throbbing behind his eyes. Tiny, enthralled by the variety and quality of the feast, ate until his large frame could hold no more. Finally, as a gesture of appreciation, he entertained his new Greek friends by belching all the letters of the alphabet.

While there was still sunlight, Wylie photographed details of the feast, pictures that Bill Mullin decided not to use. Apparently, they were too convivial, not suggesting the prowess of the Greek fighting men.

At twilight, the festivities ended and the Americans returned to their air mattresses in the Quonset hut next to Andy's billet to begin their recovery from the pleasures and excesses of the past forty-eight hours.

Early the next morning, Scott tossed their gear into the Jeep for the trip back to the 53rd. Andy and the Colonel, now in crisp Class A uniforms, stood beside the Jeep, looking like modern Spartans, and offered their hands in farewell. Reluctant to depart, Wylie promised to send copies of all their pictures. Andy was sure they would meet again soon.

As the Jeep churned along the dusty highway to 53rd Headquarters, Wylie cradled his carbine and let his thoughts wander, reflecting on their visits to the UN expeditionary forces. Beginning on a superficial level, he cataloged the exotic liquids consumed: lager tops, Turkish coffee, Elixir d'Anvers, ouzo, and retsina. He then considered the diverse characteristics of these fighting men: the prideful and well-honed killer instincts of the Brits, the family and clan relationships of the Turks, the nonchalant delight the Belgians took in blowing things up. The Greeks' fighting prowess remained something of a mystery to him, since he had seen them only in celebration, but he was sure he would prefer the Colonel at his side rather than opposing him in battle.

How diverse, he thought, yet they were all willing to risk their lives to defend a country most of them had never heard of before 1950. Having arrived in Korea against his wishes, he tried to understand the ways in which troops and their leaders were persuaded to take up arms against an ill-defined enemy in a country far from home.

His own experience providing no solution, he reviewed the stories he dashed off and suddenly found them superficial, easy, and formulaic. He failed to ask important questions during his odyssey to the expeditionary forces. He learned how they fought, but not why. He learned about their drinking habits, but not about their aspirations. What was it, for example, that changed British pub-crawlers into stone killers? He had planned to write about hobnailed boots and battle tactics, the surface stuff. He focused on the soldiers' diversity, forgetting about their commonality.

Was it possible, he wondered, to do this better, to delve deeper, to incorporate emotions and taboo "touchy feely" stuff in his articles? He was sorry Don Heron had gone stateside and that Alistair had returned to Australia. They could have advised him. They could have told him whether he was full of crap. Self-confidence, which had come with his second rocker, was under attack.

Chastened, he dwelled on his own warlike nature, or lack thereof, and puzzled whether, if given the choice, he would have volunteered to come to the aid of the Korean people. His reverie was interrupted as the Jeep crested a hill and the 53rd Division headquarters appeared in the valley below. Maybe he would have a chance to figure it out later.

Wylie was very pleased to be back at headquarters, his frolic and detour with foreign ways and cultures behind him, his battle with the solitary goat's eye won, and his notebook full of new material. It was almost as though he needed to make this journey in preparation for his forthcoming trip to Japan with Amelia. His heart leaped with anticipation.

CHAPTER 58

GOOD NEWS
ALL AROUND

◆ ◆ ◆

"The thing is, Wylie," said Beauregard Snipes, "you can read regulations up, down and sideways, and you'll never be sure what they really mean. Regulations are created by smart people for dummies like us. You gotta have an interpreter. You gotta talk to Sergeant Crammer over at I Corps. He'll 'splain it to you."

"I don't know, Beauregard. It seems clear from what I've read. It looks like my friend, Private Rowe, will have to rotate back home when his tour is up—even though he really needs to stay in Korea for family reasons."

"Like I said, there's clear and there's clear. Just get your ass over to I Corps G-2 and have a little chat with Sergeant Crammer. He's a good fren' and will find a way if there is one. That man knows more about Army regulations than Carter knows about little liver pills."

Wylie finished his coffee and pound cake and found a ride over to the I Corps compound where he located G-2 and searched for the office of Sergeant Crammer. He found him seated comfortably behind a desk in an anteroom to his Colonel's office, smoking a large cigar and reviewing a Playboy magazine nestled in a large, official looking manila folder. Crammer was a Master Sergeant, crisp and slender in starched fatigues, with sandy graying hair, close-set eyes, and a large nose. The gold rim glasses resting on that nose gave him a studious air and he looked sternly at Wylie as he introduced himself.

"So, that fat cracker sent you over to get interpreted. Settle down and tell me what the problem is."

Wylie explained Shit Dad's dilemma and pointed out that, though he wanted to help, Captain Standrich had not been able to resolve the issue at division level.

"Oh yeah, you've got Sergeant Poke and Major Brimmer up there. They're not known for creativity. You got a copy of the Private's 201 file there?"

The Sergeant puffed mightily on his cigar as he reviewed Shit Dad's file, sending flecks of ash to the exposed breasts of the Playgirl on his desk.

"It surely looks as though the Private is due to rotate in a couple weeks and that his current enlistment isn't up till next December. Under usual circumstances, he'd be on his way to Pusan and a troop ship PDQ."

However," said Crammer as he pulled out a drawer in his desk and extracted another official looking manila folder, "this latest DDO from 8th Army spells out a reenlistment policy that pays a $300 bonus and permits the enlistee to select his next assignment. They probably didn't have this up at division yet. We'll just need to make a little adjustment to these dates here and your Private Rowe will be able to buy his mama-san a new hooch. And spend another sixteen months in the land of the morning calm. Think that'll be O.K?"

Wylie was elated. He expressed his appreciation on Shit Dad's behalf and offered to reciprocate, at any time, his services in recompense for the Sergeant's help. Sergeant Crammer confirmed that the necessary paper work would be filtering its way down to Captain Standrich within a week.

There was, in fact, no Department of Defense Order that conformed exactly to the description offered by Sergeant Crammer. He had picked and chosen from the thicket of orders that crossed his desk each week to achieve what he considered an equitable resolution of the needy soldier's problem. He and his Colonel had worked together in three different posts for over five years and developed a high degree of trust in each other's judgment. They had defined a range of issues in the process, some to be solved by the Sergeant, some to be solved by them together, and some for the Colonel's attention only. Clearly, Private Rowe's problem was in the Sergeant's area of authority, and he confidently drafted a set of orders, which followed the terms explained to Wylie. His clerk typed them onto a mimeograph sheet that the Colonel duly signed.

The next day copies of Shit Dad's orders were on their way to his 201 file, retained by Corps, Division, Company, and Payroll, and ultimately crossed Wylie's desk. He gave a copy to Shit Dad who swore he would name his next child after his friend. It was all very OFFICIAL and no one questioned either the accuracy or basis of the order among the hundreds that came out on soft beige military paper each week. Back at I Corps Sergeant Crammer thumbed through his magazine with the satisfaction of a man whose job was well done.

Auntie Soo stood under the glare of a single 60-watt bulb in the secret basement of the Korean Palace examining the supplies stacked against its walls. On one side, vials of antibiotics, principally penicillin, lined the shelves along with painkillers and medical instruments wrapped in khaki cloths. Large jars of APC pills stood in a corner and anesthetics, bottles of ether, and surgical dressings were crammed on opposing shelves. To the back of the chamber, piles of olive drab canisters, holding various chemicals and explosives, threatened to spill onto the floor. Her associates had stolen them all from military warehouses and convoys over the past few weeks.

It was time to convert these supplies into cash—to send them by launch along the west coast, above Inchon, to contacts in North Korea. Pay for members of her organization was coming due and it would be improper, in her view, to divert the generous proceeds of the Korean Palace for that purpose.

She and Major Adder had spent two hours that evening going over the books and records of the Palace after its first few weeks of operation. Employee morale, based on pay and bonuses that exceeded expectations, was excellent. Clients were pleased with the cleanliness of the rooms and the enthusiasm, creativity, and agility of the employees. The Army medical staff members on call enjoyed favors supplied by their charges, and the two gigantic Korean men in charge of public relations maintained proper decorum.

Although whiskey purchased by clients for the employees was actually tea, drinks for clients themselves were watered down only slightly. No one seemed to mind. Costs for advertising were minimal since the Korean Palace relied on word of mouth to attract clientele. After the first few clients discovered the facility by stumbling across it on their way to other places, trade expanded geometrically, like mushrooms after a fall rain, as Colonel Warfinger said. After that evening's meeting, Major Adder departed with dividend payments for the investors. As the Major had predicted, the place was a goddam gold mine.

So successful was the operation that Auntie Soo called on Song Song Park once again to recruit more employees for the business. Since word of the operation and the riches enjoyed by its employees had spread to local villages, his search was much easier this time and he looked first in the little towns surrounding the Korean Palace. Within days, he had recruited two dozen attractive and eager girls for Auntie Soo's consideration. Of the eight selected, two had worked at the Chapel orphanage. They could not resist an opportunity to more than quintuple their income, and they were well suited for the work, having dealt with the demands of needy children.

Wylie sat with Amelia on a bench in the orphanage's courtyard surrounded by children who cavorted on an improvised jungle gym near the stream and played with toys provided by Marines the previous

Christmas. Little Kim repeatedly ran up a slide and descended, head first to the sand below.

Amelia was dressed in a white Korean blouse, buttoned to the collar, and dungarees. Wylie observed her russet hair glowing in the sun as she turned to watch the children. Her arm was inside his and her hand covered his where it rested on her thigh. Wylie described his recent visit to foreign units and told about the different fighting styles and personalities of their allies. When he told of his experience with the goat's eye Amelia wiped tears of laughter from her cheeks.

"I know it's sort of disgusting, Wylie, but the way you tell it, it's really funny. And, anyway, it didn't seem to hurt you at all!"

Grumbling, he admitted that was so and went on to explain that Shit Dad had been reprieved and would not have to leave his Korean family. Captain Standrich, on the other hand, would be parting from Mai Lee when he rotated in the fall. Shit Dad warned his brother in law that it was not wise to foretell his departure; Korean girls had been known to poison their boyfriends in hopes of delaying their going away. Perhaps based on that advice, the Captain purchased a modest home in the village for her.

"Mmm. I'll pack that tidbit of information away. Might come in handy if you decide to abandon me without warning," she joked.

"Never happen," he said. "I'm exclusively and permanently attracted to red headed Wellesley graduates with ample bosoms and functioning showers. I understand there aren't too many of those around here."

As she squeezed his arm, he went on, "But, listen, I think I've made some good arrangements for our R and R to Japan. If you can get away next week, my friend at Kimpo will arrange transit on a cargo plane to Tokyo. My pal, Myron Goldstein, you know, the cartoonist guy, has offered us the use of his apartment in Yokohama. I haven't seen it but it's supposed to be very nice. I understand it has a tree growing up through it.

"I'd really like to show you off to my friends at the Stars and Stripes. Then, Jules Pike suggested we go see the Buddha at Kamakura and

Mount Fuji, and then take the train to Kyoto, and watch the Ama pearl fisherwomen in Kuzaki. Jules tells me these women dive topless into the Mikomoto pearl beds and can stay under water for five minutes. I'd love to see that!"

"Sure, it's probably the topless part that got your attention."

"What can I say? I'm a normal red-blooded American boy with a tit fetish."

"Based on my experience, I can't argue with that."

She squeezed his arm again and pushed the roundness of her breast into his bicep.

He smiled in appreciation and added, "Since I know there have been delays in your receiving the whopping salary an executive director expects, I'm willing to underwrite this expedition. I am a man of notable resources just now. What do you say? Are we going?"

"Of course we're going!" She kissed him lovingly.

Shit Dad's son, the five-month-old Kim, lay burbling on a wooden cradle in the corner of the farmhouse kitchen observing his mother as she prepared the evening meal. The room was warm and steam rose from two pots placed near an open fire. He decided to suck on two fingers as he clutched his blanket with the other hand. A blissful bowel movement occurred while both hands were occupied. His enjoyment of the moment ended as the room's other occupant, his aunt Mai Lee, bent to change him.

"Standrich, he will be leaving at harvest time," she said as she attended to the squirming baby.

"Yes."

"He bought me property in the village and gave our father two oxen and money for me. Father is content."

"I know that father is content. How about you?"

"I'm not sure. He expects me to be with him in his bed as though nothing is happening. It hurts me here, in my heart, because I know he will soon leave me. He says it is the war, the Army. Says he has no choice, but your man is staying… and he has money, too."

"It is difficult to understand, yes."

"I am NOT content!"

"Look at it this way. When he leaves, you will be much better off than before you knew him. He is, after all, a round eye, not one of us. When he leaves, you will be a young woman with wealth. You can look forward to having a good family. Unless," and she looked sharply at her sister, "you have done something stupid like getting pregnant."

"Of course not!"

Mai Lee bit her tongue to avoid pointing out that the baby she was holding was the result of getting pregnant by a *waegukin*.

Changed and clean, the baby resumed sucking his fingers, watching his brooding aunt.

"I am not content," repeated Mai Lee.

CHAPTER 59

R AND R

◆ ◆ ◆

THE TWO YOUNG OFFICERS WHO chatted with Amelia on the cargo plane
flying from Kimpo to Tokyo were disappointed when the plane landed
and she took Wylie's hand and walked with him across the tarmac. It
had been some months since they talked with a round-eyed girl and
Amelia was a superior form of that species. Any thoughts of conquest
they might have had were dashed as the lanky Sergeant walked with
her toward a staff car parked near the operations center.

Jules Pike opened the sedan door for Amelia, welcoming her, smiling his approval to Wylie. He explained that the olive drab staff car
was "assigned to temporary duty" for the next few days, and Wylie concluded there must be a Sergeant's barter network alive and well in the
Roppongi district.

Amelia and Wylie settled in the back and Jules occupied the front
passenger seat, twisting around to discuss plans for the next few days.

"Amelia, it's a great pleasure to meet you," said Pike. "We've read
the stories Wylie sent along about the work you're doing at the orphanage, but his pictures of you don't do you justice. The guys at the office
are eager to talk with you, but I know it's been a long day and I hope
you'll meet with us tomorrow. We've arranged a hotel for the next
couple of nights and we have some ideas about how you might spend
the rest of your time in Japan."

"That's very thoughtful, Sergeant Pike," said Amelia. "When
Dad and I came through Sasebo on our way to Korea, we had no

time at all for a visit. I'm really excited about vacationing in this beautiful country!"

Their driver, a Corporal in starched khakis, was clearly pleased with his female passenger. Though dressed in the baggy dark green fatigues that Wylie had liberated from his supply Sergeant, Amelia was stunning, especially to young men who were accustomed to petite Asian girls with shining black hair and dark eyes. Her collar-length russet hair and emerald eyes, her even features and perennial smile gave her the look of everyone's hoped for girl next door. She grasped Wylie's hand as she looked excitedly at the narrow streets, frame houses and pedestrians in Japanese dress as the sedan moved from the airport toward the city center.

The sedan turned onto the main thoroughfare of the Roppongi district heading toward the Marunuchi Theater where the neon lights of the marquee blazed through the gathering dusk. The Ginza beckoned with its garish lights and walkways full of hawkers, B-girls and G.I.s looking for an evening's entertainment.

"Well," said Wylie, "parts of it aren't all that beautiful but Tokyo is full of life and action. We'll take it easy tonight and see more of the city tomorrow, okay?"

Amelia agreed. The sedan stopped in front of a tiny hotel situated a few blocks from the Ginza on a surprisingly quiet cul de sac. The faded English letters under Japanese characters above the entrance doors read "Hotel Belvedere."

A roly-poly attendant who, thought Wylie, bore a striking resemblance to Hai Dozo at the Stars and Stripes building, exploded through the double doors, collected the couple's duffel bags, and urged them to enter the hotel.

"Listen," said Pike, "the hotel is compliments of the guys in the office so long as Amelia condescends to being interviewed tomorrow. Corporal Flitch will pick you up at oh nine hundred tomorrow."

He waved toward Wylie and shook Amelia's hand. Then Pike and the Corporal sped off toward the main road, leaving Amelia, Wylie and his Army issue Japanese phrase book to deal with hotel arrangements.

From the lavish attention the matronly hotel manager paid Amelia, Wylie guessed she was the first American civilian woman who had visited the little hotel. The manager scolded the porter for failing to bring hot towels immediately and urged Amelia to refresh herself by cleansing face and hands.

"This feels wonderful, Wylie," she said and smiled at the manager.

"I suspect there's more to come," said Wylie, thinking of his visit to the Tokyo Onsen.

"I'm for it!" said the ever-adventurous Amelia.

The manager motioned for them to go with the porter up a short flight of stairs and followed them, puffing softly as she reached the landing. She removed a large brass key from her apron and turned it ceremoniously in the lock of a wooden door that opened to reveal a large Japanese style room with two futons, grooved wooden blocks for pillows, chairs and a wardrobe. A sink and toilet occupied an alcove and two large windows opened on to the street below where yellow streetlights shone on cobblestones. Their duffel bags rested by the wardrobe.

Amelia pulled Wylie toward a window and whispered, "Listen, I don't want to be an ugly American or anything but I'm not sure I can sleep on a wooden block. And there's no bath or shower. Is there maybe another room?"

"I think there's a bathroom somewhere. Let me see what I can do about the pillows."

He fumbled with his phrase book, but the manager guessed what the problem was and opened the wardrobe to pull out large, fluffy down pillows that quickly replaced the wood blocks. She then pulled Wylie's sleeve and pointed to the number eight on the large wristwatch she thrust under his nose. "Suppa, Suppa," she exclaimed and pointed down the stairs.

"That's quite clear," said Amelia. "Dinner at eight – very romantic, classic, even. Let me rummage through my extensive wardrobe here in the duffel bag and find the appropriate gown. Do you prefer Dior or Cardin, Wylie?"

"What?"

"Fashion designers."

"Sorry. I flunked fashion design in the fifth grade. How about that nice light blue dress I saw you pack?"

"Good choice."

Amelia descended the stairs at eight o'clock wearing the light blue dress. Wylie wore khakis, a Hawaiian sport shirt, and a huge grin. Amelia had never looked more beautiful.

Dinner was served in a traditional dining room a few steps down from the lobby. They were alone, seated on cushions around a low table. The manager and her porter appeared with trays of food probably prepared in a nearby restaurant. They offered Miso soup with seaweed and bean curd, roasted delicacies, sushi and rice, huge shrimp battered and fried, and crunchy vegetables. Amelia demonstrated her prowess with chopsticks as Wylie tried unsuccessfully to master the quick backstrokes required to cut meat and fish. The meal was excellent; the Emperor could not have eaten better.

As they reclined on cushions scooping bits of ice cream from delicate bowls, the manager arrived with two white cotton robes and towels. She made splashing motions with her hands and said "Bafu, Bafu," urging them to follow her to another room. Amelia prepared herself for their next adventure.

They entered a well-lit chamber covered from floor to ceiling in butter colored tiles. The floor felt comfortably warm to their bare feet and the humid air in the room smelled of flowers. Inside the door was a wooden bench on which the manager placed robes and towels and next to that was a large shower with multiple heads, designed to spray water on every square inch of the occupant's body. Beyond the shower, Amelia noticed a sunken pool, perhaps five-feet square, with steps descending from one side. Steam rose from the pool.

Wylie and Amelia considered the possibilities of the bathing chamber and Amelia offered Wylie a wicked smile as she knelt to test the water in the pool. As the manager left and Amelia was about to pull her dress over her head, a teenaged Japanese girl bustled into the room. She wore a simple white robe and a very serious expression.

Based on his experience at the Tokyo Onsen, Wylie understood she was the attendant, responsible for seeing they received a proper bath. It would be, he knew, a very serious matter to ignore her directions.

"Uh, you know they don't have some of our hang ups about nudity over here. At the Onsen, whole families bathe in the pools without clothes on. It's no big deal. I think this girl is sort of the bathing NCO," he informed Amelia.

"You're not going to see anything you haven't seen before, big boy, but what's with this little girl? I don't particularly think we need any help at this point."

"Just go along with it. It's a Japanese thing. I think you're going to like it."

The girl explained in Pidgin English that they must disrobe and shower before entering the pool. Amelia quickly removed her clothes and was into the shower as Wylie sat on the wooden bench, concentrating on avoiding embarrassment. Failing, he covered his lap with a towel, but not before the attendant suppressed a delicate giggle behind her hand. The girl turned rushing water on Amelia and picked up a huge soapy sponge that she applied vigorously to all areas of exposed skin, soaking herself in the process.

Shocked at first, Amelia gave in to the soft abrasions and took pleasure in them. When she reached a point where her whole body tingled, the girl shut off the water and led her to the pool. The water was hotter than she expected but she lowered herself in and let the heat envelop her. She rested, the fringes of her hair splayed on the edge of the pool.

"Wylie, you were right. This is amazing," she murmured as Wylie let the girl push him into the shower. He lost any erotic thoughts as she scrubbed him with the sponge, standing on a little stool to reach his head and shoulders. She did avoid the excitable part, handing him the sponge so he could attend to that area and frowned when he failed to maintain vigorous contact. She inspected him carefully after turning off the water, to be certain no area lacked a pink glow. Satisfied, she led him to the pool where Amelia was almost asleep and he let himself down to sit on the little underwater bench next to his sweetheart. She moved toward him and he placed an arm around her shoulder.

Amelia stirred as the attendant returned to the room carrying two wooden buckets of steaming water, both of which she poured slowly into the pool. Hot as the water already was, it became perceptibly hotter.

"Wow! This gives new meaning to the old jokes about boiling missionaries in oil. Do you think we'll be on the breakfast menu?" asked Amelia.

"I think they've figured out how much we can stand. They make it even hotter for their own people who are used to this stuff. One of the guys at the office told me they use the heat as birth control. Get it hot enough and sperm dies. But I'm not sure."

"Then I won't count on that if I ever let you have your way with me again. As wonderful and relaxed as I feel now that probably won't happen for a while."

Wylie tested that threat with a watery kiss and well placed hand movements. She rewarded him with an encouraging sigh. The attendant returned with more hot water and they sank into a relaxed daze. Time paused as they both enjoyed an out of body sensation, seeing their entwined figures from afar.

Wylie woke as the attendant massaged his neck and shoulders and suggested it was time to join Amelia, standing in a robe by the bench, and return to their room.

Amelia, sitting cross-legged on the futon in their room, seemed puzzled.

"Damn, what was that? Was that some Zen thing? I've never been so relaxed in my life. I thought I was completely washed out but now I'm full of energy, like I've been recharged!"

Wylie liked the sound of that. He was also completely recharged, and he sat beside her to suggest an energy exchange. She loosened her robe and nibbled his neck.

"How can I resist you, you sweet talking NCO?"

As promised, the sedan arrived at their hotel the following morning and took them to the Stars and Stripes offices. Within twenty minutes of their arrival, Amelia had charmed the entire staff, except for Fancher Twilly, the dyspeptic sports columnist, who hated everyone including himself. He scowled behind his glass cage at the gaggle of reporters and staffers inching ever closer to the attractive redhead.

The staff briefly acknowledged Wylie's presence, but then all eyes turned toward Amelia, who warmed quickly to this unaccustomed attention. It was a powerful contrast from cleaning up after little children and scrounging supplies for the orphanage. She answered their questions, made a few self-deprecating jokes and posed for the photographs. After last night's tryst and the current diva treatment, she was in high spirits— which expanded after Myron, Wylie's beetle-browed cartoonist friend, explained that his apartment in Yokohama was available for them to use. Amelia won his unrequited love by planting a kiss above his notorious eyebrow.

At noon, the reporters escorted Amelia to a local restaurant near the Stars and Stripes offices where she again became the center of attention. Pretty round-eyes girls were not common in this district, and a gaggle of Tokyo schoolchildren joined the procession to the restaurant. Wylie, growing accustomed to being ignored, not so graciously brought up the rear of the procession.

All questions answered, all photographs taken, the reporters released Amelia and Wylie in midafternoon, and they were on their own to explore the exotic and unfamiliar city. They found their way to the

Imperial Palace where they circumvented the moat and enjoyed the spring flowers in the gardens. Amelia enjoyed watching the young women strolling the paths in traditional clothing holding parasols, mincing along the gravel pathways.

"Wylie, it's like they are gliding along on hidden roller skates—so elegant, so feminine. Makes me feel awkward just walking normally. They are really charming," said Amelia.

"Yes," aid Wylie. "It's surprising that, even after seven years of our occupation, they still follow traditional ways. You're right. They do seem to float along."

Leaving the gardens, they walked along one of the main streets and watched pachinko players maneuver steel balls into the holes of what looked like upright pinball machines. Amelia finally tired of the bells, gongs, and loud racket in the pachinko parlor. As they walked on, a young Japanese man holding a large sketchpad and wearing a beret showed them charcoal portraits of Japanese girls, American Movie Stars, and sports figures. Wylie was impressed by his sketch of Marilyn Monroe; she was exactly as he remembered her the morning she clambered aboard the helicopter and waved to the troops below.

Amelia agreed to a portrait session and Wylie negotiated a price in yen the time-honored way—with fingers. They moved to a nearby bench and the artist began his portrait, starting with luminous eyes and generous mouth. In minutes, the portrait was complete. The artist sprayed the paper with a kind of lacquer and presented it to Amelia. Wylie saw that his swift strokes had captured her very well— the softness of her cheek, the firmness of her chin, the clear, direct gaze, her vibrant expression. Enthralled, Wylie overpaid the young man, who offered to sketch Wylie, too. Not necessary, Wylie signaled. He had the memento he wanted.

They were tired when they returned to the hotel that evening and courteously refused the manager's suggestion that they retire to the bath chamber after a dinner. They awakened refreshed as sunlight streaming through their windows the next morning. Amelia attacked

Wylie with a wet washcloth and threatened to expose him to Chinese water torture. He countered by claiming to be descended from Vlad the Impaler. Things went downhill from there.

After breakfast, the hotel manager gave Amelia a bouquet of spring flowers and helped the white gloved taxi driver stow their duffel bags in the trunk. Wylie handed the driver a card showing the address of Myron's apartment. The driver nodded in acknowledgement and sped off, circling Tokyo bay and showing them the wharfs, piers, fishing boats, and navy vessels anchored off shore. Parts of the port still resembled the fishing village it had been hundreds of years before, and in some places they saw fishermen with long poles standing along the shore, filling rope baskets with their catch.

The taxi stopped at the entrance to the courtyard of a nondescript building near the harbor. The driver talked to a box embedded in the gatepost. "Hi, Hi" said the box, and a Japanese woman who might have been the hotel manager's sister rushed from the house and pulled open the gate. She bowed profusely and deeply, saying "Golsteen-san' and motioning them to the building's entrance.

The apartment was on the second floor, overlooking the harbor. A tree grew there, its upper branches contained by a glass penthouse where they protruded above the ceiling of the apartment. The trunk was about three feet in diameter with a reddish brown rough bark. The tree's bright green leaves created dappled sunlight in the room below.

Amelia stood next to the tree and looked through large windows to the expansive view of the harbor.

"This is incredible, Wylie. Beautiful. It's just overwhelming to come to a place like this from our dusty little orphanage."

She walked to him, held him, pressed her head to his chest. Her eyes were moist.

"Thank you," she whispered.

The two lovers spent the afternoon exploring the narrow streets surrounding the apartment, peering into little shops and watching fishermen along the shore. By evening, they had located a promising restaurant nearby and joined about twenty local diners seated along a long, low table on cushions, facing four cooks who presided over gas grills and tables loaded with enough vegetables, rice, fish, and meat to feed the entire neighborhood. Wylie consulted his dictionary, squinting in the low light, and found his view blocked by a large wooden paddle placed over the paperback. The portly cook holding the paddle wagged a finger at the young Americans.

"No book. No book," he said. "House dinner. All have house dinner."

With that, he placed a frosty bottle of beer on his paddle and dexterously deposited it in front of Amelia, and another on front of Wylie. Getting into the spirit of the occasion, Amelia raised the bottle and loudly said, "Hi!" The other patrons echoed her sentiment and the cook smiled broadly. As the meal progressed, neither of the two understanding the shouted exchanges between patrons and cooks, they simply waited for the paddle to deliver more morsels of uniformly delicious food that Amelia speared easily with her pointed chop sticks.

Wylie estimated they had been sitting for almost two hours when the paddle delivered the reckoning on a yellow slip of paper. It was for three thousand yen, less than ten dollars. The cook seemed pleased with Wylie's five-hundred-yen tip and bowed deeply as they left.

Although both were ready for bed when they returned to the apartment, the twinkling lights in the harbor, the reflection of the moon on Yokohama bay, and the radiant diamond necklace strung along the crescent shore drew them to the view of the harbor. In the darkened chamber, moonlight filtering through the leaves of the tree above them, they sat, their bodies gently touching, seeing the luminous panorama before them.

When they went to bed, Amelia fitted herself to the shape of Wylie's back, like two spoons nestled in a drawer, her hand resting on his chest.

With rosy dawn, a loud clanging sound, a tenor voice signing "Oh Soba, Oh Soba," and the rumble of metal wheels on the cobblestones came from the street below. Amelia untangled herself from the futon cover, snatched on her sweatshirt, and peered from an open window. Below a man in tattered overalls pushed a cart with one hand while opening and closing huge shears to create loud clacking noises. He sang his soba song as he pushed the cart that, Amelia now saw, he had festooned with thin yellow noodles. A window across the street popped open and a kimono-clad woman lowered a basket on a string to the man below. He removed some coins and placed a mound of noodles in the basket, which she quickly retrieved. He moved on. Another window popped open. Another basket descended.

"He's like a milkman, but he's delivering noodles," exclaimed Amelia. "That's just so wonderful."

Wylie had soba soup twice before, making him a comparative soba expert. He sleepily explained that many Japanese families had it for breakfast. The idea of noodles for breakfast intrigued Amelia. During their two remaining mornings, she dragged Wylie to a noodle shop down the street for breakfast. It was hard going for Wylie who was convinced he needed a minimum of two cups of strong Army coffee to kick-start his system for another day. He made certain that Amelia understood the degree of love and sacrifice required for him to survive an entire morning on weak tea and noodles.

For two days, they commuted from the apartment to the sights of Tokyo, exploring parks, gardens, shrines, and museums, and shopping along the crowded streets. Wylie used his Nikon camera to capture many of the sights, and his pictures included many of Amelia playing the tourist in Tokyo. There was no need for nightclubs or the gaudy entertainment along the Ginza; lovemaking and long conversations filled their nights.

During their last day in Tokyo, they rode a train to Kamakura and marveled at the temples and shrines, the giant Buddha, the green and restful park surrounding it, and the beautiful beaches below. A bus took them from the temples to a view of Mount Fuji, the iconic snow-capped volcano, and they rode part of the way to its top, watching hikers descend from the peak.

Though they tried to appear blasé while exposed to sights and scenes they had only read or dreamed of, exchanged looks of awe and wonder gave them away. They were having the time of their lives.

During their visit to the Stars and Stripes office, the reporters debated whether a trip to Kyoto with its famous castles and shrines or to Nikko with its rustic scenery and national park would be more interesting. Torn between culture and nature, Amelia decided she would enjoy a trip to the sacred mountains in Nikko. Wylie agreed they could pass on the pearl fisherwomen until their next visit.

The chief of the pressroom, who knew the area, reserved three nights for them in a ryokan, a secluded country inn near Lake Chuzenji. Leaving Myron's tree apartment, they boarded a train for the short ride to Nikko armed with 3 by 5 cards with the addresses of the ryokan and local sights written in Japanese script.

They took a horse drawn cart trip from the train station to the inn that was nestled among lush green trees. The courtyard was dotted with dark volcanic rocks surrounded by a sand garden raked into intricate designs. The ornate entrance opened on to rooms delineated by shoji panels that cast soft light on highly polished wooden floors. No one was there.

Wylie placed their bags on the floor in front of a lacquered table, which held hand carved toothpicks in a stone bowl and a little gong suspended by red silk threads from its black cradle. A small hammer hung from the cradle. There was no sign of life, so Wylie shuffled his feet, cleared his throat, and coughed. He called out what he thought meant "hello." No response.

Amelia began to giggle, removed the hammer, then tapped it against the brass gong, producing a pleasing middle C tone. Immediately a panel slid aside and a young man dressed in a black suit and tie appeared.

"Syfa-san?" he asked, encouragingly, looking at a slip of paper in his hand.

Wylie confirmed he was "Syfa-san" and produced his Army I.D. card to support that declaration. The young man bowed deeply and unleashed conversational English he studied in upper secondary school.

"I welcome you to our hotel. It is the home of my parents. You will be pleased to stay here."

"Thank you," said Amelia. "Are there other guests here today?"

"Many guests. Six."

The discussion covered the weather (warm and fine), how close they were to the national park (half a kilometer), nearby places to eat (his mother's kitchen was best), the bath chamber (of course), a map of the Nikko area (sadly, in Japanese, but guides who spoke English were available), and the cost of the room (very reasonable). The young man carried their bags to a nearby room and pointed out a few of its features. Nothing in the room was higher than eighteen inches, but the futons looked very comfortable and the pillows were soft. Towels and robes rested near a washbasin and bins for their clothes were placed along a wall.

After their host left, Amelia discovered that one sliding panel concealed a window with a view of a meadow raucous with spring wildflowers, and two distant shrines. Another panel revealed a spotless porcelain water closet.

"Whoops! I was hoping we could avoid this, Wylie. It's an elephant foot toilet."

He noted the designated location for the feet and the opening in the tile floor.

"I've been told that learning how to use it is character building. They have these in the public bathroom at the Shinbashi Railroad station. I mean, it beats being on bivouac."

"Your sensitivity is so appealing," she mocked and slid the panel behind her. She wished it were a door so she could slam it. Wylie wondered what he had said to bother her.

It was a three-day idyll. They hiked to nearby waterfalls, flushing birds from trails through greening marshlands. They visited temples and mausoleums and gazed at shrines in the sacred mountains. Sour faced monkeys glowered at them from the banks of hot springs. They fished and paddled across two nearby lakes and ate food prepared by street vendors in town.

"I never want to leave," she said the evening before their departure. "I haven't worried about anything for a week!"

"Yes, I know." He held her close and caressed her hair, smelling its sandalwood fragrance.

CHAPTER 60

CATCHING UP

◆ ◆ ◆

"WE'VE BEEN UP TO OUR ass in alligators," greeted Lieutenant Bland. "Up to our ASS!"

Across the room, behind the Lieutenant's back, Tiny shook his head in denial and held his hand six inches from the floor. So, thought Wylie, they were small alligators, nipping at his ankles. That was certainly manageable. As the Lieutenant began to explain something about photographs with reversed captions, Wylie saw that Captain Standrich was in his office, a rare occurrence. He excused himself politely and rapped on the Captain's door. Standrich seemed pleased to see him, invited him into the office, and waved him to a chair. Before beginning a conversation, the Captain offered Wylie an antacid from a large jar of Tums beside his desk. Curious, Wylie accepted as Standrich popped one in his mouth as though it was a jellybean.

"Good R and R?"

"Outstanding!" said Wylie, still aglow from his romantic adventure with Amelia.

"Good time of year, I guess."

"Absolutely."

"Well, I'm glad you're back," said the Captain, riffling through clippings on his desk. "Those features you did about the expeditionary forces here got some good play, and I've been besieged by calls from other unit commanders who want us to do a story about their fighting units. I think you could be doing that exclusively from now till you rotate."

"Good to hear," said Wylie. "I'll get Corporal Takei and Jackson to carry the ball on that, I think. Be all right?"

"Sure. And maybe do me a favor and get Bland involved too. I'm getting tired of his crap about alligators all the time. Good to get him out in the field. Out of the office."

Wylie nodded affirmation

Dismissed, Wylie spent the remainder of the morning sorting through the stacks of papers overflowing his desk and engaging in various telephone conversations. He was pleased that his team had managed the office well while he was gone.

As Wylie walked toward the NCO mess, an unfamiliar soldier in fashionable sunglasses and a well-blocked fatigue hat accosted him. At first, Wylie did not recognize him. Shit Dad was shaved, dressed in sharp fatigues with polished brass, wore gleaming boots, and his fatigue hat had not a speck of grease on it.

"Sh…." he managed to say before Wylie interrupted him.

"Man, you're one squared away trooper. What's going on Shit Dad?"

"Wylie, since you get me all fixed up with reenlistment and all… man, I really appreciate that, I can tell you… thanks, man … you are one good friend, Wylie… hope you have a luscious R&R…what I mean is that it came over me that I've got responsibilities! I've got this wife and son and I have to look out for her family, too. So, I had all this re-up cash which under normal circumstances I would have pissed away on likker and such, and it was like someone grabbed me by the collar and said, Pierre, you gotta change your ways. You gotta stop being an asshole and take care of your people. Wylie, it was a revelation, a true Re.Val.Ation— like a swamp thing grabbed aholt me and shook me till I hurt."

He mimicked a hand grabbing at his throat.

"So I used the money to help out papa-san, and got nice clothes for the girls and my little boy, and I still got a bunch left which is invested in savings. And I been dry as a nun's twat for weeks. But, Wylie man, that's not what I need to speak with you about."

Wylie had difficulty accepting this miraculous conversion.

"Shit Dad, does that mean you've got religion all of a sudden?"

"Well, it's maybe something like that. Also, I must confess I enjoy messing with Lieutenant Bland's head some. He see me like this and he's trying to figure out what I'm planning and it makes him kinda jumpy. But, honest to Christ, Wylie, I have no inferior motives."

"Okay. I will try to recognize the new Shit Dad. So, what was it you wanted to talk about?"

They had reached the NCO mess and Wylie directed the Private to one of the wooden benches near the entrance.

"It's the Captain. Him being my brother-in-law, I want to keep a special look out for him and I think he is in trouble. With Mai Lee, my wife's sister. I warned him not to let on when he was going to rotate back to the States, but he went kinda stupid and noble and let on anyway. Then he promised to take care of her so she'd be all right when he left.

"I told him that my wife said she was pretty sure Mail Lee was poisoning him, little bit by little bit. I think the idea is that if she can't have him, nobody else can either. You notice all them Tums he has around; his stomach was hurting some all the time.

"But he finally smartened up and him and me told Mai Lee the wonderful news that his tour was extended and he was like me, going to stay here for the unforeseeable future. Sure as toadstools after the rain, his pains started going away. He's still chewing those Tums, but I think it's a force of habit."

"Wow, that's a lot to take in, Shit Dad," said Wylie. "I don't want anything to happen to him, either."

"Just you keep an eye on him, because I can't be there all the time. Just make sure he's not hurting. Mai Lee can be nasty but she's not too bright. I'm pretty sure she believes he'll stay with her."

Shit Dad had work to do for Sergeant Pangluss at the motor pool. He pumped Wylie's hand firmly before leaving. "Thanks, again, man—for everything."

Wylie pondered the Captain Standrich situation over a greasy corned beef on rye sandwich slathered with mustard. How he missed Japanese cooking.

His work done, Wylie decided to take an evening walk from the office to the orphanage, completing the trip by 1900 hours, with the sun still well above the horizon. Though it had been little more than two days since parting, they exchanged effusive greetings, with hugs and kisses, and with Amelia nuzzling him like a Labrador puppy. They settled on a bench in the kitchen where Amelia uncorked a bottle of red wine. They sipped from tumblers while they recounted events since their return from Japan.

Wylie had delegated most of his responsibilities before his departure, and there were no fresh disasters upon his return if one didn't count the alligators after Lieutenant Bland's ass. Wylie had returned quickly to business as usual.

Amelia spent the past two days resolving problems that arose during her absence. Two sick children required the attention of a Korean doctor located two villages away. She arranged to replenish the emergency stores caregivers invaded when needed food supplies failed to arrive from Seoul. There were continuing problems involving the young women who cared for the orphans.

Wylie saw that Amelia looked troubled when she mentioned the young Korean women who cared for the orphans.

Wylie took her hand. "Is there something I can help you with?"

"It's not that I'm a prude or anything and God knows I understand how soldiers need a woman's attention. Especially after two full weeks with you, I know that! But... there's something going on here in the village that bothers me. A lot."

He waited.

"When I returned, two of my Jo-sans, you know, the Korean girls who take care of the children, were gone. The other girls said they had found work somewhere else and just left. There was a lot of giggling when they reported that. Well, it turns out that a new whorehouse opened at the other end of the village. Those two girls decided to work there for a lot more money than the can make here at the orphanage.

"I walked over there today and discovered that it is very fancy. It's in what used to be a big warehouse and reminds me a little of some of the places on the Ginza. G.I.s and guys from the expeditionary forces were going in there as early as midafternoon"

This was news to Wylie. Somehow the advent of a new whorehouse nearby had gone under the radar.

Amelia continued, "The girls here let me know they can make more than ten times what I pay by opening their legs. I do understand that, with all the poverty and devastation here, making a lot of money can be an easy choice, especially if the girls are family breadwinners. But, it makes me feel bad to know these young girls, ones that I care for, are selling their bodies.

"The thing is, here's this whorehouse just about a stone's throw from the entrance to Division Headquarters. I'm trying to decide whether to let someone in authority know about what's going on. Put a stop to it. What do you think, Wylie?"

Except for occasional pangs of guilt about what he considered cheating on Judy with Amelia, Wylie was a stranger to moral dilemmas. Nothing in his experience and training provided him with a basis on which to weight the issues, examine the gray areas, or consider the moral implications of Amelia's question.

Right was doing the job, whether it was staying alive or trying to be an Army journalist. Wrong was making stupid and possibly fatal mistakes. Delicate or subtle moral issues were simply not part of his natural outlook. Looking at Amelia's questioning expression, he knew a glib response would not be possible. Christ, he thought, I'm really going to have to wade into this.

"Um," he said.

"Um, what?" she asked.

Hoping his befuddled brain would come to his rescue given a bit more time, he began, "Well, first of all, I do agree you have a right to be concerned here. Two of your girls are involved, right?"

Amelia pursed her lips. Why was Wylie restating the obvious?

A crack of daylight penetrated a corner of his brain. He recognized two sides of the issue.

"Some people think prostitution is a victimless crime. The girls have an opportunity to sell needed services at an acceptable price and soldiers have the opportunity to get laid. Both parties could be enjoying the transaction. It's no secret that's mainly the reason for going on R & R. You blow off steam, maybe get drunk; you get your ashes hauled. You come back relaxed, and ready to go to work. It's a morale thing."

Amelia's face began to resemble an approaching storm cloud.

Wylie continued.

"So that's the G.I.s perspective. I know it is also necessary to consider the other side of it, the girls. No question that if they are made into sex slaves, or "comfort women" as the Japanese did with Korean women during the war, that is totally disgusting and criminal. Most likely prostitution denigrates and exploits women, makes them powerless. Certainly, it is illegal and immoral back home. But, I know that lots of G.I.s have hooked up with B girls over here and brought them home. And I don't see anyone holding a gun to their heads. Like the girls you worry about—they went willingly. I am thinking about all that..."

The words stopped coming. Wylie sagged like a deflating balloon.

"This is hard. I see both sides and, the thing is, you're putting me between a rock and a hard place."

She watched him struggling. He was not like her father who easily resolved such issues with great clarity, based on faith and long experience.

"How would you feel if one of your sisters was involved?" she asked.

The abstract became concrete. That thought was shattering. Wylie looked into the embers of the kitchen fire for a long moment. Amelia held both his hands and he turned to look into her eyes.

"I'll talk to Tully about it tomorrow," he said.

"Shit, yes, I've heard of the Korea Palace!" said Master Sergeant Tully McGregor, rising from behind his desk to emphasize the declaration.

"G-2 and us MPs been keeping eyes on that operation. So far, we've kept our distance since it looks like a clean place and a whole lot better for the troops than the skuzzy ferret holes located in the other little villages around here. Funny you should bring this to my attention right now, though."

"How's that?" asked Wylie.

"You know we have ROK MPs attached to our outfit so they can help handle problems that come up involving the indigenous. Just yesterday, we got confirmation through ROK CID in Seoul that a Soo Young-le, one of your nastier gangsters affiliated with Rhee's government, runs this operation here in Uijongbu. And, get this, she looks like some harmless old mama-san you see cooking noodles in Seoul. I haven't laid eyes on her yet, but they say she gets around this part of Korea in a prewar Buick."

"A Buick, you say?" asked Wylie, wondering how many there could be. Every other car in Korea, other than military vehicles, was some crappy Japanese make.

Tully continued.

"Yeah. Anyway, our guys are real interested in her right now because it seems she's also involved in diverting some of our medical supplies across the border. Lots of them, they say."

"You say 'diverting.' What's that mean in non-military English?"

"The fuckers are shooting up our convoys and stealing from our supply depots. Set one on fire in Pusan a week ago."

Wylie felt uncomfortable. He recalled the slain driver slumped over the wheel of his truck and an ambulance carrying away a wounded soldier. He remembered the ruined bridges of Seoul as seen from the back seat of a 1939 Buick. It's got to be a coincidence; sure.

"Anyway, we…Wylie, this is way off the record, right?"

"Whatever you say."

"There is some chatter about how our own guys, officers maybe, have a finger or two in this particular hair pie. There's a Major Adder or Adler whose name comes up now and again, and I don't think it's just some joker making up that name. My Colonel has clearance to raid the place day after tomorrow night, so long as we can confirm that this harridan they call 'Auntie Soo' is there. It's going to be coordinated with the ROK Police and our Korean MPs. We have no orders to do anything about the 'clientele' but I expect they'll make themselves scarce when they see a shitload of MPs barreling into the place."

Tully offered to let Wylie come along, as a buddy, not a correspondent, but Wylie respectfully declined. It's that damned Buick, he thought. I remember seeing it there, with Kim. It was unsettling.

The next evening Auntie Soo stood in her underground chamber at the Korean Palace. The single bulb illuminating the chamber showed an empty room. Puddles of Cosmoline indicated where weapons had been stored; scraps of cardboard and a few bottles of medicine lingered on the shelves. Well, she thought, I was almost ready to bundle up everything and sent it north. A few days sooner doesn't make a difference, but it is too bad this location has been compromised.

Ah well, she sighed, as she slowly climbed the ladder to her office, not every venture is a complete success. Finding a new storage location within easy reach of the shore above Inchon was certainly possible. It was just another among niggling details that unjust gods imposed to plague her. As was her unfair and undeservedly imminent departure from the Korean Palace.

She located the little silver spittoon in the voluminous bag by her desk and released an indelicate stream of brown liquid from the corner of her mouth. That, along with the reckoning of the substantial funds she had managed to keep out of Major Adder's grasp, improved her mood. She removed a panel from the wall by her desk, scooped into her handbag more than a kilo of multihued 18 karat gold in the form of nuggets, bracelets, rings, and chains. This was her special dividend for all the hard work she had done to create the gold mine that was the Korean Palace.

Her distribution of the little "white envelopes" to the members of her extended "family" recently bore fruit. The mistress of a police adjutant learned that he had been ordered to help the ROK MPs secure the Korean Palace. The mistress promptly conveyed this information to Auntie Soo. She learned also that Song Song Park's recruitment of former employees of the local orphanage, along with concerns about all those stolen medical supplies, had contributed to this unfortunate turn of events. Regrettably, thwarting a raid by United States Army Military Police exceeded her capabilities.

Instead, she cleared out her secret warehouse and office. She ordered Kim to drive her to another of her businesses that evening, and then return the following afternoon with one of her workers who resembled her. Auntie Soo was sure the deception would work, since Americans couldn't distinguish one elderly Korean woman from another.

Though the military might catch Kim in the raid tomorrow evening, he was very resilient. He could take care of himself. Had he not survived two years of war and an airplane crash?

As she settled into the back of the Buick gliding through darkening streets, she looked for one last time at the Palace. Then she turned her attention to immediate tasks ahead, cataloguing them and assigning them priorities. As she reexamined the items requiring attention, she added one last thing. Oh yes, there is that. The orphanage in Uijongbu just lost its fire insurance.

CHAPTER 61
UNCLE HO

◆ ◆ ◆

Colonel Warfinger resisted the impulse to visit the Korean Palace often. He entrusted Major Adder to act as liaison for business operations. With glowing reports of its success, however, the Colonel could not escape a certain pride of entrepreneurship. He decided to join the Major that evening to see firsthand the results of his inspiration. As a concession to propriety, he dressed in mufti – gray slacks, white shirt and a rather garish plaid sport jacket. From a viewpoint above the reception area, he saw an orderly procession of clients who exchanged military scrip for chits, the color of which identified the specific service or services desired.

Employees in varying stages of undress waited at the bar and reclined on chaises and couches in the reception area. After an unhurried exchange of credentials, couples left the reception area for the rooms beyond. Warfinger was pleased with the decorum and the cheerful colors Auntie Soo had selected for the overall décor. This operation was even better than he had expected, and it certainly permitted his Special Services group to provide many additional benefits for the troops.

General Black had commented favorably on the quality of gifts offered to visiting dignitaries (and those he had received in return) as well as upgraded leather furniture that found its way into even the enlisted men's clubs. Colonel Cutter reported a significant drop in sexually transmitted diseases that made him a hero to the I Corps medical command. Even better, considering the contented expressions of clients departing the establishment, morale was at an all-time high. The Colonel was justifiably satisfied with his accomplishment.

"Funny thing. Auntie Soo is usually here Thursday evening, but the cashier says she came a day early and left yesterday evening," reported the Major as he joined the Colonel on the catwalk. "Everything checks out and I'm all set to go. I parked the Jeep in back, by the old warehouse entrance."

He waited as the Colonel savored the activity below. Warfinger was about to turn and follow the Major down the stairs when he saw Auntie Soo enter the building through the clients' entrance. Then the Colonel realized he was mistaken. Though she had gray hair and a slight stoop, she was taller and thinner than Auntie Soo was and seemed confused as she looked around the reception area.

Her confusion intensified as an ear-splitting whistle pierced the area and a score of armed soldiers with MP helmets, lettered in English and Korean, poured into the reception area, and stationed themselves at the exits. They surrounded the woman who immediately began sobbing hysterically. Fascinated as he was by the scene below, Warfinger finally responded to Major Adder's plucking at his arm and the two scurried down the stairs, through an unguarded hallway and escaped through the old warehouse door in the back of the building.

Meanwhile, snuffling away her tears, the Korean woman held out her identity card, waving it before the ROK MPs who held her. One of them examined it carefully and carried it over to a tall American MP who seemed to be in charge. A broad look of disgust soon crossed his face and an MP escorted the woman to the entrance where Kim was standing, manacled and under arrest. His guards took him outside to sit on the running board of the Buick, still under guard and still in hand cuffs. The woman joined him, crying softly.

Frustrated, Tully McGregor declared, "We didn't get her, so as not to waste our visit let's shake this place up a bit."

The MPs began rounding up clients and employees and herded them to the exits. One of his men rushed into the reception area and reported to Tully that he had just seen two men depart the building heading for a Jeep; he swore one was an officer.

Tully recalled reports of the mysterious Major and decided to act on this new information. Grabbing the man who reported the exodus, he raced to his Jeep and installed the soldier as his driver, pointing to the narrow alley running to the back of the former warehouse. Their Jeep charged up the alley.

Major Adder squirmed in the driver's seat of the Jeep trying to get it to start. In frustration or encouragement, he rapidly exhausted his limited vocabulary of curses as he slammed his hand against the steering wheel, demanding that the engine spring to life.

"Shit, piss, crap, asshole," he shrieked in his voice's highest pitch as an ominous grinding sound arose from under the floorboard, followed by a nasty click.

"Push in the damn throttle," yelled the Colonel from the passenger seat, pointing out a simple step the Major had overlooked.

Done!

The engine stumbled to life just as Tully's Jeep skidded around the corner of the building behind them. The Major let out the clutch too quickly, and the Jeep bucked forward, almost dislodging its passengers. Adder grasped the wheel with bloodless fingers and slammed his foot on the accelerator to engage all sixty horses under the hood. The two officers sped down the main road of the village into the dimming light of dusk, scattering chickens and the hogs lolling beside the road. Not fifty yards behind, Tully and his driver followed in hot pursuit.

Uncle Ho dozed lightly on the seat of his cart as his sturdy oxen plodded in perfect synchronization down the roadway leading to Tongdudong-ni. It had been a fruitful day of collecting and the two wooden vats gently sloshing in the bed of the cart were almost full. He was looking forward to meeting his nephew at the place where he prepared his night soil. This evening he could well employ a strong young man to shift and drain the vats. Uncle Ho was a bit hungry, so he prodded his chargers with a switch to move more quickly. With practiced indifference, they ignored him and maintained their stately pace. This is the way we always do it, they seemed to say. Go back to sleep, old man.

Ho obliged. Suddenly the distant roar of Army vehicles caroming along the streets of town shattered the stillness of early evening. Uncle Ho turned on his seat to see what was going on. In the distance, an Army Jeep swerved from a cross street and almost skidded into the vegetable stand operated by Mrs. Yung and her addled daughter. The vehicle righted itself and headed down the middle of the street directly toward him and his cart.

Another Jeep that followed also narrowly avoided the vegetable stand and churned down the road. In the gloom of twilight, dust clouds seemed to obscure the racing vehicles, which Uncle Ho watched with great curiosity. This would be something to tell his nephew.

Colonel Warfinger began to recover from the brain-numbing effects of his fight-or-flight response to the raid on his whorehouse. This situation is absurd, he thought. Why the fuck are we racing along this godforsaken roadway? Who are we fleeing from? This asshole numbers cruncher got spooked with all the MPs in the Palace and rushed out like his jock was on fire. And I jump in the Jeep and become an asshole myself. We don't need to run. I can explain whatever needs explaining. I'm a bird Colonel for chrissake!

"Stop the damn Jeep," he bellowed to Major Adder. Not understanding, the Major looked at his passenger as though requiring written authorization. After all, their pursuers were close behind them, but he was sure he could outrun them. Was the Colonel nuts? Adder was going to win this thing!

The two officers, staring at each other in mutual misunderstanding, failed to realize how close they were to Uncle Ho's cart. When the

Major saw that a collision was imminent, he followed the Colonel's order, shifted into a lower gear, and pushed hard on the brake. He failed, however, to twist the wheel to swerve away from the obstacle ahead.

A Jeep carrying two male passengers travelling at a speed of more than thirty miles per hour on a dirt road requires at least one hundred and three feet to reach a complete stop. When Major Adder applied the brake, the back of Uncle Ho's cart was exactly fifty-seven feet directly ahead.

The impact of the Jeep striking the rear of the cart pushed it forward sharply, causing Uncle Ho to topple backward. Fortunately, his foot caught the iron bar that stretched across the footrest, and he righted himself. The disturbed oxen looked back with reproachful eyes, upset with this disruption of their routine.

The contents of the barrels arched skyward, rising completely above the rims of their containers, twin geysers of noxious effluent, gelatinous, malodorous shafts of offal. The yellowish-brown mass obeyed Newton's laws; once in motion it continued in motion— forming into a mushroom shape as it rose above the vats and then descending behind the cart, seeking to come to rest a few feet beyond its point of origin.

That point was directly over the passenger seats of the now stopped Jeep. As Major Adder looked upward, he unfortunately opened his mouth to protest the looming avalanche of accumulated wastes. The Colonel ducked behind the windscreen, but to no avail. The vile contents of Uncle Ho's barrels fell generously on both men, plastering them with slimy liquid and morsels of flotsam. Little bits of detritus sloshed in the liquid flowing over the gunwales at the Jeep's sides.

Uncle Ho looked in astonishment at the two figures writhing behind his cart. Unfortunate for them, he thought, but equally bad for me. How will I recoup the fruits of today's labors? Who will pay for what I have lost? With the force of that impact, they probably broke the axle of my cart. As he counted out his woes, tears fell from his aged eyes. The oxen, now eager to move forward again, expressed no opinion on the matter.

Since the ooze covering them obscured their rank, Tully McGregor could not recognize the men as superior officers as he approached the encrusted Jeep. He was uncertain what violations of the military code of conduct had occurred during the past few minutes. However, an attempt to escape from the vicinity of the whorehouse, failing to stop when pursued by a clearly marked police vehicle, and rear-ending the cart belonging to the respected and beloved Uncle Ho were certainly infractions of SOME kind.

He had no idea what two vats of night soil might be worth, but it appeared reparations of some sort would be required. Since there was no telling what other crazy things these two morons might be capable of, he and his driver approached the Jeep cautiously. To their immediate regret, they discovered they were downwind from the Jeep. They almost gagged at the stench carried by the evening breeze. Tully paused some twenty feet from the Jeep and drew his side arm.

"Put your hands on top of the windscreen where I can see them and then get the fuck out of the Jeep."

Four beige paws reached for the windscreen and two sodden bodies descended from the sides of the Jeep. The Major spat continually and tried to clean the sockets of his eyes with his knuckles. The Colonel removed his sport jacket and stained white shirt, searching for a reasonably clean shirttail to wipe his face.

Tully backed off a few paces, for the stench increased with the movement of their bodies. He dispatched the driver to ask the Korean onlookers lining the roadway for buckets of water.

An assortment of water buckets soon arrived, and Tully addressed the two officers from the side of the road.

"Okay, there's only one way this is going to happen. You two strip down to your shorts and clean up with those buckets of water. Then we'll take you back to Headquarters."

The two officers were shivering with cold from riding in wet skivvies in the back of the MP Jeep and their aroma remained distinctly unsociable when they arrived at Headquarters. The Colonel in charge offered blankets and pretended to believe the story they quickly concocted. The official report of the incident referred only to a Jeep accident involving an ox cart and noted that the sum of six hundred and fifty hwan was paid for damages. The MPs levied a fine of two hundred dollars for "cleaning supplies." There was no official reprimand at that time.

Tully McGregor passed a copy of the official report to Wylie, who had come to inquire about the raid on the Korean Palace. He had already heard through scuttlebutt that the coda to the raid was an "actual fucking unbelievable shit storm" visited upon two officers from his own headquarters area. Both young men broke into uncontrollable laughter as Tully described in considerable detail the condition of the stopped Jeep and its occupants. He savored the excuse offered by the Major that they were on official business.

Still concerned about the Buick, Wylie questioned Tully.

"Yeah, well, since we screwed up and tried to arrest the wrong 'Auntie Soo' we all thought it best to scrape the whole nasty booger off our fingers. The driver drove the woman back south in the Buick and that was that. They're still looking for the real Auntie Soo but not much luck there."

And the Korea Palace?

"We raided the place to arrest that Korean woman. We didn't really have a beef with the place itself so we're keeping a friendly eye on it. It appears that some of the former employees left so it's not as busy as before. Also, I believe General Black himself stepped in and scotched rumors about any Army involvement in the operation. But, I won't lie to you, Wylie, I think those girls are getting medical checkups every week or so, and it's not from indigenous doctors. But, like they say, we don't make waves."

Wylie found that all very interesting. Tully's information precipitated an internal debate over how much he would pass on to Amelia. All of it, he decided.

Tully, who was due for R & R to Japan, then quizzed his friend about the places he visited with Amelia. Wylie wanted to know how the relationship with Korean MPs and Rhee's police was working out. He sensed that might lead to a new slant on friendly cooperation between the military and local forces. He reconsidered. Based on experience, he realized that sharing duties and information with Korean authorities could have negative results.

A week later, Wylie learned through a contact at I Corps what happened to the two officers involved in the collision between cart and Jeep. Within days of the incident, they had quietly resigned their commissions and departed to places unknown. Captain Anastos was promoted to Major and placed in charge of Special Services. The Captain soon discovered that Major Adder maintained meticulous and mysterious accounts involving substantial sums of money. They were set aside in a folder in the office safe labeled "KP." The newly minted Major was at a loss to understand how they related to "Kitchen Police."

CHAPTER 62

AMELIA

◆ ◆ ◆

IT MIGHT HAVE BEEN A spark carried on the wind or a G.I. neglecting to field strip a cigarette. How it began would forever be unknown.

However, it was clear that late on a Thursday afternoon the southeast corner of the thatched roof, near the bend of the stream, caught fire. Summer sun had evaporated any morning moisture by then, but the closely packed sedge and straw resisted the fire's advance. The fire smoldered at very edge of the roof for a while, creeping slowly northward. There was almost no smoke so no one looking toward the roof would have noticed it then.

Later in the afternoon, a light breeze arrived. It was just enough. The blaze ignited and coursed swiftly upward, toward the center of the roof, directly over the dormitory for the children of the orphanage.

What with gathering the children and preparing them for the evening meal, no one noticed the fire until acrid smoke descended into the anteroom of the kitchen. Even then, most of the caretakers thought the cooking fire was responsible for the smoke in the air. It had happened before. Then the Korean woman in charge of herding the children in from the playground looked up, saw the meter-high flames consuming the thatch, and raised the alarm.

Amelia, who had been working at her desk near the playground entrance, ran into the yard to see for herself. She realized immediately that their rudimentary firefighting gear would be quickly overwhelmed. Rushing back into the orphanage, she ordered the immediate evacuation of the building.

"Get the children out, out!" she called to the helpers, and toddlers were pushed and prodded to the building exits. She designated the big sand box located eighty meters from the building as the spot to corral the toddlers. The two picnic tables nearby were for little ones who did not walk. Seeing that her helpers understood where to situate the children, Amelia dashed back into the building to the dormitory. She wanted to be certain no one there was overlooked.

A two-year-old was there, lying on her cot. Her eyes were wide with terror as she stared at the widening black hole in the ceiling, watching the flames consume its edges and dropping burning shards of debris into the room. As Amelia snatched her up, she saw that bedding materials were aflame. She brushed past them to look carefully under covers and cots. No one there. She returned to the playground area, breathless and smudged.

The three and four-year-old children quickly got over their fright and treated the conflagration as a grand show put on for their benefit. The little boys tested the fire by running toward it, then skipping back, their faces ruddy with their exertions and the glow from the fire. The little girls were more circumspect, chattering in groups of two and three, pointing toward the flames and exchanging concerns. The smaller girls pulled their skirts over their faces to make the fire go away.

Flames and smoke poured from the rear windows of the building. The front remained intact, and Amelia watched one of her helpers rush from the building with one more toddler kicking under her arms. Amelia refused to panic and made a head count of helpers and children gathered in safety near the road. Everyone seemed to be there. Nearby villagers gathered and helped to console crying little ones. Those farmers who had already returned from the fields determined it would be futile to fight the blaze now. It was harsh, but it would be better to let it burn out and begin construction again from the remaining foundation and adobe walls.

Soldiers from a local engineer battalion who had been alerted to the calamity by villagers shared that assessment. They reckoned it would take almost twenty minutes for the base fire trucks to get there, by which time the fire would begin to extinguish itself for want of fuel. Nevertheless, they passed on word of the fire to division headquarters. The Army would provide needed shelter for the orphans and their warders.

The soldiers wanted to do anything they could to help the children and the shapely redhead in the smudged tee shirt in charge of the orphanage. They assured her that help for the children would soon arrive. In an attempt to minimize the impact of the destruction, they predicted it wouldn't take more than three or four weeks to "make it good as new again."

Amelia thanked them and asked if there might be some way to let her father know about the destruction of the orphanage. He was in Wonju, south of Seoul, meeting with a group of Christian Korean ministers, not scheduled to return for a few days. One of the soldiers offered to drive her to the communications center at headquarters to help contact her father.

"That's really wonderful, but I'll take a rain check. I need to stay here till I'm sure the kids are all okay." She counted heads once again to assure herself all were accounted for. One wasn't there. A chilly jolt of panic crossed her chest.

"Where's little Kim?"

No one knew. He was last seen in the vestibule, just inside the door. All the young women searched, called for him. There was no answer.

Amelia ran from the group of soldiers toward the door. Although there was no smoke in the vestibule, the fire had just reached the roof above that area. She was sure it would take just a few seconds to search the room. She waved quickly to those behind her and dashed inside.

Then the main beam supporting the roof, weakened by the fire, suddenly gave way and plunged to the floor. It fell in an avalanche of flames and cinders as Amelia entered the vestibule. Superheated air turned the room into an inferno.

The rush of flames and sparks ascending from the collapsed building reached a height of more than fifty feet. The heat from the fire washed across the aghast faces of the soldiers gathered by the play area and the sobbing young Korean women. The freight train roar of the dying blaze smothered their cries.

Little Kim thought it was an excellent game to hide in the bushes from those who called for him. However, the leafy branches obscured his view of the flames consuming his home. He ran out to stand with the other children, to see the fire more closely. How exciting! It was the most wonderful thing he had ever seen in his young life.

CHAPTER 63

AFTERMATH

◆ ◆ ◆

FATHER CHAPEL SURVEYED THE RUINS of the orphanage, wisps of smoke still rising from charred beams. An Army Major from graves registration who was unhappily familiar with such situations left moments before. The Major explained that the temperature of the fire would have taken all of Amelia. It was pointless to search for her in the ruins. This, then, Father Chapel thought, is my dear daughter's final resting place. She is with the angels and this is her memorial. He lowered his grieving eyes to the burned earth at his feet and tears fell. This is hard, my God. This is hard. He began to compose a silent prayer for Amelia.

The abrupt arrival of a Jeep interrupted him. Wylie jumped out and walked solemnly toward the minister. His eyes were red-rimmed and wet as he approached. Neither could find words of greeting. Silently, Father Chapel opened his arms and Wylie embraced him. There was comfort for them both. They stayed that way for many minutes, holding each other tight under the noonday sun. Reluctantly, Wylie moved away and the minister, his voice hoarse, whispered to him, "God must have needed a fine young woman this week. I'm sure she's with him now." Wylie took solace in that, though as time went on he wondered about God and His motives.

Tully had rushed to the Public Information Office as soon as he heard of the terrible accident at the orphanage. He took Wylie outside and, in a secluded place between Quonset huts, reported the details of the fire. As it is with terrible news, Wylie at first simply did not understand Tully's report. There was something in his nature that censored, then delayed acceptance of the sad message. This couldn't be so. He had seen her the evening before. Surely, there was a mistake.

Tully put both hands on Wylie's shoulders and brought himself closer to his friend. He said he had gone over the entire event with one of his men who had been on the scene as the building collapsed. He and other soldiers had checked every exit as soon as the heat from the conflagration subsided. There was no chance she escaped. Amelia had "passed on."

Wylie slumped into his friend's arms. He was overwhelmed with a feeling of inexhaustible sorrow. He slowly moved his head from side to side, trying to deny his loss. He straightened and moved back toward the office, only to succumb to a black rage. He pummeled the side of the Quonset hut with his fists, stopping only when the blood came and Tully grabbed his wrists. Through his pain, he burrowed his face in Tully's neck and found himself incapable of stopping the tears rolling from his eyes.

His next thought was to rush to the orphanage, to confirm, to search. He found Shit Dad and demanded the keys to his Jeep. Shit Dad had never seen Wylie in such a troubled state and realized he was probably not capable of driving himself. He placed his friend in the passenger seat and raced to the orphanage. As they turned into the lane by the ruined building, Wylie saw Father Chapel and went to him.

The passing days did not diminish the enormity of his loss. At first, he thought of her as still there. She was briefly absent but would soon return. Then his rational self reasserted itself and deep sadness set in.

During the next week, Wylie slept very little. His loss had somehow made him feel unmanned. He could not control the tears that filled his eyes as he tried to fall asleep, nor could he bring himself to eat much more than coffee and various forms of pasta. Everything tasted dry and unpleasant. The other soldiers in the office gave him a wide berth, understanding his pain but not knowing how to offer help.

He was partially successful in dulling his sense of despair by focusing on his office routine: editing stories from the divisions, reading teletypes, talking on the telephone with friends and peers, assigning stories and going over materials with Tiny and Jefferson. He did not leave to do features or travel with Jim Beam. He limited his world to the confines of his desk and his duties. In the evening, he tried blotting out his grief with whiskey, but it helped very little. He was a very sad twenty-one-year-old Sergeant with little expectation he would ever experience joy again.

Ultimately he understood that she would never again await him with loving eyes and a warm embrace, that the joining together of their spirits, their bodies, and their thoughts were lost forever. It would be months before he accepted the departure of the corporeal Amelia. But he knew her spirit and her essence would always be with him.

He thought also of Father Chapel's belief that God had taken her to Him. What could have motivated Him to curtail the wonderful work Amelia was doing at the orphanage, and what reason could there be to deny Wylie's great love? He refused to accept the concept that God worked in mysterious ways. He was beginning to suspect that He might just be a vindictive bastard.

Captain Standrich removed the jar of Tums on his desk and his complexion turned ruddy again. He extracted promises from the P.I.O. staff, under pain of death, that there would be no discussion of his imminent rotation back to the States whenever Mai Lee appeared to "straighten up" the office. It became the Captain's habit to visit the Post Exchange often to see what new silver or gold baubles had become available so he could deliver a fresh delight to his companion. He had learned that Mai Lee could forgive perceived transgressions with the liberal application of jewelry. By the eve of his departure, Mai Lee had become so weighted down with silver ornaments that she resembled the grill of a 1952 Cadillac.

Stealth was necessary to facilitate Captain Standrich's departure for Inchon and his flight to Japan.

Shit Dad arrived at their office moments before dusk with the Captain's Jeep and quickly loaded the two flight bags the Captain had deposited in the office just after Mai Lee's afternoon visit. The Captain, outfitted in his Class A uniform, soon arrived and hurriedly shook hands with the staffers, including Wylie, still in the office. "Best of luck, Sergeant," he offered Wylie who replied "Same to you, Sir." Insincerity hung in the air like diesel exhaust.

The following morning Shit Dad returned early to the office. Wylie was already there, nursing a white porcelain mug of coffee and listlessly reviewing telexes delivered by the clerk from the communications office.

"Gonna head off Mai Lee," he announced. "The Captain is more than likely on his way to Japan about now. Stayed at the BOQ in Inchon last night, Wylie. Man, was he eager to leave."

"I guess so," mumbled Wylie.

"None of my business, but you are real dark these days, and I can understand that for sure. Your girlfriend going like that, it puts a big hurting on you, and I know how that is. In combat you get real close to your buddies. It's more than a survival thing. It's sharing the danger and the being afraid. Make you real close, closer than family. Twice on Old Baldy I lost friends closer than brothers. One died in my arms. I bawled like a baby.

"They sent me back and I was all mean and dark for a long time. A long time. But you get better; you got to get better. Shit dad, it doesn't all end. There's gonna be more for you to do. There's gonna be better days. Life goes on.

"I mean, look at me now. Hog heaven. Hog heaven! Thanks to you, I'm with my wife and little Pierre Kim for a long time. I'm doing what I like; I eat and drink good. Shit dad, life goes on; there is always something to hope for. Know what I mean?"

Wylie understood. His friend had stumbled on the root of his sadness; he had been too grief- stricken, too self-involved to understand it clearly. It was so. He had lost hope. It had disappeared with Amelia's death – gone completely. Would hope return? Yes, it probably would. If nothing else, he thought, he could hope for hope. Imperceptibly he felt a little better. The pain remained, but it had lightened, just a bit.

Mai Lee appeared at the office door carrying cleaning supplies. In spite of her romance with an officer, she prudently had not left a secure position with the Army. Since the Captain was not usually in the office that early, she had no reason to suspect foul play. Shit Dad intended to let her know of the Captain's departure as gently as possible in hopes of averting self-destructive behavior. He drew her away from the office door and walked with her to an open area between Quonset huts.

Wylie saw his friend place his hand on her shoulder and speak in soothing tones. She jerked back, her face contorted. Shit Dad spoke some more, moving his hands in gentle circles. She seemed to deflate and bent over her cleaning supplies, then swiftly picked up a bucket with both hands and poured its contents over Shit Dad's head. Surprised, he stood there as gray liquid dripped from his nose and ears, watching his sister-in-law storm up the path toward her father's farm.

He poked his still dripping head around the door and Wylie had to laugh.

"She seemed to take it pretty well, didn't she?" asked his Cajun friend.

"Sure looks that way."

"Yeah. Even he's not here, I took one for the Captain. See you, Wylie."

In late spring, one of his friends in Headquarters Personnel reminded Wylie that he had over thirty days leave available and he would be rotating home in just more than six weeks. Here was an opportunity to find new places, new experiences. Here I am in the Far East with about thirty days leave and free air transportation available as long as I hang out at airports and catch rides on transport planes. He rejected returning to Japan immediately. Memories of being there with Amelia would be like an open wound.

He looked at maps of Asia and talked with other NCOs who had returned from travels abroad. He decided he would try to visit, in the next month, two famous battle sites, the island of Okinawa and Corregidor in Manila Bay. Wylie was particularly interested in Okinawa because one of his wartime heroes, the correspondent Ernie Pyle, died on that island. If time permitted, he would try to make it to Bangkok, a city greatly admired by his friend in Special Services. He searched through his papers to make sure that he had the official pardon with the royal crest of King Bhumibol provided by Colonel Kasem. That decided, Wylie set about finding civilian clothes for the trip, though it was unlikely a young American man with close-cropped hair would be taken for a civilian tourist.

A few days later, a C-124 Globemaster cargo plane touched down at the air base in Naha, Okinawa and taxied to within a few yards of the squat terminal. Wylie viewed the island from the air as the plane made its slow approach, searching for remaining signs of the ferocious two-and-a-half-month long battle for the island, the bloodiest amphibian operation ever mounted by any army. Nine years after the battle, there were still scars of raw earth on the hillsides and ruins of buildings and abandoned villages. He stepped from the plane into unaccustomed heat and humidity and walked to the terminal building.

A Marine Corporal standing behind a counter greeted him.

"You got orders?"

"Well, no. I'm here on leave. Wanted to look around the island."

The marine looked puzzled. "It's not an R & R location, you know. You're pretty much on your own here. There are a few hotels in town and a pretty nice beach and a few bars with available sporting girls, but there's no organized recreation or like that. I guess you can always stay somewhere on the base, Sergeant."

Wylie thanked the Corporal for the information and asked him what the prospects might be for getting to Bangkok.

"That would involve quite a bit of flying. You'd have to hop from here to Formosa, what they're now calling Taipei, and from there to Clark Air Base near Manila; you might could get from there to Bangkok. Or," rifling through a stack of papers attached to the clipboard before him, "you could get on Major Chord's flight Wednesday going direct to Manila."

"That gives me three days here. That would be outstanding."

For three days, Wylie explored the southern part of the island, retracing some of the deadly routes followed by Marines who fought yard by yard to extract the Japanese defenders from caves and tunnels. He wandered around the Marine base and saw skeletons of rusting armaments in the jungle and on the beaches. He took oral histories from a few Marines who had been there during the campaign and remained in the service, now providing military support to their former enemies. It was not service they relished but, as one Sergeant said, shrugging, "What the fuck; Semper Fi!"

The day before his departure Wylie bought a bathing suit at the Marine PX and waded into the gentle surf breaking onto the brilliant white beach. There was no quick drop-off as on the Jersey shore, and he moved out a few hundred yards before the water was chest high where he could swim. It had been more than a year since he had been near an ocean and a month since he had bothered with any exercise. He felt liberated in the buoyant water and stretched out full length, feeling his muscles tighten. He began a slow crawl, parallel to the shore, breathing evenly as the clear water rushed past his head. He was surprised he did not tire and maintained his pace for half an hour. He traveled more than a mile and discovered he had reached one of the initial landing sites for the invasion at Naha, and almost bumped into a rusting landing barge crushed by the explosion of a kamikaze plane deployed to defend the island from its attackers. Wylie remembered what one of the Marine veterans told him: the kamikaze pilots were locked into their cockpits when they left to deliver their ton of explosives.

He swam back. The sun was lower on the horizon. The warm water washed away his imaginings of the horrors experienced by young soldiers on both sides of the conflict and he realized those thoughts had temporarily supplanted his grief over Amelia's death. Compared to the immense suffering and loss of life on this little island, his loss, his grief meant little. But it still hurt so much. The water would not wash it away.

Wylie stayed in Okinawa for a few days before getting a ride on a C-124 bound for Bangkok, by way of Manila. Although the plane was outfitted with four turbojets, the storms they encountered over the South China Sea were so severe that buffeting caused purple bruises from the straps holding him to the side of the cargo plane. Wylie recalled jokes about white-knuckle flying and decided this must be it.

Nevertheless, the aircraft landed safely at the Don Muang airport north of Bangkok and he and another Army Sergeant on the plane hired a taxi to Bangkok and found a hotel in the center of the city. It backed up to one of the many canals crossing the capital, and Wylie awoke the next morning to the loud sputtering of outboard motors on long tail boats scurrying along the klong below his window.

The klongs, or canals, serving as major transportation arteries, were crowded with colorful boats scurrying over the water. Loaded with everything from fruits, vegetables, retail goods, automotive parts, bicycles, and people, the boats defied all nautical standards, with water just millimeters from their gunwales. Wylie expected many to capsize into the green water, but it didn't happen as he watched the scene below.

Mirroring the frantic activity on the water, three wheeled tuk-tuks scurried through the streets below, zipping in and out of alleys like minnows attacking mosquito larvae. Bright colors and gaudy designs along the streets distracted Wylie, who was now beginning to smell the mingled odors of delicacies cooked by street vendors, fumes from the tuk-tuks, the musty aroma of green water churned by outboard motors, and the powdery, earthen smell of dust raised by the activity below. In the distance, he saw the gleaming towers of temples and shrines; nearby the clamor of the streets and waterways attacked his ears. How different from Japan, he thought.

Wylie was eager to explore this exciting city. However, the guide-book he found in the hotel lobby was very confusing. The recumbent, golden, and emerald Buddhas, along with the twenty or so other major points of interest, were neither clearly identified nor easily accessible. The porter explained it would be best if he hired an official guide to navigate the numerous temples, giant Buddhas, palaces, and parks in the city. Wylie agreed to the reasonable price for that service and sipped coffee as the porter made the necessary arrangements.

Soon a young Thai woman dressed in a business suit and carrying a large handbag walked through the lobby and the porter introduced her to Wylie as his guide. She bowed politely and offered her hand. "My name is Jaidee. I am a teacher of English at Siam University and I will be pleased to show you around our wonderful city."

He expected a male guide, perhaps like Kim in Seoul, but was pleased to meet this demure young woman. She was perhaps five-feet tall, slender, but shapely. Her hair was glossy black, worn pulled back from her face. She was perhaps four or five years older than Wylie was and, though groomed like a teacher, had sparkling almond eyes and a quick smile. Involuntarily, he compared her with Amelia, noting how she was very unlike his lost love. That simple remembrance reopened unhealed wounds and he was overwhelmed with sadness. That was followed by pangs of guilt. There was tightness in his chest as he told himself that touring with this young woman could not be perceived as dishonoring Amelia's memory.

Emotionally burdened, Wylie still managed to make his way through mutual introductions and small talk. Jaidee outlined her suggested itinerary for his first day in the city and Wylie said that sounded fine.

"In that case, "she said, "shall we go outside in this lovely day to begin our explorations?"

She spoke with what Wylie thought was an English accent that seemed unusual for this Asian woman. As they reached the sidewalk in front of the hotel, he saw that the top of her head barely reached his shoulder. There was something about her he found amusing. Was it her effort to appear really grown up?

Wylie carefully examined the tuk-tuk that Jaidee had hired for the day It was a motorized bicycle with a seat for two behind the driver. Above the passenger seat was a fabric roof decorated in vibrant primary colors with bangles, sequins, and fringes. The driver smiled broadly as his passengers settled into the passenger seat, and then drove at breakneck speed to join the current of tuk-tuks eddying around the hotel.

During the day, they visited Buddhas in more positions than Wylie could remember, walked through jasmine-scented parks, and admired the exotic architecture of lavishly decorated golden palaces guarded by dog-faced warriors. Jaidee demonstrated an encyclopedic knowledge of dates, dynasties, and intimate details of the rulers' lives. By the afternoon, Wylie decided he could not absorb another detail and suggested they take a break for a drink.

Jaidee agreed and directed their driver to a bustling bar on a second floor overlooking the hectic traffic of tuk-tuks below. They found a table near the open staircase that led up from the street.

"I like Thai beer," she said. "It is refreshing after a day of looking at Buddhas and palaces. If you agree, I will order two very cold Singha lagers, so you can judge.

The reputation of Singha beer extended to South Korea. It was legendary among visitors to the Thai Regiment in Korea.

"I have heard of it. I would love to try it."

Frosty mugs arrived, and Wylie confirmed that it was excellent lager. Halfway into his second mug, feeling relaxed and comfortable, he asked, "So, what do we do tomorrow?"

She delicately wiped a drop of foam from her upper lip.

"We have seen a small portion of important temples and palaces today, so I think tomorrow we should take a long-tailed boat through the klongs and visit some floating markets and then see some of the primitive temples further from the city center. Does that seem all right?"

"Sure. Very much all right."

They arranged for the next morning's meeting.

Jaidee arrived punctually, dressed in a beige suit with a colorful scarf. Wylie noticed how the color of the scarf complemented her gray eyes and the necklace she wore. She touched his shoulder to suggest they begin the day's adventures. They visited the places she mentioned the day before. The colorful markets, the houses built on water, the clang and clamor of the crowded waterways fascinated Wylie. The activities she planned and the places they visited charmed him.

"Thank you, Jaidee," he said that afternoon as they returned to her favorite bar. "I feel like I have seen what most tourists don't see here. You are a wonderful guide."

"You are very kind to say so," she said. "I also have enjoyed your company."

She paused. "You know, I didn't properly explain the succession of dynasties relating to the temples we visited this afternoon. Beginning with…"

Wylie moved his hand across the table to cover hers, to interrupt.

"Please—the day has been filled with too many facts and figures already. Why don't we just enjoy our drinks, relax, and engage in meaningless small talk?"

She seemed relieved as she offered a bright smile, raised her glass in approval, and said, "Of course. It's just that I get involved in explaining about all the places I love. No more facts and figures today!"

As though by mutual consent, neither spoke for a while as they looked at the mad traffic rushing through the streets below.

Wylie broke the calm silence.

"So, 'Jaidee.' Is that just a pretty name or does it mean something?"

She smiled. "You know I told you that all Thai names have a special meaning. Are you joking with me?"

"Maybe I am. But I would like to know what your name means."

"My name means 'good hearted.'"

She offered a sly smile and added, "It was given to me before I proved to be otherwise."

Their conversation continued in a bantering mode. At Wylie's prodding, she told about her family, her education, and her interest in seeing more of the world. When he asked about romantic attachments, she remained quiet, then said, "No. Nothing going on right now," with a rueful grin.

She insisted that Wylie share his story. He told her about his life in New Jersey and what he did in the Army. He showed her his press card from the Stars and Stripes. She apologized and said that she had never heard of it. A bit deflated, Wylie suggested that they have some food before she returned home. They ordered noodle soup and parted soon after.

By now, Wylie was familiar with the area and decided to avoid the road traffic and walk back to the hotel. As he maneuvered the crowded, noisy streets and dodged kamikaze tuk-tuks, he smiled to himself. He realized that, for the first time in weeks, he had actually been happy with this Thai girl.

The following morning, Jaidee appeared in a sleeveless flowered green Thai dress cut on the side to reveal her legs. She wore a broad-brimmed conical hat around which she wrapped a gaudy green and yellow scarf. Wylie teased her. "Are we going to the beach today?"

"No," she said. "Today I am ignoring Western influence and wearing a typical Thai dress with a traditional head covering. I confess, though, that the scarf is my own addition. So you won't miss me in a crowd."

"Not likely!" he said.

Jaidee explained that she wanted to show Wylie artisans working on native crafts today. Carving, stonework, fabrics, intricate wood-working, and similar shops in back alleys were on the agenda. After a fascinating morning, when Jaidee suggested they stop for a quick lunch of satay and fruit from a street vendor, Wylie countered with an offer of a meal in the attractive restaurant they had just passed on their way from the latest shop. She agreed but pointed out that would interfere with the afternoon schedule; there would be less time for the stops she had planned.

"I know," said Wylie, "this is all wonderful art and history, but I've got to confess it's too much of a good thing. After three days, my head is full. I need to take a break before I can absorb any more."

Jaidee sulked, suggesting she had failed to make it all interesting, and Wylie took her hand and assured her she was the best guide he ever had.

In the languid atmosphere of the restaurant, they drank beer and consumed a little tray of peanuts before beginning their meal. As he watched his animated companion, he compared his feelings for her with the emotions experienced when he was with Amelia. They were quite different. He thought of Jaidee as a friend, a buddy like Scott or Tully. She was funny, bright, and infused their conversation with an Asian perspective that he found off beat and interesting. She was also very attractive. Wylie was impressed with the well-shaped legs dis-closed by her revealing dress, and her supple bearing.

As their meal progressed, they moved well beyond small talk and exchanged personal confidences. Without knowing why, Wylie blurted out details about his relationship with Amelia and reported that she had died. It was the first time he had allowed himself to speak of his loss.

Jaidee's eyes softened, and she told him how sorry she was. The subject once broached, it was as though an emotional dam broke and more details about Wylie's relationship with Amelia tumbled out. Jaidee reached across the table and held his hand, stroking it. Wylie paused, looking at the young woman, suspecting his story touched on an experience of her own.

Later in the afternoon they returned to his hotel and, in unspoken agreement, Jaidee accompanied him to his room. She smiled, closed the curtains, held Wylie close, kissed him, and slipped off her beautiful dress. She comforted him. The good-hearted young woman did all she could to ease his grief.

Wylie awakened, alone in bed. He discovered his cheeks were wet with tears and brushed them away with the palm his hand. Turning toward the window, he saw Jaidee silhouetted against the rays of the setting sun, her naked arms stretched above her head. He could make out the downy hairs on her arms and the small of her back.

She heard the bed creak, saw that he was awake, and walked back to him.

Later, as Jaidee lay cradled in his arms, he recalled what Shit Dad had said.

Life goes on.

CHAPTER 64

REPORTS FROM MANILA

◆ ◆ ◆

The Manila Hotel
South Port
Manila

My Dearest Judy:

I'm writing this by hand because I haven't been near a typewriter for over two weeks and a memorable time it has been. I wrote just before I left that I would be trying to use up my leave by hitching rides around the Far East and the kid has been surprisingly successful at that! Needless to say, I've landed in a really nice hotel in Manila, probably nicer than I can afford at this point, but thereby hangs a tale – which I'll tell a bit later.

As you know, I was pretty gloomy just before I left, what with the untimely death of one of my best buddies over here. We were really close and even took that trip to Japan that I wrote you about together. It really got to me; what was it the poet said – intimations of mortality? Anyway, I'm getting over it and the only dim spot so far was a stormy ride over the South China Sea where I had visions of becoming fish food, but we weathered that okay and made it to Bangkok. That was a couple days after I left Okinawa, and what a scary place that is! I took pictures of both places and even sprang for a roll of color so you can see how beautiful the water and shore are around spots where so many of our people died just a few years ago. That was Okinawa, not Bangkok.

There wasn't much to do in Okinawa so I hung out with some of the Marines stationed there and hiked around the places where the Japanese had dug tunnels and caves and held the Brits and us off for more than two months in 1945. There's a black market in Naha where they have human skulls the locals still find buried on the sides of the mountain there. I know I got shot at a little in the land if the morning calm, but that was probably nothing compared to the poor buggers who fought on that island. But I digress.

Except that the swimming was nice; I did that twice and had to think about the time we went to Long Beach Island and you looked so great in that black bathing suit. But I still digress. There really weren't any worthwhile souvenirs in Naha, but I made up for that when I was in Bangkok. I've got to tell you that is a fabulous and exotic city; I liked it better than Tokyo. They have these little motor bikes called tuk-tuks there and it just costs a few pennies to ride anywhere in the city and any place you go there's another temple to Buddha or a crazy gold palace. The tops of their buildings have these upside down funnels covered in gold and there are funny warriors with animal faces all over the place. I hung out for a while with one of the guys on the plane with me and we did some shopping in the native markets.

You probably haven't received it yet, but I sent you a package with some native silk materials and a Thai dress with a slit down the side that I'm sure you will look terrific in. And I hope to see you in it soon! There were also some silver pieces and a couple of pearls in the package; don't overlook them.

There was so much to see and do in Bangkok that I stayed there a whole week. Except for one rainy day, the weather was really beautiful, not as hot as I expected this time of year. The people are very friendly and seem to move at a much faster pace than the folks in Tokyo. Prices for everything were very reasonable but, between sightseeing, buying souvenirs and running up a hotel bill, the kid was a little, as they say, short when he landed at Clark Air Base, which is several miles north of Manila.

Anyway, I rode a truck into downtown Manila and got let off at the west end of Manila Bay – just me and my duffel bag. This hotel, which is pretty fancy, was a couple of blocks away and I went through their ornate lobby to the counter sort of as a lark. They charge fifteen dollars a night! I was looking at about fifty dollars in my wallet but figured I could splurge for one night. The guy at the desk asked for ID and I showed him the Stars and Stripes press card that I keep with my Army ID. It was a surprise to see he knew all about the paper and offered me a special press price of four dollars a night. He said it would be nice if I mentioned the hotel in one of my stories. Judy, my love, it is the first time being a reporter paid off financially! There may be a future in this.

Anyway, I'm sitting in a chair on the balcony of my room looking out over Manila Bay and it's a clear and sunny afternoon. I have a corner room so if I go to the edge of the balcony I can see the ruins of buildings and a church right in the middle of town behind me. What little I've seen of the town so far looks pretty depressing. They haven't cleaned up the place anywhere near as well as they have in Tokyo. I took a short ride in a Jeepney this afternoon over to the Magsaysay Palace, which also looks dingy. The Jeepneys are Jeeps left over from the war that have been taken over by the locals and they dress them all up with bold colors and tinsel and fringes and turn them into taxis. They're bumpy, but better than those tuk-tuks in Bangkok.

It looks as though I'll be able to stretch my dollars a little further than expected, so I plan to stay in the hotel for a few more days and take the boat to Corregidor tomorrow. They have some nice parks here too, so I certainly don't think I'll be bored. But, best of all, is that every day I spend here on traveling is a day closer to the day I get back to the States, and see you again. It's now been more than fifteen months since I left and I know lots of new things have happened to both of us. I can't tell you how much I'm looking forward to getting reacquainted. And I do think of you a lot – especially in the black bathing suit.

All my love – Wylie

P.S. I almost forgot – congrats on the summer job at the hospital. It should be a great experience for you and really look good on a resume.

M L-W.

The Manila Hotel
South Port
Manila

Dear Mom and Dad, Betty, and Ellie,

As the old writers say, I'm taking pen in hand to bring you up to date about the recent peregrinations of your son and brother. In my letter before I left for this Far East adventure I said I hoped to get to Okinawa, Bangkok and the Philippines and, after almost three weeks, I've done it. I'm living beyond my means in this hotel right on Manila Bay, thanks to a very nice press discount. This is the end of my second day here and I've had a chance to wander around the old town, which remains severely damaged (The Japanese certainly succeeded in reducing the city to rubble) and have just come back from an emotional visit to Corregidor Island, which I can actually see from this hotel balcony.

Backing up a bit, though, you've probably received the postcard I sent from Okinawa, so you know I was there for a few days. I got to see a few rusting landing barges and military equipment along the shore. As it turns out, the Japanese attacked the landing craft mainly with kamikaze planes and spent more than two months attacking us and the British from caves and trenches on the island. I wandered around some of those places and took some pictures that I'm sure Dad will be interested in. The Naha area is mainly a Marine base now so I spent some time with the "gyrines" and listened to their stories. Those guys are pretty much all volunteers and extremely gung ho, even though there's no action there now.

It took a while to get from there to Bangkok since it is a pretty long way. I went from Okinawa to Clark Air Force base on Mindanao and hung out there for about a day before catching another flight to Bangkok. That was a smaller cargo plane, a C-123, and we got knocked around in bad weather over the South China Sea, but all ended well, as this letter testifies. Mom, I think you would love Bangkok. It's incredibly colorful and has the most exotic buildings, shrines and palaces I've ever seen. They also have really nice clothes for women there and you can expect a little care package for you and the girls. I'm not a big shopper but I was intrigued by these really pretty silk blouses they wear over here and picked out a few for you. They have high collars and lots of embroidery. I think I got the right sizes. I've never seen anything like it in the States. Dad, the only thing I saw you might have liked was the pretty girls, but I couldn't fit one in the package.

The weather in Thailand was just about perfect, cooler than I expected, but then it's sort of winter time over here. It's been much cloudier in Manila. Anyway, I spent a whole week in Bangkok and absorbed as much of the culture as I could. There was so much to see that I hired a guide and we got along very well. The guide was an English teacher at one of the better local colleges and knew just about everything of importance. It was a real learning experience. I would go back there at the first opportunity.

It was a much smoother flight back to Manila, where I arrived yesterday morning. I plan to be here a few more days, but I wanted to go to the island where we surrendered to the Japanese in 1942. I still remember seeing the movie about it when I was about ten and it made a big impression on me. I learned that a combined force of Marines, Army, Navy and Philippine troops held off Japanese invaders from the end of December, 1941 to the beginning of May, 1942. Those troops suffered constant bombardments and lived for months in caves on thirty ounces of food a day, with very little water. After our troops surrendered, thousands more died on the Bataan Death March as the Japanese forced them to trek inland.

Riding the boat out there today, it was easy to see that the island controls Manila Bay. There were still remnants of big guns there and I could see the caves the soldiers used while they were being pounded by enemy artillery. You can see graffiti scratched in the stone walls. I know it's a cliché, but you have to wonder how it is that we are now defending people who tried to slaughter us and sent the defenders of Corregidor on a totally cruel death march, and that was only about ten years ago. If that's a question for philosophers, I plan to look into it when I return to college.

The postcards I'm enclosing with this letter show what the Jeepneys that race all around town look like. They're really gaudy and the people seem to compete to see who can out decorate the others. I rode two of them today (to the boat and back) and I've got to say they are fun! On the picture of the bay, you can see Corregidor like a small spot and I've marked it with an "x." Quezon Park is on the other card. I hope to go there tomorrow. I picked it out because it looks a lot like the scenery you see on the way to town from Clark base. I also hope to get a few pictures with the Nikon in the next few days. I only have black and white film, though.

I'll still have enough leave days saved to spend at least a week with you when I come home next month, and you know I'm looking forward to that! I know I've changed some over the past year and a quarter – I actually noticed crow's feet when I was shaving the other day. (I have to shave every day these days). Being in the Army I don't have all that much control over my life but I realize that when I get out I'll be in a better position to influence what happens according to choices I make. I'm hoping you'll help me with that, noble parents. Really!

I wrote earlier about how bad I felt when I lost my best friend in a fire on base. I don't think I'll ever forget, but the change of pace and the new places I've seen have made me feel a little better. One of my muscle-bound buddies, Scott, says "no pain, no gain." I hope he's right.

Anyway, it's time to stop rattling on. It looks as though I'll be returning in about three and a half weeks and I'm going to try to get assigned to a base in or near New Jersey. I'm hoping they'll need a newspaper editor at Fort Dix!

So, love to you all. I'm counting the days till I see you again.

Wylie

CHAPTER 65

GOLDEN GATE

◆ ◆ ◆

AN IMPECCABLE SHIT DAD AWAITED Wylie as he poked his head through the door of their Quonset hut and tossed the duffel bag on his bunk. Wylie almost didn't recognize him in the dim light of the room. He wore pressed and starched fatigues, the trousers neatly bloused in spotless boots. He was clean-shaven and his hair was trimmed.

"What the hell is that?" asked Wylie. "Is that a stripe on your sleeve?"

"Shit dad, it is! Captain Bland, he said he was keeping an eye on me and he was beginning to like what he saw. So, I got promoted. First time for me in almost five year. I believe I am becoming more responsible. Anyway, that's what the Captain says."

Wylie congratulated his friend and asked whether anything of note had happened during his three-week absence.

"Not much. There's talk about the Captain and Major Barbara over at MASH sneaking off to do the nasty, and Jefferson found a new guy to do typing since Lamar got caught playing patty cake with one of the cooks and they got themselves discharged. The general's gonna retire, and he's got himself a new job running a beer factory in Milwaukee. Captain Standrich sent us a letter says he's enjoying being out of the Army and he's got a business running a skeet range in Wisconsin. And, lemme see," he considered whether to bring it up and decided he could, "there were a lot of us guys helping out the engineers work on the orphanage. Looks like it'll be all done, like before almost, in a couple weeks. There's already a sign says it's the 'Amelia Chapel' orphanage. Got a Korean lady from down south to run it. You could go over."

Wylie continued unpacking his bag.

"Like I said, not much going on. But, yeah, there's one thing. My wife is starting to swell again; I'm gonna be a double daddy 'bout six months. Responsibilities, man, responsibilities!"

In Cajun, each syllable was drawn out and each vowel enunciated Louisiana style.

"That's really great!" and he hugged his friend.

"Makes me think. Still owe you for cigars from the last time."

"That's okay. Consider it a baby gift."

Auntie Soo had enlisted one of her younger nephews as her new driver. He was infatuated with the Buick and polished and greased it so it slipped through the air like a bird's wing. The Buick no longer journeyed to the Korean Palace since the area authorities were still very interested in speaking with her about numerous matters, most importantly her involvement with the diversion of medical supplies. Nevertheless, she retained a strong interest in its operation and a portion of its substantial profits found its way to her by various routes. She grumbled more and more about the aches and pains of advancing age, but continued to supervise her numerous business endeavors with powerful attention to detail and ruthless efficiency.

Her former driver, her nephew Kim, became resident manager of the Korean Palace. It was operated on a smaller scale and with great discretion. Kim realized the political and economic danger of maintaining a monopoly so near the military base and arranged for the local ROK police to sponsor a smaller establishment nearby. High standards of hygiene and cleanliness were observed and Colonel Cutter, who maintained a peripheral influence over the operations, returned to a post in the United States with glowing recommendations in his personnel file. He was soon promoted to Brigadier General.

Uncle Ho settled into a golden retirement. The money provided after the unfortunate accident to his cart was sufficient for him to live comfortably with his wife of many years in his little home in Tongdudong-ni. He enjoyed rice wine and providing details of the defining moment of his life to his neighbors. No matter how often the story was told, his description of the two officers covered with excrement as they sat shivering in their Jeep always raised raucous laughter. It was very Asian to find humor in the misery or bad fortune of others. The family business continued with his nephew driving the now repaired cart behind the long-suffering pair of oxen. Every afternoon his nephew, Jin Park, returned to town with the night soil. Life went on at a stately pace.

The troop ship crossed the calm South Pacific seas toward its dock in Oakland without incident. It may have been anticipation of a combat-free posting or the placid waters, but no one became seasick. As a non-com, Wylie enjoyed quarters less crowded than on the trip west and edited the ship's newspaper. The paper was prepared on blue mimeograph sheets and run off by hand for delivery to the passengers. Wylie and others concocted stories from materials received over ticker tape in the communications shack. The most popular items were baseball scores as time for the World Series approached.

Corporal Scott McIlvane returned with Wylie and the two men swapped stories and drank near beer with other returning soldiers. The ship also carried a compliment of Marines and the monotony of sailing the smooth seas was broken with friendly games of volleyball between men of the two services. Customary horseplay by servants of the kingdom of Neptune occurred as they passed the International Date Line and sailors demanded to be honored for arranging to give the troops back the day they lost on the westward trip. From somewhere a vast kettle of grog appeared and the sick bay added APC tablets for hangovers the following day, to go along with the customary zinc oxide cream for soothing sunburned shoulders.

The first sixteen days on the General Freeman passed very slowly, uneventful and tedious. On the last two days, however, a wave of anticipation swelled. Boots and brass were polished and stubble disappeared. Duffel bags were organized and reorganized. Home addresses were exchanged and gambling debts paid. On the evening of the seventeenth day, the intercom announced the ship would be entering San Francisco bay early the following morning and docking at Oakland by noon.

Before dawn the following morning the foredeck of the General Freeman was crowded with soldiers peering into the foggy gloom ahead, waiting for first light, searching for a glimpse of the Golden Gate Bridge. Wylie was among them. As he waited, he pulled a prized possession from the pocket of his fatigue shirt. It was the charcoal drawing of Amelia created by the street artist in Tokyo. He looked at it often. It was his entry point to the myriad visions he retained of his departed lover. His thoughts would wander from the picture to see her lying softly beside him, hear her laughter as she ran across an arched bridge in a Japanese garden, watch as she shooed little children onto the playground of the orphanage. As on his recent trip to new places, he sensed his recollection of moments with her fading. All he knew of her was becoming consolidated into a single Amelia construct. He thought of it as a crystal that produced shimmering bands of color depending on how it was hit by light. That was she, his eternal band of bright color. He turned the paper toward the ship's running light and looked at it once again.

Standing among other soldiers in the moist darkness, listening to the slap and splash of water under the ship's bow, he recalled his voyage on a similar ship to Korea. Was I really that naïve, that green just sixteen months ago? Losing Amelia had changed him, as had his experiences in combat, with foreign troops, in Japan, in other Asian places. Fulfilling the responsibilities of a noncom, a Sergeant, also matured him. As had the many occasions when he found himself challenging some of his core beliefs. So many questions, so few answers.

His thoughts of Amelia shifted to his expected first meeting with Judy after those long months away. Elated as he was to be returning home, he worried about how that meeting would go. Had she changed as much as he had? Was she as unfaithful to him as he had been to her? Had their amorous spark extinguished? Excited but troubled, Wylie pulled up the collar of his field jacket and stared ahead, searching for glimmers of light.

The horizon glowed pale pink, barely distinguishable through wisps of fog. The light expanded like a filling balloon, revealing headlands in the distance joined by a graceful black form suspended from slender twin towers.

"There it is! There it is!" voices called and echoes of "Boo-yah!" rang out. The sun rose and shone in their eyes as the ship closed on the bridge, offering a black silhouette. Wylie looked forward to seeing a great golden structure, shining in morning light, welcoming him back home.

When the ship was about a quarter mile away, the bridge was struck fully by the morning sun, revealing its red orange color. Where's the gold, wondered Wylie? Why would it be called the Golden Gate and be painted that funny brick color? He expected his first view of the bridge to herald and confirm a turning point, a gilded new beginning. Soldiers around him were equally disappointed. But they were inured to disappointment and their grumbling quickly subsided.

As the ship cruised under the bridge, it was caught by the morning breeze rushing from the expanse of the bay through the narrows. It dispelled the remaining wisps of fog still clinging to the water. The breeze caught the portrait Wylie held loosely in his hand, dislodged it and sent it flying upward as though to carry it to the bridge. He watched as it fluttered through the air, descended behind the General Freeman to settle in the foamy wake.

He turned and saw the great expanse of the bay. Already there were boats with white sails scudding and tacking across sparkling waves on the deep blue water. To his right, the city of San Francisco awakened with the dawn, its spires illumined by slanting rays of morning sunlight.

There, thought Wylie, there. I see it. There is the gold.

For more information about the author and other of his books,
please visit www.frogworks.com

www.ingramcontent.com/pod-product-compliance
Lightning Source LLC
Chambersburg PA
CBHW050022030726
47506CB00001B/68